The Fightback

Alex Kane is a crime writer from Glasgow. She lives with her husband and three-year-old daughter and in her spare time likes to read as much as possible.

Also by Alex Kane

No Looking Back
What She Did
She Who Lies
The Angels
The Housewife
The New Friend
The Family Business
The Mother
Janey
Two Sisters
A Mother's Revenge
The Second Wife
The Fightback

THE FIGHTBACK
ALEX KANE

canelo
HERA

First published in the United Kingdom in 2026 by

Hera Books, an imprint of
Canelo Digital Publishing Limited,
20 Vauxhall Bridge Road,
London SW1V 2SA
United Kingdom

A Penguin Random House Company
The authorised representative in the EEA is Dorling Kindersley Verlag GmbH. Arnulfstr. 124,
80636 Munich, Germany

Copyright © Alex Kane 2026

The moral right of Alex Kane to be identified as the creator of this work has been asserted in accordance with the Copyright, Designs and Patents Act, 1988.
All rights reserved. No part of this publication may be reproduced or transmitted in any form or by any means, electronic or mechanical, including photocopy, recording, or any information storage and retrieval system, without permission in writing from the publisher.
No part of this book may be used or reproduced in any manner for the purpose of training artificial intelligence technologies or systems. In accordance with Article 4(3) of the DSM Directive 2019/790, Canelo expressly reserves this work from the text and data mining exception.

A CIP catalogue record for this book is available from the British Library.

ISBN 978 1 83598 341 6

This book is a work of fiction. Names, characters, businesses, organizations, places and events are either the product of the author's imagination or are used fictitiously. Any resemblance to actual persons, living or dead, events or locales is entirely coincidental.

Cover design by Head Design

Cover images © Alamy, Shutterstock, Getty Images

Printed and bound in Great Britain by Clays Ltd, Elcograf S.p.A.

Look for more great books at
www.herabooks.com | www.dk.com

For my dad – Cheers

PROLOGUE

2025

Lori Graham and Steph Lyle sat on Lori's veranda and stared out over Blackhill Court. The shithole they'd grown up in, raised their boys in. The place had them in a death grip and no matter what they'd tried over the years, it just wouldn't let go of them. But this was the only place either of them had known as home. Best friends since they were just little, they'd stuck by each other. They'd given birth to their boys just days apart and they'd grown up like brothers. If nothing else, they all had each other.

Steph gripped the wine glass in her trembling hand and her eyes darted between Lori and the estate. A sense of overwhelming dread sat heavy in the pit of Lori's stomach.

'They'll never believe us,' Steph said.

Lori bowed her head. Steph was right. 'We can't just wait for this to blow over, Steph.'

Steph raised the wine glass to her mouth and glugged it down. Lori sat back in her seat.

As they both glanced over Blackhill Court, Lori watched as Steph's son, Reece, walked towards their building. Glancing further back, she saw Jay sitting in the driver's seat of a van. His expression spoke a thousand words and Lori's stomach dropped. Something was wrong. *Very* wrong.

Then out of nowhere, three loud shots rang out. Lori threw her arms up over her head, but the shooting stopped as quickly as it started. When she looked out, Reece was on the ground.

The van that Jay had been in sped out of the estate and Steph was already on her feet, running out towards the green where her son lay bleeding to death.

ONE

2001

Sixteen-year-old Lori sat on her bed and listened to the silence in the house. The place was usually filled with the noise of drunk adults, partying and taking drugs. The silence now was thick and almost sinister. The family home that had never truly been a home. She had never felt like she belonged, not with the family she'd been born into. Her parents were addicts, her eighteen-year-old brother Kev was an addict and in and out of prison constantly, and her fourteen-year-old sister Charley was a shell of herself.

The bag she'd found under her bed certainly hadn't been put there by her, or Charley. And if her parents had found it, then there wouldn't be anything left of it and they'd probably be dead by now. It had to be Kev. And with the amount she'd discovered, she knew it couldn't possibly just be for him. He had to be dealing it for someone. The only person more stupid than Kev to think that was a good idea was the dealer themselves. If they thought that money was going to be paid back to them, they'd highly overestimated her brother. He'd do the off with that money, or make a decent dent in the drugs himself.

As she stared down at the bag, she didn't care what kind of drugs were inside. Could be anything, but by the looks of it, it was likely heroin; or *brown* as her brother called it. She'd seen enough of the stuff in her short life to know the difference in colour between that and cocaine. What mattered was that it was under *her* bed and she wanted it gone. Living with addicts and seeing what it did to them as people, never mind what it was doing to their health, was enough to stop her from putting anything in her body that could do the same to her. Her parents were like zombies, her brother much the same. Lori didn't want that life for herself.

The silence and her thoughts were disturbed as her bedroom door burst open. Her brother swayed in the doorway.

'What the hell are you doing?' she asked, but he didn't respond.

She noticed how his eyes fixed on the bag on her lap and widened; just a little, though. He was too off his face to truly elicit any emotionally charged response.

'This yours then?' she asked, getting to her feet and clutching the plastic shopping bag in her hand.

'Aye,' Kev said. 'Gies it here.' He held out his hand and beckoned as though the bag would free itself from Lori's grip and toddle on over to him like a loyal little puppy.

'What's inside?' she asked. Lori wanted to see if he'd tell her the truth. Were drug addicts capable of the truth? Her parents certainly weren't. They were constantly lying to her and Charley about why there was barely any food in the house, how their benefit money hadn't come through yet, or the shop had run out of stuff they needed... when they had the ability to speak. When they were on a drug high, they were mostly unconscious. In reality, it was all because the little money they did have went to drugs and alcohol.

'It's nothing for you to worry about. I said gies it,' Kev said, swaying a little more. His bloodshot eyes glowed a pinkish red behind blinking lids and Lori raised a brow.

'You're dealing for someone, aren't you? I mean, this can't all be for you unless you're planning to kill yourself?'

Kev frowned and laughed in that fake, slurred way that she'd become accustomed to. She'd known of a few addicts in Blackhill Court and they all had that same laugh. They slurred their speech the same way too. Were they ever sober, or was that just how they sounded now? Her parents' laugh was identical to Kev's too. The sound made her skin crawl.

'What's so funny?' Lori pressed. 'I'm being serious. Are you dealing drugs for someone?'

He moved closer, tried to snatch the bag off her. 'Lori, I swear to *fucking* God, you don't give me that bag, I'm going to wrestle it out your fucking hands.'

Lori smirked. 'Are you kidding? You can't even stand up straight. Look at the state of you, Kev. You're a fucking disaster. In and out the jail constantly, not giving a fuck about us or yourself. In fact, you're so smashed you probably couldn't even find your own hands.'

Nostrils flared, Kev staggered back a little and pulled a quarter bottle of vodka out from the pocket of his jogging bottoms.

'Ah, so you're pissed today too. Brilliant. Well, I'll tell you this. You ever stash this shit under my bed again, I'll set it on fire. You got me?'

Kev unscrewed the cap on the bottle, tutted and glugged back a mouthful of vodka. Swallowing hard before wincing, he wiped the back of his hand across his mouth and said, 'You've no' got the fucking baws to do that, Lori. You're just a daft wee lassie who doesnae have a clue what the fuck real life is.'

She stared at her brother and a sudden fiery rage exploded in her chest. 'Just a wee lassie?' she repeated. 'I've got more balls than you realise, Kev. My life is a shitshow because my parents and my brother are junkies! I've had to raise Charley because our parents would rather get off their face. And you're telling me I'm just a daft wee lassie without a clue of what real life is? *This* is real life, Kev. Trying to survive living with you!'

Kev blinked slowly and stretched out for the bag again, but Lori pulled it back, slid around him and headed for the bathroom.

'What you doing?' he called after her as she moved through the hallway.

'Getting rid of this shit. Fuck knows who you're involved with, Kev, but I don't want anything to do with it. Like I said, I'm surviving.'

She sat the bag down on the filthy bathroom floor and opened it, revealing individually wrapped bags of brown powder.

Quickly, Kev's hands were on her shoulders, pinching at the skin as he pulled her back from the toilet pan. 'Are you insane? You'll get us all fucking killed,' he shouted in her ear, making it ring loudly.

'You're the insane one, Kev. You need to get a grip of yourself and stop all this chaos. Me and Charley are still just kids, and we're having to grow up too fast because our parents are a pair of wasters. You should be the one stepping up for us: your little sisters. Instead, you're getting fucked up every day and now you're stashing drugs under *my* bed. What the hell do you expect me to do?'

Kev kept hold of Lori's shoulders and stared her down. His eyes glistened, although she didn't know if it was from tears, or anger. Maybe fear that she was going to flush the lot?

'Lori, if you do this, my death is on you. You know that, right? If you get rid of these drugs, I'm a dead man walking.'

Lori glared at her brother. He was utterly pathetic. Maybe she'd be better off if he was dead. In fact, she'd be better off if they were all dead. She and Charley would be able to start again without them.

'Fine,' she said. 'I won't flush them. But you need to get rid, Kev. If you don't, I'll do it myself.'

Kev nodded and grabbed the bag up as quickly as he could. 'Stay out of my business in future.'

Lori glared at him. 'Then stay out of my bedroom and keep that bag of shit out from under my bed.'

Kev turned, moved through the hallway and went into his own bedroom, slamming the door behind him. Stepping into the hallway, she glanced across at the living room and saw her mother, spark out on the sofa with a lit cigarette in her hand. Sighing, Lori moved towards her before taking the cigarette out from between her mum's fingers and stubbing it out in the already full ashtray on the arm of the sofa.

Glancing across at the armchair on the opposite wall, her dad had passed out with a bottle of Buckfast between his knees; empty, of course. His head lulled, chin touching his chest as he snored like a bull.

The TV was on but had been muted, and the blinds were still closed. They'd been closed for years, allowing the build-up of cigarette smoke and nicotine to give the curtains a bile-like yellow tinge, as well as the ceiling and the walls.

She glanced between both parents and shook her head.

'What a waste,' she said quietly, before retreating to her bedroom.

–

Lori woke to the sound of rustling plastic beneath her as she lay in her bed. She didn't move, frozen in fear for a few moments before she realised. It was Kev. Back to put another bag of drugs beneath her bed; or possibly the same bag. He'd either forgotten their conversation earlier, or was just so lacking in respect for his younger sisters that he didn't give a shit.

She would stand by her word. She'd warned him what would happen. Lori wasn't one to be messed with when she was backed into a corner. None of the adults in her life were capable of being adults and looking after her or Charley, so she would have to do it herself.

Lying perfectly still, Lori waited until Kev left the room. He probably thought he was being quiet but he was far from it. Still, she remained as though sleeping, even for a further ten minutes after he'd left.

Then she heard the front door close and Lori got out of bed before padding across the room towards the window. She peeked out the edge of the sheet, which had been hung to act as a curtain; not by her parents, but by Lori herself. They didn't give a shit about their own dignity, never mind that of their two teenage daughters.

She watched as Kev stumbled along the pavement and out of the estate. *Good*, she thought, before returning to her bed and pulling the bag out from beneath. She stared at it. Same drugs as earlier.

Picking it up, she carried it down the hallway towards the bathroom and closed the door quietly behind her. She used the tweezers on the mirrored shelf above the sink to pull open the plastic and began pouring each bag of powder down the toilet pan, flushing every few pours. No one in the house would care if they heard the toilet flushing a million times. All anyone in this house cared about was drugs, alcohol and how to get more of it.

She got to the last bag, and poured the remainder of the contents into the pan. When she was younger, she used to watch the toilet paper disappear when she flushed and she'd cheerfully say, 'Bye-bye, toilet paper, have a nice holiday.' The memory made her smile. It was one of the very few happy memories she had as a child. One which came before her parents turned to drugs. That was something she'd never understood. Why they'd gone down that path. Living in Blackhill Court likely had a lot to do with it. The families in every second or third house were in the same position as the Graham family. Maybe her parents just followed the crowd. It could have started off as a casual line here and there before addiction really took hold. It was all a guessing game to Lori.

Watching the last of the powdered drug dissolve in the water, she gave the toilet one last flush and whispered, 'Bye-bye, heroin, good fucking riddance,' in the same sing-song tone she'd used as a child.

There was a possibility that Kev wouldn't even remember placing the bag back under Lori's bed, but if he did come looking for the drugs, she'd pretend that the last time she saw the bag was when he'd taken it back to his bedroom.

In reality, by the time morning came, Kev could be back in prison, but being the one to call the police on him was not an option. He might be a waste of space but he was still her brother.

Kev was never out of jail for long, forever getting lifted for shoplifting, assault, breach of the peace. A few weeks here, a few months at max. Prison could be the safest place for him right now, considering he'd said that if she flushed the drugs he'd be a dead man. She'd acted out of anger at his drug-fuelled comments towards her. She hoped that wasn't something she lived to regret.

She prayed for her brother that, one day, he'd get clean. Maybe he'd get clean while inside and would be able to come out and start a new life.

What she'd done was helpful. He'd thank her for it one day; she was sure of it.

TWO

The next morning, Lori glanced down at the needle lying on the floor beside her parents' bed and then up at the bed itself. Her eyes rolled over their bodies. Dressed in the same clothes for the last few days. Her mother hadn't washed her hair in weeks. They looked much like they did when they were on a high. The difference now was their skin colour. A bluish tinge to their hands, their feet. Their lips were almost dark blue in colour, their eyes wide. Dried saliva trailed down from both their mouths to their necks.

Lori stared at them, her body still, her heart thrumming in her chest. They were both dead and she didn't know what to do. Glancing at the digital clock on the bedside table, she saw it was only 6:36 a.m. and wondered how long they'd been dead for. It couldn't have been more than a few hours. She'd gone into the living room at eleven or so the night before and they'd been on the sofa. They must've moved into the bedroom during the night.

'Lori?' Charley called, her voice penetrating the horrors in front of her eyes.

'Don't come in here,' Lori called back.

But it was too late. Charley was already in the room. She stood by the door, looking at Lori who was stood in front of the bed, trying and failing to conceal her dead parents.

'Charley, please get out of here. You don't need to see this.'

Charley ignored her and moved further into the room. She walked to the bottom of the bed and stared at her parents. Lori took a deep breath and tried to stop the tears from falling. She had to be the strong one in this, for Charley's sake.

'Oh my God!' Charley shouted. 'Mum? Dad?'

Lori went to her sister, pulled her around so she wasn't facing them any more. 'They're dead, Charley. Come on, we need to get out of here.'

Charley was crying hysterically now. Tears pouring from her eyes as she kept trying to pull away from Lori.

'No, they're not. They're not dead. They're just on a bad high, that's all. Wake them up, Lori. Wake them up.'

All her efforts not to cry failed in that moment and the emotion came in waves. 'I can't, Charley. They're gone.'

Charley screamed, a high-pitched sound that would have alerted the neighbours that something was wrong.

'What's going on?' Kev said, suddenly appearing in the doorway of the bedroom. Lori looked at him, and when he saw that both his sisters were in tears, he glanced down at the bed and his eyes widened with shock. 'Oh fuck,' he said, stepping forward. He stood next to his mother – his *dead* mother – and kneeled down on the floor. 'Oh, no.'

'Kev, please, wake them up,' Charley was shouting, wriggling out from Lori's arms and going to her brother. 'Please, Kev. Wake them up.'

There were tears in Kev's eyes, but he got to his feet and ushered both girls out of the room. 'I'll phone someone,' he said. 'I don't know who. An ambulance?'

He looked at Lori, as though she'd have the answers. She simply nodded and pulled the door closed behind them. 'Come on,' she said to Charley. 'Let's go into the living room.'

They sat down on the sofa and Charley continued to sob. Lori listened to her brother phone for an ambulance and the emotion in his voice caught her off guard. It seemed that he did still care about something other than just drugs.

Kev sat down on the sofa next to Lori and said, 'The ambulance is on its way.'

Lori nodded.

'Will they help Mum and Dad to wake up?' Charley asked, sounding desperate and hopeful all at once.

Kev blinked away tears and shook his head. 'Nah, pal. They're not going to wake up. The ambulance will come and take them away, I think.'

Charley started wailing again and the sound crushed Lori's soul. She began sobbing silent tears and turned her face away, not wanting Charley to see her cry.

'I'm going to wait outside,' Kev said, getting to his feet and leaving the girls alone.

'What's going to happen to us, Lori?'

The question stopped her in her tracks. What *was* going to happen to them now? Were they going to be any worse off than when her mum and dad were alive? They didn't do anything to help look after their kids; hadn't done for years. Now they were dead, surely things couldn't get any worse?

'I don't know, Charley.'

They held each other's hands and cried together.

—

The ambulance pulled out of the estate and Lori watched as it left. Kev stood next to her, his hands in his pockets as he kept his eye on the ambulance.

'Hey,' Stephanie's voice filtered through the chaotic thoughts in Lori's head, 'what's going on?'

Lori turned and, when she laid eyes on her best friend, all the bravery she'd put forward melted away as she fell into Stephanie's arms.

'Oh my God, what's happened?' Stephanie said, holding Lori in her arms.

'It's my mum and dad,' Lori sobbed. 'They're dead.'

Stephanie held Lori out and looked at her face, then over at Kev. 'What do you mean they're dead?'

'Lori found them early hours. Looks like they OD'ed,' Kev said, before going back into the flat.

'Jesus Christ, I'm so sorry.'

'You got a fag on you?' Lori asked, trying to compose herself as she remembered they were standing in the middle of the estate.

Stephanie frowned. 'You don't smoke.'

'I do today.'

Stephanie pulled a cigarette out from the breast pocket of her denim jacket, along with a lighter. Lori took them, lit the cigarette before she began coughing and spluttering.

'See, told you, you don't smoke.' Stephanie smiled.

Lori looked her best friend in the eye and shook her head. 'I knew this day was coming, you know. Given all the shit they pumped into their veins and all the crap they sniffed up their noses. But I didn't think *I'd* have the pleasure of finding them myself.'

'Where is Charley?' Steph asked.

Lori thought back to Charley's reaction and it summoned more tears. 'She was so scared, Stephanie. She kept telling me to wake them up. She asked if the people in the ambulance would wake them up. She just couldn't understand they were gone.'

Stephanie puffed out her cheeks and breathed out slowly. 'That sounds horrible. Where is she now?'

'She's gone to her wee pal's house at the end of the estate. I don't know how she's going to get through this, Stephanie.'

Stephanie nodded. 'I know this is going to sound harsh, but in some ways, you guys are free.'

Lori shot her a look and for a brief moment felt angry. The image of Charley, breaking her heart and telling Lori to wake them up, came to mind. Charley was devastated by their deaths; deaths that could have been avoided had they just got sober.

'Yeah, I suppose we are. Free from seeing our parents slowly kill themselves. Now we just need to deal with the aftermath. And I don't know what that's going to look like.'

They were quiet for a moment, Lori thinking about the future, and it seemed Stephanie was doing the same.

'It could be your guys' ticket out of here,' Stephanie said, her voice a little quieter than it had been.

'What about you?' Lori said. 'I don't want to leave you behind.'

The thought of not having Stephanie in her life felt wrong. They were like sisters. Growing up together, they knew they were different from the other kids at their school. The others were clean, with nice clothes that didn't have holes in them. Their hair was always clean and shiny. They always had school bags that didn't look like they were falling apart, as well as their school shoes. Stephanie wasn't as unkempt as Lori and Charley, but close enough. Stephanie was the only person who got Lori, who understood what it was like to come from a family like she did.

'Och, don't worry about me. I'll be fine,' Stephanie said, unconvincingly.

'I never thought I'd say this, but I don't want to leave Blackhill Court. This is the only life I've known. I don't know if I could survive life without you, Steph.'

'Yeah, I feel the same. Still, I won't stop trying to get out of here once I'm old enough.'

They were both quiet for a few moments. Lori reflected on the last few hours and how much her life could possibly change now. What would happen to her? To Charley? Would they be kept together or split up? Would they be taken away from Dunreath or kept close to the life they knew?

'Why did life deal us such a shitty hand?' Stephanie asked, breaking the silence and Lori's train of thought. 'Both born to junkies who gave zero shits about us. And where's the fucking help? I mean, at least my gran had the decency to take me on after my junkie mum abandoned me. She's a good gran really; or at least she tries to be. A big drinker, but stays away from the hard stuff as much as she can. Being an alcoholic is bad enough.'

Lori shrugged and continued to smoke. 'It's this place. It's a shithole. It eats you up, but instead of spitting you out, it holds you in its rotten guts. Parents are supposed to care about us, aren't they? But all mine cared about was drugs and getting high and it eventually killed them.'

Stephanie was quiet, probably because she knew it was true. At least Steph lived with her gran, away from the drugs. Not that her gran was any better. She was never in; always out working the streets to make cash for her own alcohol fixes and the odd bit of cannabis.

'We won't let any of it happen to us, Lori,' Stephanie finally said. 'We won't become our parents.'

Lori glanced down at the cigarette in her hand and stared at it for a few seconds before dropping it on the ground and stamping on it with her foot.

'I don't want to end up like my brother either. I've tried to tell him to stop, you know? That's why I did what I did last night.'

Stephanie gave a quizzical look. 'What did you do?'

Lori sighed. 'I did something stupid, Steph. But for good reason.'

Steph raised a brow and waited for Lori to continue.

'He's been dealing for someone,' she said quietly. 'I found the drugs under my bed yesterday, threatened to flush them down the toilet; or was it set them on fire? Anyway, he convinced me not to, but I warned him that if he didn't get rid, I wouldn't hesitate.'

Steph sucked on the end of the cigarette and expelled a cloud of grey above them. 'So, what happened?'

'I woke up during the night and he was putting them back under my bed. He'd either forgotten our conversation because, of course, he was pissed, or he just blatantly disregarded everything I'd said to him and thought I wouldn't notice.'

'You didn't get rid of them, did you?'

Lori nodded. 'I flushed them. All of them. He'd begged me not to, said he'd be a dead man walking if I did it. He's a dead man walking anyway, Steph. He's going to die from his addictions, just like my fucking parents.'

'But he told you he'd be killed if you got rid of them. Did you not think about that?' Stephanie asked, her expression one of shock.

Lori shook her head and sighed loudly. 'I didn't know what else to do.'

'Well, let's hope the worst doesn't happen then. Sorry to say it, Lori, but you might have just signed Kev's death certificate.'

Lori shot her a look, but she knew Stephanie was right. 'I don't think he's realised yet. He hasn't said anything and I know Kev: our parents dying this morning wouldn't have stopped him in his tracks if he thought his bag of heroin was missing,' Lori said.

Again, they were both quiet for a while, Lori silently panicking about what she'd done. Was Stephanie right? Had she signed her brother's death certificate?

'You and Charley could come and live with me at my gran's house,' Stephanie said, the sudden change of subject easing Lori's anxieties. 'I mean, she's never in; always out on the street trying to get money. She wouldn't even notice, if I'm being honest.'

The idea of living with her best friend seemed better than any other alternative. But she knew it wasn't realistic. If Stephanie's gran even agreed to it, it was unlikely there would be room for both Lori and Charley.

'Thank you,' Lori said, her voice small and weak.

'I'll phone her now,' Stephanie said, pulling her Nokia 3310 mobile phone from the breast pocket of her denim jacket. 'I have about a tenner in credit thanks to good old Gran's purse left lying on the kitchen table when she was passed out on the sofa last night. I'll ask her. She'll say yes to keep me quiet.'

Lori wiped her tears away with the back of her hand and was so thankful for Steph: her friend, and now the only person she really had left that she could count on.

THREE

Charley sat on the chair and stared up at the ceiling, trying her best not to cry. She'd had plenty of practice over the years being brave while living in chaos. Being brave was all she had now that she'd been separated from her sister, Lori.

'I don't want to live in a children's home,' Charley said to her social worker as the tears streamed down her face. 'I won't know anyone. Why can't I just live with my sister at Stephanie's gran's house?'

Janet's expression was soft, and it made it harder for Charley to keep her emotions under control.

'If that was at all possible, you would be there now. Stephanie's gran only had room for one of you. I'm so sorry this is happening to you, Charley. I really am. You deserve so much better. But I'm hopeful that it will only be for a short time. We have a foster family who have one of their kids moving out in the next month or so. They're getting ready to go away to university and so, their bedroom is going to be free. This is just a stopgap. And you'll be able to keep in touch with your sister as often as you would like.'

A deep sense of helplessness came over her and her instinct told her to get up and run away. The reality was unbearable. Lori was the only person in Charley's life who'd ever tried to look after her. She was the only one who'd ever tried to mother her. Charley's own mother couldn't even keep herself alive in the end. The images of her parents, lying dead on that bed back in the flat they all shared, were still very strong in her mind. Home life hadn't been good, but was it as bad as this? Being separated from the only family she had left? Her big brother was in prison – again – and Lori was living with a friend. It all caused such a knot in Charley's stomach that she permanently felt sick. This wasn't happening, it was just a horrible nightmare she was going to wake up from. Yet here she was, sat in front of her social worker, a bag at her feet with the very few possessions she did have and the choice being made for her.

She thought about the moment she'd had to say goodbye to her sister. She'd managed to stay at Stephanie's for three nights but there had only been one bed and Charley had to share the single with Lori. Janet was right, there wasn't enough room for both of them. But because Lori and Stephanie were best friends, that was how the decision had been made. Lori had tried to be brave, like she always was. She hadn't cried when Janet had come to collect Charley, but Charley had cried every tear she had in her and hadn't stopped from the moment her sister had let go of her. Now she felt drained and helpless.

'What if I refuse to go?'

Janet was silent for a moment. It was as though she knew that Charley's question wasn't fully loaded. And it wasn't. There was no way she was going to refuse to do anything because where would that get her?

'How long?' she asked, feeling defeated.

'Two months,' Janet said.

Nodding, Charley took a deep breath and leaned down to pick up her bag. She wanted to channel her emotions in another way. Being sad wasn't going to get her very far. She wanted to take a leaf out of Lori's book. She wanted to be brave. Lori wasn't there to protect her now. Charley would have to protect herself.

Charley wiped furiously at her tears and shook her head. 'I want to change school. Everyone there knows what happened to me and it's embarrassing and horrible and just another reminder of it all. I don't want people constantly asking me about it.'

Janet stood up, pulled her lips into a thin line, turning her expression solemn. 'We can organise a school transfer if you think that's wise. The foster family you'll go to are in another local authority, so you'd have to move eventually anyway.'

Charley rose with Janet, and in her bleakest moment, said, 'I wish I'd never been born, you know that? My mum and dad didn't want any of us. They only ever wanted drink and drugs.'

Silence again as Charley followed Janet out of the office and to the car. Climbing in, she clipped her seat belt into place and felt her stomach roll with the anticipation of going somewhere new to live. To survive.

Janet pulled out of the space and headed along the street in the direction of the city; away from Dunreath and Blackhill Court. Away from all the horrific things she'd endured while living there.

Maybe going into care was Charley's silver lining. Maybe one day, she'd look back at this and she'd be able to smile, to thank her fucked-up family for setting her free.

FOUR

'Want a fag?'

Charley had been staring out of the window when the question came, barely present in her surroundings. She'd been in the children's home for just three days now and she was counting down the weeks until she could get out of there and on to the foster family Janet had told her about. The place wasn't as bad as she thought it would be. There were only around eight occupants, all of various ages. The people who ran the home were all right. They were kind enough and made sure that Charley had everything she needed that she'd barely experienced at home, like fresh bedding, clean clothes and hot meals, although she – along with the other occupants – were expected to chip in and do a lot for themselves; which she did have experience of because, at home, if she didn't do anything for herself, she'd have had nothing to eat and no clean clothes. They said it was all life skills and she knew they were right. It was nice to be able to keep her space clean and tidy; to be in control of how hygienic she and her belongings were. It was nice not living in a filthy house. Still, she wanted to keep her head down and do her time.

'Oi, deefy, I said do you want a fag?'

Glancing up, Charley noticed Maria perched on the opposite end of the windowsill of the room they shared. The window was wide open and Maria's arm hung out of it, said fag between her fingers.

Maria was a girl who'd arrived apparently two weeks before Charley had. They hadn't spoken too much in the three days

Charley had been there, but she seemed the same as everyone else: all right.

'Nah, don't smoke,' Charley replied. 'Cheers, though.'

Maria tutted. 'Who doesnae smoke these days?'

Charley raised a brow. 'Are you taking the piss out of me for *not* tarring my lungs?'

'What are you, a posh wee fucker or something?' Maria tutted again.

As much as the girl tried, her ability to intimidate Charley wasn't working.

'Not posh, just don't smoke.'

Maria flicked the ash and Charley watched as it fell onto the flat roof of the porch beneath. 'Nah, you wouldn't be in here if you were posh. I've smoked since I was eight.'

'Is that right?' Charley replied, unimpressed.

'Aye, and I've been drinking since I was ten. Mainly voddy, but I'll take whatever's going, you know?'

Charley refrained from rolling her eyes as she studied Maria's face. Her foundation did not match her skin; it was orange in colour and it made Charley think of the Tango advert from when she was younger.

'You drink?' Maria continued. 'I've got some voddy stashed under my bed if you want some?'

Charley shook her head. 'Nah, you're all right.'

Maria straightened her back. 'What, you think you're better than me coz you don't drink?'

This time the eyes rolled involuntarily. 'Did I say I thought I was better than you?'

The radio was set to Clyde 1, and Five's 'When the Lights Go Out' started to play, which was followed by Maria getting to her feet. Charley thought she was going to get a slap, but instead, Maria started dancing. She pulled Charley to her feet and smiled.

'Come on, loosen up a bit. This place might be a bit of a shithole, but at least we've got each other, eh?'

Stunned by the sudden change in her demeanour, Charley couldn't help but laugh. 'You're mental.'

'They don't call me Mental Maria for nothing,' she said, reaching under her bed and pulling out a bottle of vodka. She unscrewed the red lid and drank straight from the open top.

'Who calls you Mental Maria?' Charley laughed.

'Everyone. Got kicked out of my last place, and the place before that. It's why I'm in here. Cannae control my temper. Mind you, if you had parents like mine, you'd be an angry fucker an' all.'

Charley blinked. 'Why? What are they like?'

Maria screwed the vodka lid back on and slid the bottle back under the bed. She sprayed some perfume on her T-shirt and returned to the window.

'My dad's in the jail and my mum's in the loony bin.'

'Loony bin?'

'Aye, you know, locked up for her own good. She's got something wrong with her brain that makes her do mad shit. She was sectioned. I'll probably never see her again and even then it'll be too soon. She dangled me out the window when I was a wee lassie apparently, trying to shake the devil out of me, my granny told me.'

Charley couldn't hide the shock from her face. 'Fuck sake,' she muttered.

'And my dad's in the jail for armed robbery. Stupid bastard shot and killed a polis, so he's not getting out anytime soon.'

As much as Charley wanted to tell Maria that she could do one better, she decided that she didn't want to tell her story to Maria; not yet, anyway. She barely knew her, and baring her soul like that required knowing someone longer than she'd known Maria. 'How do you feel about it?' she asked.

Maria shrugged. 'My social worker said I don't know any different, so for me it's normal. But that's bullshit. I had pals at school, I saw their normal lives, steady homes. I knew what I was dealing with meant I was the odd one out. No one's lived a life like mine. I'm only fourteen and I've seen more shit than most adults probably have. I mean, have you ever been dangled oot a windae by your own maw and lived to tell the tale?'

Charley shook her head and thought to herself, *No, but I have had to lock myself in the bathroom while my dad's best pal got high on ketamine and thought everyone in the house wanted to kill him, including me.*

'Aye, well, I'm not going to let my sad excuse for a mum fuck up my life. When I'm old enough, I'm out of this place and I'm going to be a model.'

Again, Charley was quiet. She didn't want to say what she was thinking: that if she didn't stop smoking and drinking while she was young, she wouldn't have the chance to do much in her life.

Charley didn't know Maria from before she'd been placed in the children's home. Maybe if she had, they'd have been friends. On some level, they could relate to one another but, again, she didn't want to tell Maria her story.

A knock at the door made Charley tense as Maria moved towards it. 'Who is it?'

'It's me. Need a fag, got any?' a male voice called through.

Maria rolled her eyes and shook her head. 'If Michael down the stairs hears you at this door you'll end up in the shit.'

'Then hurry up and give me one,' the voice replied.

Maria pulled the door open and handed a cigarette to the older boy. Charley caught his eye but quickly looked away. She didn't want to be involved with anyone in the home. Not even Maria, really, as much as they shared a room. She just wanted to keep her head down and get through the next two months before being moved to the foster home.

'You new?' he asked.

'Aye,' Maria replied for Charley. 'And she's never going to be interested in you, so you might as well fuck off.'

The boy glared at Maria, tucked the cigarette into the pocket of his joggy bottoms and turned to smile at Charley. 'How long you here for?'

'Too long,' Charley replied.

'Like I said, fuck off,' Maria said again. 'And if you don't leave, I'll shout on Michael. I've got plenty of shit on you, all I have to do is pick one story to tell him and you'll be out of here quicker than you can light that fag. Got it?'

Charley stared at the pair of them. Was this some kind of wind-up between the two? Were they actually friends and this was their way of showing it? The older boy took a step into the room and leered over Maria, his nose almost touching hers.

'Who d'ya think you're talking to, *Manky* Maria?' he sneered.

'You really want me to answer that?' she replied, squaring up to him. 'And it's *Mental* Maria for a reason, you prick.'

Maria and the lad locked eyes for a few moments and, suddenly, they were both laughing. It unnerved Charley.

'You're fucking mental all right,' he said, and Maria playfully slapped him on the arm.

'Seriously, you better do one or Michael will do his nut,' she said.

He glanced over at Charley. 'Nice to meet you,' he said.

Charley smiled thinly at him and watched as he closed the door.

'What was that all about?' Charley asked.

Maria shook her head. 'He's a pal. He's a bit of a lad, but he's a laugh.'

Charley narrowed her eyes. 'Who is he?'

'He's just a pal. He's been here for a couple of years, makes money dealing, you know? Gets me my bevvy and fags when I want them. If I'm honest, he's the only decent human I've ever met in my life.'

Charley stared at Maria and wondered what kind of people she'd met in her life to warrant *that* guy being the most decent.

Sighing, Charley sank back down onto the bed and said, 'I hate this place.'

'Aye, tell me about it. Least you've not got long before you're moved on.'

Charley sat down on her temporary bed and picked at her thumbnail. 'How come you know I won't be here for long?'

'I overheard your social worker talking to Michael downstairs when you first got here. You've got a foster home lined up, haven't you? Sounds better than staying in care. I mean, out of all the homes I've lived in, this is one of the better ones. Even though I say that, I'd rather a better existence than this. But I'll never get out of the system because no one will have me. And when I do get out, I'll be on my own with nothing.'

'You make it sound like the jail,' Charley replied. She looked around her, knowing in that moment that existing in a care home like the one she was in now was better than back home, even if that did mean being split up from her sister.

'Oh, I'll end up in there one day, just like my old man. Or the loony bin like my mum.'

Charley had the urge to reassure Maria, to say that she was sure it would all work out for her. But how could she say that when she didn't know how things would turn out for herself?

'Maybe we could stay friends?' Maria suggested. 'You know, swap mobile numbers and that?'

Smiling, Charley nodded. 'Yeah, we could do that.'

Maria pulled the bottle of vodka from under her bed again, opened it and drank back another mouthful. Swallowing and wincing from the taste, she smiled back and said, 'That's it then. Best mates *for life.*'

Charley lay down, stared up at the ceiling and, for a split second, she felt sorry for Maria. But she felt sorry for herself more. Pulling out her mobile phone from under the pillow, she sent a text to Lori.

> Hi. I miss you. I hate this place. Hope I get to see you soon. Love you. Charley x

She needed to get the fuck out of this place and start her new life with the foster family. Whoever they were. She just hoped that whatever life they could provide would be better than the one she came from.

FIVE

SIX WEEKS LATER

Charley was finally free from the care home, but it didn't feel like she was free at all. Janet had said the foster family were ready and had a place for her, and now Charley Graham stood in the hallway of her new foster family home and took in her surroundings. She'd never seen anything like it in her life. The sage-green-coloured walls looked freshly painted and the cream carpet brand new. The entrance hallway was filled with natural light and Charley was astounded by the place.

Finally, she was out of the children's home, away from strangers she had to share a house with and about to start a new life in a place like this. And as much as she'd had her guard up about Maria initially, she'd grown on Charley. Best mates for life, she'd said to Charley on her third day in the home, but she had known deep down that she might never see that girl again. Something in her gut told Charley that Maria would forever be stuck in that cycle of chaos of moving from place to place. She'd said it herself: no one would have her.

'Charley, this is Margaret and Ronnie,' Janet said, interrupting her train of thought. 'They're going to be looking after you for the foreseeable. They've many years of experience in foster care and I can genuinely say, hand on heart, that you're going to be well cared for here.'

Charley didn't smile, only said hello in the meek voice she'd used her entire life due to trying her best to stay unseen and unheard by the adults around her.

'Charley,' Margaret said, her tone soft and her eyes a piercing blue. 'I would like to show you to your bedroom, if that's okay?'

The man, Ronnie, smiled at her and it was the gentlest, most sincere smile Charley had ever seen. All the adults in her life only smiled when they were on one of their many drug highs, or about to be. And usually in those situations she'd smile back out of fear.

'I'm the cook of the house,' Ronnie said. 'I can turn my hand to anything, so whatever you fancy for your first meal with us, I can do.'

Charley's stomach groaned in protest for food. She hadn't realised just how hungry she was. She'd barely eaten a thing in days due to all the stress of knowing that she was being moved again. In fact, she'd barely had an appetite since her parents died.

'I'd love a Pot Noodle,' she replied.

A raised brow from both Margaret and Ronnie and a shared look of confusion.

'You sure that's all you want?' Janet asked. 'Ronnie's speciality here is spaghetti bolognese, I've had some myself.'

She looked at Ronnie, who seemed hopeful she'd take him up on the offer. Charley didn't even know what spaghetti bolognese was. Surviving on toast, and sharing Pot Noodles with her sister, along with dry cereal and the odd can of Irn-Bru, had been her only diet up until she'd gone to the home. Then she'd branched out to things like fish and chips, which she didn't particularly like, or steak pie and potatoes.

'What is it?' Charley asked.

'Spaghetti bolognese?' Ronnie asked, the surprise clear on his expression.

She nodded.

'Why don't I make some, with garlic bread on the side, while Margaret shows you to your bedroom?'

Charley nodded, not knowing what she was agreeing to eat but not caring. She didn't care much about anything any more. Not since her life as she'd known it had been turned upside down.

Margaret led the way upstairs and Charley reluctantly followed, with Janet close behind. Charley noticed the framed photographs on the wall as she climbed the stairs to the first floor of the house. Each one was an image of kids of various ages, with both Margaret and Ronnie smiling beside them. Happiness beamed from each image and Charley didn't know what it was to smile or to trust. The only person she'd ever truly trusted with her life was Lori and they'd been pulled apart.

'Are they all yours?' Charley asked, nodding at the photos.

Margaret stopped and smiled. 'Ronnie and I have fostered over thirty children in the last fifteen years. We've kept in touch with every one, and some of them have gone on to do amazing things, Charley. Some have their own children, two are teachers, one is at university studying to be a doctor.'

Charley felt a pang of sadness hit her then. She couldn't imagine achieving great things. Where she came from, people became addicts and then died. They didn't go on to become anything else other than failures.

They walked along the hallway towards a closed door at the end of it. Charley counted the doors. There were eight, four on either side.

'How many bedrooms are in this house?' she asked.

'Eight on this level, four above, and there is a master room on the bottom floor,' Margaret replied.

Charley felt her eyes widen. 'And there are light bulbs in each room? Like, they all work?'

Margaret and Janet exchanged a glance and Charley waited for an answer.

'Yes, my love. Each room has a working light.'

She looked down at her feet, feeling the thick carpet beneath her worn socks. 'Do all the floors have carpet too?'

Charley felt Janet's hand rest on her shoulder and she turned to see her social worker's eyes were glistening against the lights above them.

'Sweetheart, you'll have every essential you *should* have had right here. Carpets, light bulbs, home-cooked food, clean clothing, a clean bed. It's all yours.'

Charley turned upon hearing a bedroom door open. Margaret stepped aside and gestured for Charley to go in ahead of her. Again, she hesitated. This was more like a dream than reality. She'd never had so many adults be so kind. It set off an uneasiness in her, because she was used to surviving on her own or with her sister. She always thought the world was like Blackhill Court, even though most of the kids at school were different to her. But now she was out here, seeing it with her own eyes. It was hard not to wonder if it wouldn't all be snatched away from her.

When she stepped into the bedroom and saw where she'd be sleeping every night for the foreseeable, she gasped.

'This is *my* room?' Charley said, her voice cracking with the emotion of it all.

A double bed sat in the centre of the far wall, a bedside table on either side. The fresh lilac sheets neatly tucked under the corners of the mattress smelled so clean it almost stung her nostrils. Three fluffy white towels were folded into a pile on the bottom of the bed and a pair of slippers sat beside them.

To the right, an oak double wardrobe stood against the wall, with a full-length mirror on the side of it. A dressing table with a chair stood next to that and a shelf on the wall housed a radio and a small jewellery box.

'Is that a television?' Charley pointed towards the chest of six drawers, noticing it sat on top.

Margaret nodded. 'It only has the five channels, but I've also linked up a new DVD player for you. We've got some films and box sets downstairs that you can have, if you'd like?'

'Do you have the *Friends* box set?' Charley asked. 'I've always wanted to watch it but...' She trailed off, thinking about how her parents had always had the TV on in the living room, but Charley was never allowed in the living room to watch it because she'd get in the way of the party.

Margaret nodded. 'Yes, we have the first three series, I think.'

Charley straightened her back as she felt emotion swell in her throat. To anyone else, feeling overwhelmed with happiness about having the freedom to watch a box set of a series most people in her age group had already seen would seem stupid. But to Charley, this was something huge. It was the first time an adult had said yes to her without condition. There was no 'You can watch TV but go to the shop and get me a bottle of vodka first' or 'Go to the ice-cream van and get my cigarettes'. The shops around Blackhill Court didn't care much about age-restrictive laws. It was a case of serving people because they didn't want the backlash of saying no.

'Thank you,' Charley said, staring back at Margaret. She felt her eyes pool with tears and turned away to face the TV again. It was overwhelming to be shown kindness without condition.

She thought about Lori, still living in that awful estate Charley used to call home. Was she happy? Because Charley was. She rubbed her hand across the fresh bed linen and drank in the beauty of her new bedroom. She missed her sister terribly but was so grateful that she no longer had to endure Blackhill Court as her home. She hoped that, one day, that place would become a distant memory.

SIX

Two months had passed since her parents had died and Lori's life had changed drastically and not particularly for the better. Yes, she was out of that horrible flat that she once was expected to call home. Yes, she no longer had to worry about what state her parents and brother were going to end up in on a daily basis. But she missed her younger sister, Charley, so much. She hadn't seen her in almost two months. They'd spoken on the phone and via text message, but that was it. Was this how it was going to be now? Dead parents meant the rest of the family were separated?

'I'm so glad you got to stay here,' Stephanie said, interrupting Lori's thoughts.

'Yeah,' she replied with a solemness to her tone that she hadn't meant to come out.

'You all right?' Stephanie asked.

Lori pulled two chicken and mushroom Pot Noodles from the cupboard, peeled back the lids and a memory came to her. This was Charley's favourite flavour. A sadness washed over her and a tear dropped down her cheek.

'Hey, what's wrong?' Stephanie asked, placing an arm around Lori's shoulders.

'I know, it's so stupid crying over a bloody Pot Noodle. It was Charley's favourite.'

Stephanie sighed and hugged Lori tighter. 'She'll be living on fancy meals now, given what she's told you about her new place.'

Lori was glad for her sister. She deserved so much better than what Blackhill Court had to offer her, or Lori, for that matter.

'I wish we could have stayed together, that's all. If Kev could just get his shit together and be the big brother he is meant to be, he could have taken parental responsibility and we could all still be together. He's a fucking idiot.'

Stephanie pulled away and gave a thin smile. 'How long is he away for this time?'

'Three months, but he'll get out and just reoffend and end up back in there. I sometimes wonder if he does it with the intention to go back inside because at least there he doesn't have to think about where his next meal is coming from.'

'Or maybe it's the safest place for him since he doesn't have the money for those drugs? His dealer is probably full-on raging because of that,' Stephanie pointed out.

Lori sighed and folded her arms across her chest. 'Yes, I know. I regret it now, okay? You don't have to keep bringing it up. I know what I did was stupid but I was angry and desperate, Steph.'

'Hey, I wasn't having a go at you. I just think it could be one of the reasons why he has ended up back inside. It makes sense,' Stephanie suggested.

'None of my life makes sense. I'm glad Charley got away from it all, though.'

'When did you last speak to her?'

'Maybe a few days ago. But she had to cut it short because she and her foster carers were going out for the day. Some boat trip down at Loch Lomond or something. I kind of get the feeling her foster family don't really want her in touch with anyone from this cesspit, and I don't blame them.'

'I doubt they'd stop Charley from having anything to do with you. It's in both your best interests to stay together as much as possible, is it not?'

Lori shrugged, feeling sorry for herself. 'If I'm honest, I wouldn't be surprised if Charley loses interest in me and this place altogether. I could understand why. We've all abandoned her. She'll feel sent away, if that makes sense.'

The kettle rumbled before clicking off and Lori poured water into the two Pot Noodles on the counter. She stared down at each chicken and mushroom pot and felt an overwhelming sense of disappointment for herself. Pot Noodles for dinner. *Again*. Charley would be having something much more nutritious, and she was happy about that. The sacrifice Lori had made to stay behind so that Charley could go to a better place was something she didn't regret. Not one bit.

'Okay, so to try to get away from all the heavy shit and cheer you up a bit, I have something to tell you.'

Lori raised a brow and handed one of the Pot Noodles to Stephanie. 'Oh aye?'

'We've been asked to go on a double date.'

Her raised brow became a narrowed look of suspicion. 'With who?'

'So, you know that guy I've been chatting to from the chippy?'

'He's not *from* the chippy, Steph. He hangs around *outside* the chippy with his mate. But yes, I know who you mean.'

Stephanie rolled her eyes. 'Yeah, Peter. Him and his mate asked if we fancied going out with them and I said yes.'

Lori pulled two clean forks from the drawer under the counter and handed one to Stephanie.

'First of all, thanks for speaking on my behalf... *not*. And secondly, I don't think standing outside the chippy with a bag of chips and a pizza crunch with two guys really counts as a date,' Lori teased, and she couldn't help but laugh.

'Ha. *Ha*. Very funny. Seriously, they want to take us out for dinner. Or the cinema. And I didn't speak on your behalf, I just said yes because I was excited. I've fancied this guy for ages. He's a bit of a bad boy.'

Lori rolled her eyes. Steph did like a bad boy, but Lori most definitely did not. 'And what age are these guys? Peter and... what's his pal's name?'

'It's Jambo. And they're both almost eighteen.'

Lori laughed. 'Aye, so they say. They *definitely* look older.'

'So what if they are? They're taking us out and paying for it. What's there to say no to?'

She shrugged, unsure how to answer. Was Stephanie right? Was there any harm in going on a double date with someone she'd never met? Of course, she knew of them, had seen them around now and again. But she'd never had a conversation with either of them.

'I'm assuming Jambo's a nickname?'

'*Obviously.*'

'And his *real* name?'

'Jamie Marshall,' Steph said. 'Apparently he's one of the Marshall family. You know, the ones who went missing a few years ago.'

Lori rolled her eyes. 'Fuck sake, Steph.'

'What?'

'You know about the Marshall brothers, don't you? They were dodgy. More than dodgy. I've heard so many rumours about them.'

'Yeah, and so what?' Stephanie asked.

'Are you joking? Have you not heard the story about one of them cutting off someone's hand because they owed the Marshalls money for coke?'

Stephanie rolled her eyes. 'Yeah, but we don't know it's true.'

'Maybe not, but everyone knows the Marshall guys were murdered by...' She stopped herself from saying it out loud even though there was no one else around to hear it.

'The Fyfe brothers? Aye, but that's all just rumours too. And Jambo's like a second or third cousin or something and *he's* never come out and said that it's true.'

Lori shook her head. 'Of course he hasn't. Do you think he wants any comeback? The Fyfes are mental too.'

Steph frowned. 'Anyway, that's got nothing to do with what we're talking about. Are you coming on the date? I think you and Jambo would get on great.'

Lori let out a long breath. 'Are you going to go in a huff if I say no?'

Steph smiled. 'Definitely. I've already said we'll go and I *really* want to. It's only once. If you don't like him, we don't have to do it again.'

'Why can't you go out with Peter on your own?'

'Well, because they asked us both out, and I'm nervous. If it doesn't go well, we can use a code to get out of it. Like, I could say I don't feel well and you could go to the bathroom with me, then we just do a bunk.'

Lori was nodding slowly. 'Fine. I'll go. We just getting the bus?'

'No, Ped has his own car.'

'*Ped?*'

'That's Peter's nickname.' Stephanie smiled, spinning her noodles on her fork and shoving them in her mouth.

'Right, no way. I'm not getting in a car with a couple of guys I don't know, Steph, especially not ones called Jambo and Ped. Are you mental?'

'It's fine. I've got my gran's penknife, just in case. Any funny business and I'll slash the tyres and we'll be gone before they can ever catch us.'

Lori stirred the Pot Noodle slowly. Suddenly, she'd lost her appetite. 'Okay, fine. I'll go. But if things go well with you and Ped, you better not fucking ditch me, Steph. I mean it.'

Steph gave an excited little jump and then she clapped her hands. 'I won't. I'd *never* abandon you. There is no one on this planet who could ever make me do that. And there never will be.'

SEVEN

Lori slipped the mascara across her lashes and glanced at the final look in the mirror. She'd decided against a lot of make-up as she didn't want to give this Jambo guy the wrong impression. She didn't want to go on this stupid double date at all, but she was doing it for her friend and it would be a good distraction from her current situation.

'What do you think? Too slutty?' Stephanie asked, staring at herself in the mirror.

Lori looked at her friend, who was wearing a black miniskirt that zipped entirely from top to bottom, a black backless halter-neck and slip-on heels. Stephanie had a figure to die for and her skin was perfect.

'For the dancing, no. For a date at the cinema...' Lori let the words hang there and she watched as Stephanie's grin grew wider.

'So, I'm noticeable then?'

Lori nodded. 'If noticeable is what you were going for, then yeah, that's what you are.'

'Good,' Stephanie said, turning to admire herself from the back.

'But he noticed you when you had joggies and a jumper on. Why all this effort now? What sort of effort is he putting in for you, Steph?'

Stephanie laughed. 'He has a car, Lori. And cash. If I can keep hold of that long enough, he might be my ticket out of this fucking shithole.'

Lori bowed her head. 'What about never abandoning me?'

Stephanie spun around, placed her finger under Lori's chin and pulled her face upwards. 'You're my shadow, Lori. Where I go, you go. Remember? But there's only one front passenger seat. You need to ride in the back.'

Lori felt her stomach flutter at the prospect of getting away not only from Blackhill Court, but Dunreath altogether. It seemed like one of those dreams that you grasped at after waking up. You knew it was a good dream, but you couldn't remember anything about it. An impossibility.

'So long as you don't put me in the fucking boot,' Lori joked.

'Hey, I'll toss *Ped* in the boot and I'll take the fucking wheel before I ever let that happen,' Stephanie laughed.

Lori didn't want to appear desperate, not at all. But Steph was the only good thing she had left in life. She'd fight tooth and nail to keep anyone from ruining that, especially a guy like Ped.

Stephanie looked down at Lori's outfit choice. Boot-cut jeans, trainers and a pink T-shirt. 'You look nice.'

'But not noticeable?'

'Sorry,' Stephanie said, pouting her lip. 'I didn't mean it like that.'

'No, it's fine. Unnoticeable was what I was going for.'

A car horn sounded and Lori felt her stomach flutter again, though not in excitement. Stephanie flew across her bedroom to the window and peeked out through the blinds.

'They're here. You ready?' she said, without turning. Almost as though she feared that if she did, the car would disappear.

Lori moved across the room, stood next to Stephanie and peered through the gap in the blinds too. The car was a statement piece. Blacked-out windows, huge alloys that looked ridiculously oversized, and stickers from a *Max Power* magazine on the back passenger windows.

'Wow, talk about overcompensating,' Stephanie laughed.

'I thought you fancied this guy,' Lori said, stepping away from the window.

'I do. But you can fancy someone and still think they're a bit of a dick at the same time, can't you?'

'Well, yeah. But surely if he's a bit of a dick then you should stay clear?'

Stephanie shrugged. 'But he's stunning.'

Stunning wasn't exactly the word that Lori would have used to describe Ped or Jambo. There was something about their faces that automatically made her recoil. They looked like thugs; both had a glint in their eyes that told her they were wannabe hardmen and it put her off immediately.

'Ever look at a guy and, just by their face, you can tell they're a bit of a tool?' Lori asked.

Stephanie laughed. 'Yes, but Ped isn't one of them.'

Lori and Stephanie had very different tastes when it came to guys. In fact, Lori wasn't hugely interested in finding a guy at all. Her experience of men throughout her life hadn't exactly been decent. Her dad: a drug and alcohol addict who couldn't have cared less about himself let alone his daughters and son. Her brother: exactly the same, plus in and out of prison more times than Lori thought possible. Stephanie had much the same experience of men, yet she seemed more determined than ever to get herself a boyfriend.

'Isn't he?' Lori pressed. 'I mean, if you're a dick, your looks eventually go and all you're left with is a guy who treats you like shit. We both know we deserve better than that.'

Stephanie expelled air slowly and rolled her eyes. 'What age are you, Lori? What we deserve after everything we've dealt with is a bit of fun. Two guys with a car and their own cash can give us that.'

Yeah, Lori thought, *that among other things*.

'What's that look?' Stephanie said. 'You don't want to go, do you?'

'No,' Lori sighed. 'I don't, but I'll go for you. But it's a one-time thing, Steph. I won't do this again.' She didn't want to admit it out loud, but her gut was telling her *not* to go. Not that she just didn't want to. But she knew her best friend better than she knew herself. Steph would go by herself if it came to it. And getting into the car with two guys on her own was not something Lori could stand back and allow her to do.

'Okay then, let's go, because we've already kept them waiting long enough.'

Lori watched as Steph grabbed her tiny leather bag, hung it over her shoulder and headed down the hall towards the doorway. Taking a steadying breath, Lori followed her, and when they stepped outside, Ped and Jambo were in the car, smoking with the windows down and music pumping from the speakers.

Lori turned, stared at Stephanie and couldn't stop the smirk that followed. 'They're listening to Westlife? *Seriously?*'

Steph returned the smile. 'Could be worse. Most guys are blasting Eminem and D12 these days.'

Lori nodded. She'd have preferred a bit of Eminem and D12 herself. The fact that they were listening to a boy band aimed at teenage girls did not soften her thoughts about them. If anything, it made her more wary.

Steph walked towards the car, leaned on Ped's door and smiled. He turned down the music a little and smoke billowed up around Steph's face.

Lori glanced down at the passenger side as Jambo smiled widely at her. She had to refrain from rolling her eyes at his nickname. If Steph thought Ped was a bit of a dick, then it was likely that Jambo was much the same.

'Hop in,' Ped said as he got out of the car and pulled the driver's seat forward for Steph to get in. Jambo did the same, although he didn't say anything to Lori, simply continued to smile in that weird, wide-mouthed way. It made her skin prickle.

Lori hesitated. She hadn't noticed that the car was only a three-door. That meant if there was a reason to get out of the car without having to explain herself, then there was no way of doing it.

No way of escape, a menacing little voice in the back of her head whispered.

Steph climbed in without a second thought, and Lori stepped forward, climbed in and felt Jambo's eyes on her. *All* over her.

Before she could change her mind, Jambo was back in his seat, the door was closed and the music was blaring again.

Steph was giddy as she sat forward, chatting to Ped. No seat belt. None of them wore a seat belt, Lori noticed as she pulled her own one across her body.

Jambo was smoking. Steph was flirting. Ped was driving out of the estate a lot faster than was necessary.

'Right, ladies,' Jambo said, his voice slithering through the humid, smoky air inside the car. 'Here's to a great night.'

'Aye,' Ped said. He picked up an open can of beer, which Lori hadn't noticed when she first climbed in, and took a long slug.

Steph didn't seem to care that the person in charge of the car was drinking, nor did she notice when Ped locked the car doors. But Lori did. Something deep inside told her she should have listened to her gut the first time.

41

EIGHT

Steph drank greedily from the can of beer that Ped had cracked open and passed back to her. Jambo had offered one to Lori too but she'd refused. It was clear Steph had every intention of getting hammered. But Lori didn't want to do that. One of them had to be sober. She was on high alert, waiting for whatever was going to go wrong to happen. She wanted to be able to deal with it properly.

Steph was dancing in her seat to Fragma as it blasted out of the speakers, and Lori kept her eyes on the road ahead. Darkness surrounded them and she realised that they weren't on their way to the cinema. They were headed in the wrong direction entirely.

'This isn't the way to the cinema,' Lori called over the music.

Ped kept his eyes on the road. Jambo said nothing. Steph continued to drink and dance. It was like she was invisible.

'Ped?' Lori shouted. 'The cinema?'

Nothing.

Shit. They weren't going to the cinema. They were never going to the cinema.

She turned, touched Steph on the shoulder.

Steph looked at Lori, but her eyes weren't focused. They were swirling in her head and her head itself was beginning to roll.

'Steph, look at me,' Lori said, giving her friend a shake, but she could barely hear the sound of her own voice over the thumping music.

'Stop the car,' Lori said, leaning forward and shaking Ped's shoulder.

'Why?' Ped said, and she detected a smirk in his tone.

'Steph's being weird. Something's wrong with her. Stop the car.'

'She'll be fine,' Jambo said. It occurred to Lori it was the first time she'd heard him speak; heard his voice. It was as creepy as his face made her feel when she'd first set eyes on him.

Scowling, Lori shoved Ped as hard as she could and said, 'I said stop the *fucking* car.'

It happened in slow motion and top speed all at once. Jambo spun on his seat and punched Lori in the eye. She flew back, her head bouncing off the headrest. Her hand immediately went to her face and she was stunned into silence.

She tried to gather herself, waited for the next blow. Instead, the music remained at an unbearably loud volume and, when she slowly turned to look at her friend, what she saw made her stomach drop.

Steph was unconscious.

—

Breathe, Lori told herself. She had to stay calm. Had to make sure she was clear and able to get them out of this situation. Whatever this situation would turn out to be.

The car moved along the road at speed. The music blared; this time Public Domain, 'Operation Blade'. The bass thumped in her chest and made her skin prickle.

As she tried to remain calm and stare out at the road to work out where she was, it didn't take long to recognise those six looming tower blocks ahead of her. Clydeview Towers. All derelict.

There would be no one there. No one to help her. How the fuck was she going to be able to get away? *Would* she be able to get away? And what about Steph? She was completely out cold.

'Why are you taking us here?' Lori heard herself ask.

No answer. The silence was the worst part. It meant her imagination doing overtime and she didn't want to go to that dark place in her mind.

Turning, she gave Steph another shake in the hope that she would wake up and help Lori to work things out. She didn't move.

'What did you give her?' Lori asked, knowing that her questioning was futile. These guys weren't going to tell her anything; nothing she wanted to hear, at least.

Suddenly, the music was low, the headlights were off and terror set in Lori's chest as she realised that what she was about to face would be nothing short of hell.

Pulling up outside the third tower, Ped killed the engine and got out of the car. Slamming the door shut, he went around to the boot, opened it and then quickly closed it again. Jambo got out too. But he left the door open.

Lori glanced over at the steering wheel in the hope that Ped would have been stupid enough to have left his key in the barrel. He hadn't. That would have been too easy. She imagined jumping into the driver's seat and driving them away from what fresh hell awaited them. It wasn't to be.

'Get out,' Ped said, leaning in and pulling the passenger seat forward.

Lori shook her head.

'I said get out,' he snarled, leaning in further and pulling at her arms. She wasn't strong enough to fight him off and had no choice but to move.

She stood in front of him, darkness surrounding them with the towers looming over them like midnight monsters.

Lori tried to breathe through the rising panic.

'Your brother, Kev, this is all his fault, you know?'

Fuck. What the hell had Kev done to this guy to make him want to hurt Lori?

'Aye, Kev's been a bit of a silly boy. Owes me money, so he does. A *lot* of money. *Apparently* lost something that belongs to me. Then goes and gets himself the jail. Someone needs to pay his debt, Lori.'

The panic turned to nausea. She immediately knew what he was talking about. The drugs she'd flushed down the toilet, they belonged to this guy. And now Lori was stood in front of him while he said someone needed to pay his debts.

'And I'm sure he will when he gets out,' Lori said, gritting her teeth and hoping she wasn't about to throw up. She couldn't admit to being the one who had got rid of his drugs. He'd kill her on the spot.

'I need payment now. He's already overdue,' he said, so matter-of-fact.

'I'm sorry, but I don't have any money and certainly not enough to pay you for whatever he owed. I'm a sixteen-year-old girl from Blackhill Court, did you expect me to have thousands stashed away somewhere?'

'But the payment is due. And I take what's due to me, Lori,' Ped said, taking a step closer to her.

The sound of movement to her right made her turn and she saw Jambo pulling Steph out of the car. She was starting to come round a little but still very groggy; unaware of what was happening to her. Lori stared at her, horrified by what could happen. Her best friend was extremely vulnerable and in so much danger. She saw how Jambo's eyes rolled over Steph's body and it made Lori feel sick.

Lori made a move to go to her, but Ped was in front of her, his larger hands on her shoulders, holding her in place.

'Let go of me,' she said, trying to shrug out of his grip.

'I said I need payment.'

He stared deep into her eyes and she could do nothing but stare back at him.

'I know people, Lori. People who would pay good money to spend time with a beautiful young lady like yourself. You might not have the money your brother owes me, but there are other ways for his debt to be paid.'

She could almost see her reflection in his eyes and he seemed to revel in her terror. Then his face came full force at her, his head butting into the bridge of her nose so hard, she fell to the ground.

'I'm not letting you go until I've taken what's owed to me.'

NINE

Lori woke and, before she opened her eyes, she knew it was going to be as dark as it was behind her eyelids. Pain seared through her cheekbones and nose and she struggled to move.

Opening her eyes and giving herself a moment to adjust to the darkness, Lori noticed the low ceiling. The smell surrounding her set her on edge. A damp, mucky scent like mould coupled with a coldness that licked at her skin.

'Urgh,' she groaned as she tried to sit up. Everything ached: her bones, her muscles, her groin, even her skin, like that feeling you get right before flu sets in.

Her clothes were wet and torn and she immediately wondered if that was because she was or had been bleeding.

She remembered the last thing Ped had said to her; how he'd insinuated that he had people who would pay to rape her. Because that's what it would be, wasn't it? Rape? The memory made her shudder and her body rattled with pain.

'You've been out for a while.'

It was Steph's voice.

'Steph?' Lori said as her eyes flew open. 'Where are we?'

Steph sighed. 'We're in one of the towers...' Her voice trailed off. 'Feels like we've been down here forever.'

Frowning as her eyes adjusted to the dark, she said, 'What do you mean, down here?'

'They've locked us in the basement. Do you remember what they did to us, Lori? Because I don't. But I know it can't be good because I'm sore, Lori. *Everywhere* hurts. And given what I'm wearing...'

That word. *Hurts*. Lori felt it. All over. She panicked, checked that she could actually move and get up from where she was sitting. She wasn't going to stay here a second longer than necessary. 'Oi,' she snapped. 'Doesn't fucking matter what you're wearing. They'd planned this before you decided what you wanted to wear. So don't fucking do that to yourself.'

Steph let out a sob and then sucked it back in, composing herself. Lori could just about make out her friend's silhouette.

'I'm not tied down. Are you?' Lori said.

'No.'

'Then let's get *the fuck* out of here,' Lori said, moving towards her friend. 'I'm not hanging about here to let him go through with his threat. I'd rather die than let him turn us into some fucking sex slaves.'

Her eyes adjusted a little more. She could just about make out objects around her. Boxes. Old wooden pallets. A set of stairs.

'They'll find us,' Steph said.

'Then we fight,' Lori said. What she really wanted to say was that she knew they should never have got in that bloody car. Her gut had been right. But now wasn't the time for I told you so. Now was the time to survive. To fight.

The shuffling of feet above made her breath catch in her throat. She looked up at the ceiling and froze. Footsteps overhead, muffled voices and the sound of laughter made her stomach roll.

'They're here,' Steph whispered.

'Hide,' Lori said, feeling around the small room with her hands. Rough concrete walls encasing them in the damp space told her all she needed to know. There was nowhere to hide. They were stuck in a box and Ped and Jambo had them right where they wanted them.

Almost half an hour had passed since Ped and Jambo had been above the basement. They hadn't entered, hadn't come for Lori and Stephanie – this time. This was the most terrified she'd been in her entire life. The smell, the darkness, it clawed at her throat and all she wanted to do was scream. She recalled nothing. At least, her memory recalled nothing. Her body, on the other hand, ached from the abuse she'd suffered when that part of her brain had shut down to protect her.

'Stephanie?' Lori whispered into the darkness, hearing a scritch-scratching sound coming from the top of the stairs.

She heard an urgent hiss, followed by her best friend's voice. 'I've almost got it.'

'What are you doing?' Lori pressed.

'I'm trying to pick the lock, *shoosh*.'

Lori's knees trembled beneath her. 'We shouldn't have got in that car,' she said, her voice trembling with worry. 'We're never going to get out of here alive, are we?'

At that, the sound of a click, followed by the screech of metal, halted her voice.

'Yes, good old Gran's penknife to the rescue. Hurry up,' Stephanie said, as a sliver of light crept into the basement. Lori felt her friend's hand grip her own and pull her towards the door.

Lori counted the stairs as they climbed.

One. Two. Three. Four. Five.

As they reached the twentieth and top step, a tall, dark silhouette blocked the doorway.

'And where do you two think you're going?'

It was Jambo.

He rushed down towards them, arms outstretched. Steph moved her arm across Lori's body, pushed her into the wall and stuck her foot out. Jambo stumbled over it, causing him to stagger forward.

'Shit, my penknife,' Steph said as the sound of it skittering across the floor made Lori's heart sink.

Jambo fell down the twenty stairs into the depths of darkness below. He landed with a deep thud and Lori held her breath.

'Go,' Steph said, pushing Lori ahead of her and out into another tiny space, although lighter than where they'd been kept for however long it had been.

'Get the knife,' Lori said, but just as she did, the sound of rushing feet in their direction made Lori's heart jump in her chest.

'I should have fucking killed you both when I had the chance,' Ped's voice hissed as he knocked into Lori. She fell to the ground, and Ped pulled her up quickly. His hands were around her neck, urgently squeezing her windpipe.

'No!' Steph shouted. Lori could just about make out her friend's face at Ped's back. Hands scratching at his cheeks.

He let go of Lori, pushed her so hard she fell backwards through the doorway and into a pile of old, broken pallets. There was a scuffle, Steph was silent. Lori could see he had his hands around her neck now. Where was the penknife? It was too dark to see.

She got to her feet, her body screaming in pain as she bent down and felt around for something she could use as a weapon. Then she felt a broken piece of pallet big enough to do some damage.

Her hands gripped around the long, jagged piece with nails sticking out of it. She raised it above her head and swung as hard and fast as she could, aiming for the dark outline of Ped's body.

She felt the impact vibrate through her arms, heard the crunch against the back of his skull. Steph took a long gasp of air. He'd let go.

'Run!' Lori said as she watched Ped stumble back from her.

She kept an eye on Ped, hoping that her best friend had done what Lori had said and got out of there. All she cared about was putting an end to this ordeal.

'Bitch,' he hissed. She swung again; this time she could make out the whites of his eyes. The nailed pallet connected with the side of his face, and as she pulled it away, she felt a resistance.

Ped let out a yelp like an old dog. The nails had embedded themselves in his face on impact, and the yelp came once she'd pulled the pallet plank away from his face.

He was on the ground, crawling away from her. Crawling towards the open door to the basement. Jambo was still down there. Possibly still alive.

'That enough for you? Prick? Is it?' Lori said, her voice weak.

Ped was getting to his feet, and his face was a mess. One of his eyes was swollen almost completely shut and blood poured from his face and the back of his head. He resembled something from a horror movie and, as much as it horrified Lori, she knew he wasn't going to give up. He was stood in front of her, wobbling and swaying. She'd done damage. But not enough to put him down for good. He had fight left in him, but so did she.

She swung again, caught him on the other side of the face. Her arms were beginning to tire, but the adrenaline fuelled her to keep going. This was about survival.

Ped stumbled backwards and the darkness swallowed him. As he fell down the stairs to the basement where she and Steph had been imprisoned, the sound of his bones crunched under the impact with each step. Silence followed. It didn't fool her. She wasn't convinced they were dead.

'Let's go,' Steph spluttered behind her, trying to regain her breathing.

'No,' Lori said, spinning around to face Stephanie. 'We need to check they're dead.'

'We need to go. Now,' Steph pleaded. 'If we go back down there the only people who are going to die are us.'

Lori shook her head, kept her eyes on the black space in front of her. 'I don't remember what they did to us, Steph. My imagination is doing that for me. But I *need* to know that I've made sure they can't do it again.'

TEN

Lori felt around the wall for a light switch or cord. Anything that could provide some form of light so she could check if the two pricks in the basement were dead or whether she had to finish the job.

She found the switch she hoped would be there, and when she pressed it, a dull light flooded the basement beneath them. It seemed there was still electricity to the building even though no one lived there any more.

'Jesus,' Steph whispered.

Lori glared down at their bodies, lying deathly still at the bottom of the stairs. A pool of blood seeped out from beneath Ped's skull, with more smeared across his face.

Jambo's eyes were shut, his face slightly turned away from the angle where Lori stared down at him.

'Are they dead?' Steph asked from the top of the stairs.

'I think so. Surely you can't lose that much blood from the back of your head and live to tell the tale.' She rubbed her hand in circular motions on her chest as she tried to stem the horror and fear rising inside her.

'Okay then, let's go,' her friend said in a hiss.

Lori hesitated. 'No. We have to know for certain.'

She took one more step, two, three. She stopped, seventeen steps above their captors, and took a long, deep breath. She peered down at them. Jambo's leg jerked. His eyes flew open and Lori jumped.

'Fuck,' she hissed. 'Not quite dead.'

He sat up slowly, as though he was cautious of causing any more damage. Then he craned his neck and looked up at her with that creepy smile he had on his face when she first met him.

'Don't fucking move,' Lori said, her voice shaking.

Jambo got to his feet, pulled a penknife from his pocket. Her stomach lurched. He'd somehow managed to grab hold of the knife when it fell from Stephanie's hand.

'Lori,' Steph said, her voice strained. 'Come on.'

Heart thrumming in her chest, she kept her grip on the wooden slat in her hands. He moved towards her, taking each step slowly.

'Do you want to die, or something?' Lori asked, trying to sound braver than she felt. 'I said don't move.'

'Or what?' Jambo challenged. 'You going to hit me with that crumbled old piece of wood?'

'It did the trick on your mate,' she retorted.

He was now three steps below her, knife pointed in her direction. She jabbed the slat at him, caught him in the throat. A nail embedded itself and blood spurted from his mouth as he fell back, grasping at the hole where his windpipe was.

Steph sobbed behind her, repeating the words 'Oh my God, oh my God' over and over.

He landed back where he'd started and Lori listened for last breaths – *hoped* for them more than anything. They came in wet, gargled sounds and Lori knew he wouldn't survive this time.

Silence followed.

Stephanie sobbed hysterically and Lori simply took her hand as they stood over the bodies of the dead.

Lori was quiet, her mind whirring at what could have happened to them. They'd been so close to death and it could easily be them at the bottom of those stairs. But it wasn't. And for that, Lori couldn't be more relieved.

'We survived, Steph. We're going to be okay.'

Those words had no weight to them. Because they weren't going to be okay. Not by a long shot. How the hell could they be? They'd just killed two people. For survival, yes. But it was murder. That would follow them wherever they went for the rest of their lives.

ELEVEN

2025

DUNREATH GAZETTE

WEST AND CLYDE COUNCIL AGREE DUNREATH TOWER DEMOLITION CONTRACT

West and Clyde Council have awarded a contract for the demolition of the Clydeview Towers, south of Dunreath Village. Greer Demolitions Ltd will begin works on the towers, stating that the demolition will be carried out within two months. The agreed contract amount has not yet been stated; however, Greer Security Firm Ltd has also been awarded the contract for security of the site, due to issues of fire-raising, looting and other crimes.

A spokesperson for West and Clyde Council said, 'Rehoming of tenants was not necessary as the towers have been abandoned for many years, although some of the properties were privately owned. Work to buy back said properties took a long time, but now the demolition works can commence and, hopefully, property developers can begin construction on new, affordable homes for tenants of the council area. Of course, this is all due to the completion of surveys done on the land to ensure it is suitable for future construction.'

Mr Logan Greer, the owner of Greer Demolitions Ltd and Greer Security Firm Ltd, has been living in Dunreath for the last two years. We spoke to Mr Greer following the announcement, and this is what he said:

'I grew up in Dunreath but moved away when I was younger. Hearing that the village wasn't doing so well, I wanted to inject some happiness back into it. I began buying some of the businesses that were failing and decided that I wanted to start cleaning the place up a bit. I've been back two years, and I am confident that Dunreath is on its way back up. The area will be a better place for people to live and work, and I am happy to be the one to raise it up. The Dunreath Arms is back to being a well-used public house, as it was back in my day. And I've just opened up a café which has West End vibes but Dunreath prices. I want this to be a place people are proud to call home. I know I was when I lived here all those years ago. Pulling those towers down will get rid of the eyesore and create new jobs as well as new amenities for the people living in the area.'

The Dunreath Gazette will continue to follow the progress of the village and report on new and exciting ventures coming your way.

TWELVE

Logan Greer sat on his office chair at the back of the Dunreath Arms and watched on the CCTV as the delivery van arrived.

Getting to his feet, he moved out of the office and through the pub. The punters raised a glass as he passed them, some giving him a nod. He was respected here and it was something he would never get bored of. Rising up the ranks hadn't been easy, especially doing it alone. But he'd managed it and now he was reaping the rewards.

Once outside, Logan headed towards the van just as the driver got out.

'Boss,' Davie said in acknowledgement. 'How's things?'

Logan shook his hand. 'Aye, all good, mate. Your journey all right?'

Davie nodded and led Logan round to the back of the van. Davie had been his pickup and delivery driver for three years now, but they'd been friends for over two decades. He was one of the only people in the world Logan could trust.

'Aye, no bother at all. That was the one good thing to come out of us not getting independence: nae fucking border control between us and England.'

Logan smiled in agreement. Independence from England would have caused many a problem for moving drugs up and down the country.

'And it's all there?'

'It's all there. I checked each case myself before heading off,' Davie said, opening up the back door. Logan glanced inside and smiled when he saw the cases. Fifty in total, all containing another payday.

Pulling open the shutter to the back entrance of the pub, Logan and Davie began unloading the shipment one case at a time and carrying it down to the cellar.

Once the last case was in the cellar, Logan slipped Davie a handful of cash. 'A thank you for keeping things running smoothly. And for helping me all these years. I wouldn't have survived without you, mate. I really wouldn't have.'

Davie patted Logan on the back and smiled. 'No need to thank me. You'd have done the same in my position. I wasn't going to leave you on the street, was I? Not when we'd become mates.'

Now that Logan had his feet firmly on the ground in Dunreath and he knew that he was eventually going to own the majority of the place, he would be able to earn money from both sides of society here. There was the income from the security and demolition firm, as well as the café and the pub. But he knew that he'd make so much more from selling drugs to those living in the estates around Dunreath; those who just couldn't go without. He had a plan to buy up some of the flats from the council – he'd be able to rent them out to some of the girls he knew on the streets. Their rent would be paid through entertaining some of his clients, those with very specific needs. Then he'd be able to launder the cash through the café and the pub, as well as the many other businesses he had planned for the future.

'Your street team ready for this? It's the biggest shipment we've ever done here,' Logan asked Davie. 'I mean, I know you've managed plenty of runs before, but this is bigger than either of us has put out there.'

'They're ready,' Davie replied confidently. 'And there are plenty of people ready and waiting for some of the best cocaine they'll ever get their hands on. You know what this place is like: full of people gagging to stuff gear up their nose, and I'm happy to deliver on your behalf, Logan.'

Logan nodded. He believed every word Davie said. He was a good worker, someone Logan knew could get the job done and the money in.

'The heroin's a first for you, isn't it?' Davie stated. 'You think it'll sell?'

'Well, this place is full of junkies. So, it's not like it'll sit there stagnant. And it's good shit, by all accounts. I personally wouldn't go near the stuff; far too addictive and I don't want to do anything that will fuck up my future. But one hit of the stuff and the punters will be begging at our feet for their next hit, Davie.'

Davie laughed as Logan pulled a set of keys out of his pocket and jabbed one of them into the seal of the box nearest him. Dragging it along the seal, he pulled the top flaps open and peered inside. Packages of cocaine and heroin lined the box, separating the bottles of beer.

'Ooft, would you look at all that money, just lovely,' Logan said, pulling one of the packages out. 'This lot won't last long in this place. I'm sure I'll be able to put in another order within the month.'

Logan took his phone out of his pocket, pulled up the number of one of the lads working for him and hit call.

'All right, lad,' he said. 'It's all here. I want all of you down at the pub tonight. You've got a sales target to hit. Bring Andy and keep your mouth shut, understood?'

He hung up and perched himself on an empty beer keg.

'He's no idea?' Davie asked.

'Not a clue. The fact that he's been undercutting in small amounts shows he's clever, but not that clever if he thought he'd get away with it for so long. Stupid prick. Hope it was worth it for him,' Logan said.

'I just cannae believe he had the balls to do it at all. I mean, it's brazen, I'll give him that.'

Logan sneered. It took a lot for him to trust people and taking on young lads from the estates to sell his gear was hard for him. And now, this little shit had proven him right. You can't always trust people.

'What you going to do with him?' Davie asked.

'Haven't decided yet. Depends on how honest he can be with us. If he lies, then it's game over for him. I've got somewhere I can leave him. Somewhere no one would ever find him.'

Davie raised a brow. 'The towers?'

Nodding, Logan thought about it. Would that be a good idea? So close to the demolition? Maybe not.

'There's always the Clyde?' Davie said, as if reading his thoughts.

'Aye, true. I'll tell you this, though. I'm not going to let some wee fucker from this place screw me over. Not with all the plans I've got for the future.'

He thought about that. With the income from the demolition, the pub, the café, his security firm and now some of the best cocaine and heroin in the country, soon Logan would be the king of Dunreath. And that was just the start. He wanted to expand, rise up the ranks in more towns. He wanted to take Glasgow. He'd be better than all those before him: Ricky Fyfe, Janey Hallahan, Donnie Black, Terry Reid, the Brysons. He'd do it right. Once Logan was kingpin, all those names would be forgotten.

—

Davie's team of dealers were stood in the cellar at the Dunreath Arms. Everyone was silent as Logan eyed them all. Some were clearly nervous, some weren't. As Logan began to slowly pace the floor in front of them, Andy kept meeting his eye.

'You good there, mate?' Logan asked.

'Aye, boss. Never better,' the young lad answered. Andy, who'd been a dealer from Davie's hand-picked lads from the estates in and around Dunreath for the last two months, was stood there, brazen as ever, and Logan felt his blood begin to boil.

'So,' he began. 'You all know why you're here. We have a new shipment and Davie here is going to delegate. But before he does, I've got one question I need to ask you all. I want a straight yes or no answer. And I'll know which of you, if any, is lying.'

The ten lads, including Andy, gave each other a look of confusion. It seemed Andy was a good actor. For now.

'Davie, fancy doing the honours?' Logan asked, sitting down on the empty beer keg.

Davie stepped forward, stood with his feet apart and folded his arms across his chest. 'You've all been working for Mr Greer for the last two months. And you've all been earning a decent wage from it. He pays well if you sell well. And so far, no one has had any complaints. But it seems as though we have a thief in the team and we need to get to the bottom of who it is. Mr Greer can't have that. It's not good for business, and it's not good for morale. So, my question is, have any of you been undercutting Mr Greer? Particularly in the last month.'

The lads' faces said it all. Shock. Disbelief. Some gave an incredulous laugh.

'Who the *fuck* would be daft enough to do something like that?' one of them asked, and Logan smiled.

He got to his feet and raised his arm, pointed a finger in the face of Andy. 'You,' he said calmly. 'Wee specky Andy. You look innocent, couldn't even pass as a dealer, never mind a dealer who'd undercut his boss.'

Andy stared at him, his eyes huge and round behind his circular-framed glasses. 'Not me,' he simply said.

'Well, it's none of us,' one of the other lads called out. 'I always thought you were a dodgy wee bastard, Andy. You've just signed your death certificate there, mate, and you've put us all in the firing line.'

Andy spun around and stared at the lad challenging him. 'I'm not dodgy and I'm not lying.'

'If you're not lying, where's my missing gear, Specky?' Logan pressed.

'He's probably sniffed it himself,' another lad piped in. 'Check the size of his nostrils. That beak was made for snorting.'

The rest of the lads began roaring with laughter and Davie raised a hand to quiet them. They all did so immediately.

'You see, I think he's right, Specky. The boys have had complaints about cost versus volume, and we did some digging. We've had eyes on you for a month now and you've been taking a little for yourself each week and selling the remainder at the same price. Haven't you?' Logan said.

Andy blinked rapidly before he shook his head. 'No.'

'He's a wee coke-heid, you can tell just by looking at him. He's always *pure* wired,' someone else said.

Logan brought his arm back down to his side, and Andy was visibly angry. Logan had two choices here. Set the mob of dealers on him, or deal with the little shit himself.

'You've pissed off your colleagues, Specky,' Davie said. 'You're all meant to work as a team, and you've not just let us down, you've let the lads down too.'

Logan watched as Andy eyed each of his peers. He stood taller, shoulders pushed back as if he was ready for the fight that was coming.

'Can you prove you've not been stealing from the boss?' Davie asked.

Andy shrugged. 'I didn't think it would be an issue.'

Logan frowned, flexed his fingers. 'You didn't think it would be an issue to steal my gear?'

Muffled words of disbelief came from the rest of the lads and Logan himself couldn't believe how upfront Andy was being.

'You're heavy minted,' he continued. 'I thought a wee line here and there wouldn't make a difference.'

'You've been taking a gram from each of your orders, Specky. We've had them check after you've delivered. You've got ten orders on your run. That's ten gram per week.'

Someone gasped. 'Ten gram a week? Fuck *sake*, how the fuck have you even got a beak left after all that?'

Logan raised a brow. 'Unless you're selling it? Going rogue. Is that it? You fancy yourself as a lone wolf, Specky?'

Andy raised a brow and shook his head. 'We all have bills to pay.'

Logan nodded. 'Oh fuck off, Specky. You're a seventeen-year-old lad who lives in a tiny bedroom in his mammy's hoose. You're hardly independent.'

A low thrum of laughter came from the rest of them.

'You know what happens to people who steal from me, Specky?' Logan asked. He glanced up at the group of lads in the cellar and gave a nod.

They descended on Andy like a pack of wolves. Kicking, punching, stamping. Andy barely made a sound as Logan and Davie climbed the stairs and stood outside.

'He might not make it out of there alive,' Davie said.

'That's the price you pay for stealing from me,' Logan replied.

After a few minutes, one of the lads opened the door and gave Logan an icy stare. 'Done.'

Logan approached the door and held out his hand. The lad placed Andy's broken glasses into his palm and glanced up at him. 'What do you want us to do with him?'

Davie stepped forward and said, 'I'll take it from here. You boys get back to work.'

Logan gave Davie a nod and tossed the glasses into the back of the van, before heading round to take his place inside the Dunreath Arms.

THIRTEEN

Lori stepped out of the shower and wrapped the towel around herself before heading through to her bedroom. Sitting down on the edge of the bed, she began to rub the rough fabric across her skin in an attempt to get herself dry as quickly as possible. She didn't often look at herself in the mirror; at least not her body. Taking in the reflection of her own face wasn't something she could avoid and that was fine. Her face wasn't where the scars were.

Pulling on her jeans and jumper, Lori ruffled her hair with the towel and then her fingers. With natural curls, there wasn't much styling involved. Back in the day, she'd straightened her hair so much she wondered if the curls would ever return. But they had, with some retraining. It changed the shape of her face and she looked a little different than she did when she was a teenager.

Curls and a few extra lines around the eyes don't change what happened to you, a voice at the back of her head whispered.

She wished that it was as simple as that.

A sharp buzz from her phone as it vibrated on her bedside table startled her from her thoughts. Reaching for it, she picked it up and read the text from her son, Jay.

> Got the job. Start tomorrow. Chinese takeaway on me when I get my first wage.

Smiling, Lori hoped that Jay's new job would allow him to escape from Blackhill Court. And Dunreath altogether. Anyone from the area was tarnished by their roots. No one who ever tried to get out was ever successful; except for Charley. Not that she'd wanted to leave. She'd been forced by social services. But Lori knew it had been the right thing for her.

She typed out a text in reply.

> Congratulations. I knew you'd get it.

Not that she even knew what the job was. Jay hadn't told her. His reasoning? In case he didn't get it. He'd been for a few job interviews. Had never been successful. As soon as you mentioned you were from Blackhill Court, no one would touch you. Of course, that was never stated as the reason, but it was blindingly obvious.

A rhythmic rattle from the front door followed by a click and, 'Helloo? You in?'

'Just coming,' Lori called back to Steph as she opened the bedroom door and headed into the hallway. Steph had let herself in, as she always did.

'You heard from Jay yet?' Steph asked.

'He got it.' Lori beamed. 'Honestly, Steph, I'm so bloody happy for him. It means he has a way out of this dump.'

Steph's grin widened. 'Reece got a job too.'

Lori stared at her, jaw dropping. 'Oh my God! That's amazing. What is it? The job?'

Steph cleared her throat. 'Security. That's all he said.'

A surge of happiness filled Lori's chest. 'We need to celebrate.'

They headed to the kitchen and Lori opened the fridge. She pulled out the bottle of Prosecco that had all but one glassful missing from it and placed it on the worktop. Steph was already in the glass cupboard, pulling out two glass flutes as Lori reached for the lemonade for herself.

'So, did Jay tell you what the job was for?' Steph asked as Lori poured the Prosecco into one of the glasses, the bubbles fizzling up her nostrils. She didn't dislike the smell, but even after all these years, she still couldn't bring herself to put alcohol into her body.

'Not yet,' Lori replied, placing the bottle down and pouring some lemonade into her own glass. 'But I honestly don't care what it is. It's income; an opportunity. Something *we* never had at his age.'

'Aye, but not for lack of trying, eh?' Steph said.

That was true. Lori had been offered an opportunity to get into a childcare apprenticeship after she'd had Jay.

'Yeah, that early-years apprenticeship was great. But I was looking after children for forty hours per week and the college were paying for Jay to be at nursery. I wasn't getting to spend any time with him at all, and when I wasn't at the nursery, I had coursework to do. All that on top of being a mum and still navigating through the fucking trauma, it just wasn't something I was able to manage. And I was gutted when I gave it up. So were my management team and my tutor. I still think about that job all the time; wonder where it would have taken me if I'd stuck at it.'

Stephanie shook her head. 'It's not like you just gave up, Lori.'

They moved through to the living room and Lori opened the veranda door. The sun hadn't quite reached her side of the building yet, but she could already feel its warmth as it stretched around the estate.

'Mind that time I went for that apprenticeship job when I was nineteen? The one at that hair salon in Glasgow city centre?'

Lori nodded. She did remember. And she also recalled how Steph came back in floods of tears.

'Stupid bitch was all up for me getting the job until she read my address on my already sparse CV. Then told me that she'd be in touch but there had been a lot more people before me who had more experience. Fucking arsehole. I could have done her for discrimination, but what would have been the point? I swear, all this place gives you is grief and fucking trauma.'

They fell silent for a brief moment. Trauma was one word for it. Not a day went by that Lori didn't feel the weight of the horrors she and her friend went through. They'd tried to make as decent a life for themselves and the boys as much as they could. Growing up and living in Blackhill along with what happened to them made it hard. But the hardest part was trying to be good parents to their boys while carrying the weight of what they had done to survive. It seemed that night had ruined their future, no matter how hard they tried to change that.

She pushed the thoughts out of her head. Today wasn't about her. It was about Jay and, now, Reece.

Steph raised her glass and Lori clinked hers against it.

'Have you heard?' Steph said after a moment of silence.

'Heard what?'

'The Clydeview Towers are being torn down.'

More silence followed and a strange sensation tightened in Lori's chest. Panic? Relief?

'Fuck,' she whispered.

'It's a good thing,' Steph said, her volume almost matching Lori's. 'Honestly, it is.'

'But, what if someone finds them?'

Steph puffed out her cheeks. 'As morbid as this is to say, there won't be much left, Lori. And if anyone was going to find them, it would have happened by now. Don't you think?'

She wanted Steph to be right more than anything in the world.

'Sometimes I still wake up in a cold sweat,' Lori found herself saying out loud, just as Steph lit a cigarette.

Lori closed her eyes briefly. She could still smell the basement. Still smell her own sweat; her own blood and the dust that clung to her skin.

'Why did we never get out, Steph?' she said, opening her eyes. 'You know, after we got away from that place. Why didn't we try harder to get out? I only ever gave it one shot.'

A long, exasperated sigh followed. 'Because this shithole, Blackhill Court and Dunreath, once it has a grip on you, it doesn't let go; sinking its filthy claws into your skin, your bones. You know what it's like, Lori. We've both watched family members get caught up in shit that was bigger than them. Yeah, we might have been able to steer clear of becoming heroin addicts, but look at the rest of the shit we had to deal with. No money, no jobs.'

It was Lori's turn to sigh in exasperation. 'Yeah, but we're of this new generation, Steph. You hear people talking about breaking the cycle. Why aren't we trying to do that?'

Steph shrugged; her expression pained. 'Because it's not just about our behaviours towards our kids, and how we role model, Lori. It's about money; let's not pretend it isn't. We don't have any. And you need it to get away from places like this. Even if we did have jobs, which is impossible around here, then we still wouldn't make enough to get away. And I'm sorry to say it, but it might be too late for the likes of Jay and Reece. They're here, living and breathing this place. It's in their bones, jobs or not. I mean, look at us. Full of regret now, and we're in deeper than the boys are.'

Lori closed her eyes again, shook her head. 'It's almost not worth going on.'

'Okay, if you're going to start that shit, then I need to remind you of something. We've been through *the* worst thing anyone could imagine. And we survived. We are doing okay, Lori. As much as this place is the pits of hell, we're doing all right. And so are the boys. It's our job to convince them to get the hell away from here once they have enough money. It's just a question of if they want to. They're good boys, Lori. Despite where they're from.'

The front door clicked open and two sets of footsteps padded into the flat.

'All right, Maw and adopted Maw,' Jay laughed, swaggering into the living room. 'How's it feel to have two wages coming in now?'

Lori rolled her eyes at the cocky attitude, but it put a smile on her face. Steph laughed loudly as she hugged her own son, Reece.

Born just weeks apart, the two young men had grown up like brothers. Becoming young mums at the same time had been one of the hardest yet best things that could have happened to Lori and Steph. It gave them something to focus on other than their trauma.

'So,' Lori said, ruffling Jay's hair. 'What is the job?'

Jay and Reece sat down on the sofa, side by side, each grinning ear to ear.

Lori and Steph gave each other a glance.

'We got a job working together,' Reece said.

'You're both working in security?' Steph asked.

'Aye,' Jay replied. 'For the firm in charge of the Clydeview Towers site until it's ready for demolition.'

Another fleeting glance, although this time Lori saw the fear in Steph's eyes.

Lori cleared her throat. 'That's…'

'We're getting twelve quid an hour. Time and a half for night shift. Once the towers are down, the firm will move us on to the next job. So, we might actually get the fuck away from this place,' Jay said, his voice booming with excitement.

'That's great, son. Really great,' Lori said, hoping that her voice didn't carry the tremor felt in the rest of her body.

'The only thing is,' Reece said. 'Our boss is Logan Greer. And we've all heard the rumours about him. So, not sure how that will pan out.'

Lori and Stephanie glanced at each other again.

'Logan Greer is your boss?' Lori asked, hoping she'd misheard but knowing she hadn't. 'Oh, I don't know about this, boys. You know what people say about him.'

'Och, Mum. Don't worry about it. It's only rumours. And if I'm honest, if the rumours *are* true, I'd rather work for him than not,' Jay said.

'Hmm,' Stephanie chipped in. 'Just be careful around him. Do what he asks, don't be late and make sure you do your job well and you both should be fine.'

Jay rolled his eyes and gave a wide smile. 'Money, Mum. It means money. At this point I'd work for the devil and not care, so long as I'm working my way up to getting the fuck out of here.'

Lori raised a brow and refrained from saying that he might as well be working for the devil from the stories she'd heard.

'Like Steph said, just be careful.'

'Right.' Reece rubbed his hands together. Turning to Jay, he said, 'Pub?'

'Aye, but no' too late,' he said, rising from the couch. 'We need to get into the night-shift routine, so I want a clear head for that.'

The boys left the flat, and once the door was closed behind them, Lori watched as Stephanie glugged back her Prosecco, took a long draw on her cigarette and bowed her head.

'Fuck,' she said quietly.

Lori nodded her head.

Fuck indeed.

FOURTEEN

Logan Greer got out of his van and looked up at each tower. One to six. All dark. All derelict. His top lip curled up, revealing bright white teeth. He licked his tongue over them, adjusted his high-vis jacket and reached into the van for his hard hat.

He'd arrived at the site earlier than his new employees to make sure that he could take in every one of their faces. He wanted to know each and every one of them. Who he could truly trust. Of course, he'd already interviewed them, hence why they had the job in the first place. But interviewing someone and getting to know someone were very different things.

Placing the hard hat on his head, Logan slammed the van door shut and strode towards the main entrance of the demolition site.

He glanced up again and smiled. Soon enough, those towers would be brought to the ground and he'd get to watch. That was all he'd ever wanted.

Stepping into the makeshift office in the form of a metal container, Logan sat down at the desk and leaned back in his seat. He now owned Clydeview Towers. All six of them. He was the one who would get to bring them down. Watch them fall, piece by piece. Once flattened, he was going to begin plans for new construction. A new housing scheme. Maybe even a shopping complex. The opportunities were endless. The *income* would be endless. Not that he was in any way struggling financially. He was the biggest business owner in West and Clyde. A legitimate businessman who owned pubs, cafés, a demolition and security firm. One who was flourishing and creating jobs and he didn't need a single qualification in any of it. Anyone could own those types of businesses and he *was* anyone. An all-round good guy, looking to regenerate the area of Dunreath for the people who lived there.

Logan slid open the drawer to his right and pulled out the envelope of security lanyards for each of his new team. Ten in total. Five for day shift, five for night shift.

He looked over them carefully. Took in each name. Each face. He *never* forgot a face.

A gentle tap on the door made him look up. Logan got to his feet, straightened his high-vis jacket as though it was an expensive suit and moved around the desk towards the door.

The door opened outwardly, and as he pushed it, all ten faces belonging to his new security team stared back at him.

'Did you all hire a bus to get here?' he laughed.

The young lad at the front laughed loudly. Everyone else smiled.

'Right, in you come. We've a few things to go over before I assign you all to your shifts.'

Logan stepped aside and they all filtered through. Young, tall, some a little skinnier than Logan would have liked. Doing a job like this for a man like him required a physical presence. Security guards needed to be looked at and feared. Not all of them would last, he thought.

'Mr Greer,' the one who'd laughed loudly started. 'When is the demolition taking place?'

Logan raised a brow. 'Call me Logan. And that's one of the items on our list.' He walked around to the desk, stood behind it and removed his hard hat. He picked up the lanyards and began handing them out, calling their names one at a time.

'Reece Lyle?' he said, handing the lanyard to Reece. 'And lastly, Jay Graham.' He glanced at the lad's face. The one who'd laughed. The one who'd asked the first question. The one who clearly *wanted* to be noticed.

'So, a bit of background about me. I'm Logan Greer. I own a lot of land and a lot of premises within the village. Once these towers are down, I aim to build upon the land, creating more jobs and opportunities for financial growth for the village. If you lot play your cards right, your employment with me could last a long time post-demolition.'

He regarded each of their faces. All enthusiastic, some quietly so. But Logan couldn't help but notice the look on Jay Graham's face. He wasn't just enthusiastic. He was excited. Impressed.

'I understand some of you are from Blackhill Court?' Logan probed.

Jay Graham and Reece Lyle nodded. Jay seemed proud. Reece, not so much.

'You've found it tough to get a job because of that?' Logan asked.

'As soon as you mention Blackhill Court, no one wants to know,' Reece replied. 'Not that they ever say it obviously because they'd get into bother for it, but you can see their enthusiasm for you drain from their face, like you've just told them you're a gravedigger or something.'

A few of the lads gave a nervous laugh. Logan nodded. 'Right then, boys, why don't you go outside, take a walk around the site. Familiarise yourselves with the place and the towers. Come back to me in about half an hour and we can move on to discussing job descriptions.'

Everyone nodded and began to shuffle out of the door.

Logan cleared his throat and said, 'Reece, Jay? Stay behind, please.'

They glanced at each other nervously but stood still as everyone else left the Portakabin.

'I get it, you know? The stigma attached to Blackhill Court. The place doesn't have the best reputation. Although, from what I hear, it's a bit better now than it was back in the day?'

Jay sniggered. 'Not sure that's the case. The place is brutal. I am proud of where I come from, but I want out. That's why I have this job. Going to make something of myself, you know?'

Logan looked at Jay. Then to Reece. 'And you?'

'Aye,' Reece replied, albeit a little hesitantly. 'The sooner I can get away from this place, the better. I don't want the estate hanging over me and tarnishing my name forever.'

Logan clicked his fingers, pointed at Reece and then Jay. 'That's what I like to hear. Ambition. It's what got me to where I am now. I went through a shitty situation when I was younger. A series of bad decisions which could have led me down a bad path. In fact, it did for a long time. I won't go into detail, but I decided that when life gave me a second chance, I wasn't going to let that opportunity go. It doesn't matter where you're from, what your background is. If you put your mind to something and work hard, you can achieve anything.'

Jay was nodding like an excited puppy with treats dangling in front of its nose.

'If you boys want to make your lives better, then you stick with me, you work hard and you'll go places.'

Reece stared at him through narrowed eyes.

'You seem, sceptical?' Logan asked, taking in the look on his face.

'Not sceptical. Just... It's nothing.'

'You don't believe you'll get away from this place?' Logan asked.

Reece shrugged. 'No one does and I never have, so why would now be any different?'

Jay nudged him. 'Oi, that's not very positive.'

'Sorry, but good things don't happen to folk from the estate. Just my take on life,' Reece replied.

Logan cleared his throat. 'We all have to start somewhere, Reece. And this is your stepping stone to better things. It might just be a security job now, but in a few years it could be something much bigger. Demolition, for example. I could help get you into that, if it's something you're interested in? There's money to be made there. We're going to make Dunreath great again.'

This had been a long time coming. Being back in Dunreath as the person he was today, a wealthy and successful businessman with close connections to the hierarchy of Glasgow, felt brilliant. In fact, it was almost euphoric. But none of that compared to how he felt about being able to bring those towers down. That meant more to him than the mountains of money he'd made. Bringing those towers down would be his greatest achievement to date.

FIFTEEN

Lori paced the living room floor with her coffee mug in hand. Not that she'd taken a sip in a while. She felt sick.

'Would you sit down? You're making me dizzy,' Stephanie said.

'I can't. It keeps me from going to a really dark place. If I'm moving, I'm fine. If I stop...' She let the words fade. She didn't want to relive that night. Not now.

'There's nothing we can do, Lori.'

'That's the problem.'

'Look, those remains, they'll have been discovered a long time ago by some junkie who'll have shat themselves from saying anything in case it got them banged up, meaning no more drugs. It's been twenty-four years. It'll just be bones now. Yes, they were reported missing; yes, it was in the local news briefly; but you know what the police are like round here. As soon as Blackhill Court or Dunreath are mentioned, they don't bother their backsides. They did a half-arsed job and the case was closed. Once those towers are down, those bones will be dust; if they're not already and—'

'Can you stop!' Lori said, her voice a lot louder than she'd intended. 'Just *stop*, Steph.'

'Sorry.'

Whispering, she said, 'You're not the one who killed them. It was me.'

'They fucking deserved it, Lori,' Steph gasped. 'You know they did. And anyone who thinks otherwise is just like them. Fucking monsters.'

Lori shook her head. 'That's not what I'm worried about, Steph. What if Jay and Reece find out about what we did?'

Steph frowned. 'Why would they? No one knows what happened. No one even knows we went with them that night. It was the turn of the century, Lori, and we lived in the shittiest area in the country. That's why we could get away with burning out the car, which they'd stolen anyway. Stuff like that happened *all* the time. The police never set foot near the towers, never mind the estate; like I said, they half-arsed it. No CCTV, no smartphones. If you ask me, that night never happened at all.'

Lori sniggered. 'Try telling that to my fucking brain.' Stopping at the veranda door and looking out onto Blackhill Court, she shook her head. 'You know, I thought I was fine; thought I was doing okay. After all this time, I really thought the trauma was slowly leaving me. Then bang, our boys get a bloody job on the site and it all comes flooding back. What are we doing, Steph? Allowing them to set foot in that place after all we know?'

Steph sighed, got to her feet and placed her hands on Lori's shoulders. 'Again, what happened was justified, Lori. And they know nothing about it and never will. Our boys are going to be fine. The towers are coming down, Lori.'

Lori felt sick. She wasn't convinced that things would be fine. Things had never been fine.

'Look, the only surviving people who knew about that night are stood right here. The ones who could ruin our lives are already *dead*. That's thanks to you, Lori. You don't have to be scared. You should be proud that you saved our lives.'

Lori narrowed her eyes. What she wanted to say was that if Steph hadn't been so bloody keen to get in that car, then none of it would have happened at all. Instead, she bit her tongue, took a deep breath and nodded. There was no point placing blame. It was simply a need to lash out, and she'd already done that twenty-four years ago. Those two monsters paid the price for it.

'I just can't help worrying. That's all. It was bad enough knowing the towers were still standing, hiding our secret. But now they're coming down and...' She stopped herself. And what? She didn't know.

'We've never gone back,' Steph said. 'Maybe we need to face them before they're demolished.'

Lori's eyes widened at the absurd suggestion. 'Are you insane?'

'No, but I can see that this is tearing you up inside, Lori. Maybe we could watch the towers come down?'

Lori thought about it. 'You can do that?'

'Yeah. There's stuff on TikTok about all the high-rises in Glasgow that have come down over the years. Like the Red Road flats? There was a big crowd for that one. Actually, one of the towers never properly collapsed. Just stood at half-mast.'

Seeing the towers coming down did appeal to her. 'Maybe watching history crumbling to the ground would heal me from what I did.'

Steph frowned. 'From what *you* did? What you did, Lori, was *save* us from the depths of hell. Christ only knows what those animals would have done to us if you hadn't picked up that wooden plank.'

Lori closed her eyes. Remembered the sound of the wood smacking off the side of his head. The nails embedding themselves in his skin.

'But yes,' Steph continued. 'You're right. Maybe you would heal from seeing them come down. Knowing that the hell they inflicted on us will never happen to anyone else because those bastards will be buried in there forever.'

Lori nodded. 'Yeah, forever.'

But forever would never be long enough.

SIXTEEN

As Reece Lyle sucked on his vape, he stared up at the third building from the left and squinted in the sunlight. Clydeview Towers were like evil giants, spoiling the view of the River Clyde and Greenock in the distance.

'Good fucking riddance, I say,' Reece said, blowing out a huge cloud of raspberry-scented smoke. 'They've made the place look like a shitehole for years. I don't think anyone's ever lived in one since I've been alive.'

'Aye,' Jay said as he pulled his hard hat off and chucked it into the back of the van. 'Apparently they've not been lived in since the late Nineties. They'll not be missed, that's for sure.'

'Bet they don't get demolished for ages yet,' Reece continued, before slipping his vape into his pocket.

'Well, the longer they stand, the longer we're in work,' Jay said. 'And you better not let Logan Greer hear you say that. He owns the demolition company too, you know? Don't want him to know you think his company is full of shit.'

Reece grimaced at the thought of staying in the job longer than necessary. They'd already been working there for a week and, almost as soon as they'd started, Reece knew he didn't like it. The place had an eerie feel to it. Plus, it was boring just doing perimeter walks all night long. But worst of all, it meant working for Greer. He was a self-assured prick. So certain he was going to make Dunreath a great place to live and work, and that in itself was a good thing, but it came with a cocky attitude. As much as he went on about being there to make things better for his workers and the residents of Dunreath, he always managed to make Reece feel as though he saw himself above everyone else. Reece hated that about him.

'I never said it was full of shit. And anyway, I'm not sure I'll do this for long. The money's not the best,' he said.

Jay turned and gave a quizzical look. 'Are you shit at maths? The money's brilliant.'

'Don't think I'm the one bad with numbers, Jay. If you think twelve quid an hour is good, then you need your head seeing to.'

'Aye, but I've not got bills to pay and neither have you. We're free men, living under a free roof with no responsibilities. That twelve quid an hour will get us everything we need, from bevvy, to vapes, even drugs if we want them.'

Reece stared at him for a moment and wondered what was going on with him. Was that all he wanted to be? Free from responsibility, with as much drink and drugs at his fingertips that he could ask for? 'I thought you said you wanted to make something of yourself outside of Blackhill?' Reece asked.

'I do, but I'm allowed to have fun first, am I not?'

Reece narrowed his eyes. That kind of attitude was what resulted in people never getting out. The fun and the partying lasted too long, and then it became the norm.

'Well, all that shit's not for me. Working for someone like Logan Greer isn't something that I want long-term. You've heard the rumours about him. You do know he fancies himself as a gangster, Jay?'

Jay laughed loudly. 'He doesn't fancy himself, Reece. He *is* a gangster. He owns every pub in Dunreath, as well as Clydebank, along with the security and demolition firm, and fuck knows where else.'

'He doesn't just own pubs, Jay. He owns the security company that guards the doors of other pubs. Have you not heard the stories about the owners getting threats? Punters being forcibly removed if the security guys don't like what you're wearing, or what you're talking about? And did you hear him that first night on the site? *We're going to make Dunreath great again*. Aye, nae *bother*, Donald Trump.'

Jay scoffed, but Reece kept his expression straight.

'If you're so against the guy, then why'd you go for the job here?' Jay asked, his face now devoid of humour.

'Because my mum is struggling to pay the rent in our shitty flat and I said I'd help her. Fucking hell, Blackhill Court itself is just as bad as Dunreath as a whole. The whole area should be flattened, not just the fucking towers.'

'All the more reason to keep this job. Then you get to spend every shift away from the place and with your best pal,' Jay said, giving Reece a playful dig in the ribs.

Reece smiled a little and stared out of the front windscreen of the van. Why did no one from Blackhill Court ever want better for themselves? Why did they always stay? Generations of people lived and died there and Reece didn't think he wanted to be one of them. It seemed clear to Reece that Jay was much the same, was quite happy to stay in Blackhill and spend his time wasting away, using his money to get drunk or off his head. If he did that for too long, he'd end up never getting out. His own mum was going to be stuck there forever. And his dad? Well, neither he nor Jay knew who their dads were and, according to their mums, they both just upped and left when they found out they were expecting. Much like most of the men in Dunreath. Deadbeats.

'Aye, maybe. I'll see how things go,' Reece said, pushing thoughts of his dad out of his head.

'That's my lad.' Jay slapped his shoulder and then started up the van. 'Now, brekkie? I'm starving.'

Nodding, Reece pulled on his seat belt and Jay drove the van away from the derelict hell towers and along the main road towards Dunreath Café, which was situated in the east side of the village, next to the football pitches and dog fields. A passer through might take in their surroundings and believe the place to be a picturesque village. Reece knew differently. As did most of the sober residents; not that there were many.

Jay killed the engine and got out of the security van: a perk of the job which hadn't been in the advert when they'd applied for the job and none of the other employees seemed to have. Only Jay, and that alone didn't sit well with Reece.

Reece followed Jay into the café, and a familiar, booming voice came shooting through the crowd noise.

'Boys! Come over and join us.'

Reece's stomach lurched. It was their boss.

Jay looked like a kid who'd just seen Santa Claus for the first time. Reece had to stop himself from rolling his eyes at how pathetic he looked. He couldn't understand what it was about Logan that Jay thought was so wonderful. The guy was a prick.

'All right, Logan,' Jay said, stood by the edge of the table.

'Jay boy. How are we? Good shift last night? Reece?' Logan peered around Jay's tall yet slender frame and smiled widely at Reece.

'Quiet. No issues on our end.'

Logan nodded as he shovelled a forkful of food into his mouth. Suddenly, Reece wasn't hungry any more.

'Good,' Logan said. 'Take a seat, boys. What you having?'

Jay sat down opposite Logan and Reece slipped in beside him.

'Coffee for me, please,' Reece replied.

'I'll have the full Scottish, extra hash brown,' Jay replied.

Logan raised his hand and made eye contact with the waitress, who scurried over quickly with a beaming smile on her face. And in that very moment, Reece's stomach rolled as his ex-girlfriend, Sammi Connolly, stood at the table. He stared at her, eyes wider than usual. He hadn't seen her since she'd abruptly ended things with him; so abruptly that he'd never truly understood why. Right now, he could be looking at his answer.

'A'right, babe,' Logan said. He reached around, grabbed her backside and jiggled his hand. 'Look at that arse, it's a belter.'

Reece kept his eyes on the table and refused to react to what Logan was doing. Doing that to her in front of everyone in the café didn't make him look like a big man, it only made him look like a bigger prick than he already was.

He gave their order and then said, 'Boys, this is Sammi. She's my fiancée. Running this place for us, aren't you, babe?'

Reece glanced up at her, taking in her face. The face he'd fallen for very quickly when he'd been younger. She'd broken his heart when she'd ended things. He'd always suspected that she'd gone off with someone else. But Logan Greer? He was at *least* forty. Could be younger, but the well-groomed beard made it hard to tell for sure. It just showed the kind of guy he was, having a girlfriend that young. What did a forty-year-old man want in a girl half his age? What a creepy bastard.

'Hiya,' she said sweetly, barely making eye contact with Reece before Logan tapped her on the hip and sent her on her way.

Reece kept his eyes on the table, not wishing for Logan Greer to think he was staring at his girlfriend. It took all his strength not to steal a glance at her. He still felt the same way for her as he had back when they were together.

The problem was, no one knew about them. He'd kept it all to himself because he'd fallen so fast. As much as Jay was his best friend, he'd have taken the piss out of Jay for being in love with someone. And telling his mum would have resulted in Lori finding out, therefore Jay discovering their relationship. Now more than ever, what they once had would have to stay a secret. If Logan thought he'd employed one of his fiancée's ex-boyfriends, he probably wouldn't be best impressed about it.

'So,' Logan said, taking a large mouthful from his coffee mug. 'I've got a proposal for you.' He was staring at Jay.

'Who, me?' Jay replied, looking a little worried.

Reece struggled to concentrate, his mind a mishmash of thoughts.

'I want you to be site supervisor of your shift. You've done a brilliant job and shown true leadership skills. If you do this well, you could rise up the ranks, maybe at one of my other businesses.'

Reece groaned in silence. *Here we go*, he thought.

'Are you serious?' Jay beamed. 'Site supervisor?'

'Aye. Good money in it. How's eighteen quid an hour sound? And you get a bonus for every little bastard you find snooping around the property.'

There's never anyone snooping around, Reece thought. No one in their right mind went near the place. It was rat-infested for a start and Christ knew what else lurked inside.

'That's...' Jay faltered. 'That's brilliant.'

Brilliant wasn't the word Reece would use. But then, it seemed he and Jay were becoming different people as they got older.

Reece turned to see Sammi coming towards them with their order. She sat the coffee in front of Reece and the breakfast plate in front of Jay.

'Cheers,' Reece said quietly, and she disappeared again. It was like they were complete strangers. Logan hadn't acknowledged her this time.

'Supervisor.' Jay turned to Reece, giving him a jovial nudge. 'That's fucking brilliant.'

Reece reached for his steaming-hot mug and smiled. 'Sure is, mate. Congratulations.' He sipped slowly at the coffee and felt Logan's eyes on him. He peered across the table and their eyes met. Did he know?

'You're probably wondering why I haven't promoted you,' Logan said.

'Not really. You think Jay's good for it. It's your business at the end of the day. What you say goes.' As soon as the words were out of his mouth, he could have kicked himself. As much as he genuinely didn't care, and would never want a job as a supervisor with Logan Greer, the way he'd said it made him sound bitter. And he was; especially now, knowing that Logan was engaged to Sammi.

Logan stopped, a piece of toast hovering by his mouth, and smiled. 'Ha. I like that.'

Aye, you would, Reece thought, before setting his mug down. Something about Logan didn't sit right with him. It wasn't just that he was a gangster; although Logan always referred to himself as a multi-business owner, there was something else. Reece sensed that Logan was a lot more dangerous. He imagined Logan causing physical harm to anyone who would try to get in the way of his plans, business or personal. The rumours about him being a criminal yet hiding it with all these legit businesses were bad enough. Adding Sammi into the mix made him feel sick.

'You're both discreet. You've demonstrated that since you've been working for me. That's exactly what's needed from security staff. Discretion and loyalty to the job.'

Jay sat forward, ready and eager to please his new boss with whatever he needed. Reece raised a brow and wondered why the pep talk was necessary now. Why not have this discussion in the interview process? It was almost as though he was giving them a warning. Be discreet or else. Discreet about what? Had he had this chat with the rest of the security staff? Or even the demolition staff?

'Discretion and loyalty are our middle names,' Jay said. 'Aren't they, Reece?'

Reece refrained from the instinctual eye roll. 'That's us,' he replied instead. Discretion was Reece's number-one quality. He'd kept a huge part of his life a secret for so long. How he'd managed it, given that Sammi had ripped his heart from his chest when she'd ended things, he'd never know.

'Jay, I need you to do something for me,' Logan went on.

'Anything at all,' Jay said.

Here it comes, Reece thought. The favour that would seem like nothing, but coming from a man like Logan Greer, could mean all sorts of things.

'Be at the site three hours before your shift tonight. You come along too, Reece. Means if Jay's ever unable to attend his shift, you'll know where to pick up.'

So, essentially the deputy to the deputy? No thanks, he thought.

'Ah, sorry, boss,' Reece said before he could be sucked into anything. 'I've got to take my mum to her doctor appointment before I start my shift. Sorry to let you down.'

Logan was nodding slowly, as though he was deciding whether to let Reece away with his defiance; because that was how he'd see it. Reece didn't even know what would come of the request to go in early, and he didn't want to know.

Reece could feel Jay's eyes boring into the side of his head, but he chose to ignore him.

'Ah, family come first, eh?' Logan said, but his demeanour had changed, just enough that only Reece would have noticed.

'Glad you understand,' Reece replied with a smile.

Logan didn't respond; instead, he turned to Jay and said, 'You in?'

Jay nodded like an emphatic puppy and Logan gave a sneer. It made the hairs on the back of Reece's neck stand on end.

Whatever it was that Jay would be getting dragged into later, Reece had to find out what it was and try to warn him of the dangers of getting in deep with Logan Greer.

Reece would never admit it out loud, but Logan scared him. Behind the expensive suit he was wearing, and the perfectly groomed beard, there was something very sinister about him, and Reece wanted nothing to do with any of it.

SEVENTEEN

Sammi Connolly watched as her fiancé and ex-boyfriend sat at a table together and she felt sick. She hadn't seen Reece in two years, since she'd ended things with him to be with Logan. Now he was right in front of her and she couldn't react. Logan wouldn't like it. Logan looked up at her and smiled, the lines around the corners of his eyes creasing a little. She was once madly in love with him; she'd even go as far as to say she'd been obsessed with him. Not now. She knew she needed to get out of this relationship. He was dangerous, unpredictable. Someone, she knew now, she should never have got involved with. She should never have left Reece for Logan. But she was young when it happened: only eighteen years old. At first, he'd been charming, kind and all things she'd wanted in a man. She'd been taken in by him quickly and suddenly everything she'd loved about Reece became nothing. Reece was a boy. Logan was a man. She'd thought a man was what she needed.

Logan's good traits had lasted for the best part of a year. He'd showered her with compliments, made her feel special, wanted.

Now, two years down the line, Sammi had a ring on her finger and so much had changed from the moment she'd met Logan. All slow, minuscule changes which she hadn't noticed until it was just that little bit too late. Telling her she was prettier without make-up, saying that she should show off her true beauty. Then came the first time she'd gone to leave the house and he'd taken her hand, held her out in front of him. He'd glanced over her, told her that he didn't think the outfit she was wearing suited her. Told her to change. Then quickly, he started picking out some of her clothes for her. All the signs had been there, she just hadn't seen them until she couldn't stop it. Control, passive aggression, his ability to make her feel two inches tall if she wanted to do anything that didn't involve him. Then the passive became the blatantly obvious. His ability to terrify her to her very core just by giving her a look was just as scary as when he shouted in her face. Logan was not a partner. He was a monster and was very clever about only showing it behind closed doors.

She met Reece's eye and Sammi felt like he was reading her every thought, watching every memory play out in her mind. There was a sadness in his eyes that riddled her with guilt. She'd left one of the good ones to be with the bad guy. Their relationship had been a secret and she was glad now that was the case, because Logan would make it very obvious how much he disliked the fact that he was faced with her past.

Jay seemed to be lapping up every word Logan said. But Reece wasn't. She recognised the look on his face. No one knew she understood Reece on a deeper level than everyone else. She could tell that he was very cynical about whatever words were coming out of Logan's mouth. And he should be. A strong sense of regret washed over her for how things ended between them. Reece was a good person; a million times the man Logan would ever be.

'Hey.' Her friend, Dionne, nudged her, pulling her from her thoughts. 'How are the wedding plans coming along?'

Sammi turned to face her and plastered on a big smile, mostly for Logan's benefit, but also for Reece's. She needed to pretend she was happy. 'Oh, we haven't really started yet.'

Dionne's brow creased. 'You've been engaged for ages now. What's the hold-up?'

Sammi shrugged, tried to keep her expression neutral. The idea of marrying Logan terrified her. Tied to him forever? No thanks. And now she was staring into the eyes of Reece Lyle and everything he was to her came rushing back. She didn't know what she had back then until she gave it up for a monster. 'There's no rush. And Logan is busy working. He's got lots of different things on the go. I don't want to bore him with wedding stuff and add to his plate.'

Dionne's disappointed expression didn't last for long as her attention turned to a customer approaching the counter.

Sammi turned to see Reece standing in front of her and her stomach lurched.

'Sammi, can you serve him, please, I'm heading on my break,' Dionne said.

Clearing her throat and trying her best to put on a brave face, she smiled like she would at any customer and said, 'What can I get you?'

'A slice of school cake, please,' Reece replied. 'It's for my mum.'

Sammi nodded. 'I don't need to know who it's for. You sound like the wee guys who used to get sent to the icy for fags for their mum.' She immediately regretted engaging in conversation with him. It might give him a false impression. Stealing a quick glance in Logan's direction, she was relieved to see that he hadn't seemed to notice. She was always being accused of flirting with other men and it just wasn't the case. Of course, Logan never needed an excuse to start a fight with her, but if he saw her chatting with Reece then found out who he was, all hell could break loose.

Reece chuckled and his shoulders relaxed. Sammi felt a mix of emotions.

'How are you?' Reece asked, his voice low.

Panic set in and all she wanted was Logan to hear her speak highly of him, of their relationship. 'Brilliant,' Sammi said. 'Really happy. About to start planning a wedding and running this place. What's not to be happy about?'

He raised a brow as if he knew what she was trying to do but said nothing to allude to it. Instead, he smiled and said, 'You look well.'

Sammi wanted the ground to open up and swallow her. She didn't deserve for him to be kind to her.

Ignoring him, she turned, made up a cardboard takeaway box and slipped the slice of cake inside.

'It's on the house, big man,' Logan's voice boomed from behind Sammi, and immediately her stomach felt like it was going to fall away from her. Had he heard Reece tell her she looked good?

'There's really no need,' Reece replied as Sammi turned to hand the box over, making sure that she kept her eyes on her fiancé.

'There's *every* need. You're my employee and that's one of the benefits of working for me. You get freebies sometimes.'

Logan's arm was hanging around Reece's shoulders and he was leaning in towards the counter.

'She gets freebies too, don't you, Sammi?' Logan laughed loudly and Reece seemed to wince.

The crap pun made her skin prickle. No longer being attracted to or being in love with the man who was abusing you didn't make it easier to walk away. The fear of what might happen to her if she did walk away had been the reason she'd stayed for as long as she had.

'I eat so much free cake I'm a bit sick of it, if I'm honest.' She smiled. She and Logan locked eyes and Sammi could clearly see that Logan was annoyed, yet his smile widened. As soon as the words were out of her mouth she regretted saying them. She was insinuating that she wasn't grateful and that would have got his back up.

'She's teasing. She loves it all, really. She'd have nothing if it wasn't for me, let alone cake, isn't that right, babe?'

Sammi wanted to smash the cake dish over his head. *Aye, certainly none of the aggravation*, she thought. Instead of biting, she smiled sweetly and said, 'Absolutely *nothing* at all. I couldn't be more grateful to have Logan as my future husband.'

Again, regret immediately followed.

Why couldn't she just keep her mouth shut? That sounded incredibly sarcastic and Logan wouldn't appreciate it. An awkward silence hung over them, and if she didn't know any better, she could have sworn she saw Reece try to wriggle out from under Logan's grip. She didn't blame him. Logan made her skin crawl too. Was that hurt she saw in Reece's eyes? Surely after all this time, he wouldn't still have feelings for her, would he?

'Right then, I'd better head off. I'll see you guys later,' Reece said, finally breaking the silence and slipping out from Logan's arm hanging around his shoulder.

Logan shot her a glance. 'You're a cheeky wee bitch,' he whispered with a smile.

'Sorry,' she said quietly. Then she internally recoiled for apologising. Why couldn't she be cheeky when he behaved so appallingly? Grabbing her backside in front of his employees, speaking about her as though she was a piece of meat, as though he *owned* her. Was now the time to start speaking up for herself? She knew Logan well enough to know that he'd punish her for that; there was no point in reacting if it was going to result in a bigger blow-up.

He smirked then turned away from her before heading back to join Jay. As she watched him go, she wondered if she'd ever be free from him.

EIGHTEEN

Reece walked through the flat he shared with his mum, the cake box in one hand and his phone in the other. He tried to put Sammi out of his head. It shouldn't be too hard, he'd had enough practice over the last few years. Being at school together, he'd always fancied her but never had the guts to say anything. They'd been friends before they'd got together; good friends. Walking home from school together sometimes when Jay wasn't around. Then they'd fallen for each other, with Logan very quickly taking her from him. Pretending she wasn't on his mind was a skill Reece had perfected.

'How was work?' his mum asked as she emerged from the kitchen with a coffee mug in one hand and a cigarette in the other.

'Shite. Boring,' Reece replied, and held the box out to her. 'Your favourite's in there.'

She smiled. 'What is it about the job that's so boring? Surely if you're making your own money, it can't be *that* bad?'

'It's far from good. But that's not the problem.' Reece watched his mum place the cigarette between her teeth and take the cake box with her free hand. 'My boss is a dickhead.'

'Aren't bosses supposed to be dickheads? It's how they get the workers to get the job done,' his mum replied. 'Trust me, if I could be your age again and be *sober*, with a job, I'd take any boss being a dickhead if it meant I had opportunities ahead of me.'

His mum wasn't even forty yet and she looked like she was closing in on fifty. Life for her had been rough and he was quite sure he didn't even know the half of it. She never opened up much about her past. All that he really knew was that she had lived with her gran most of her childhood and teenage years because her own parents were addicts. Reece had never met either of his grandparents and, from what he did know, it sounded as though his mum was better off without them. He barely remembered his great-gran, given that she died when he was two.

'You could always cut back on the bevvy, if that's worrying you?' he suggested, not knowing how she'd take it.

She shrugged. 'Aye, I could. But it's a bit late in the day now, isn't it? Whatever damage is done is done. And it's not like I know any different, is it? I mean, I grew up with an alcoholic for a gran and, in this estate, every second person is a drinker or likes the gear. It's normal to be a drinker in this day and age, isn't it?'

Reece wanted to argue the point, but chose to keep the conversation moving forward. 'Would you go back and change things, if you could?'

They both sat down on the sofa and Reece glanced out over the estate. No matter whether the sun was splitting the skies or if there was a grey blanket above them, Blackhill Court screamed depressing and oppressive at the same time.

'Knowing what I know now? Yeah, I'd try a bit harder to get the fuck away from here,' she replied, placing the cake box on the coffee table in front of them and taking the cigarette from her teeth. 'The only thing I wouldn't change is having you. Because you were my little ray of light in all the darkness.'

Reece blinked, turned away from the window and sank into the sofa. 'You deserve better than this place, Mum. *We* deserve better.'

'I know. But things were different back then, Reece. It wasn't as easy to up and leave and, with no real prospects, it was difficult to get anyone to even look at you for a job. You know the story about me going for the apprentice hairdressing job in the city; bitch practically threw me out when she realised where I was from.'

Reece sighed at the thought of what it must have been like. What he couldn't help but think of was that she hadn't tried again. She'd just accepted that people thought you would amount to nothing if you came from Blackhill Court. She'd sat back and allowed that perception to become a reality.

'This is why you're doing this shitty, boring job with the dickhead boss in the first place, Reece. You're doing what I couldn't. It's your foot on that first step of the ladder out of here. If you look at it that way, then you'll stay focused.'

Reece narrowed his eyes and laughed. 'What podcast did you pick that line up from?'

She laughed and he liked the sound. 'Look, me and your Aunty Lori came from a different world. We had scumbag family members who didn't care about us. You and Jay have mums who care about what you do with your life. We're proud of you both and we never had that growing up. We had to scrape through every minute of every day to survive. When you were born, I promised myself, and Lori made the same promise, that we would go without if it meant you boys got what you needed. And now, here you are: an adult with your own job. You're already winning in life, Reece. You're alive, you're healthy and you're earning.'

Reece rubbed his hands on his work trousers and sighed loudly. 'Aye. You're right. I just need to stay focused. I suppose working for a dickhead like Logan Greer is better than not working at all. When you put things into perspective, I see it your way. Living here is like living in stagnant water. The place is disgusting, it's depressing and I want us both out of it, Mum.'

'I know you do, son,' she said with a tinge of sadness to her tone. She stared down at the cake box; stared at it hard as though she wanted the thing to open up so she could jump inside and avoid the conversation.

'Mum, can I ask you something?'

'Anything.'

'Why did you never try to find someone? You know, a boyfriend? Other than Lori, you seem lonely. You've seemed lonely for a long time.'

His mum sighed and then a smile crossed her face, although Reece could see there was no happiness there; no humour.

'Reece, sweetheart, you not included, but men are absolute arseholes. The majority of them are narcissistic, evil and all take, take, take. I raised you to be none of those things and I think I can safely say that I did a good job. You're a gentleman who genuinely cares for others. But most men are awful and I don't need that in my life. And no, I don't think I am lonely. I have you and I have Lori. That's all that matters to me.'

Reece nodded. That was a fair explanation and yet, somehow, Reece wasn't sure he believed that his mum wasn't lonely. Yes, she had Lori and, yes, Reece was there. But you can be in a crowded room and still feel lonely, can't you?

'Anyway,' Stephanie continued. 'I'm going to eat my cake in peace and assure you that everything is and will be fine.'

'Yeah, I'll be fine once I'm away from Logan Greer. Honestly, Mum, Jay thinks the sun shines out of his arse and I just can't see it. It's actually quite sad to watch Jay sucking up to him. It's like he's worried that, if he doesn't, Logan will sack him or something.'

Stephanie sighed. 'Maybe that's how he feels, though? Maybe he thinks that he has to behave a certain way because the guy gave him a job?'

'It's bullshit. Jay's the hardiest guy I know. I've never seen this side to him. And already he's been promoted. I'm not jealous, by the way. I just wonder if Jay wasn't such a fan of his, if he'd have been promoted at all.'

Stephanie was quiet and Reece closed his eyes briefly.

'Sorry, I'm just knackered. You know what I'm like when I'm tired, everything pisses me off.'

'Well, you should get some sleep then. And you shouldn't let this stuff get to you. This might not be your dream job, Reece. But it might be Jay's and you need to respect that.'

He glanced at her and smiled. 'Yeah, you're right. I better get to bed. On the night shift again tonight.'

He got to his feet and his mum remained on the sofa, beginning to pick at the cake.

'I'll get us out of this shithole, Mum,' he said, placing a hand on her shoulder and giving it a squeeze. 'If it's the last thing I do.'

She finally looked up at him and her eyes were glassy from tears, which he hadn't expected, yet she still smiled. 'It won't be the last thing you do, son. It'll just be the start.'

He walked through to his bedroom and shut the door, but just before he did, he heard the sound of his mum's muffled sobs.

NINETEEN

Stephanie clasped her hand over her mouth so that Reece wouldn't hear her cry. How she'd managed to raise such a polite, caring young man in the middle of an estate like Blackhill Court was something she'd never understand.

How had she and Lori survived this place? After what they'd been through at those towers? Not that either of them could truly remember other than that final night. If it hadn't been for Lori, they'd both be dead long ago; both Reece and Jay wouldn't exist.

Stephanie tried to compose herself, reminded herself that her son didn't need to hear her cry. No child should bear witness to their parents' problems. Shame the ancestors of Blackhill Court couldn't have thought the same thing. People like Lori's parents had left a trail of destruction after their deaths; and when they were still alive. It was a wonder that Lori had chosen the sober route in life. She could have easily gone down the same path as the rest of her family, but instead she'd chosen to try to break the cycle; not that she'd known that was what it was called back then.

Stephanie had always been good at keeping her feelings about what had happened to them hidden. Although, it had manifested itself in other ways. Stephanie drank away the already hazy memories to the point where she now knew she had an alcohol problem. Following the trend in her family. Parents, grandmother. Now Stephanie. She was glad that Reece didn't seem to be following on that same path. She'd get a hold of it one day; she would. She wished she could be more like

Lori. Sober and able to cope with whatever life threw at her without the need to drink herself to the bottom of a bottle.

What happened was my fault. If I hadn't agreed to that date, if I hadn't forced Lori to go, none of it would have ever happened. That same thought had plagued her every single day for the last twenty-four years. It was because of Stephanie that Lori had killed Ped and Jambo. It should have been Stephanie's job. But she'd been too much of a coward.

Taking a deep breath, she let the air out of her lungs slowly, tried to stop the terror she felt in her chest and her thoughts sending her into a spiral. Reece was working on the demolition site, on top of the bodies she and Lori had left behind. The thought made her sick to her stomach, yet she had to be calm for Lori's sake.

Getting to her feet, Stephanie moved towards the veranda door and opened it wide. The fresh air hit her in the face like she hadn't been outdoors in days. The sound of kids out on the estate kicking a ball off the neighbouring flat's wall echoed around her. She welcomed the sound, allowed it to occupy her mind.

'Morning.' Lori's voice came from the balcony next to Stephanie.

Stephanie opened her mouth to speak, but fear captured her voice and she closed it again.

'What's wrong?' Lori said, a look of terror washing over her.

'Fuck fresh air,' Stephanie whispered, pulling her cigarettes out of her dressing gown pocket and lighting her second one of the morning.

'Has Reece said something? Does he know?' Lori panicked.

Stephanie shook her head. She whispered, 'No. He doesn't know anything. And even if *they're* found, I doubt it'll ever come back to us.'

Lori moved towards the railing closest to Stephanie's veranda and leaned against it. 'You sound so sure. I'm not.'

'No one missed them, Lori. Yes, they were reported missing, but if the people who'd reported it really, truly cared about what happened, then the police would have done a better job in finding them.'

Lori looked out at the estate as Stephanie spoke. 'Yeah, I suppose you're right. And if they were found, then we'd have heard about it, right?'

'*Exactly*,' Stephanie said, keeping her voice low. 'So, it means their remains are still down there and even if they are found, *and* they are identified, there doesn't seem to be any reason why we'd be linked to them. We never made it to the cinema that night. And anyone in this estate who might have seen us getting into their car won't remember because they'd have been drunk or off their face. So, I'm not worried about Reece or Jay finding out.'

Lori turned her back to the estate and looked at Stephanie. 'So why do you seem so stressed? You've been crying, I can tell.'

'I haven't been crying,' Stephanie replied defensively.

'You forget I know you better than anyone.' Lori smiled. 'You've got hives all over your neck. That's a sure sign you're upset.'

Stephanie pulled her dressing gown tighter around her, as though that would eliminate the fact that Lori was right. She did know her better than anyone else, and vice versa.

'Can I come over?' Lori asked.

Stephanie nodded, stood back, and Lori climbed across from her own veranda to Stephanie's. They'd been doing this since they'd both got a flat next door to each other when the boys were just babies.

'You know, this gets a bit scarier the older we get,' Lori laughed as she placed both feet on the concrete beneath her.

'It's only about half a metre.' Stephanie smiled, sucking hard on her cigarette. 'A goldfish could jump it.'

'So,' Lori said, sitting down on the seat next to Stephanie. 'What's upset you this morning?'

Stephanie blew out a plume of blue smoke and tapped the build-up of ash into the ashtray on the table. Then she went on to talk about Reece, how he knew that his mum had gone through something traumatic, how he wanted to get them out of Blackhill Court.

'He hates his boss,' she continued, purposefully leaving out everything else she'd been thinking about. 'Said he was a bit of a dickhead.'

Lori raised a brow. 'Jay seems to think the sun shines out of him. I can tell he's impressed by the guy's lifestyle. It's like he's thinking he can have that life if he puts the work in. He might not be wrong.'

Stephanie pursed her lips. 'Aye, he definitely could. They both could. But not here. Not in this shithole. Reece is right, we need away from this place. Reece and Jay have prospects, but do they really want their old maws following at their back?'

Lori puffed out her cheeks, and they were both quiet for a while. Then Lori said, 'So, you still haven't told me why you're upset. And don't tell me it's because Reece thinks his boss is a dickhead.'

Stephanie was suddenly sick of smoking and stubbed the cigarette out but said nothing.

'Is it because of the towers coming down? You're worried, aren't you? I mean, you talk a good talk, Steph. But I know you're not made of stone. This has to be worrying you the way it's worrying me.'

Breathing out as much air from her lungs as possible in the hope it would take the stress away, she nodded. 'I can't help thinking it's my fault. All of it. I was the one who set up the date. I was the one who insisted we go. It's because of me. All of it, Lori. And don't say it's not. Every time I look in the mirror, I see their faces and those fucking scars they left on our bodies, Lori. And it's all my fault.'

Lori's expression was tinged with sadness. 'You didn't make them do what they did to us, Steph. That was their choice. If it's anyone's fault, it's mine. I was the one who flushed away their drugs. If I hadn't done that, Kev might have been able to pay Ped back.'

Stephanie was unable to hold back any longer and the tears were coming thick and fast now. Lori cried with her.

'Can we just stop blaming ourselves?' Lori cleared her throat. 'They did this. Not us. And we're only going over it all because the towers are finally coming down. If they weren't being demolished then—'

'Then what?' Stephanie cut in, swiping at her cheek with the back of her hand. 'Then we wouldn't be talking about it? The hell of what we went through would stay buried?'

'The hell of what we went through,' Lori said calmly, 'will *always* stay buried. Whether those towers remain standing or not.'

Stephanie rolled her shoulders, sat forward and rubbed at her face. 'I hope so.'

—

Lori went into the bedroom and took off her dressing gown and pyjamas. She stared at herself in the mirror and tried to blink away the thoughts of what had happened to her.

Lori didn't need to remember what had happened that night. And she didn't particularly want to remember. The scars, the fact that she'd killed the two of them, were enough. 'And I'd do it again if I had to,' she said out loud.

She glanced out of the window and in the distance she could just see the tops of each of the six towers down in the outskirts of Dunreath.

The idea that they would be coming down soon, that they'd be razed to the ground, was enough to help her realise that the past was going to stay in the past.

She'd murdered two men when she was just sixteen in order to save their lives. Lori would never apologise for that. She'd *never* feel guilt or remorse and she'd make sure Steph didn't either. Neither of them deserved to feel anything other than safe and proud that they'd managed to escape the clutches of those nutcases.

Taking the towel from the back of the bedroom door, Lori took one last look in the mirror and saw the scar of the saltire on both inner thighs: the diagonal cross, raised and puffy on her flesh. One on the outer side of each breast. The bastard, Ped, had branded her like a fucking notch on a bedpost.

TWENTY

Sammi stepped out onto the street to have her cigarette break and Logan was right behind her.

'You're a cheeky wee bitch, do you know that?' Logan whispered in her ear.

'That's twice you've said that now. Is that meant to be a compliment?' Sammi sniggered as she placed the cigarette between her lips. She knew it was a risk, giving him backchat, but she couldn't help herself. He was the biggest narcissistic arsehole out there and he needed to be taken down a peg or two.

'You get a kick out of it, don't you?' Logan said, ignoring or seemingly missing her sarcasm.

'I think you're the one who gets a kick out of it, Logan. You love trying to put me down in front of people. But you also love it when I fight back. That's why you fell for me in the first place. You loved my fiery personality and, guess what, I'm still fucking in here.'

They stared at each other for a few seconds before Sammi drew her eyes away from him. It was true, he did love a fight. But never with men, it seemed. Only ever with women. She'd never seen Logan speak to another male like a piece of shit. Was that because he didn't have the balls, or because he saw men as equals and women on the lower end of the scale? Most likely the latter.

'I saw the way Reece Lyle was looking at you. He fancies you, doesn't he? And you were admiring him the same way.

You two at it behind my back? Is that it? Because you couldn't keep your eyes off him. I'm not blind.'

Fuck. Did he know, or at least suspect that she and Reece were once a thing? Why would he? She'd kept it quiet, he didn't even know she had a boyfriend when they first met.

'Well, how do you expect me to serve customers? With my eyes shut?' she said, trying to keep up the pretence.

She knew she was pushing her luck with the amount of cheek she was giving him, and later on, when there was no one else around and they were within the walls of his flat, he'd punish her for it. It could be anything from a slap to a full-on battering. And he could make her wait for it for days on end; torturing her with the *will he or won't he* thoughts.

Logan bared his teeth a little. 'You know exactly what I fucking mean,' he said, his voice a low growl.

'No, Logan, I don't know what you mean. Why don't you spell it out for me? Are you saying I was looking at him in the way I *used* to look at you when we first got together?'

His body shifted then, spinning so that he was stood in front of her and her back was against the wall of the café. In the middle of the main street of Dunreath. In plain sight for everyone to see, yet Logan would make it look as though there was nothing to see. Just a couple having a cosy chat.

'*Used* to look at me?'

His nose was so close to her own she could feel his breath on her face.

She thought about Reece and the relationship she had with him. He'd treated her perfectly: with respect and kindness. Reece had grown up with just his mum to raise him and Sammi often wondered if that was the reason he was so good to her: he just knew how women should be treated. Logan, on the other hand, had ideas about women that scared her. He saw Sammi as beneath him, most likely saw all women as beneath him, like they were there to serve men and that was it. She'd left a good, kind-hearted man like Reece for Logan. What the hell had she been thinking? The memory of doing that stirred up anger, not at Logan but at herself. She'd binned a good guy for a scumbag and now she was dealing with the fallout of that.

'Yes,' she said, blowing smoke into his face. 'Because you were good to me back then, Logan, you were. Promised me the world, looked after me. Told me that I'd have everything that I should have had growing up, everything that I deserved as your fiancée and wife. Now you're abusive and controlling. I don't like it, Logan. I miss the old you. If you want me to stick around then you need to treat me better. I think you're forgetting who I am, Logan. I grew up with *nothing*, had to survive on my own for most of my life. A druggie mum, a dad in the jail. I had nothing before you came along and I was just fine. I can be fine on my own again if need be.'

Logan took a step back, his expression neutral. Often the look on his face just before he'd explode on her. But not this time. He took the cigarette from her hand and took a draw before handing it back to her. Every organ inside her body rattled from the fear of speaking against him. She was going to be punished for her attitude. Why couldn't she just keep her mouth shut?

'Is that right?' he said, blowing the smoke back into her face. 'Well, let me remind you of a little something, Sammi. I own *everything* in this little village, and more. You *won't* get far without me. You think life was hard back then? You're used to my money now, it would be far more difficult going back to that life after what I've done for you. So, speak to me like that again, and you'll find out what it's really like to be on your own; you think rock bottom was bad before you met me? I'll show you what rock bottom really means. Just remember this: I'm about to bring in a shit ton of money with the towers coming down. I'm going to be generating a lot of money from the land and, if you leave, you won't see a penny of it. I'm going to build, lease properties for business and I'm going to have so much money you'll be able to fucking sleep in it. You want to leave, go for it. But you'll regret it in more ways than one.'

Sammi kept her eyes on his. Unblinking. The bastard, she hated to admit, was right. She was used to his money and it would be far more difficult to start again. She'd have to start from the bottom. How would she be able to get her life together if she didn't have a roof over her head? Or money to buy food so she could merely survive? Not only did she want away from Logan, but she wanted away from Dunreath too. There was nothing here for her; or anyone else, for that matter. But this was the only place she'd ever known. She was stuck here. Going off into the big, wide world without his money behind her would be almost impossible. The only job she'd ever had was working at the café. Logan would never give her a reference. If she left him, if she left Dunreath, she'd most likely end up in a worse situation than the one she was in now.

Tutting, she raised the cigarette to her mouth, poised at her lips. 'I'm not going fucking anywhere,' she said, her words sitting heavy on her chest.

'Thought as much. And keep your eyes on me at all times. You're marrying *me*, no one else. I catch you looking at Reece Lyle like that again, I'll fucking kill you. And him. Got it?'

He leaned in, pressed his lips to her cheek and held them there for a few seconds. Then, pulling away, he glanced up and down the street before turning his face towards her. His eyes were dark, almost black, and a deep sense of fear rushed through her. He slipped his hand around the back of her neck and pulled her face closer to his, pressing his lips to hers so hard that his teeth crunched against her own. Then he took her bottom lip between his and bit down hard before letting go after just a second. His fingers pinched the back of her neck and his eyes were wild.

'Logan, you're hurting me,' she said, her voice trembling.

'Just a quick taster of what will happen to you if you fuck me over, Sammi. You don't want to know what would happen. All I'll say is, your tiny little body wouldn't cope with it.'

He let go of her and went back into the café. Once she was sure he was completely out of sight, Sammi sucked in a large mouthful of air and tasted blood.

His aggression, his anger, she was used to it all, but that didn't make it any easier to deal with. It wasn't the first time he'd tried to hurt her. It wouldn't be the last.

Growing up around men who thought women were a possession had been exhausting, but also made her determined not to let them bully her. If her dad had been around, she suspected he'd have been much the same. Sammi had had very little contact with her biological dad over the years. One call from prison every so often and one meeting. A general chat which truly meant nothing. The usual, *Hi, how are you? Yeah, fine, how are you?* The conversations never lasted long. And he always said that he'd get better, he'd get out and they'd get to know each other. Sammi never believed him and, so far, she'd been right not to.

Men didn't ever paint themselves in a good light when it came to women, whether it was father figures, brothers, boyfriends or just acquaintances, and especially not the ones in and around Dunreath.

Sammi closed her eyes and tried to allow the anger and fear to pass her by. Logan was a nutcase. His own mind would be the death of him if he wasn't careful.

Then she smiled, licking the blood from her bottom lip. Maybe that wouldn't be such a bad thing. Then she'd be free.

Sammi couldn't remember what it felt like to be free. Maybe because throughout her whole life, she'd never experienced it.

There had always been a man holding her back. Other than Reece, why did she always pick controlling men? Ever since the age of fourteen, she'd had boyfriends who liked to try to control her and she'd always walked away from them, but she kept going for the next bad boy; it was like she couldn't help herself. With Logan, it was different. She feared her future more as a woman with nothing. Not like back then, when she had nothing, so had nothing to lose. Perhaps she knew more of the world now, knew the dangers of being a woman out there on her own. But she wouldn't let that stop her from leaving. If she stayed with him, he might kill her one day.

Her phone vibrated in her pocket. She pulled it out, noticed that an unsaved number was calling. She hit the answer icon, placed the phone to her ear. 'Hello?'

A moment of silence passed before the caller spoke. And when they did, her stomach lurched.

'Samantha?' the voice said. Only one person on the planet ever called her by that name.

'Dad?' she said, although the word didn't roll off the tongue too easily. He'd never been a dad to her. But calling him by his given name felt wrong somehow.

'How are you?'

Here we go, she thought. *Empty conversations which will result in absolutely nothing once again.*

'I'm out,' he said.

Sammi cleared her throat. She'd never spoken to the man who'd fathered her while he was on the outside before. Not once. It was always while he was in jail. 'Out? For how long?'

'Hopefully, permanently. I've been out for almost a year.'

He'd been out for almost a year and this was the first time he was contacting her? Why had it taken him so long? Why wasn't she the first person he'd thought to get in touch with back then?

'I'm clean and sober,' he continued.

Raising a brow, she couldn't help the scepticism as it washed over her. 'You're sober? For how long this time?'

'Have been since I last went back inside.'

'And how long has that been?' Sammi asked. She genuinely couldn't remember purely because she never tried to. She never kept track of her dad's prison / real world timeline. What was the point?

'I've been sober for almost two years now.'

Sammi bit her bottom lip and closed her eyes. 'And why are you telling me this now?'

'Wondered if we could grab a coffee? Get a chance to talk? I could explain everything then?'

Sammi dropped the cigarette on the ground, stubbed it out with her foot and straightened her back before she responded. 'See, thing is, I don't know you all that well. In fact, I don't know you at all. I've spoken to you a handful of times in my life. Fuck, I don't even speak to *her* any more. You both kinda fucked me over when I was young and I've floated my way through life without really knowing what I'm doing and without anyone to turn to. So, if you don't mind, I'll pass.'

Before her dad had the chance to say a word, Sammi ended the call and breathed out a long, heavy sigh. She couldn't decide if it was relief, anger or something else.

She felt a sudden pang of guilt hit her but she quickly shook it off. Why should she feel guilt? He'd never done anything to warrant any emotion like that from her.

Shoving the phone back into her pocket, Sammi turned and braced herself for having to face Logan, before heading back into the café.

She'd made her decision. She needed to leave.

TWENTY-ONE

As Jay approached the site, his boss was stood outside waiting for him. He had a smile on his face while smoking a cigarette.

'Jay boy, how's things?' Logan asked.

'A'right, gaffer? Aye, no bad, thanks,' Jay replied. 'What's this all about then?'

Logan opened the cabin door and gestured for Jay to head inside. 'Take a seat, Jay.' Logan closed the door behind him and Jay sat down on the seat opposite Logan's side of the desk. 'You were promoted to site supervisor this morning,' Logan continued, as he moved around the desk and sat down. Jay couldn't keep the smile from his face. 'I have more businesses to take care of around Dunreath and I can't be present in all of them at the same time. I've got the pub to think about, plus the café as well as this place. I need someone running this place that I can trust.'

'Aye. I'm buzzing, gaffer. I'll do you proud, I promise.'

Logan sighed. 'I don't need you to be a suck-up, Jay.'

Jay's expression fell then, but he tried to keep the embarrassment from showing. 'So, what do you need me to do?' he asked, clearing his throat, trying not to sound too desperate.

'I need you to read this file. It's like a policy and procedure manual. A pain in the arse, but necessary to the job. Then I need you to do a walk-round of the site. Check all the towers, make sure they're secure. Any issues, report back to me. That way, I can note things down and report them on to the demolition team. You're like a second eye. Keeps us right with any inspections prior to the buildings coming down. The demolition team are due to start the soft strip in two days' time, so everything needs to be confirmed as safe. Understood?'

'A soft strip?' Jay queried.

'Aye, taking out the glass panes, the doors, any partitions, that kind of thing. Means the internals of the buildings are basically bare before the they're pulled down.'

Nodding, Jay thought about what Logan said and a feeling of concern washed over him. 'Hang on, are you saying that I'm the only person that is here to deem if each building is safe to enter?'

Logan laughed. 'You think I'd give you that responsibility? This is your first job, Jay. You've never worked a day in your life before this. It's me who has overall responsibility. Despite folk thinking I'm not always a legit businessman, let me assure you I am. I don't want SEPA and HSE coming for me because I've not done my job properly.'

Jay waited for Logan to explain the terms mentioned. When he didn't, he said, 'I don't know what those are.'

Logan's eyes flickered in frustration. 'Scottish Environment Protection Agency and Health and Safety Executive. They're the regulatory bodies. So, like I said, you're just a second eye. I'm asking you to basically check the security of the tower blocks. Make sure no one's hanging around, there are no leftover needles, no dead animals, etcetera. Again, I've already checked, you're just confirming *my* checks. Understood?'

Jay hesitated. It all seemed a bit above his pay grade. He wasn't working for the demolition side of things. He was just a security guard. But he wasn't about to argue with his boss and certainly not when his boss was Logan Greer.

Keeping his thoughts to himself, Jay nodded and said, 'Aye, that's fine. How long will that take?'

'Well, I called you in three hours before your shift for a reason. Ideally, I wanted Reece in with you so you could get it done quicker. You know what it's like. Two sets of eyes are better than one, three are better than two and all that.'

Jay glanced down at the manual and nodded. 'Shall I do the walk-round first?'

'Whatever suits, mate. Just make sure you get it all done before the rest of the shift arrive.'

'Okay,' Jay said. 'If you don't mind, I'll do the walk-round first; stretch the legs a bit.'

Logan gave a nod and glanced at the door, silently willing Jay to get on with it. Jay stared at him with curiosity and Logan seemed to pick up on it because the corner of his mouth raised in a slight smile. 'What is it, Jay?'

'Can I ask you something, about business? You don't have to answer if you don't want to.'

Folding his arms across his chest and resting against the edge of the desk, Logan raised a brow and said, 'Aye, go for it.'

'When I first started, you said you had a bit of a rough start like the rest of us. How did you get into all this?'

Logan looked around before raising his hands in a quizzical gesture. 'All this?'

'Aye, like, how did you start up? I mean, it must cost money to start, does it not?'

Jay stared at his boss and wondered if he'd gone too far. He was curious and genuinely interested because, one day, he wanted to be independent. Owning your own business was the route to freedom, wasn't it? No one to answer to. Being your own boss had to have nothing but perks, surely, money aside?

'You're a right nosy wee bastard, aren't you?' Logan said with a wide grin. 'Ach, mate, I get why you're asking. I wish I'd had someone to look up to at the start. But if I'm honest, I was just lucky. I worked in scrap metal, buying and selling. I made a mint. Then I invested the money I'd made in other things.'

Jay raised a brow. 'Like what?'

Logan laughed again, this time his smile not as wide as it was a baring of teeth. Jay got the impression he was annoying his boss.

'Listen, Jay, I've got this reputation of being a bit dodgy. Back in the day, aye, I was. I was in with some dodgy people, making money in ways I'd rather not discuss because I'm not that person any more. And I'd love to sit here and give you an unofficial degree in starting up your own business. But you'll learn better by figuring it out on your own, legitimately. So, if you just get on with the job in hand, watch how I handle things from my end, you'll pick it up. One day, you'll be your own man.'

Jay had never been inspired before. Not by anyone or anything. But right then in that moment, Jay had never been surer of anything in his life. He *was* going to be his own man one day, just like Logan had said. He'd own his own business, whatever that would be. And he'd earn his own money. He was sure of it.

'Cheers, boss. I appreciate the honesty,' Jay said.

'Don't worry about it. Now go and do your walk-round. You've still got that bastard binder to get through.'

Getting to his feet, Jay smiled, headed out of the Portakabin and walked towards the first tower. If he was honest with himself, he couldn't be bothered with this. Each building had thirty properties inside and there were six of them. But if he wanted to get on in life, then he supposed he'd have to start at the bottom. Logan Greer had and now look at him. Multi-business owner and probably minted more than anyone from Dunreath could imagine.

Pulling out his phone, Jay opened the calculator app and did the sums. Glaring down at the result, he groaned. 'That's one hundred and eighty properties I need to check. Fuck's sake, that'll take longer than three hours.'

As he approached the first block, Jay wondered if he could get away with checking every second or third? Maybe even fewer? But what if he missed something that Logan had logged down for the demolition team? He'd get a kick in the balls for that, at the very least. And it wasn't a very good start as site supervisor. He'd promised to make Logan proud to have promoted him. He'd have to do his best.

Staring up at tower one, Jay sighed and pulled his earbuds from his pocket. He selected his favourite playlist on Spotify, and Yungblud started blasting in his ears. He closed his eyes and entered the building.

—

'Fuck *me*,' Jay sighed as he stood outside tower three. He hadn't taken into consideration that each building's lift would no longer be working, given the electricity supply had been cut many years previously. Climbing the stairs in each of the first two towers had shown him that he might look the part in terms of fitness and stamina, but he was by no means fit.

'I'm fucking gubbed,' he gasped, pulling the earbuds out and placing them back in his pocket. He tried to regain some composure before setting foot inside the third tower.

As he entered, he glanced at the first set of stairs to his right when something to the far left of the entrance caught his eye. A partially boarded-up doorway. He moved towards it, trying to work out if the first two towers had possessed such a door. If they had, he'd have noticed them, would he not?

As he stood in front of it, he felt a chill run down his spine. He pulled it open. Inside was a dead, dark space which roughly only measured about four feet by four feet but was tall enough for him to be able to stand at full height. The space made his skin prickle. Then he noticed the second door. This one was made of metal, by the looks of it. He pushed it.

Nothing happened.

He pushed it again, harder this time. It didn't move.

Then he placed his hand on the steel handle and pulled it. A little wiggle of movement. Pulling harder, it scraped along the concrete and, slowly but surely, began to open towards him. The sudden smell overwhelmed him.

'That's got to be rats,' he whispered before raising his arm and covering his nose. He stopped, pulled out his phone with his other hand and turned on the torch. He shone it into the space behind the door and realised he was at the top of a set of stairs.

The first two buildings *definitely* didn't have a basement.

He stepped down, taking each stair slowly. Once halfway down, the sound of tiny scratches on concrete immediately gave him a surge of adrenaline. Definitely rats. He'd heard the place was full of them. He held himself on the fourth step down.

Shining his light down towards the bottom, he squinted. Taking two more steps, his eyes adjusted to what he was seeing and, this time, he did not remain in place.

'Holy *fuck*!' he shouted, spinning on the stairs and taking them two at a time until he was in the four-by-four space. Slamming the metal door behind him, he ran out of tower three faster than he thought possible and didn't look back until he was at the Portakabin.

Bursting through the door, he found Logan was sat in the same place as he had been when Jay first left.

'You did that in record time, Jay boy,' Logan said, before frowning at the state Jay was in.

Bent over, Jay placed his hands on his knees as he tried to catch his breath.

'What's up with you?' Logan asked, his tone a little fiercer than Jay deemed necessary.

Jay couldn't speak, couldn't get his head together to get his words out. But Logan was in front of him now, his hands on Jay's shoulders and raising him to the upright position.

'What the fuck happened to you? You see one of those industrial-sized rats or something?'

Swallowing hard, his throat scratched with how dry it was. Jay parted his lips and said, 'There's something you might have missed in the third tower.'

Jay's brow furrowed; his expression serious. 'What do you mean, *missed*?'

Jay shook his head. 'I can't even say it. You just have to look.'

Logan raised a brow. 'No, you'll fucking tell me first.'

Jay sucked air in through his nostrils and stood up straight. He had to get himself together. Had to show how much of a man he could be in this situation.

'I wasn't sure I was seeing properly at first. There are human remains in the basement of the third tower.'

The corner of Logan's mouth raised in mock humour. 'Oh, fuck off, Jay. You had me there, I'll give you that.'

'I'm being *serious*.'

Logan's smile diminished, his eyes narrowing as he continued to stare at Jay. 'What *exactly* did you see?'

Jay closed his eyes and immediately the pile of bones at the bottom of the stairs flooded his mind. He quickly opened them again and tried to push the thoughts out.

'Please, just go and look for yourself.'

Logan gave an exasperated sigh and shook his head. 'Fine. Show me.'

—

Jay stood behind Logan outside the first door that led down to the basement. His legs began to tremble with the idea that he was about to see the dead once again.

'Hold your breath,' Jay said. 'The stench is pretty fucking awful.'

'Down here, you said?' Logan turned to him, ignoring what Jay had said.

'Aye. At the bottom of the stairs.'

Opening the door, Logan stepped into the small space and pulled on the second door. Jay had to stop himself from wincing at the smell; irrationally half expecting a pair of hands to appear from the darkness and pull them down to the basement. How could rats leave such a stench behind?

'Where?' Logan shrugged, staring down.

Jay pulled his phone out from his jacket, switched on the torch and shone it down to the bottom. 'There,' he said, annoyed that he was having to prove he wasn't lying.

Glancing down, Logan fell silent as his eyes scanned over the scene in front of him. All Jay could hear was the rush of blood in his ears as his heart thrummed in his chest.

Logan took a few steps down, just like Jay had. He stopped about halfway, shone the torch down to the floor. To the bones. To the *dead*.

'Fucking hell,' Logan whispered, although Jay noted it wasn't in disbelief, or in empathy. It was as though he was annoyed, like it was an *inconvenience*.

After what felt like a long bout of silence, with Jay's thoughts running wild while his skin prickled, he said, 'What do we do now?'

Logan climbed back up the stairs and closed both doors. He stood, almost nose to nose with Jay, and looked him dead in the eye. 'You speak of this to no one. Do you understand? *No one.*'

Jay blinked and responded with, 'You're not going to report this?'

'That's not what I said,' Logan replied. 'What I said was, you speak of this to no one. I need to hear you agree to that, Jay.'

Jay's frown deepened. 'Why?'

'Because I need time to think about this; to process it. I want to know what happened down there.'

Jay's stomach rolled. 'Could it be murder, boss?'

'We don't know that for sure, Jay. You've heard what this place was like: hoaching with junkies back in the day. They could have died from an overdose or anything. Let's not go to the darkest scenario, eh?'

Jay felt a brow raise in astonishment. 'There could be people out there, looking for—'

Logan raised a hand in protest. 'I said, you keep your mouth shut. For now. Let *me* handle this, Jay. It's my site. My job. My responsibility. Understood?'

Blinking again, Jay nodded slowly and backed away from Logan and the basement door.

'Now, get back to work. Inspect the last three towers, go back to the Portakabin and read over as much of that manual as possible. I don't want to hear another thing about this unless I mention it to you, got it?'

Jay gritted his teeth but refrained from showing his frustrations. What the hell was wrong with this guy? Surely anyone in their right mind would report something like this, especially if it was happening on their property? 'Got it.'

Upon exiting the third tower, Jay watched as Logan headed back towards the Portakabin. His walk was slow, calm. Unlike someone who'd just uncovered... Jay couldn't even think it.

He wanted to run from the site and never go back. But he didn't have another choice. This place, the job, Logan – they were his only lifeline. His only means to make a better life for himself.

He turned, stared up at the remaining three towers and reluctantly headed in their direction.

TWENTY-TWO

Jay stepped into the Portakabin having completed his checks of the last three towers, and sat down on the seat opposite Logan.

Logan shot him a glance, raised a brow and waved his hand in an upward motion. Jay immediately got to his feet and stood to attention as though Logan was the field marshal and Jay the lieutenant. When he did, Logan returned his gaze to his phone and said, 'Done?'

Jay nodded. 'Done.'

'No more dead bodies?' Logan asked. Jay looked at him, shocked he'd joked about the whole thing.

'Everything seemed fine in the other towers.'

Logan shook his head. 'Mate, try not to let this worry you. I told you, I've got it covered.'

'But, shouldn't we report what we found? There could be people out there looking, wondering what the hell happened.'

'I doubt that very much.' Logan shrugged.

Jay felt utterly speechless. Was Logan really going to let this go in silence?

'You see, Jay. Those remains, they're old. Really old. I'm talking decades. If anyone was out there, looking, they'd have been discovered long ago.'

Jay felt his frustration grow, and then something deep within reminded him of who he was talking to, who his boss was. Not just Logan Greer, owner of the security and demolition companies responsible for the site, but gangster – as much as Logan said he wasn't one. If Logan didn't want Jay to speak of what was in that basement, there would be a very good reason for it, and Jay wasn't going to question him any further on it. Not if he wanted to keep his job.

'Okay,' Jay simply replied.

As though he knew what Jay was thinking, Logan said, 'Jay, the date for the demolition will be pushed back by a considerable number of weeks, if not months, if I report this. And if I'm honest, I don't have the funds for that. I'm looking to rebuild on this land as soon as the rubble is cleared so I can create jobs in the area, create a better life for the people of Dunreath, and Blackhill Court in particular.'

Jay nodded, hoping that Logan would accept he would be silent as asked of him.

'So, being site supervisor, it's your job to protect the plan. I need this to go smoothly and, with your help and support, that can happen.'

'But what if someone else finds them?' Jay couldn't help but ask.

'It's your job to make sure no one else does, Jay. Do you understand how important your role is here at the site now?'

Puffing out his cheeks once more, his eyes widened with the realisation. Logan didn't just want Jay's silence; he wanted, *needed*, his co-operation.

'Jay, I don't intend on this getting out. And you'll help with that. But if you don't do your job properly, there will be consequences for all of us here.'

Jay was quiet. He didn't want to be the reason people lost their jobs.

'Jay? Are you listening to me? Do you understand the importance of keeping this under wraps?'

'Aye, gaffer. Understood.'

'You'll be paid handsomely for this. I can guarantee it.'

'What do you mean?'

'Call it a discretion bonus. How does ten grand sound?'

'Ten *grand*?' Jay said, almost choking on the words.

'It would be enough for you to be able to make a better life for yourself. You know, you wouldn't have to go into scrap metal to get started like I did. And like I said on your first day, if you do your job well, there's plenty more opportunities for you to progress with my company. Any one of my companies.'

Logan's eyes were fixed on Jay, full of expectation. Expectation that he'd agree and not make any trouble for his boss.

'I... I don't know what to say,' Jay said, his voice almost quivering.

'Hey,' Logan said, getting up and moving around the desk. He placed a hand on Jay's shoulder. 'I get it. This is probably the last thing you were expecting. It's not easy. It wasn't easy for me either, to see those bones down there, on my site. Harder for me; I fucking missed them completely. But I wouldn't ask you to oversee this if I didn't think I could trust you. And I can trust you, Jay, can't I?'

Jay shot him a look. He'd just been offered ten grand to keep quiet. That kind of cash would make a considerable difference to Jay and his mum. He could help them get out of Blackhill Court. Maybe a flat in Clydebank, maybe even further afield? Suddenly for Jay, his morals fell down a step on the ladder.

'You can trust me with your life,' he replied.

Logan nodded slowly. 'That's what I wanted to hear, Jay. In business, especially in my line of work, there aren't a lot of people to trust. Thankfully, you're one of the people I can. That means a lot.'

Jay stared at his boss, hesitant on saying anything more in case it was the wrong thing. He didn't want to mention the police again in case it upset Logan, and equally, he didn't want to mention the money in case Logan changed his mind. Also, there was an overwhelming feeling inside that Jay wanted to make Logan proud. He had confidence enough to make Jay site supervisor. He trusted Jay with the position, and if he let Logan down at the first hurdle, it would break that trust.

'You came to me first, Jay,' Logan continued. 'When you found those bones, you didn't go running to the coppers and you certainly didn't start shouting about it. I appreciate that more than you know. You remind me a lot of myself when I was younger. People think they know you just by looking at you. You're from a rough area, so people automatically think you're going to try to fuck them over. When all you really want is a decent life.'

Jay looked down at his feet, Logan's hand still gripping his shoulder. 'Everyone thinks I'm scum because I come from Blackhill Court. I mean, Dunreath is a shithole in its own right, Blackhill is just smack bang in the middle of it. And yeah, I do want a better life for myself. But I'm not ashamed of who I am or where I'm from. I'll wear this place like a fucking badge of honour, but it won't stop me from going somewhere in life.'

Logan nodded. 'I'm from a shithole too, not too far from here. Grew up a bit of an arsehole, did some shitty stuff to people who didn't deserve it. But I learned from my mistakes. I might be seen as someone who people would cross the road to avoid. I wear that with a badge of honour because it means that the time-wasters stay out of my way, the ones I could never trust and, believe me, there are a lot of those people. But like I said, you're not one of them, Jay.'

'No one will ever know those bones are down there. And anyone who finds out won't live to tell the tale.'

He knew that last sentence was just to please Logan. Of course it was. Jay didn't have it in him to threaten that kind of violence, let alone carry it out. Smiling, Logan shook Jay's hand and said, 'No need for any of that, Jay boy. And no one will find out if you do your job as well as I *know* you can. Like I said, Jay, I'm counting on you.'

—

Jay sat in the work van outside the site, waiting for Reece to arrive. He'd only just managed to stop himself from shaking. Finding human bones wasn't what he'd expected at the start of his shift. His boss asking him to keep it quiet he'd expected even less. When Jay thought about it, his skin crawled.

Sighing, Jay rolled down the window and opened his pack of cigarettes. He often vaped, but now was the time for a proper smoke. Tobacco was the only solution in this instance.

He lit the cigarette and took a long, deep draw, savouring the fullness of his lungs.

Unlike the lungs of the dead in that basement, he thought.

He shivered, the image of the bones making him feel sick. He couldn't help but wonder who they belonged to. Were there people out there, wondering what had happened to them? Based on Logan's estimation on how long they'd been down there, it was unlikely, surely?

'A'right?' a voice said, jolting Jay from his thoughts. The cigarette fell from his fingers to the ground as his hand hung out the window.

'*Jesus*,' Jay hissed, the smoke rushing out of his mouth. 'You nearly gave me a fucking heart attack, Reece.'

Reece raised both brows and a sly smile pulled at the corners of his mouth. 'What the fuck's got you all jittery?'

Jay considered spilling it all to Reece then thought better of it. Logan trusted Jay to keep quiet and, in doing so, Jay would be rewarded with a shit ton of money. He wasn't going to risk that.

'Nothing,' he lied. 'What you doing here so early?'

'I could ask the same of you?' Reece replied. 'The boss asked us both to come in early, remember?'

'Aye,' Jay said, a little snappier than he'd intended. 'And you said you had to take your mum to a doctor's appointment. Which we both know is absolute bullshit. Cannae get an appointment in that place for love nor money.'

Reece looked away momentarily. 'Aye, well. I didn't want to come in earlier if I wasn't getting paid for it. I'm only here to see what's going on with you and him.'

Jay stared at Reece.

'So, what was it all about?'

'Just about the promotion.'

'Really?' Reece queried.

'Aye, really. Just wanted to go over the job with me. Had a policy and procedure manual to read now that I'm supervisor. Had to check the towers, make sure Logan hadn't missed any security issues prior to the dem.'

'Come on, Jay. He wanted you to check he hadn't missed any security issues? *You?* What, are you some security expert or something?'

Jay shook his head. 'That's what I thought. Asked him if I was solely responsible, but he laughed and said that two pairs of eyes are better than one.'

'And did you do a check?'

Jay nodded. 'Aye. Bloody lifts are off, aren't they? Legs are fucked after it.'

Reece walked around to the passenger side and climbed into the van. 'What's going on, Jay? What have you been dragged into?'

Jay shook his head and laughed. 'Do I seem like the type to be forced to do something I don't want to?'

Reece stared at him, his eyes searching Jay's face as though he would find the answer to his questions stamped across his forehead. 'You tell me?'

'There is *nothing* to tell and, even if there was, I wouldn't betray the gaffer's trust like that.'

'Oh, so you're his little puppy dog then?'

Jay pulled another cigarette out of his packet and lit one. *This little puppy dog's just earned ten grand*, he thought. 'Aye,' he said, inhaling deeply. 'If that's what you want to think.'

The silence that grew between them was deafening. But Jay was determined to keep his mouth shut. Reece was the better one of the two of them. If he knew what was lurking in that basement, he'd try to encourage Jay to report it. Not because he was a grass but purely because he would think it would be the right thing to do. Jay couldn't allow that to happen. Not now. Not ever. If it got out and the demolition was delayed, therefore delaying Logan's purchase of the land, that would all be because of Jay. He'd lose his job, he'd lose his bonus and his ability to be trusted. He couldn't risk that. Nothing but good would come from keeping quiet. He was one step closer to getting out of Blackhill Court.

'Fine, Jay. If you're determined you're not going to tell me what's going on, then at least know that you can change your mind. If you're deep in some shit with our boss, then the earlier you get out, the better.'

Jay thought about that and realised that, yes, seeing those bones wasn't ideal and he'd likely never get the images out of his head. But then, he'd never have the chance of ten grand being injected into his bank account.

'I'm not in deep shit. I'm just his supervisor. End of.'

Reece sighed and the sound made Jay think that he was finally giving up.

'I'm going to grab a coffee before we're officially clocked on. You want one?' Reece asked.

Jay hoped that Reece wouldn't think anything untoward was going on. After all, he was the closest person to Jay other than his mum. If Reece thought there was something wrong, he'd try to get it out of Jay, and he couldn't risk that. Nothing could come in the way of such life-changing money. Nothing.

Jay glanced down at the burning embers on the end of his cigarette and flicked the ash out of the window. 'Aye,' he said. 'Make mine black, two sugars.'

TWENTY-THREE

'Looks nice from out here,' Steph said. 'Should we try it? Tea? Cake? A fry-up? Whatever you fancy, it's on me.'

Lori looked at her and laughed. 'Did you win the lottery and forget to tell me?'

'You'd know if I won the lottery. If I did, we'd be in a bar in Ibiza, not a café in fucking Dunreath Village owned by Logan Greer.'

'Practically every business in this shitehole is owned by him,' Lori replied. 'Every time he snaps one up the local papers are all over him. It's pathetic, like he's the only news around here. And now our boys work for him. Not ideal but at least they're out earning money.'

Lori looked at the entrance, taking in the round sign with backlighting that lit up the words, *Dunreath Café*. An artificial green vine arch was attached to the wall around the entrance door, and it gave off a very West End of the city vibe right in the centre of the shittiest village in the west of Scotland.

'Why would anyone want to invest in a business here?' Lori asked. 'It sticks out like a sore thumb.'

'For that exact reason? Maybe the rumours are just that, and he wants to better the place?' Steph suggested. 'Maybe he can see the potential this sad, depressing little place has to offer and he's going to try to make a difference.'

'Aye,' Lori spluttered with laughter. 'I doubt that very much. He's probably using it for money laundering, like the rest of them.'

Steph raised a brow. 'Feeling very optimistic today, are we?'

Lori shook her head. 'Och, no wonder, Steph. The only decent thing about that guy is that he's bringing the towers down.'

Steph fell quiet. 'Let's not talk about that any more today, Lori. I can't cry any more. I honestly thought I had my shit together about all this.'

Lori felt suddenly guilty. 'Sorry. But don't worry about having a bad day. Some days I need to support you and others you need to support me. We went through hell, Steph. We're going to feel it sometimes. We're only human.'

Steph smiled. 'This morning was a heavy one. But I'm okay now... I think.'

Lori returned the smile and let out a breath of relief that Steph was feeling better. 'Okay, let's go in. The food can't be worse than the location, surely?'

Steph smiled, linked her arm through Lori's and pushed open the door. Stepping inside, the café resembled a West End eatery: tall green plants in oversized plant pots were dotted around. The place was furnished with dark oak tables featuring coffee menus, most of which Lori had no idea what they were.

'Hi,' a young, chirpy woman around the same age as Jay and Reece smiled. 'Table for two?'

Lori glanced at her and felt empathetic for yet another young person being stuck in Dunreath. This place might look like it would create opportunities, but Lori knew that Dunreath was like superglue.

'Please,' Steph replied.

The girl showed them to a small booth at the far side of the café. A dark wooden table with leather-bound benches awaited them. A plant with little pink flowers sat in the centre, and more artificial vines ran up the centre of the wall.

'Our soup of the day is lentil,' the girl said. Lori caught a glimpse of her name tag.

'Thanks, Sammi,' Lori said, before the girl smiled and pulled out a small notepad.

'Can I take a drink order first?'

'Black coffee for me,' Steph said.

'Same,' Lori replied.

Sammi moved towards the counter at the other side of the café and Steph raised a brow.

'You know her?'

'No. Why?'

'You said her name,' Steph replied.

Lori pulled at her shirt. 'It's on her badge. I was just trying to be polite.'

Steph nodded. 'She reminds me of us when we were young.'

Lori couldn't help the frown which took over her expression. 'She's nothing like us at that age. First of all, she has a job. Second of all, she still has light in her fucking eyes.'

Steph burst out laughing. 'Aye, I suppose you're right. Jesus, if you don't laugh you'll cry.'

'And you've done plenty of that the last few hours.'

'Try the last few years, for both of us.'

Lori sighed and felt ready to cry herself but the sight of Sammi approaching with two coffee mugs in hand stopped her.

'Here we are,' Sammi said, her voice chirpier again. 'Ready for a food order?'

'Oh,' Steph said, 'we haven't even looked at the menus yet. Too busy gabbing.'

'Ha, I'm the same. Such a chatterbox. Especially in here. But don't tell the boss, he's my fiancé. Don't want him thinking I'm taking the piss.'

Lori raised a brow. This young girl was engaged to Logan Greer? She looked a bit young to be with a man his age, let alone be engaged to him. Yes, she smiled widely and seemed happier than Lori had ever imagined a person could be. A job? Engaged to the man who owned the place? She was set for life.

'Our lips are sealed,' Steph replied.

Lori and Steph looked down at the menus and suddenly a male voice called out across the café.

'Sammi?'

The girl turned and Lori noticed how her shoulders drooped when she looked up.

'Ah, speak of the devil,' Sammi replied. 'Here he is.'

Lori peered down to the entrance of the café to see a man in a high-vis jacket and a hard hat stood by the counter, with a thick, well-groomed beard and a smile on his face. As much as he looked like a builder, he seemed to carry the outfit well. He looked like the kind of man who liked to show off his success.

'I'll be back in a moment,' Sammi said, moving towards him quickly.

Steph looked up at Lori while lifting her mug. 'That's a perk of the job, isn't it? Getting to shag the boss while he pays you to run his business for him.'

'Pretty sure you could class that as prostitution.'

Steph laughed loudly and almost spilled coffee on the table. 'He might well be dodgy, but he's handsome. No one can deny that. I could be convinced if he didn't have such a reputation.'

Lori couldn't help the smile that crept onto her face. 'You could be convinced of pretty much anything if it meant enough money to fuck off out of here.'

'Ha, true.'

They fell silent again, and Steph kept her face turned to the front counter of the café.

'Could you be more obvious?' Lori whispered.

Spinning round in her seat, Steph raised a brow. 'I'm a people-watcher.'

'You're a man-watcher more like.'

'Not any man. Just the ones worth looking at. And let me tell you, men are only worth looking at. Start stripping back the layers and they're all the same piece of shit as the next.'

Lori couldn't help the chuckle that rose from her chest. 'Couldn't agree more.'

She watched the conversation between Sammi and her fiancé, unable to hear what was being said. Something seemed off. It looked as though Sammi was annoyed, and he looked hostile. Certainly not the happy young woman who'd first greeted them.

Sammi and her fiancé were closer now, noses almost touching. Sammi looked uncomfortable. The fiancé, Logan, looked hostile. The interaction piqued her interest; something wasn't right between them.

'What you having?' Steph asked, oblivious to what Lori was witnessing. 'I might have the fry-up. Can't go wrong with that, if I'm honest. I'm not a smashed avocado kinda girl. I don't think anyone in Dunreath is. In fact, I don't think anyone anywhere likes it. Tastes like hedges if you ask me.'

But Lori wasn't listening, she was too busy taking in what was going on. She'd seen this before in couples in Blackhill Court. The man being domineering, the woman backing away like a small, petrified animal.

'Lori?' Steph asked, glancing up from the menu and seeing that Lori wasn't choosing what she wanted to eat from it. Turning, Steph was now watching them too.

'He's jabbing a finger into her chest,' Lori whispered. 'Jesus, he's not even trying to be subtle about it.'

'Excuse me?' Steph suddenly called out, putting her hand up. 'Sammi?'

Lori felt a twist in her stomach. 'What are you doing?' she whispered again.

Sammi turned sharply, but Logan didn't move other than to lower his hand.

'Hi, sorry to interrupt but we're ready to order now?' Steph said, loud enough for everyone in the café to hear her.

Everyone was now looking at Sammi. Logan took a step back, muttered something that Lori couldn't quite make out before he left.

Sammi straightened her back and put on a smile before walking towards Lori and Steph's table. Clearing her throat, she pulled out a small notepad and didn't look either of them in the eye. 'What can I get you?'

'Are you all right?' Steph asked, her voice quiet enough for only Sammi and Lori to hear.

Sammi blinked and rested her eyes on Steph. Lori felt her stomach lurch.

'Yes. Why?'

Sammi pulled her lips into a thin smile but the light that had been in her eyes when they'd first arrived had gone out. 'Because you didn't look okay just a few seconds ago.'

Sammi's eyes flittered to Lori. 'Are *you* ready to order?'

Lori gave a silent sigh and looked down at the menu. 'I'll have the egg and bacon bagel with fries on the side, please.'

Sammi scribbled the pen across the small notebook with fury and Steph raised a hand before placing it on her forearm. '*Are* you okay?'

Sammi jolted away just ever so slightly before raising a brow. 'And I asked if you're ready to order?'

Steph blinked a few times before nodding. 'Full Scottish, extra hash brown, no beans. Please.'

Another furious scribble on the pad before Sammi tucked the pen into the pocket of her apron. 'And I already said, yes, I'm fine.'

Steph nodded. 'Okay. Just wanted to check. It's not every day you see a man his size hover over a woman your size while jabbing his finger into her chest. But, if you're okay, then you're okay.'

A heavy silence settled over the table and Lori bit down on her lip. 'Look, we don't want to upset you. We just... we just wanted to check.'

Sammi turned on her heel and headed away from the table.

'Jesus,' Steph said, puffing out her cheeks.

'You really put her on the spot there, Steph.'

A deep frown line appeared between Steph's eyebrows. 'Are you serious? You don't think I should have said anything? After everything we've been through, you expected me to just sit there and say nothing?'

Lori closed her eyes briefly. 'That's not what I meant, Steph.'

'There was no one there to help us back then, Lori. No one there to stop us from going through hell. A hell we don't even fucking remember properly. And you think I should have just turned my back? Fuck that.'

Taking a breath, Lori realised she was right. There hadn't been anyone there to help them all those years ago. No one at all. There were a million things Lori wished she'd done differently on the day she'd got into that bloody car. She wished she'd gone with her gut and said no. She wished someone would have at least called out to her; tried to distract her from going. But no one ever did because there was no one. Parents dead, brother in prison – again – and Charley in a care home.

'I'm sorry. You were right to call over and stop that from escalating. But that doesn't mean it won't escalate for her later, when we're not here to stop it again. We might have just made it worse for her.'

Steph's face flushed a deep crimson, her cheeks glowing under the artificial light above. 'Men like him infuriate me, Lori. I hope we've raised our boys well enough to treat women with respect.'

The words sat heavy on her chest. She hoped for nothing more.

A few minutes passed before Sammi reappeared at the table with the food orders. She set them down in front of Lori and Steph before sighing. 'Sorry for being so snappy. And thank you for your concern. He's just a little stressed because this place has just opened and he's worried I've taken on too much by running it myself. He lashes out when he's stressed. It's all good, though. He knows I can handle it.'

Lori and Steph exchanged a glance and Steph smiled a little.

'It's okay to get stressed. But you shouldn't have to put up with that at all,' Lori said.

'I know,' Sammi replied. 'I can handle it.'

'Good. But our point, again, is that you shouldn't have to,' Steph pressed.

'Suppose it's just men, isn't it? They're all the same.'

Sammi did have a point.

Before walking away, Sammi shrugged and said, 'Enjoy your food.'

'I can't get my head around this is the same guy who employs Reece and Jay,' Steph said as she picked up her fork. 'Young lads like ours are easily influenced by men of his power, Lori. That's *also* why I said something. I want them to know that women can and will stick up for themselves and one another. It's important they turn out to be one of the good ones, Lori. Don't you think?'

Lori looked down at the plate and, suddenly, she wasn't very hungry.

TWENTY-FOUR

Sammi closed up the café for the evening and headed along Dunreath Main Street, taking each step as slowly as possible. The longer she walked, the more she could think and the longer she'd be free from Logan.

Getting that call from her dad earlier had thrown her off. She hadn't been expecting it because she hadn't heard from him in years. If she was honest with herself, she hadn't expected to hear from him ever again. The man had been in prison all of her life. She'd been told he was many things – druggie, thug – but she was never sure what was true. Her mum, if she could call herself that, had bashed his name from the moment Sammi could remember. She had a cheek herself; she'd never been a good mum. In fact, she'd never been a mum in any sense of the word. Sammi was passed from pillar to post, from her gran, who couldn't cope, to mates who were just as much a failure as her mum had been. That's what happens when kids have kids, especially in places like Dunreath. Sammi questioned herself. Was rejecting his request to meet the right thing to do? She'd survived this far without her parents; did she need them now? It might be nice to try to have some kind of contact. Perhaps it would work out? Then her logic kicked in. Nothing had ever worked in her favour, so why would seeing her dad be any different, especially after years of absence?

Her mind wandered to what had happened in the café earlier in the day. Those women had really got under her skin. They'd seen what was happening between her and Logan, and Sammi had played it down to them. But Sammi knew they hadn't bought it. They had years on her, had probably seen a lot of what she was dealing with. It was embarrassing to be treated that way and for people to see it in person. Up until recently, she'd managed to hide their volatile relationship and no one on the outside had ever seen what things could truly be like. But after Logan's accusation that she'd been flirting with Reece Lyle, he'd been like a dog with a bone. It was all that came out his mouth, and now he didn't seem to care that people could see that he was acting like a dick.

'Hey.' A familiar and reassuring voice woke her from her thoughts. 'How you doing?'

Sammi looked up to see Reece stood in front of her after he'd walked out of the local shop on the main street. He had a newspaper under his arm and a packet of cigarettes in his hand. Suddenly, she felt like she was in a strange space; safe and dangerous at the same time. Reece was a safe person, a kind person. She'd treated him terribly back then when all he'd done was show kindness to her. She'd thrown him away for Logan. What an idiot she'd been.

'Oh, hi,' Sammi said, with no intention of stopping. Not only out of concern that Logan could drive past in his van and see her, fuelling his already ridiculously huge fire about them, but also because all she wanted was to be alone with her thoughts. Speaking to anyone right now was the last thing she wanted, and she feared she'd be taken in by Reece's kindness.

'You just finished?' Reece continued, not reading the look on her face or the tone of her voice.

'Yep,' she said sharply, before trying to move around him.

'You all right?'

'Why the fuck do people keep asking me that? Look,' Sammi said, finally realising that the nice-girl act wasn't going to cut it. 'We both know standing here talking to each other is dangerous. So, let's do each other a favour and just fuck it off, shall we?'

Reece's eyes widened and his jaw loosened a little. 'Brutally honest – nice. Wish you'd been this honest when you ended things between us. Then I'd have known where I stood with you.'

The kindness in his eye twinkled as she looked at him and the guilt began to set in. She was being a bitch to the wrong person.

'I'm sorry, Reece,' she said in an almost whisper, making sure that there was a considerable amount of physical space between them. 'I'm sorry,' she said. 'For how I treated you.'

'Why?' he said softly. 'Why did you end things? Was it to be with him?'

Sammi nodded. 'I was fooled by his charm. He sucked me in and I thought he was what I needed in a man. I'm annoyed at myself for treating you that way. But I'm more annoyed at myself for thinking I need a man at all.'

A pained expression flickered across Reece's face and he glanced down at the ground.

'Look, it's just been a long day and I'm sure you'll understand me just wanting to get home.'

Reece pulled his lips into a thin smile, but she could tell he was not happy. The sadness on his face, in his stance, made her feel the weight of her guilt. 'Yeah, I get it. Night shift is a bastard and all I want is to crawl into bed at the end of it. In fact, all I want to do is crawl into my bed right now.'

'Hmm,' Sammi said, glancing down at the time on her phone. 'Speaking of night shift, aren't you supposed to be starting soon?'

'Not for another hour. Need company on the way home?'

Sammi's face crinkled, her eyes narrow as she stared at him after the question. The way Reece had said those words, it wasn't a loaded question, in the hope that she was interested in him in *that* way again. At least she didn't think it sounded like that. It was more a friendly tone and she appreciated it. But it was coming from the wrong person. She couldn't risk his safety – or hers.

'Sammi?' Reece said, and she realised she hadn't said anything for a few moments.

'Reece, you know I'm engaged to your boss.'

Reece nodded. 'Of course I do. All the more reason for me to check you're all right?'

Sammi sighed. 'No, I'm not all right. He seems to think that you are a bit of a problem.'

Reece's shoulders slumped. 'What do you mean, problem? Does he know I'm your ex?'

'No. He'd have made that very clear. But he did say that he saw something between us. Accused you of fancying me and said I couldn't keep my eyes off you. He also straight out asked if we were at it behind his back. Which I told him was absolutely not the case. Me and you have been done for years now and it can never go back to how it was. Not ever. You do get that, don't you?'

They both stared at each other and Sammi realised that Reece looked very concerned. Not because there would never be a chance for them again, but for her.

He gave a silent nod and his shoulders slumped. 'Are you okay, Sammi? With him, I mean?'

'Och, Logan is...' She looked for the right words. *A bit of a dick? Paranoid? A bully?*

'Dangerous,' Reece said, his voice low and full of frustration. 'But he plucked this thing out of thin air. We weren't flirting and we're certainly not seeing each other. I was just shocked to see you and wanted to ask how you were. Things were left...'

'I know,' she said, thinking about the text she had sent him to end their relationship. 'It was shitty of me to text you. I should have told you to your face. I'm sorry.'

Reece was quiet again and she imagined him playing the text over and over again.

> I'm sorry. We're done.

And then she had blocked him so he couldn't contact her. She'd been all consumed by Logan and his charm. What a horrible idiot she'd been.

'He doesn't trust many people. Always going on about trauma from long before I met him, so he's a bit paranoid about me talking to another man.'

She knew it sounded pathetic. But what else was she supposed to say? That Logan would pick a fight in an empty room if it meant he came out looking like the better person?

'Well, if he really thinks that I'm a problem,' Reece said, waving his hand between them, 'then if you don't mind, I'll take back my offer to walk you home. Don't want to cause any arguments and I certainly don't want him thinking I'm trying it on with you.'

She nodded, smiled thinly and replied, 'It doesn't take much to create a fight with him, that's for sure. You're best on his good side, Reece. Stay away from me, even in the café, and you're good.'

'But that's ridiculous. Every second person on the planet is a guy. Surely he doesn't expect you to avoid males altogether?'

She stared at him, blinked and shook her head. 'Reece. That's exactly what he wants me to do. And yes, that is utterly impossible. It makes it easier if the guy in question is a complete arsehole, one worse than Logan. But that's never the case. And the longer we're stood here together, the harder it's going to get. I don't want him finding out about our past otherwise he'll use it as a stick to batter fuck out both of us with. Trust me.'

'Then leave? I mean, you found it easy enough to dump me by text. You can't do the same to him?'

Sammi glanced up at the sky and then back at Reece. She had to be more forceful to protect him.

'Excuse me for being rude, but my relationship with Logan really has fuck all to do with you, Reece. And the more you poke your nose in, the worse Logan's suspicions will get.'

Reece shrugged. 'I know I've done nothing wrong.'

'You don't have to have done anything wrong for Logan to think so.'

'Are you telling me to watch my back?' Reece asked.

'Yes. Just like I do, every single day.'

Sammi took a step closer to Reece, then proceeded to move around him and head along the main street. She didn't turn to look back, she didn't know if Reece was watching her, waiting to respond. She hoped her warning was enough to make him back off.

The whole way home, all she kept hoping for was that none of Logan's people, employees, had seen her talking to Reece. Because if they had, he'd know about it before she even set foot through the front door.

TWENTY-FIVE

Lori stood in the kitchen and stared out of the window as she stirred the teabag around her favourite mug. The estate was busy as usual. Kids kicking balls off the side of the building opposite were being extra rowdy this evening, a sound she was able to block out after years of practice. A group of teenagers sat at the bottom of the stairs leading up to the flats at the top end of the estate. They were chatting, drinking from two-litre bottles of Coke and Irn-Bru, which Lori knew fine well was mixed with some form of spirit. Cheap vodka or whisky, most likely. They'd be rowdy later, probably bring out the Bluetooth speakers and blast their music loud enough for people from the main road through the village to hear.

The flat was quiet as she went over the events from the café earlier in the day, when she heard a grunting coming from Jay's bedroom. She turned and moved out to the hallway. It came again, although this time it was more like a distressed moan.

Stepping closer to his bedroom door, she raised her fist to knock, when he became more vocal.

Lori placed her hand on the door handle and opened it gently. Peering her head around the door into his room, she saw Jay thrashing around on the bed, but he was still asleep.

'No, *no*. I can't... Urgh. Get them away from me. The bones. Get them *away*. I'm not going. The basement. Urgh. Argh.'

The words were clear as day, and Lori froze, her eyes wide with horror.

Jesus fucking *Christ*.

She couldn't move, frozen by the words which had just come out of her son's mouth. The son who worked as security at the demolition site of the towers in which Lori had *murdered* two people in self-defence.

She parted her lips to speak, but jumped as the alarm on Jay's phone started to ring furiously.

Lori quickly stepped out of the room before he came around and saw her standing there. She had to gather herself together, try not to look as terrified as she felt.

Get them away from me. The bones. The basement.

She heard Jay switch off his alarm and yawn loudly. Closing her eyes, Lori couldn't get the words out of her head. If he was saying those things while he was sleeping, then it meant he'd discovered the bodies. He *must* have. It was too much of a coincidence.

'Hey,' Jay said, opening the door and meeting her in the hallway.

Lori put on her best *I've not just shit myself after what you said* smile and offered to make him a coffee.

'Aye, going to need it. Slept like absolute shit today,' Jay replied, rubbing his eyes furiously. 'And now I need to go into work for a twelve-hour night shift. Fun times, eh?'

Lori made a coffee and handed the mug to Jay. She stared at his face, studying to see signs that he remembered the words that had left his mouth while he slept.

'What?'

'You were talking in your sleep.'

'Was I?' Jay asked, seemingly unfazed. 'Hope I didn't say anything too inappropriate for my wee mammy's ears.'

Should she tell him what she heard? Should she ask what he had seen in his dream, what he'd possibly discovered in real life?

'Are you all right, Maw? You've gone really pale.'

Lori felt sick. The same nausea that had come over her that night in tower three when she...

'Maw?'

But it was too late. Lori's knees had already buckled, the terror too much to bear.

'Fuck!' Jay was on his knees, arms out to catch her. 'Jesus, Mum, what's wrong?'

She drifted out of consciousness, but only just. She could hear her son saying her name, over and over, trying to get her to wake up.

'Mum, can you hear me?'

Mum. The only time he used that was when he was worried, or in trouble. Other times, it was always Maw.

Forcing her eyes open, she looked up at his worried expression and her heart sank.

'I'm okay,' she replied. 'I think.'

Jay helped her to her feet and led her into the living room before gently lowering her onto the couch. 'I'm phoning an ambulance.'

Lori waved her hand. 'No need. I'm fine.'

'You don't just randomly pass out if you're fine. I'm getting you help.'

'No,' Lori replied, firmer this time. 'Just go and get your Aunty Steph for me, please.'

'Since when was she a doctor?' Jay scoffed.

'Just go and get her, Jay. You need to get to work,' she said, forcing out the words.

'I'll phone in. The boss will understand.'

Lori raised a brow. Logan Greer. The guy who'd publicly scolded his young fiancée in front of a café full of people.

'No, you will not phone in.'

Everything she was saying was going against her wish to keep Jay as far away from the towers as possible. But if she started telling him to stay away from them, then she'd have to give an explanation as to why.

Jay shook his head, turned and headed out of the flat. She heard him knock on Steph's door and it quickly opened.

'Can you come in for a second? Ma maw's fainted.'

'She's *what*?' Steph's voice was shrill, her footsteps rushing from her own flat through the hallway and into the living room.

Lori looked up and saw Steph rush into the room and stop in front of her.

'Jay said you fainted? What happened?'

Lori shrugged, glanced behind her at Jay and then said in an ill attempt at humour, 'I fainted.'

'She won't let me phone an ambulance.'

'I'm fine. Don't worry about me, Jay. Just you go to work. I'll see you when you get home. If I need you, I'll phone you.'

Jay hesitated.

'I'll get in touch if it happens again,' Steph said, her voice reassuring. 'You don't want to be late. You're the supervisor. That wouldn't look good, would it?'

Jay nodded. 'Reece about ready?'

Steph shrugged. 'Reece left ages ago. Think he was going to the shop before heading in.'

Jay huffed in annoyance, turned and said, 'If she becomes ill again, phone me straight away, okay?'

'I will.' Steph smiled.

Once the door was closed, Lori glanced up at Steph and burst into tears.

'What the hell happened?' Steph asked, sitting down on the couch beside her.

Lori tried to breathe, taking in long, slow breaths to calm herself.

'He was talking in his sleep,' she said. 'He said...'

Steph took Lori's hand and squeezed it gently. 'What did he say?'

'He said, *get those bones away from me. I'm not going into that basement*. Or something to that effect.'

Lori looked into Steph's eyes and saw the same terror she felt.

'It could mean nothing,' Steph replied, trying to sound reassuring and failing terribly.

'Or it could mean *everything*.'

Steph shook her head. 'No. If he'd uncovered anything, he'd have told you.'

'Would he, though? He's a young lad, Steph. What if he's scared?'

'Did you ask him about it?'

'I didn't get the chance. I was too busy fainting from the shock.'

'Are you going to ask him about it?'

Lori puffed out her cheeks and sighed. 'I'm scared what the answer might be.'

Nodding, Steph let go of Lori's hand and got to her feet. 'I think you have to. I mean, to be fair, those towers have been derelict for so long, the bones could belong to a dead animal. Maybe multiple. He could have found a dead fox, a dog. Maybe even another person entirely; you know how many druggies used those buildings back in the day. Any of it would be enough to cause a nightmare.'

Lori closed her eyes. Maybe she'd overreacted.

'Ask him,' Steph said. 'It'll be nothing, Lori. Please try not to worry. If your brain starts working overtime, you'll end up back there, in that dark place. Neither of us needs that.'

If she was honest with herself, Lori had never left. Those moments of her life had stayed with her; while she was awake and while she was asleep. Mostly, it was at the back of her head, blocked out by everyday things. But since finding out that the demolition was due to take place, her trauma had reared its ugly head. And now there was the fear that Jay was one step closer to Lori and Steph's horrific secret.

TWENTY-SIX

Sammi sank into the bubbles in Logan's Jacuzzi bathtub and allowed the hot water to wash over her. The Jacuzzi bath *looked* the part, but the jets didn't work. Not that she cared. It was more than she'd had growing up.

Still on high alert after her altercation with Logan earlier in the day, her mind wandered back to Reece. Why was she thinking about him so much now after all this time? Was it because she still cared about him, or because he was being nice to her? Lads around Dunreath and especially Blackhill Court weren't nice to women like her without an agenda. It was why the single mum rate was so high in the area. She'd seen it time and time again: young women walking around with their newborns or young kids, no dad to be found. They say it takes a village to raise a child. These girls had no one, and Dunreath Village was *not* the place. But Reece was different; he was nothing like his environment. He was one of the good guys.

She reached for her phone, which sat on the side of the bath, and opened up her Instagram account. Scrolling aimlessly, she realised that she had a message. Tapping on the icon, she noticed that the message was in the requests folder. Most likely another stupid collab invitation from a fake account. They were rife these days.

Tapping on the requests folder, she quickly realised that the message was not another collab invitation. It was from Reece.

'He doesn't take a telling,' she whispered, opening it to read the entire thing.

> I hope I haven't caused you any problems.
> Reece.

Sammi read the message twice and shook her head. Reece clearly didn't understand the real danger he was putting himself in; or her, for that matter.

She began to tap out a reply.

> You will if you don't back off. Messaging me is the last thing you should be doing.

She hit send and stared up at the shower head.

Thoughts of leaving Logan crept back in and she started to think about what it would be like to be on her own. She could survive, couldn't she? It was all she'd ever done. Logan had just somehow managed to dig his nails in and she couldn't break free from his grip. She wasn't ashamed to admit she'd become accustomed to the fact he had money and she was better off financially. But the money wasn't hers and it never would be. That same image of her being homeless on the street, with no money and no prospects, kicked in. That would be her reality.

Her mind wandered back to her dad. Maybe she *should* get back in touch with him: take him up on his offer to meet. If he was clean almost two years, maybe he had his own place? Maybe he really was trying to make amends? Maybe he could put her up for a while. Perhaps they could build a relationship?

Or perhaps, she was just utterly delusional to think that would ever happen. No man with Dunreath blood in his veins was anything other than scum. The more she remembered that, the better.

TWENTY-SEVEN

Lori had finally managed to convince Steph that she was feeling much better after fainting, even if she was still riddled with fear about what she'd heard.

Lori got up to close the curtains when there was a gentle tapping at the front door. She moved through the hallway, half expecting to see a worried Steph at the door, hoping to be able to get back in and probably stay the night.

'I said I'm fine,' Lori said as she opened the door.

She stopped, took in the face of the man stood in front of her.

'All right, sis?'

'*Kev?*'

He was well turned out. He looked healthy, his skin was clear, his eyes bright. Nothing like when she'd last seen him, which had to be close to five years ago during one of his release periods. He hadn't seen her, though. She'd been in the city centre and he'd walked past her, off his face. She'd wanted to stop, wanted to speak to him. But Steph had told her not to. The memory almost brought tears to her eyes.

Brows raised, eyes wide, she couldn't get her words out. Was this really happening, or had she fainted again?

'Yeah, it's me,' he replied.

Lori took in his appearance once more. His clothes were clean and she noticed his build had changed. He'd clearly been using the prison gym, given that his upper arms were being tightly hugged by his jacket.

'You look so... different. What are you doing here?'

Kev took a breath as if hesitating about whether he should speak. 'Can I come in?'

Lori frowned. As much as he looked well, she'd never known Kev to have anything other than an agenda. Nothing he did was without a plan on how to get a fix.

'Why? What do you want?'

'I want to talk, that's all. No hidden agenda,' he said, like he'd heard her inner voice. 'And certainly, no trouble following me. I just want to see how you are.'

Lori bit the inside of her cheek. She wanted to believe him. She'd always wanted to believe her big brother. But he'd let her down so many times when she was younger and always during crucial times. Too busy doing drugs whether he was in prison or not.

'Why now?' she asked, her tone a little harsher than she'd intended. 'Why has it taken you so long to get to this point? I mean, you look the part, Kev. But can I trust you?'

Kev pulled his lips into a thin line and nodded, as though he agreed that he deserved the attitude she was giving him. 'I don't want to wake up one day when I'm old and regret never having tried. As far as trust goes, that's something I need to earn from you. I don't expect it to come straight away.'

The words hit her hard. She'd never expected to hear him say anything like that and it made her heart ache for all the years she'd missed out on with her brother, with the family she should have had. But what if he did this and then, a few weeks down the line, he let her down again? He wasn't exactly known for his loyalty.

Against her better judgement, Lori stepped aside and allowed Kev into the flat. She avoided looking across at Steph's door in case she was stood there, peering through the peephole, ready to launch a tirade of abuse at him.

'So,' he said as Lori closed the door. 'You're still in good old Blackhill Court then?'

'Good isn't the word I'd use for this cesspit.'

Kev shook his head. 'Prison was better than this place. I remember it clear as day.'

'Do you, though? Because from what I can recall, whenever you were out, you were off your face,' Lori said, although without much venom in her voice. As much as he deserved it, she couldn't bring herself to be cruel to Kev.

'I was an addict, Lori. Our parents were the only role models we had. I thought getting smashed every day was normal. I didn't know any better and we all suffered because of them.'

Lori glanced down at her feet. He didn't have the first clue about suffering, not really. Especially not at the hands of someone else. Not when you had to fight for your life as a sixteen-year-old girl.

'So, what are you here to say?' she said, switching the topic. 'After *all* this time, what is it you felt you had to show up to say?'

Kev puffed out his cheeks. 'Can we sit?'

Lori led him through to the living room and they sat on opposite sides of the sofa. She stared at him, barely seeing the version of Kev she'd always known. Drunk, high, dirty and desperate. She'd never been to visit him in prison. Hadn't seen him sober since she was a child. This was a completely new experience for her and it had thrown her. She didn't know how to react, how to behave.

'I'm sorry,' Kev said.

She heard the crack in his voice and a sudden, involuntary need to suck in a large lungful of air took over.

'I'm sorry for *everything* I ever did to make your life harder than it already was. I was the older brother, and I should have been there for both you and Charley through Mum and Dad's addiction issues. I should have been the one looking after you both. Instead, I was fighting active addiction myself and I didn't even know at the time that's what was happening to me. I mean, in this place, everyone was on drugs. Everyone was drunk or high, all the time. I thought I was just doing the same as the rest of them. It wasn't until I did my last stint in prison that I really saw myself for what I was. A failure. A let-down. I got help and I got clean. It took me most of my life to do it, but I did it. And now I want to make things right.'

She watched as he sat forward, hands clasped between his knees, head hanging low. A lump formed in her throat but she was damned if she was going to let her tears flow now. She didn't want to be distracted from his apology by crying.

'I just left you two to rot here.'

Lori cleared her throat, waited until her emotions had settled before she opened her mouth to speak. 'Not her, just me. Charley went into foster care at fourteen. She's never come back here. Not that I blame her. I'd have run a thousand miles to get away from here if I could have.'

Kev kept his head low, his hands clasped together – tightly, she noticed: his knuckles were white; the tips of his fingers bright red. She still couldn't compute how long Charley had been gone for. Even harder to believe was that Kev had no idea. He'd been too enveloped in his life as an addict that all he'd cared about was himself. He knew nothing of Charley's life, or Lori's. He should have been the next adult in line to take care of them and all he'd wanted to do was take drugs to stop withdrawal.

'Fuck,' he whispered, before looking up at the ceiling. He was quiet for a moment and Lori wondered what was going through his mind. His youngest sister? In care. It was partly his fault. He could have been there to stop it, but what good would that have been for Charley? She'd just have been stuck here like Lori. 'Just shows you the state I was in all my life to only just know about this now. Do you have any contact with her?' Kev asked.

Lori nodded. 'Very little. A few texts back and forth every year. Like, I know the basics of her life. She's married to a guy I've never met because I didn't get an invite to the wedding. Got two kids who I've never met and lives somewhere near the

Borders. I mean, in a car it's only a few hours, but for someone like me, with very little money and no car, it's a difficult place to get to and she'd never come here to visit me. Why the hell would she after what this place did to her? Not that she wants me around anyway; if she did, we'd be part of each other's lives. She has a good life from what I know of. Seemingly her husband has a really good job and works away a lot.'

Kev was quiet, taking in all she'd said. It was likely that Charley wouldn't want anything to do with Kev either, if he tried to contact her. She had got away from Blackhill, got away from the hell the place dished out. Their parents dying of drug overdoses was probably the best thing that could have happened to Charley. Sometimes, Lori wished she'd been underage too. That way, she'd have been taken into foster care, probably alongside her sister, and she wouldn't have gone through all the shit she'd endured.

'Well,' Kev said. 'For what it's worth, I'm sorry you got left behind. You didn't deserve that.'

Sighing, Lori shuffled along the couch to be closer, reached out her hand and placed it over his. 'I didn't get left behind. I wanted to stay here with Steph. Charley did too, but there wasn't enough room. As much as I want to blame you, it's not your fault. Not really. It was Mum and Dad's. As an adult, I understand addiction now; I did my research a few years after they died. I was angry at them for dying, for not being better for us when they were alive. I mean, why would you not want to be the best version of yourself for your kids? And I was angry at you too. You abandoned us when it was your turn to step up. But I know now that you didn't have much of a choice in leaving us. You were ill. I still want to be angry at you, but I can't. Because...' She stopped, the emotion catching in her throat so quickly it rendered her unable to speak. 'Well, look at you. I can see you as you were meant to be, Kev. Clean. Sober. Free. Not many people get out of addiction alive.'

Kev raised his head, turned and met her eye. 'I'm still fighting every single day, Lori. I still have that crippling need to drink and to use, even though I almost died. *Twice*. The first time, I got complacent quickly. I was like, I *could* have died, but I *didn't*. The second time scared me more than I thought possible. I'm not out of the woods yet. My liver is fucked. And I mean *fucked*. One more drink, one more hit, and I'm done for. And when I was literally on my deathbed in hospital with the consultants telling me the severity of my disease, I realised that I didn't want to die. Not like that. I didn't want to leave this world with nothing to show for myself except a lifetime of drug debts and jail stints as a fucking junkie. Being told your liver is going to die before you do is one of the most sobering things I've ever heard in my life.'

Lori felt tears spill over and cascade down her cheeks, but she held in the need to break down. This wasn't about her, this moment was about Kev and his redemption. She'd get her chance to speak. 'That must have been terrifying.'

'It was,' Kev replied, staring through the window out to the estate. 'I genuinely can't believe I'm still walking around, if I'm honest.'

'How long have you been clean?'

He sat up straight and Lori removed her hand. 'I've been out of prison for a year. It was my two-years-clean anniversary, yesterday.'

She couldn't help but smile. 'One year? That's the longest you've ever been out of prison?'

'Yeah.'

'And two years clean? Is this your longest stint?'

'Before that was four days,' Kev said. 'Even in prison I was using. I always remember you saying you'd never touch anything because of our childhood. Did you stick to that?'

'I'm sober. Don't smoke either. Never wanted to be out of control of my own body.'

'I wish I'd had your strength, Lori. I really do. If I could go back and change it all, I would. I would never have left you behind to fend for yourself. I'd have fought my demons and…'

'There's no point in going back over it. The past has already happened, Kev. It can't be changed. But what we do now is what counts,' Lori said, reaching for his hand again.

The years of addiction had aged him. He was only forty-one, just two years older than Lori, and he could easily pass for fifty. She could only imagine what he'd looked like at the peak of his drug and alcohol abuse. But even with the ageing, he looked so healthy. She was proud of him, for the first time in her life.

Kev puffed out his cheeks and glanced up at the photo frames on the walls. He stared at the pictures of Lori and Jay and it was then she realised that he had no idea she had a son. Of course he didn't. He didn't even know his youngest sister had gone into care.

'Who's that?' Kev asked, his voice quiet as he turned to look at her.

Lori pulled her lips into a thin line and said, 'That's my son. Jay.'

The look on Kev's face was like a kick to her gut. She had nothing to feel guilty about but, for some reason, the feeling was overwhelming.

'You have a son? What age is he?' Kev asked, sounding utterly dumbfounded.

'He's twenty.'

Kev fell silent for a few moments, as if processing it all. Then, a smile lit up his face. 'I have a nephew?'

Lori smiled with him and nodded. 'And he's such a brilliant young man, Kev. Very resilient growing up in a place like this. He's just recently got a new job and he's doing well. I'm really proud of him.'

The smile remained on Kev's face but she could see a sadness in his eyes. She could only guess what was going through his mind. Excited to have a nephew, sad that he'd missed out on the first twenty years of his life.

'Does he know about me?' Kev asked.

'He does. The sugar-coated version, anyway.'

Kev smiled and was quiet again, but Lori couldn't stand the silence.

'Kev, nothing's changed here, you know. The estate, it's still the same. It's still a shit tip, full of addicts and thugs. There are still some good people, but we don't get very far in life living here. I tried when I was younger to start a career, but with Jay as a baby, I just couldn't do it, I couldn't leave him all week. So I sacrificed the opportunity to work, which could have resulted in getting us out of here.'

She'd been stuck between not wanting to leave her baby and wanting to get out of the estate.

'Do you think life would be different if you'd carried on? You'd have got away from this place?' Kev asked, and the question hurt.

'Maybe,' she replied. 'But we didn't. We're still here. Faced with the past, staring out to our old flat every single day. The memories of what we all went through staring us right in the face all the time.'

Kev took Lori's hand. 'All that you went through was my fault. I want to make things better for you, Lori. And your son. If you'd let me, I'd like to get you and Jay the fuck away from this place.'

Lori bit the inside of her lip and furrowed her brow. 'Oh, come on, Kev. How are you going to do that? You've not even met Jay yet. What makes you think he'd even go for that?'

He shrugged. 'Well, yeah, he might not. But surely if you've been wishing for a better life out of Blackhill, then this could be your opportunity to give that to him? I trained as a chef during my last jail stint and really wanted to learn about nutrition and good, healthy foods. Like I said, I've done so much damage to my liver, I wanted to understand ways to keep myself as healthy as possible. I've got a job in a restaurant in the city centre. I've got my own flat, three bedrooms. No point those two extra rooms going to waste? Why don't you both come and live with me?'

Lori's eyes were wide. She couldn't believe this was her brother she was talking to. He was the polar opposite of the man she remembered. 'Are you serious?'

'Never been more serious about anything in my life.'

'But like I said, you and Jay have *never* met. You don't know each other. Fuck, I barely know you any more, Kev. Don't get me wrong, I'm happy you are where you are in life. But we can't just up sticks and move in with you.'

'I get that, Lori. But do you really want to stay here? This is your chance to get away from here.'

She stared at him, then turned to face the veranda door, so many thoughts running through her mind. The one she kept coming back to was the only reason she could never leave Blackhill.

'I can't. I'm sorry.'

'Why not?'

'I can't leave Steph behind. We made a promise to each other when we were teenagers that we would always stay together. And we have. I can't break that promise, Kev. You might not understand it, but we went through some shit after Mum and Dad died. And we only survived it because we had each other.'

Another lump formed in her throat and, this time, she was openly crying.

She supposed that addiction didn't just come in the form of drugs or alcohol. It came in the form of best friends staying together. And dying together. Lori couldn't live without Steph. She knew that. And Steph wouldn't survive without Lori.

'Steph Lyle? You're still best mates with her?' Kev frowned.

'She's my sister. The only family I've got. And I'm *not* leaving her.'

There was a silence between them for a few moments before Kev nodded. 'Yeah, I get that. Fine. Maybe I was a bit premature with suggesting it, sorry. But I'd still like to rebuild some kind of relationship with you, Lori. Get to know your son, Jay. I mean, I'm trying with everyone in my life I've ever let down.'

Lori frowned. 'Everyone?'

'Yeah. I've fucked my entire life up, but I've fucked up everyone else's too. Yours, Charley's, Samantha's.'

'Who the *hell* is Samantha?' Lori asked, staring at him with wide eyes.

'She's my daughter.'

Lori's jaw fell open. 'You have a fucking *daughter*? Since when?'

'Since twenty years ago. I haven't had anything to do with how she grew up because I was in jail for the majority of it. But yeah, I have a daughter. I've missed out on years of her life and it was all because I was too busy being a druggie. We've had minimal contact over the years. A few phone calls here and there. I've met her once when I was out years ago. I don't think she'd know me if she fell over me in the street. In fact, I know she wouldn't. There have been times when I've passed her in the street and she's had no clue who I am. Only reason I knew her was because she was with her mum; who didn't recognise me or just blatantly ignored me. I've got so much to put right.'

Lori couldn't speak. How the hell had she gone through her entire life not knowing that her brother had a kid of his own? Then again, Kev hadn't known she'd had a son either.

'I can't believe I never knew about this,' she said quietly.

'To be fair, I was off my face when she was born, probably when she was conceived too.'

'Who is her mum? Do I know her?' Lori pressed, with all sorts going through her mind. Had she walked past this woman and her child in the estate, in the village, and never known? Had she known who Lori was and never come forward?

Kev sighed. 'Her name is Lisa Connolly. I don't know where she is these days, certainly not Dunreath. Not sure what happened to her, if I'm honest. And I don't think Samantha has any contact with her either. Another example of *phenomenal* parenting to come out of this place.'

Lori didn't recognise the name, thankfully. She didn't know how she would have reacted if she'd known who the girl was.

'I can't believe this is happening.'

Kev nodded. 'Me either. People like me should have been sterilised.'

Lori sighed. 'You're not that person any more, Kev.'

'He's still in there. But I fight every single day to be a better version of myself. I want to be a good brother to you, Lori, because you deserve it. I want to apologise to my daughter for missing out on her life.'

Lori didn't want to say out loud what she was thinking. But Dunreath Village was the type of place where trauma cycles weren't broken. If he did meet his daughter, chances were she'd have her own issues to deal with. If that was the case, Kev would be hit with even more guilt. Would he be able to handle that and remain clean and sober at the same time?

'Let's just take things slowly, eh?' she suggested. 'You're back here with me. You've explained your side of things. I get it.'

'Yeah,' Kev replied. 'Let's just hope she does too.'

Lori looked at Kev and, for the first time in her life, she was hopeful that things could be about to get better. The offer for Lori and Jay to move away from Blackhill Court, to get away from the looming towers and for Jay to start a new life, was like a fever dream. Was it all some kind of delusion? Or would Kev really pull through for her this time?

TWENTY-EIGHT

Jay and Reece were doing their first perimeter walk of the night. They walked in silence at first and all Jay could focus on was the churning sensation in his stomach as he glanced towards the six towers. All due for demolition and not soon enough. Jay couldn't get the images of the bones out of his head. Human bones. Who did they belong to? How long had they been down there? It struck Jay that perhaps the reason no one had come looking for them might be because they didn't matter to anyone. In a strange way, that made Jay feel a little less shaken about the whole thing. And Logan seemed completely unfazed by it all. His boss was someone he looked up to, someone who inspired him. If Logan could brush it off, then so could Jay. He needed to be as tough as his boss because if he wanted to be like Logan, then he needed to start acting like him.

'Oi.' Reece gave Jay a playful shove.

Jay stopped, stared at his best friend. 'What?'

'I've just spilled my guts to you and you've not so much as blinked.'

Jay frowned. 'Sorry, I was miles away, mate.'

'Miles away? You weren't even listening to me.'

Jay stopped walking and kept his eye on his best friend. They were like brothers, him and Reece. Their birthdays were in the same month, they lived in flats next to each other, their mums were best friends. Reece was trustworthy. So much so, Jay would trust him with his life, with his biggest secret. But could he trust him with something this big? Something that would line Jay's pockets with ten grand?

'What's up with you?' Reece asked. 'You look ill.'

Sometimes, Reece knew Jay better than he knew himself.

'I'm fine. What were you talking about?' Jay asked, trying to switch the attention away from him.

Reece looked at him with a suspicious glare in his eye. 'Is this about the other day when Logan asked you to come into work three hours early?'

Jay wanted to tell Reece. But he couldn't. There was ten grand at stake here. If Jay spilled his guts, he'd lose that money.

'No. Nothing happened,' Jay said, but his voice cracked and he could kick himself for being such a fucking weakling. 'Like I said, it was just about my promotion.'

'I don't believe you. You forget we know each other better than ourselves and I know when something is bothering you. You've not been the same since Logan asked you to come into work early.'

Jay shot him a look. 'I said I'm *fine*.'

'You're lying.'

'I'm not fucking lying. Stop pushing me to tell you something when there's nothing to tell.'

Reece shook his head. 'Okay, fine. Let's just get on with the shift, eh?' He walked on ahead but Jay put on a jog to catch up with him.

'Tell me what you were saying back there,' Jay persisted, hoping that the change in subject would be enough to derail Reece's thinking.

Reece shoved his hands into his pockets and glanced around. 'I was talking about Sammi Connolly.'

Jay blinked before it clicked in his head who Reece was referring to. Then his eyes widened. 'Logan's missus?'

'Aye,' Reece replied. 'I don't like them together.'

'What do you mean, you don't *like* them together?' Jay asked, although from what Reece had said, he could gather where this was going. 'Are you going to try to fire into your boss' fiancée? Are you fucking mental?'

Reece stopped walking and turned sharply. 'Did I say that I was going to fire into her?'

'No, but you said you don't like them together and, if I'm honest, I don't see where else that could go.'

'I don't fancy her. Well, I don't any more. Look, I just don't think she should be with him,' Reece said.

Jay couldn't help but smile, but not in humour – in disbelief. 'You don't any more? So when did you fancy her, Reece?'

Reece stood still, glanced up at the sky and muttered, 'For fuck sake.' He lowered his face to the ground and sighed. 'If I tell you this, you need to keep it quiet. Sammi and I, we used to go out. A couple of years ago. Before she binned me for Logan.'

Jay stared at Reece, his eyes narrow before he started to laugh. Reece couldn't get his head around what was funny.

'That's some fantasy you've created,' Jay said. But when Reece didn't respond, Jay's expression straightened. 'Are you kidding?'

Reece shook his head. 'No. We were together for about six months. Spent a lot of time together. We had plans to get out of Dunreath. I swear to God, I'd have done anything for that girl and she patched me. Dumped me through text message then blocked me. Haven't heard from or seen her since. Then the other day in the café, she served us, and I just about shat myself when she showed up at the table. Didn't know where to look or what to say.'

Jay was shaking his head, his eyes darting all over the place. 'How the fuck did I not know about you being loved up for six months? When was this?'

Reece shrugged. 'She ended it about two years ago and, from what I can gather, went straight from me to him.'

'What a bitch,' Jay sneered.

'Oi, watch your mouth. She gets enough of that shit from Logan.'

Jay began pacing back and forth slowly. So many things running through his mind at the same time. The money.

The bones. Now this. He needed to make Reece realise how dangerous this information would be if it fell into Logan's hands.

'Look, Reece, I mean this in the nicest way, because in all honesty, I don't want you to get a tanking off the boss, but stay the fuck out of their relationship.'

Reece grimaced. 'Aye, she kind of said the same thing, although not in as many words. He's old enough to be her dad. You saw the way he behaved towards her in the café the other day. Spoke to her like a piece of fucking meat rather than his fiancée.'

'She's not your bird any more, Reece. Do yourself a favour and get over it,' Jay said firmly. 'And why did you not tell me about this at the time?'

Reece rolled his eyes. 'We wanted to keep it quiet. Our plan was to just see how it went. I didn't want anyone coming in and putting pressure on it and neither did she.'

'Well, she's engaged to your boss now so you best stay away from her.'

Reece's face flushed a little, but he kept his composure. 'She looks terrified of him, Jay. I can't just stand by and let her be scared of him, can I?'

Jay laughed. 'Are you trying to lose your job *and* your legs at the same time?'

'You know she said that to me? That he expects her only to talk to women. That's fucked up.'

Jay glanced down at the ground, then setting his expression in as serious a manner as he could, he looked up at his best friend. 'Why is that your problem? She dumped you by text, you should be glad you got out when you did. She seems like a bitch to me to be able to do that to you.'

'Stop calling her a bitch,' Reece sneered. 'She's vulnerable.'

'Trust me, stay away from her. You said it yourself that he doesn't want her talking to other men. If that's true, then don't be *other men*.'

'So what? I just stand back and let something bad happen to her?' Reece asked.

Jay slowly shook his head. 'Jesus Christ, mate. It's not your problem. Get a fucking grip of yourself, eh? She's an ex for a reason.'

Silence fell between them and Reece took a deep breath.

They continued walking in silence, making their way around the exterior perimeters of the towers. They reached the third building and Jay stopped outside the entrance. He stared inside and he could feel Reece's eyes on him.

'Why have you stopped?' Reece asked, following his gaze.

Jay didn't respond and continued to stare. The images in his head were taking over now. You could only fake bravery for so long before it started to eat you up inside. As much as Jay acted like a tough nut, he wasn't sure he was in reality.

'Is there something in there?' Reece pressed when Jay didn't answer.

'Nah, mate. Come on,' Jay replied, while making a move towards the next tower.

Reece didn't follow. He kept his eyes on the entrance of tower three. 'There is, isn't there? Is this what's been up with you? Did something happen here the other night? I swear to God, Jay, you've gone white as a sheet. What the fuck is going on?'

Jay closed his eyes briefly, but when he opened them again, Reece was already making his way towards the tower.

'Wait, Reece.'

'If you won't tell me what's going on in there then I'll go and see for myself. I told you my biggest secret, Jay. Least you can do is tell me what's up with you.'

Catching up with him, Jay reached out and spun Reece around to face him. 'Don't do this,' he said desperately. 'You can't go in there.'

'Tell me what's going on. You've been weird since you were promoted and I need to know why. I only want to help you, Jay.'

Jay sucked air into his lungs and breathed out slowly. There was no getting out of this. He couldn't lie. And even if he did, Reece wouldn't believe him.

'Okay. If I tell you, you have to know that it can *never* be repeated.'

'Why? Would he kill me to keep me silent or something?' Reece joked. 'I'm already on his fucking radar because he thinks I was flirting with Sammi; even though I wasn't. And he even said to her that he thought we were at it behind his back. So, he wouldn't need much of an excuse anyway.'

Jay raised a brow. 'This isn't a joke, Reece.'

'Have you found a sex dungeon or something?'

Sighing, Jay started to walk towards the entrance door to the third tower. 'If only.'

They walked in silence and Jay could feel the tension in his neck, in his shoulders. His heart shuddered in his chest. Jay led Reece inside and headed towards the basement door.

'What's down there?' Reece asked, the sound of his footsteps stopping behind Jay.

'You wanted to know what happened the other day, so I'm showing you. But only because you won't let it fucking go, not because I want to,' Jay replied, opening the door and pulling the torch out of his high-vis jacket pocket. He switched it on, shone it down the stairs and, just as the bones came into view, he turned his face back to Reece, unable to believe he was looking at the damn things a third time round.

Reece hesitated, before taking a step forward and peering down the stairs.

Jay took in his best friend's expression as the realisation set in of what he was staring down at. His face contorted; his head tilted to the left a little.

'What am I looking at here? Is that...' Reece's words trailed off. 'Jesus *fucking* Christ,' he said, stumbling back.

'That's pretty much what I said too,' Jay replied, pulling the door closed and switching off the torch.

Reece turned away, his shoulders rising and falling with slow, steady movements. 'What the fuck, Jay?'

What the fuck, indeed, Jay thought.

'What are you involved in, Jay?'

Reece's voice was a low whisper, but to Jay the words echoed around the basement so loudly he worried that someone would hear them.

'I was doing the security checks to see if I found any security issues he'd missed before the demolition, like he asked,' Jay replied. 'All was fine until I found this. I went to him about it and he told me to keep quiet.'

'Keep it *quiet*?' Reece stared at him incredulously. 'As in don't go to the polis about it?'

Jay nodded. 'Said it wouldn't be good for business.'

'He's right about that,' Reece spluttered. 'What about reporting it because it's the right thing to do?'

'Apparently it would push back the demolition date. He wants it all to go ahead so that he can use the land for building works to create jobs.'

Reece stuck his jaw out, raised a brow. 'You're telling me that Logan isn't going to report this because he wants to make money? I mean, he's a fucking gangster, so yeah, I can believe that.'

'Would you keep your voice down, anyone could hear us,' Jay hissed, spinning around to check they were still alone.

Reece shook his head with a look of despair. 'What else did he say?'

'He said I'd get a bonus if everything went smoothly.'

'What kind of a bonus?'

'He called it a discretion bonus. Ten grand.'

Reece laughed incredulously and shook his head again. 'He's paying you to keep quiet about a murder he's committed, you do realise that, don't you?'

'There's no proof he killed anyone,' Jay scoffed. 'If he did, why would he ask me to do a check and risk me discovering that kind of secret?'

'To get you onside. To get you to believe he's the good guy; an innocent party in all of it. And you've fallen for it, Jay. Are you thick?'

Jay gritted his teeth. 'Far fucking from it, you cheeky bastard.'

'Then walk away. You don't need this in your life. Living in Blackhill is bad enough without this hanging over you.'

'I'm not walking away from ten grand, Reece. That money will help us get out of Blackhill,' Jay said.

'It's blood money, Jay. You need to get out of here. Chuck this job. I'm going to. In fact, I'm off the site right now. I'm not hanging around here a second longer than I have to.'

Reece turned his back on the basement door and headed for the main exit and, in a state of panic, Jay ran after him and pulled him back. Spinning around, Reece glared at Jay.

'You can't just walk off-site.'

'Watch me,' Reece said, jabbing his finger into Jay's forehead. 'If you've got any sense left in that head of yours, you'll leave with me and you *won't* take that money.'

'I can't do that.'

Reece pulled his lips into a thin line. A moment of quiet, then he ran a hand over his face. 'Jesus. I knew he was a dodgy bastard, but this?'

'Are you honestly going to leave?' Jay asked in the hope that he'd stay. Because Jay could not walk away. He simply couldn't.

'I can't stay here, knowing what I know, Jay. I'm not saying it's right, but I do get why you're staying.'

Jay closed his eyes. He was living a nightmare. 'Money talks, Reece. If it had been you, would you walk after being offered that kind of cash, if it meant the chance of a decent life?'

'I don't know,' Reece replied solemnly. 'But I can't stay here. I just can't.'

'What are you going to tell Logan?' Jay asked.

'Dunno. That I've found another job? That I'm leaving Dunreath altogether. Not such a bad idea, actually. Me not being around might actually do Sammi a favour; at least until the next guy comes along and causes her problems.'

They both headed outside to the grounds of the site and back towards the Portakabin in silence. And all Jay could think about was that, without money, Reece would be going nowhere.

TWENTY-NINE

'What are you doing back?' Stephanie asked as Reece walked through the front door nine hours before she'd expected him.

'I quit,' Reece replied, closing the door behind him.

Stephanie stared at him, waiting for more, but instead he kicked off his boots and walked into the kitchen.

'Any dinner left over?'

Narrowing her eyes, Steph followed him and stood in the doorway. 'There's a couple of slices of that pizza from Aldi that you like in the fridge. Couple of minutes in the air fryer should do it.'

Reece opened the fridge door, pulled out the plate wrapped in cling film and placed it on the worktop.

'So, are you going to tell me why you quit?' Stephanie pressed.

'Can't work for someone like Logan Greer. He's a...' His words trailed off and he started to unwrap the pizza. 'I just don't like him.'

'Why?' Stephanie asked again.

Sighing, Reece pulled the air fryer drawer open, placed a slice inside and tapped the digital pad before the machine started to whir. 'You ever just get a feeling about someone? That they're not right? I think he's more trouble than anyone really knows and I don't want to be a part of it.'

Folding her arms over her chest, Stephanie nodded slowly. She wished she had a sixth sense like that. Her life could have been so much more if she'd felt that way about Ped back in the day.

'Well, everyone's heard the rumours about him being trouble, so you already knew that. What's changed?'

Reece shrugged. 'Me, I suppose.'

'So what did you say to him?'

'To who?' Reece frowned.

'Your boss? What did you say to him before you walked off-site?'

Reece stared at the air fryer, as if somehow it was going to answer the question for him.

'Did you leave without telling anyone?'

'Jay knows. And he's the site supervisor. So, technically I told *a* boss.' A smile raised the corners of Reece's mouth, but Stephanie knew her son well enough to know that it wasn't in humour. It was out of nerves.

Stephanie uncrossed her arms and felt a tightness in her chest. She was worried for her son.

'Reece, you can't just walk off a job like that, not when the boss is someone like him. He's dangerous.'

'I know. That's why I left.'

'How do you know?' she asked. 'I mean, have you witnessed him first-hand?'

'Have you?' Reece challenged.

'I have, he was very unpleasant towards his fiancée and, trust me, if he can do to her in public what he did today, then Christ knows what he'd do to an employee who leaves him in the shit.'

Reece looked up at the ceiling and groaned. 'He's a fucking dickhead for treating her like that,' he said quietly, before balling his fists.

Stephanie frowned at the reaction. 'I agree. That's why I want you to be careful.'

'Mum, he's got skeletons in the closet.'

'I don't fucking doubt it, Reece.'

'No, I mean that *literally*.'

Stephanie felt her stomach roll; her chest constrict. 'What are you talking about?'

Silence, followed by the ping of the air fryer, which made Stephanie jump a little, weighed heavy in the air.

Reece was quiet, hesitant even. Glancing down at the floor, he said, 'Nothing. What happened with his fiancée today?'

'Hang on, you just said he had *literal* skeletons in the closet. Explain.'

Shaking his head, he said, 'Less you know, the better, Mum. Trust me on this.'

Her stomach lurched again. She knew exactly what he meant. He'd seen something, or at least heard something. This, coupled with the fact that Lori had heard Jay talking in his sleep about bones, could only mean one thing, and a sudden nausea took over.

'Reece. I'm your mum. And if I think you're in danger of a nutcase coming after you, then I need to know what the fuck it's for. So, you'd better open your mouth and start talking, right now.'

He stared at her and she couldn't read his expression. He sat down, glanced up at her and said, 'You're going to want to sit down for this one.'

THIRTY

Stephanie barely made it to the sofa before her legs gave way. Reece must know about the bones. Why else would he have said what he did?

'Has something happened?' she asked, her voice quivering. She had to keep herself calm. So far, there was no concrete evidence to suggest anyone had found human remains, and she had to hold on to that for as long as she could.

'Okay, so what I'm about to tell you is pretty awful. Jay knows about it too. And Logan told him outright to keep it quiet so the demolition could still go ahead. Said it was bad for business; fucking prick.'

So Jay did know about the bones. Of course he did, it was the only explanation for what he'd said when asleep. Stephanie's saliva glands were working overtime, ready to help empty her stomach. She would have to pretend she was fine, that this situation wasn't making her feel like she was going to die.

Swallowing and trying to breathe as slowly as she could, Stephanie turned, took Reece's hands in her own and looked him in the eye. 'What would be bad for business?'

'There's human remains in the basement of one of the towers.'

She closed her eyes, as though not being able to see would mean that this wasn't happening. The truth was beginning to crawl out of that basement and her entire life was going to come crashing down on top of her. Lori's too.

'Which tower?'

'Three.'

'How do you know for sure?' she asked, finally opening her eyes. She dreaded his response.

'I saw them.'

Shitshitshit. This couldn't be happening.

'*What* did you see?'

'Bones. And before you ask, yes, they were human, although I was hoping even when I was looking at them that they weren't. Maybe a dog or a fox, but definitely not.'

'Jesus,' Stephanie whispered. Her nerves were shot but she had to keep a lid on the panic threatening to bubble over. 'Are you *absolutely* sure?'

'One *hundred* per cent sure. Jay showed me what he'd found, told me that Logan said if Jay keeps it quiet, if the demolition goes ahead on time because of his silence, then he'll get a ten grand *discretion* bonus.'

Steph's palms began to sweat and her stomach churned as though she was on the roller coaster of death. She couldn't throw up, couldn't show signs of fear. The question posed now was, how the hell was Stephanie going to break this to Lori? It was one thing for her to hear Jay distressed in his sleep about it, but to know that he'd discovered them himself and was being offered money to keep his mouth shut was something else entirely.

'The fact that he's offering Jay that amount of money screams that he's responsible, Mum, don't you think?' Reece pressed. 'And Jay's going to do it; he's going to keep it a secret. He said he needs that money.'

In a perfect world, that would be the best explanation. But the human remains in that basement were there because of Stephanie and Lori, not Logan.

Swallowing down the lump in her throat from the fear of her secret coming to the surface, Steph attempted as brave an expression as she could and said, 'It doesn't matter about that money, Reece. What matters is that Jay's right. You *can't* tell *anyone* else about this. Do you hear me, son? We don't want Logan Greer coming after you.'

Reece nodded. 'But I've already walked away. He's going to want to know why, Mum.'

Stephanie got to her feet and breathed out a lungful of air as slowly as she could. 'We'll figure out an explanation together. You can tell him you've had to walk away to care for me, or something. You don't have to let on that you know a thing.'

'I'm not worried about me. Also, no one seems to have mentioned the fact that there might be people out there looking for answers. Does anyone care about that?'

Stephanie shrugged her shoulders and began pacing the floor. 'That's not your concern, Reece. And clearly it's not the concern of your boss.'

'Ex-boss.'

Glancing out onto the estate, life went on as normal for the rest of the residents. An evening of survival, finding their next hit and wondering how they were going to pay for it, or get away without. For Stephanie, she was faced with how she would keep her son safe from the gangster who was going to ask a million questions and likely not be satisfied with any answer he was given.

All this time, it was only ever Lori and Stephanie who had known that Ped and Jambo were down there, rotting away.

Now it seemed as though their secret was very slowly making its way out of that basement. Soon, everyone would know, and Lori and Stephanie would have to make sure that the mystery of who they were would remain just that.

Raising her hand, Stephanie pulled down the handle of Lori's front door and walked into her flat. She could hear Absolute Radio playing some Nineties dance music and it made Stephanie frown. Was Lori having a party to herself?

'It's me,' she called, walking through to the living room. 'We have a problem that can't wait.'

'Steph, what's up?' Lori said, getting to her feet quickly. Shock peppered her expression and Stephanie realised that Lori wasn't alone.

'Are you all right, you know, after earlier?' Stephanie asked, but she wasn't looking at Lori. She was staring at the man sitting on the sofa.

'I'm fine. Look, this isn't a good time.'

The man got to his feet, stared at her with a smile on his face. 'Steph? Steph Lyle?'

'Aye, who wants to know?' Stephanie asked, a little more venom in her voice than she'd meant.

'It's me,' he said, his arms stretched to the side a little, as though he was presenting himself to her.

Shaking her head and feeling the frown line between her brow deepen, she said, 'Does me have a name?'

'Steph, it's Kev,' he replied.

Eyes wide, Stephanie's mouth fell open as she took in the face of the man in front of her. 'Kev?' she asked, but turned to Lori. 'As in your brother, Kev?'

Lori nodded. 'The very one.'

Turning back to face him, Stephanie placed her hands on her hips and glared at him. 'If you're here for money for drugs, you can rest assured she doesn't have a penny to waste on that shit, so you can just fuck off.'

Kev smiled a little. 'You've not changed a bit. And that's absolutely not why I'm here.'

'Oh aye? And where the fuck have you been all this time?'

Kev laughed and replied, 'In the jail, out the jail.'

'Is this for real?' Stephanie turned to Lori again. 'He's actually back?'

'Aye, I'm actually back. And you can ask me yourself, you know?'

'Sorry, mate, but you've never been the most reliable person. So forgive me if I speak like you weren't here.'

'Steph!' Lori exclaimed. 'That's just *fucking* rude.'

'And he's just been *fucking* absent your entire life. Sorry for keeping my manners for someone who deserves it.'

Kev raised his hands. 'It's fine. I get it. You're being protective of her. Something I should have been as a brother.'

Stephanie stared at Kev, took in his features. He looked different, yet the same. His face had aged; all those years of drugs and being in and out of jail would do that to a person. But his eyes looked the same as they had when Stephanie last saw him.

'There's something different about you,' she said to him, her tone a little softer now, and almost forgetting why she'd come to see Lori in the first place.

'He's sober. Has been for two years,' Lori said in his place.

Pursing her lips and raising a brow, Stephanie nodded slowly. 'Sober for two years, eh? How long you been out?'

'A year,' Kev replied.

'And you're only just showing up now?' Stephanie said judgingly.

'Wanted to make sure I had my head straight before venturing back into this place. The nostalgia can get you, help you forget why you're trying to better yourself. I didn't want to risk going back into my old ways by coming back too soon. If I came back before I was ready, I'd be dead. And by the looks of the place, nothing's really changed.'

Lori rolled her eyes. 'Got that right. Place is exactly as it was. Just different people from when you were last here. Apart from us, obviously.'

Stephanie regarded Kev's explanation and realised it made sense. 'So, why now?'

'Making amends. Or at least trying to. Got two sisters, a nephew and a daughter to make up to.'

Stephanie frowned. 'A daughter?'

'That's right.'

'She's twenty,' Lori interjected.

'Bloody hell, you've missed out on a lot,' Steph replied.

'Aye, and I don't intend on missing anything else. I want to know how life's been, Lori. How the hell have you survived Blackhill after all this time?'

Lori blinked and stole a glance at Stephanie. Clearing her throat, she asked, 'So, what was this problem that couldn't wait?'

Stephanie's stomach flipped at the harsh reality of why she was stood in Lori's flat. But how could she tell her now, with Kev there? She couldn't.

'It's nothing,' Stephanie replied. 'It can wait.'

'But you said it couldn't?' Lori replied, a slight smile on her face.

She gave Lori a stern look, a warning with her eyes that, hopefully, she would understand. Kev was only just back. Who knew how long he'd hang around for? Two years sober and one year out of prison wasn't something anyone could have imagined. She didn't want to go blurting everything out in front of him when he'd only been back a matter of, what, hours?

Lori seemed to take the warning and cleared her throat.

'Steph?' Kev said, interrupting her thoughts. She turned to look at him, tried to keep her composure. The last thing she needed to do now was fall apart because of what was about to come out.

'Yes?'

'Thank you for sticking by my sister's side when I couldn't. You're more like family to her than I ever could be and you'll never know how ashamed I am of abandoning her.'

Stephanie hadn't expected that. What's more, she hadn't expected the tears that filled her eyes in that moment. But she wasn't crying about what Kev had said. The tears were for Reece, for Jay. They were for Lori and herself. Their secret was about to come out and, when it did, it could destroy everything.

THIRTY-ONE

'Davie?' Logan said, placing the phone to his ear.

'Mate,' Davie said. 'How's things?'

Logan looked through the window of his van up at the towers and nodded. 'Aye. The demolition is well on its way. How's things your end?'

There was a brief pause and Logan knew that was never a good thing.

'There's a bit of a problem, actually. That's why I'm phoning.'

Logan kept his eye on the towers. 'Go on.'

'More drugs have gone missing,' Davie replied, and the silence that followed was deafening.

'Hang on, so you're telling me that even with Specky out of the picture, my drugs are still being fucked with?'

Logan's blood began to boil. Had they got it wrong with Specky? No, that wasn't possible. He'd admitted it before the team attacked him.

'It seems we've got another thief amongst the boys. Don't worry, I'll deal with it. I just wanted you to know. I'll figure it out quickly.'

Logan pinched at the bridge of his nose and shut his eyes. 'You better, mate. And when you do, tell them I'll be the one dealing with them. Ungrateful little fuckers. They've got fucking balls, I'll give them that; especially after seeing what happened to Specky.'

'Aye,' Davie said. 'I mean, they would have been part of what happened to him. I don't get it. But I will sort this.'

Nodding, Logan hung up the phone and got out of the van. He began to walk towards the entrance, the gravel crunching under his steel-toecap boots. Boots that had met the faces of those who didn't follow his rules. And Jay would be no different to the little bastards who were stealing his gear.

Pushing open the entrance gate, Logan didn't bother to close it behind him as he walked towards the Portakabin. The light was on inside, the door slightly ajar.

Stepping inside, Jay was stood facing the door, his phone in his hand and a tormented expression on his face.

'Boss, what you doing in so late?' Jay asked, startled. 'I mean, I wasn't expecting you. I thought you were at the pub tonight.'

'Just thought I'd come in and see if there have been any issues tonight. Any staff phoned in sick? Not showed up? Or just fucked off for the night?'

Jay took a breath, his eyes darted back and forth before resting on Logan. 'Erm, actually, Reece had to go home.'

Narrowing his eyes and raising his brow, Logan lifted his chin. 'Oh? Why's that then?'

Jay fell silent. Terror shone out of his eyes and Logan detected a tremble in his hand as he slid his phone into his pocket.

'He said he had to leave,' Jay replied.

'*Why* did he have to leave early?'

Shrugging, Jay said, 'Didn't say.'

Logan bit the inside of his lip. The little bastard was lying and not very well. He'd seen Reece and Jay on the CCTV. He'd seen them go into tower three and, when they came back out, Reece had walked off-site.

'Let me ask you something, Jay. Do you know anything about my Sammi and Reece getting a little closer?'

Jay frowned, but there was a flicker in his eye. 'What do you mean, closer?'

'Come on, Jay. You're his best mate. Let's not pretend he hasn't said anything to you about it?'

Jay shook his head. 'I swear to you, I don't know what you're talking about.'

Logan cracked his knuckles together and sighed. 'Fine. Maybe I'm just imagining it then. You know, imagined Reece flirting with her while she served him. Imagined her flirting back. Just like I must have imagined seeing you and Reece leaving tower three together?'

Jay's eyes widened and the look on his face told Logan that he knew he couldn't lie his way out of this one.

'Anything to say for yourself, Jay?' Logan asked, his voice light in a way that would leave Jay feeling uncertain.

'We were just doing our usual perimeter checks, that's all.'

'And that involves going *into* the buildings themselves, does it? Specifically tower three?'

Jay's eyes darted down to his feet, unable to look at Logan.

'Did you show him, Jay? Did you show him what was down there?'

Jay glanced up, shook his head, but his eyes were glassy, as though tears were beginning to pool. The little shit would only be worried about losing his measly ten grand. What was it with these little estate bastards trying to screw him over? First Specky, now Jay?

'I don't believe you, Jay. I really don't. So, I'm going to ask you again and I want the truth this time. Did you show Reece the basement of tower three?'

Jay's fingers locked together, his knuckles white. 'No.'

'Lie to me again, Jay. I *dare* you.'

Jay closed his eyes, fingers released from one another. His arms were by his side as he remained silent.

'Reece knows what's down there, doesn't he? That's why he left?'

Jay's eyes flickered open and he nodded.

'And didn't I tell you to keep that to yourself?'

'You did.'

'So, why did you betray me? Why did you go running to your best pal the second my back was turned? I thought I could trust you, I thought you were trustworthy, Jay. What's that about, Jay? Go on, tell me. Tell me why you couldn't keep this between us? You do realise you've put the jobs of your colleagues at risk, don't you? If this gets back to the authorities, the site will be shut down, the dem date postponed. I won't be able to pay your workmates because of this, Jay.'

Logan had fired the words at Jay quickly enough that he wouldn't be able to answer each question before the next came, and Jay began to tremble.

'I'm sorry. He kept asking me what was wrong. He went to go into the tower to inspect it and I told him to stay out. He wouldn't listen. I didn't have a choice. He'd have found out himself. I'm sorry. But Reece can be trusted, boss. I swear he can. He won't say a word to anyone.'

Logan began pacing the floor. 'Is that right? Trusted so much that he walked off-site, without so much as a second thought? Nah, we need to get him back here. Now. We need to talk to him. If he blabs, you'll all be out of a job. I was the first person to give you and Reece a proper chance, Jay. No one else would entertain you because of where you're from and you've gone and fucked that up.'

Jay held his hands up in defeat. 'Right, okay. I'll get him back. I'll go and get him.'

'No, you're not leaving. You're on shift. You'll phone him; you'll tell him I want a word. With me right in front of you.'

He could tell Jay was stressed and rightly so. He'd broken Logan's trust. He'd tried to lie about it. And what's more, his best friend, Reece Lyle, was trying to get closer to Sammi. And he could tell her about what he'd seen.

The anger bubbled inside him and his mind whirred. Who the fuck did these little scrotes think they were? These bastards were a bunch of nothings from a council estate and there was absolutely no way he was going to let any of them get away with behaving like they were invincible. Not the dealers, not Jay or Reece and most definitely not Sammi.

'Phone him,' he growled. 'Now.'

THIRTY-TWO

Reece paced the kitchen floor, trying to work out what he was going to do, when his mobile phone rang. Glancing at the screen, he saw Jay's name.

'Jay?' Reece answered.

'Aye, it's me. Listen, I need you to come back to the site.'

Narrowing his eyes, Reece frowned and asked, 'Sorry, mate, but I can't be there.'

'Logan wants a word. He knows you've left; just wants to know why?'

Jay's voice was strained. Something wasn't right and Reece knew fine well what the problem was. Logan had put him up to this call and he was stood in the same room as him.

'Am I on loudspeaker?' Reece asked.

'No.'

Reece took a long, silent breath. He knew Jay wasn't lying. There was no distant echo to tell him he was on loudspeaker. But that wasn't to say that Logan wasn't stood in front of Jay, listening in on the conversation.

'Is your audio volume down as low as it can go?' Reece asked quietly.

'Aye.'

'If the answer to the next question is yes, tell me you think I owe Logan an explanation, okay?' Reece didn't wait for Jay to say anything. He continued. 'Do you think Logan wants to silence me because of what I saw?'

Jay was quiet for a few moments before he said, 'Mate, I think Logan would appreciate your resignation in writing, if I'm honest. He just wants an explanation.'

Fuck, Reece thought.

Reece wasn't going to risk going anywhere near Logan. The reputation he had around Dunreath was real. He might well have legitimate businesses to make him look the part, but Logan was an out-and-out psycho and Reece wanted nothing to do with him.

Reece almost dropped the phone. Once upon a time, not so long ago, Jay thought Logan was the coolest guy on the planet. Was he still thinking the same thing now? Knowing that Logan probably wanted to kill Reece for knowing. And what about Jay's part in it all? Why would he hang around Logan, knowing what he might do to his best mate, his brother? Jay would never admit it, but he was terrified of what Logan would do to him.

'Jay, mate. I'm going to hang up now. I need to figure out how I'm going to deal with this. You should get the fuck away from him. It's not right that he's asking you to keep this quiet in case the site gets shut down for a couple weeks while the polis do their jobs. There's a hidden agenda in there somewhere. Tell him what you have to so you get out of there in one piece. Don't take his money. Please. For all our sakes.'

Reece didn't hesitate to hang up the phone. As he ended the call, he sucked air into his lungs and felt a wave of despair wash over him.

'He's not coming,' Jay said, barely able to look his boss in the eye.

Logan was staring down at the floor of the cabin in silence and it made Jay nervous. Was he going to explode? Was he going to lash out at Jay since he was the only one there? Logan was blocking the only exit and there was no way Jay would match up to Logan's strength. If anything was going to happen, Jay would have to do his best to survive it.

'He bare-faced said no?' Logan asked, and Jay saw a rage in his eyes he hadn't seen before.

Nodding, Jay gripped his phone in his hand and hoped that, if he needed to use it, it would do enough damage to allow him to get out of the Portakabin. He imagined having to hit Logan back, what it would feel like to go up against a man of his size. It terrified him. Was the money worth this?

'What does he think I'm going to do, Jay? Does he think I'm going to hurt him? Because that's ridiculous.'

The incredulous look on Logan's face took Jay by surprise. He wasn't expecting it. But the words still didn't match the fiery rage in his eyes.

'Well, no. I mean, we're both just worried about how this is all going to turn out for the future of your business; you know, your plans.'

Logan stared, unblinking, right into Jay's eyes. He was silent, his expression so still it was like he'd frozen on the spot.

'Bloody hell,' Logan said loudly, before he began to laugh. 'What do you two take me for, some kind of psycho killer? Jay, all I want is for your job to be safe. I just wanted to tell Reece it's okay. I understand why he left.'

His laughter continued, somewhat manically, and Jay didn't know whether to laugh along with him or simply stay silent. If anything, he wanted to run away. Psycho? Quite possibly.

'Look, Jay. Just get back out there and finish your work. We can talk about this later. A'right?'

Jay's heart was in his throat, the phone still gripped tightly in his hand.

Logan stood to the side and gestured for Jay to head back out to the site. He did so without hesitation and it took him every fibre of his being not to run home. Not just because Logan was now beginning to scare him, but also because he needed that money. He just hoped that the offer still stood. Because Jay knew he'd failed to keep his end of the deal. Reece knew now, and it was possible that Logan could withhold the money. Jay just had to hope he wouldn't.

THIRTY-THREE

'Lori, wake up.'

Steph's voice jolted Lori awake and she sat up in bed. Steph was stood by the bedroom door and her expression was solemn.

'What time is it?' Lori asked, reaching for her phone.

'Just gone six,' Steph replied.

'Have you been here all night?'

'Slept on the couch. I didn't want to leave you in case you took unwell again, plus Kev was here for ages. No offence, I know he said he's sober, but it's going to take a while to trust him, Lori.'

'Yeah, I get that. It's not just going to happen overnight, is it? Did you manage to get a sleep? You look knackered.'

'Not a wink. I've been holding this in all night and I just have to get it out.'

Lori yawned loudly and stretched out her legs, relaxing quickly when she felt a cramp coming on. 'What's wrong?'

'You're not going to like this, Lori. You're *really* not.'

Steph sat down on the bed beside her and her eyes were glassy, but not from tears. From something else. Terror.

'Reece quit his job last night, came home early,' Steph said.

'Right,' Lori said, stringing the word out.

Steph took a breath, looked like she was going to be sick. 'Reece knows about the bones.'

Lori felt her stomach lurch. 'Oh, Jesus. How?'

Steph took Lori's hand. 'It was Jay who found them, he showed Reece.'

Lori shot out of bed, gripped her hair by the roots and stared down at Steph. 'Tell me you're fucking joking, Steph.'

Steph got to her feet, shook her head. 'I wish I was. But I'm not. It'll be the reason he was talking about them in his sleep yesterday.'

Her head started to spin and her legs felt like jelly. This wasn't happening. This couldn't be happening.

'It gets worse.'

'How the fuck can it get worse?' Lori squealed.

'Logan apparently told Jay to keep his mouth shut about his discovery, and because he told Reece, I'm now worried Logan's going to come after him. Jay accepted the bribe. But I think it's probably through fear more than anything else. We all know about Logan's reputation; the whole village does and probably beyond. And we witnessed first-hand how openly horrible he was to his fiancée in that café yesterday. He pretty much owns everything in the area.'

Lori began pacing the floor, hands still gripping her hair at the roots. 'I need to talk to Jay. I need to hear from him what the *hell* is going on.'

She picked up her phone and rang Jay. When he answered, she almost lost the ability to stand.

'Jay, are you all right?'

'Aye, I'm just on my way home. You feeling better after last night?'

Lori frowned. He didn't sound like someone in fear of speaking out against someone like Logan.

'Yeah, I'm fine. I need to talk to you. You need to get home as soon as you can, okay?'

'I'm only two minutes away. What's wrong?'

'I'll just see you when you get here,' Lori said, before ending the call.

'Do you think we should get Reece in here?' Steph asked.

Lori nodded, and Steph rushed to her flat, reappearing in the living room quicker than Lori could blink. Reece stood beside her, bleary-eyed and almost swaying with tiredness.

Steph wrung her hands together. Just then, the sound of the front door opening set Lori on edge. This conversation was about to happen and there was no possible way to put a pleasant spin on it.

'Mum?' Jay called before entering the living room. He stopped upon seeing three sets of eyes on him.

'Right,' Reece said, turning to Steph. 'What the hell is going on?'

'You and Jay are going to explain what happened at the site last night before you decided to quit,' Steph said with force.

Jay shot Reece a look of what Lori could only describe as anger. 'Are you actually *fucking* kidding? You ran to mummy about this?'

'Oi,' Lori shouted. 'Don't be so cheeky. Reece had every right to tell her what happened. And now you're going to tell us. What is going on down there, Jay?'

Jay shrugged off his jacket and dropped it over the back of the sofa. Sighing, he sank down onto the seat and his hands covered his face. 'I was supposed to keep my mouth shut but Reece was like a dog with a fucking bone.'

Reece shook his head, a look of disgust crossing his face. 'I was fucking worried about you.'

'Why?' Lori asked, hoping that the tremble she felt all over her body wasn't present in her voice.

'Because Logan doesn't want people to know he's a fucking murdering bastard, that's why,' Reece sneered.

Jay raised his head and he frowned. 'We don't *know* he's a murderer, Reece.'

'You keep telling yourself that, Jay. But from where I was stood last night, it seemed very obvious to me that Logan murdered that person and left them there in the hope that, once the buildings were down, they'd never be found.'

Jay sighed loudly. 'You're so sure of yourself. It was a pile of bones, Reece. If he did kill them, it would have been years ago. It doesn't make sense for it to have been him. He's only just come on the scene.'

'Tell me this, if Logan didn't kill that person, then who the hell did?' Reece pushed. 'And why *the fuck* would he offer you a discretion bonus of ten grand to keep quiet?'

Jay's eyes darted towards Lori and a slight look of shame washed over his expression.

Her eyes widened, her jaw relaxed and she felt like she was going to throw up. 'I already know about that too. And you bloody well accepted it? What the hell is going on in that head of yours, Jay?'

'It's not like I fucking asked him for it, is it? But yeah, I did. And we need that money, Mum. Don't deny it. I found the body and then he said we had to keep it quiet to protect the site and the other boys' jobs. Then the demolition would go ahead on time, he wouldn't lose out on any money owed, then he'd be able to go ahead with the land purchase once the towers were down.'

Lori glared at him. As did Steph. But Reece rolled his eyes.

'He's fucking with you, Jay. That's what his kind are like. Jesus, you've grown up on one of the roughest estates in the country, and you're still blind to how it all works. You can't seriously think he's innocent in all this, surely? And you can't believe he's actually going to give you that money? Even if he did, you're locked in after that. He'll expect more from you; you'll be like his personal secret keeper.'

Jay glanced down at the floor and merely shook his head.

Steph cleared her throat, turned to Reece and said, 'Hang on, did you say one body?'

Lori's stomach lurched. She'd heard it too. Body. Person. Singular. Not plural. At first she thought she'd imagined it.

'It wasn't a body. It was a skeleton. I think I'd know if there were two deid folk in that basement. It was bad enough seeing the skull of just one never mind fucking two.'

Jay hadn't noticed the glance between Lori and Steph. Nor had Reece, for that matter.

'I take it you didn't bother to tell them about your ex-girlfriend?' Jay said, and Reece raised a brow.

'That's a fucking low blow, Jay. You know nobody knows about her.'

'I'll tell them for you, shall I? Reece's ex-girlfriend is Logan's fiancée,' Jay said.

Both Lori and Stephanie groaned.

'For fuck sake, Reece,' Stephanie exclaimed.

'What? It's not like I fucking planned this, is it? It's not like I looked into the future and made all this happen on purpose.'

'And now,' Jay went on, his fists balled and his shoulders up round his ears, 'Logan knows I showed Reece and that Reece fucked off from the site. The cherry on the cake now is that you two know. Fuck, I'm a dead man. I'm a *skint* dead man.'

Lori closed her eyes and all she kept thinking was how there was only one body. *One.* Not two. Not Ped *and* Jambo. Just one of them. But which one?

And where the *fuck* was the other one?

THIRTY-FOUR

Sammi lay in bed, her phone in her hand above her face. Logan was away overnight for work, and when Sammi thought about it, she had no clue what that work was. All his businesses, that she was aware of, were in Dunreath. She dared not question him, though, and she was at ease having her phone out and able to respond to any messages without Logan giving her a hard time about talking to other people.

The text had come through early, just past six a.m. A simple request to meet. From her dad. That was the second in forty-eight hours. He was persistent, she'd give him that.

The first time he'd called, she'd pretty much told him to fuck off. But now, reading that text, she felt her heart soften a little. Why now? Was it because she wanted away from Logan? Maybe she saw her dad as a means to an end? But getting away from one man and going to another, was that the way to do it? She didn't know her dad at all but now she was curious.

She'd never had much of a relationship with him. Her parents had never been together and, from what Sammi could remember, her mum never had a nice word to say about her dad. It had been him who'd reached out all those years ago; her mum would never have arranged a meeting and not just because she never liked him, purely because it would have taken away from other necessities like drugs and alcohol. Much like most people in Dunreath. To give her mum her due, Sammi remembered how her mum hadn't fought against the idea of meeting Kev. Although, in hindsight, it probably shouldn't have happened. She remembered the first time meeting her dad. He definitely was not sober; even as a kid she could see that. But Sammi was an adult now. She could control the situation to go in the direction of her best interests.

Now there was a potential to get to know him properly. She supposed the potential had always been there, but she'd stayed away because going to a prison to visit a stranger – because that's what he was – just because he created you didn't seem like the right way to go about things.

Tapping out a reply almost half an hour later, Sammi agreed to meet and suggested a neutral spot outside Dunreath altogether. She knew a place in the centre of Clydebank. It was far enough away and not owned by Logan, so it meant it was less likely he'd know she was even there.

Her dad's reply came through quickly with a thumbs-up emoji and a thank you. For some reason, it made her smile. She was in contact with one of her parents and, for once, it wasn't a screaming match with her mother. Not that the woman deserved that title. Much the same as everyone else in Dunreath: an addict who only thought about herself. Not once had she ever put Sammi before her own needs. Sammi didn't have much to go on but, as far as motherhood was concerned, the child should always be the number-one priority, surely?

Seconds later, another message came through, bringing Sammi back to the present.

> Hi. You all right?

It was from Reece. Again.

'Jesus, this guy's on a death wish,' Sammi whispered, before tapping out her reply.

> I can't say this any other way. Stop contacting me. You're putting us both in danger.

A few seconds later, she could see he was typing back a reply and she rolled her eyes. She should have blocked him immediately like she had when she ended things with him. It would protect both of them.

> I will. But there's something I want to talk to you about. I think you're in danger. Can we meet?

Sammi bit the inside of her lip. Had Logan already said something to him? What else could it be?

> Why would you say that?

She sat up in bed, staring down at the message.

> The man you're engaged to is hiding a body in one of the towers.

Her eyes scanned the words from Reece's last message and she raised a brow. As much as the words should have shocked her, they didn't. She knew what kind of man Logan was. He was ruthless. She also knew what kind of person Reece was and he didn't deserve to be caught up in any of this.

> Best keep out of it if you don't want to end up down there too. Don't contact me again, you know what could happen to us otherwise.

She selected all the messages between her and Reece and deleted them.

Sammi knew what Logan was. A gangster. A multi-business owner. Someone who claimed to want the best for Dunreath and Blackhill Court, yet he was the one keeping it in the state that it was in. He'd never told Sammi straight what he did outside the legitimate businesses, but she wasn't deaf or blind. She'd heard the whispers, the rumours about where the drugs came from. People knew who they were buying from but no one in Dunreath would ever say anything concrete for fear of reprisal. She didn't blame them for that. Logan was a dangerous man; Sammi lived with him. She saw it first-hand; had witnessed it for herself. And as for Reece's comment on Logan hiding a body? Logan was capable of it. He was a gangster and killing people just came with the job title. But Sammi didn't want to be involved. She wanted to remain blissfully ignorant, and that was the way she intended it to stay until she could figure out a way to free herself from Logan. He didn't seem to be aware that Sammi knew that he was part of the underworld, and that suited her fine.

If Reece valued his life, he'd keep his nose out.

THIRTY-FIVE

Lori sat on the seat on the veranda, staring out at the estate while Steph poured herself a second measure of gin.

'That'll do your liver in, you know,' Lori said without looking at Steph. 'Sorry. None of my business what you drink.'

'Rather a fucked liver than getting done in by some gangster,' Steph replied before knocking it back. 'I'd offer you one but I know you won't have it.'

Lori took a breath, pursed her lips and said, 'It's not like I haven't thought about it. But now, more so than ever before, I need a clear head.'

Steph placed the glass on the table in front of them, lifted the lid and screwed it back on – reluctantly, Lori noticed.

'What are we going to do?' Steph asked.

'About the fact that one of them is missing?' Lori raised a brow. 'I mean, there's not a lot we can do, unless we go to Logan himself. But what are we meant to say? Hey, see that body in your basement, happen to know if there were ever two?'

Lori noted how Steph's knee juddered under the table. She was a mess, even with two large measures of gin in her veins. It reminded Lori of how she had been once they'd got back to Blackhill Court that night. She was a trembling mess for months afterwards.

'What if they didn't die? What if those remains are someone else entirely?' Steph suggested.

'The thought crossed my mind also, but if that was the case, why didn't they come after us when they had the chance? Why wait all this time?'

Lori pictured them, Jambo lying at the bottom of the basement, Ped challenging her. She remembered vividly, smashing him over the face with the plank of wood with the nails sticking out. She remembered how the nails embedded themselves into his face. How he'd fallen down the stairs. How he'd lain there, next to Jambo. Both very much dead.

'What if Logan is some distant relative, out for revenge?' Steph asked, and her face paled as the words trailed from her lips. 'What if someone out there knew what was supposed to happen to us and then found them? Helped the one still alive out?'

'Again,' Lori said, 'why not come for us right away? Why not finish the job back then? I mean, it's not as if they both didn't know where we lived at the time.'

Shrugging, Steph sighed loudly and picked up the cigarette pack from the table. 'If I can't drink away the memories, then at least let me have a smoke without judging me.'

Lori smiled without the humour. She lowered her voice and said, 'Hey, no judgement from me. I'm the murderer here, remember?'

'It's not funny, Lori,' Steph said, giving her a glare.

'You don't have to tell me that. I have to think about what I did every single night, when I try to go to sleep. I have to look at that fucking scar on the inside of my thigh every time I'm in the shower. I have to see those fuckers' faces every time I close my eyes, or when I blink. So, no, Steph. It's not funny. It's far from fucking funny and I wasn't insinuating it ever was, all right?'

She knew she was being too harsh on Steph. They were both faced with a situation that they had known might come eventually, but there were only remains of one body. Getting caught was always a possibility. Someone discovering Ped *and* Jambo's bodies had *always* been a possibility, but for someone to find just one? What did that mean for them? Had one of them survived and was plotting revenge? The thought was too horrific to comprehend.

'Our boys finding out wasn't on my 2025 bingo card,' Lori said with a smile, trying to lighten her tone and push the thoughts out of her head. 'And now we find out Reece used to go out with Logan Greer's ex. I mean, what the fuck?'

Steph's eyes softened. She sighed, rubbing at them. 'I think that's just bad luck. My head's all over the place.'

Lori raised a brow, nodded and turned her attention back to the estate. As much as the place was a shithouse, there were some good people living in Blackhill. Not all were lost causes to drugs and alcohol, although most families were definitely rough round the edges. She glanced down to the green to see a group of kids kicking a ball around, laughing and having a carry-on. Across at her old flat where she grew up, two women sat on the stairs outside their doors, mugs in hand and chatting. They looked free, like they didn't have a care in the world. Lori didn't know what that felt like. Would she ever?

'What are we going to do, Lori?' Steph asked, her tone full of worry.

The question snapped her out of her trance. 'We do what we have to. We protect our boys. I've killed two fuckwits before and that was for my own survival. If I have to kill again to protect my son, I'll do it without so much as blinking.'

She noted the look of horror on Steph's face. And she knew it wasn't because of the prospect of having to kill, it was the idea that they weren't just protecting themselves this time.

'Do we go to him first?' Steph suggested. 'Maybe we could try to make him see that Reece and Jay aren't a threat.'

A thought suddenly occurred to her and Lori closed her eyes, a feeling of dread washing over her. 'What if it's him?'

'Who?' Steph asked, sounding confused.

'Logan. What if *he* is Ped or Jambo? I mean, we both know only one set of bones was found. It would make sense.'

Steph stared at her. 'No. No way. We've seen him around, Lori. We'd know. *You'd* know because you've come face to face with both of them. You're trying to tell me that all this time with Logan here, you wouldn't have recognised him? Not a chance. Their faces are embedded in my mind, Lori. I'm sure yours too. Nah, they're both dead, Lori. You *killed* them.'

Lori scoffed. 'Aye, I thought I did. Seems one of them survived. And what if it's Logan? Don't tell me it's not impossible. It was over two decades ago, Steph. People's faces can change a lot. Hair colour, everything.'

Steph lit a cigarette and drew on it a lot longer than Lori thought possible. Exhaling loudly, her words carried on the plume of smoke as she said, 'We'd know. And a man like him, *them*, would never be able to control himself if he knew who we were. Not after what we did to survive. He'd take revenge on us as soon as he could, Lori. Nah. Not a chance.'

Lori tapped her index finger on the table, one, two, three times, took a deep breath. Steph's words had somehow eased her nerves. 'Okay, well, whoever Logan is to this situation, he's going to make sure he covers his own arse. Paying Jay a bonus to keep quiet means he's dangerous whether he knew of Ped and Jambo or not. They're young, impressionable lads, Steph. He will do whatever it takes to keep that body buried.'

'Yeah, *one* dead body. We left two down there,' Steph said. 'As much as I don't think Logan is one of them, where the hell is the other one?'

'Maybe the foxes and the rats got to him?'

Steph snorted. 'Aye, but not the pigs.'

Lori stared at her, confused.

'Only pigs clear up an entire body, Lori. They eat everything, including the bones.'

Nausea washed over Lori and she got to her feet. 'Jesus, Steph. That's grim.'

'Not as grim as not knowing who got up that night and walked out of that basement.'

An icy chill ran down Lori's spine. 'He could have gone anywhere, Steph. He could have woken up with amnesia, forgotten completely who and where he was. He could have woken up, tried to leave and died somewhere else.'

'That's wishful thinking,' Steph scoffed. 'Nah, something about this whole situation doesn't add up. Logan Greer...' Her words trailed off.

'What? Have you changed your mind? Now you're thinking he could be one of them?'

'Och, I don't know what I think. All I know is we need to keep Reece and Jay safe. I just don't know how to do that right now,' Steph said, sucking on the cigarette again.

It didn't matter to Lori that Steph didn't believe that Logan could be their missing body. It was still the closest thing Lori could get to an explanation. Again, just not why he'd wait so long to do anything about what had happened.

Kev entered Lori's mind then. He'd offered to take Lori and Jay to his new place, for them to live with him. If he knew how desperate they were, maybe he'd take Reece and Steph in too; until they could figure things out.

'Lori?'

'Yeah?'

'I'm scared.'

Lori reached over and took Steph's hand. 'I know. Me too.'

THIRTY-SIX

The café came into Sammi's line of sight as she walked through the shopping centre from Sylvania Way South. She passed the nail bar on her right and stopped, breathing in the scent of the chemicals which the artists wore masks to protect themselves from. Secretly, she loved that smell. It reminded her of when she first started to get her nails done, long before Logan was on the scene and long before he started buying nail bars to bulk out his business portfolio. He had to have as many legit businesses on the go in order to clean his dodgy money. Thankfully, the nail bar in the centre she was in right now wasn't one of his. Sammi might be young, but she was far from stupid. Dunreath Café was one of those businesses, and she was aiding Logan's lifestyle. She sickened herself at times, staying with a man like him.

Sammi stared in through the window of the nail bar and watched as each woman worked on the nails of a stranger. No words were exchanged between any of them. All in their own worlds; in their own heads, working out their own problems while the smell of the chemicals floated around them.

Everyone had their own shit going on, so much so that no one ever seemed to notice the next person. But Sammi did. She was a people-watcher. Always had been. Perhaps it stemmed from being on her own a lot of the time while she was growing up.

Turning her face away from the nail bar, and over to the café on the corner of the centre, she took a deep breath and headed towards it, where her dad would be waiting. Or maybe he'd changed his mind and she'd wait at an empty table for an hour before leaving.

Pushing the door, she stepped inside and, from the far corner, she saw a man get to his feet and raise a hand. It was strange, she'd only ever met this man once before, but she recognised him.

'Samantha?' he said, and she nodded before heading in his direction.

'Call me Sammi,' she said, and he nodded, a small smile raising the corners of his mouth.

Stood in front of her dad, Sammi felt every word she had stored in her brain fall away from her.

'Thank you for agreeing to meet me,' he said. 'Do you want a coffee? Tea?'

A wine or a vodka would be better, she thought to herself. Sammi nodded again, cleared her throat and said, 'I'll have a latte, please.'

Kev ordered and then they sat in silence for a few moments before Sammi decided she needed to start talking.

'So,' she began. 'How's things?'

He gave a tight-lipped smile and blinked. 'Yeah, things are good. Well, they're much better than they've ever been.'

Sammi raised a brow. 'Sorry, I feel really awkward.'

'I get it,' Kev replied. 'You've basically met a stranger for a coffee. That stranger just happens to be your dad. So, yeah. I understand if you don't have a lot to say.'

Nodding, she felt a little relief wash over her before the waitress appeared at their table, placing her latte in front of her. She mouthed a thank you before wishing the mug was big enough to swallow her.

'How are you?' Kev asked.

How was she? Well, she was in a hellish relationship with a lunatic gangster who happened to own most of the village where she grew up. She had no family or real friends to turn to and her only source of income was from the man she wanted to get away from.

'Yeah, I'm okay,' she replied, lifting her mug. Straightening her back, she smiled widely and continued. 'I'm really good, actually. Life is great. I'm engaged and I run my fiancé's café for him. I'm the manager, so the buck stops with me. I love it, though.'

Silence followed and the lie she'd told so easily sat heavily between them. She didn't want to be dishonest, but what else was she supposed to say? She didn't want to tell her dad that because he and her mum abandoned her that her life had gone to shit. Sammi wanted to prove to them that she had managed fine without them. But because the lie was so obvious to her, was it obvious to Kev too?

'That sounds brilliant. I'm so pleased for you. I really am.' Then he hesitated, as though trying to work out how to word what he was going to say next.

'Life couldn't be better,' she said again, the lie rolling off her tongue. If she said it enough, she might start to believe it herself.

Kev stared at her, his eyes soft and his expression sad. 'I'm sorry, Samantha.'

She held up a hand. 'I prefer Sammi.'

He swallowed and corrected himself. 'Sammi. I'm sorry I wasn't there for you.'

'No. You weren't. But it's fine. I survived on my own.'

Silence grew between them and Sammi glanced out of the window, across to the canal. She watched as the bus for Glasgow city centre headed down Kilbowie Road and, in that moment, she wished she was on it, travelling far away from Clydebank and Dunreath. Away from Logan, and Reece. Her present and past. She imagined herself getting to Central Station and stepping onto the London train. She could start a whole new life there. No one would know her. Logan wouldn't be able to find her in a city that huge, would he?

'Do you still have contact with her?' Kev asked.

Sammi pulled herself back from her daydream and frowned. 'Who? My mum? God, no. She's a narcissistic witch, I wouldn't piss on her if she was on fire.'

Kev pursed his lips. 'I don't remember much about her, if I'm honest. Was either in the jail, or when I was out, I was off my face or being a thieving little ratbag.'

'So, it was a one-night thing then?' Sammi asked.

'Not a one-night thing, no. We saw each other on and off briefly for that one period of time I was out. But it was never serious. Sorry, that must be hard to hear.'

In that moment, Sammi realised just how unscathed she'd come out of life with parents like the ones she had, or at least was related to. A narcissist for a mum, a druggie for a dad and brought up in the hellhole of Dunreath. If she didn't have Logan in her life, things would actually be quite good for her, she could be proud of keeping herself afloat without relying on anyone.

'No need to apologise. You're lucky not being able to remember much about her. I'm sure if things had been different with you, if you hadn't been an addict at the time, you'd have seen her for what she was quite quickly. I grew up with all sorts coming in and out of our flat. As soon as I was old enough, I got the fuck out of there.'

Kev glanced down at his mug, like he was unable to look her in the eye. 'I'm pretty ashamed of myself, Sammi,' he said. 'I'm glad you have such a good life. I wasn't expecting that, to be fair. I was expecting for you to have a go at me for being the reason things are bad. I'm glad I was wrong.'

Sammi swallowed down the hard lump in her throat. She couldn't cry and let on that she'd been lying about how great things were for her. If she did, her walls would come down and, at the moment, she was struggling to keep them up.

'I'd like to spend time getting to know you. I'd like to be some kind of a dad to you, if it's not too late?'

Something in her chest felt heavy. A sadness mixed with gratitude. Why couldn't he have been this person back then, when she was little? More to the point, why couldn't her mother have cared about and for her?

Nodding, Sammi bit back tears and said, 'I never, *ever* thought I'd say this. But I think I'd like to get to know you too.'

'Good. This is good. Better than I expected, if I'm honest. I thought you'd either not show up, or tell me to bugger off.'

Sammi laughed. 'The thought had crossed my mind. But I've had such a shit time of it over the years, I decided that passing up on the chance to meet you could be a mistake itself. I've made too many of those over the years.'

They both stared at each other and Kev frowned. 'I thought you said things were good?'

Sammi scolded herself. It seemed her walls had already come down and she'd let the lie slip away from her quicker than she'd hoped. 'Yeah, I'm good now. Life has its ups and downs, doesn't it? If it was all good, it wouldn't be real, eh?'

Kev shifted in his seat. 'I don't even want to go into how many of the downs were directly my fault.'

Sammi took in his features. He looked healthier than she expected. All those years on drugs would take their toll on anyone's appearance. She had questions for him, questions that had never crossed her mind until now. 'You're not the only person to cause me problems, trust me. Can I ask you something?'

'Ask away,' Kev said, interrupting her thoughts.

Puffing out her cheeks and releasing air slowly, Sammi looked into the eyes of the man who'd abandoned her to drugs and asked, 'What happened to you? Like, what happened to make you the addict you were?'

Nodding, Kev smiled. 'Wow, straight for the jugular.'

'Sorry,' Sammi lowered her eyes, 'I just need to know what happened to you so I can somehow begin to understand why you abandoned me.'

She watched as he sat back in his seat, his lips slightly parted as he considered how to answer her.

'I suppose it's that old cliché, *it was my upbringing that caused it*, things you probably don't want to hear. But in all honesty, I had drug addicts as parents. I didn't know there was a different way of life out there, waiting to be lived. When you're a kid, you believe everything you see and hear. And all I ever saw, all I ever heard was people taking drugs, fighting over drugs, stealing money to be able to buy drugs. I don't think I ever encountered a sober adult in the entire time I was a kid, unless I was at school, and that was rare.'

Sammi was about to ask why the teachers hadn't involved social work, then she remembered where they were both from. Dunreath and especially Blackhill Court weren't the types of places where people cared about each other. She wondered if it was worse now than it had been back in Kev's day.

'Do you have other family? Anyone you could have gone to for help?' Sammi asked, feeling genuinely interested.

Kev cleared his throat, shifted in his seat. 'I was the oldest sibling. Two younger sisters. Our parents kind of left us to it pretty much from the day we could look after ourselves, which was younger than you'd think. When they died, I ended up going off the rails even more than I had previously, and I abandoned my sisters.' He shook his head and she noticed the flicker of sadness in his eyes.

'Where are they now?'

Kev glanced up at her, as though he'd been far away in his own thoughts and had forgotten he was even sitting with her.

'My sisters?' He puffed out his cheeks. 'Well, my youngest, Charley, she was taken into foster care and I've not seen or spoken to her since. And Lori still lives in Blackhill Court.'

Sammi nodded. 'Seems no one ever gets out.'

'I did,' he replied. 'And trust me when I say this, if I can get out and get sober, anyone can.'

Sammi swallowed down the lump in her throat again. She'd gone through life with a mum who couldn't have given a damn and a dad who she never imagined ever having a relationship with. The word family had been so far removed from Sammi that she never thought she'd understand its meaning. Now she *knew* she had family out there. Two aunts, possibly cousins; and one of them was living in Blackhill Court in Dunreath. Right on her bloody doorstep.

'I've come up from nothing, Sammi. And look, I'm not saying it was easy, far from it, but getting sent to prison that last time was actually one of the best things that could have ever happened to me. Christ knows where I'd have ended up if I hadn't been banged up; dead most likely. And look, I got to meet you. Properly, I mean. Not like before, when I passed you in the street when you were wee and your mum didn't even recognise me. Not when you were older and I'd see you walk past the Dunreath Arms and you didn't know who I was. Jesus, how awful is that? To have your daughter pass you in the street and not know who you are.'

Sammi cleared her throat and straightened her back. 'Well, we did have chats on the phone once a year, and we met once. So there's that.' She smiled, attempting humour and failing terribly. 'Look, I'd like to meet my family. What's the point in having a great life if I don't have any family to share it with?'

Kev nodded and gave a smile. He hadn't picked up on her lie. Yet. 'I think she'd like that. You'll get to meet your cousin too. Jay's the same age as you, I think.'

Sammi blinked, then blinked again. 'Hang on. You're not talking about Jay Graham, are you?'

'You know him?'

Sammi bit her tongue and nodded. 'I'm engaged to his boss.'

THIRTY-SEVEN

Logan stood in the centre of the bandstand. He was facing the café and watched the back of his fiancée's head as she spoke to the man across the table. Who was this guy? And why was she meeting him outside Dunreath? Was she having an affair with this guy? If she was, she'd pay for it.

Logan's phone pinged in his pocket, pulling his attention away from the café.

Taking it out, he noticed it was a private message on Instagram. He didn't have an Instagram account of his own. Social media wasn't something that had ever interested him and it wouldn't be good for someone like him to have.

> Hi. How are you today?

As his eyes scanned over the message which had been sent to Sammi's inbox, Logan felt a fire begin to burn in his belly, in his chest. The brazen little bastard was openly trying to crack on with Logan's fiancée even when she'd warned him that it would be the end of him if he continued. When Sammi had blocked Reece from sending her more messages, Logan had decided to unblock him, just to see if he would continue to reach out to her. And he had.

Logan had to give it to Sammi, she'd been straight with Reece. But just how long would it be before his words started to have an effect on her? Before she started to listen to Reece? There was another problem, though. Messages had been deleted.

Logan decided to leave the message as unread before tucking his phone away. It wouldn't take much more to push him over the edge, and with Reece now aware of what was in tower three... well, it was the perfect excuse to show him he shouldn't fuck with Logan.

Sammi got to her feet and Logan kept his eye on her. He knew her every move, her every conversation. Keeping her close, knowing what she was doing, where she was going and who she was seeing was something that just had to be done. Soon, she'd be his wife, and he couldn't allow that without knowing every inch of her movements when he wasn't around. It was hard enough having a wife and a fiancée on the side. How much harder would it be to have two wives?

Speaking of wife number one, he realised he hadn't checked in with her for a while. Best keep her sweet. What was that saying? Happy wife, happy life?

He pulled his phone out again, continuing to keep an eye on Sammi, while he pulled up his wife's number and hit call.

'Logan?' she said sweetly as she answered. 'How are you?'

'Ah, all the better for hearing your voice,' he replied. 'How are the kids?'

'They're great. Callan is currently watching *Bluey* and Thomas is in a milk coma.'

Logan smiled and his heart felt full. 'Glad to hear it, gorgeous.'

'Logan, when are you able to come home? The kids need to see you. I need to see you. We miss you. Surely the place won't fall down without you?'

He closed his eyes briefly and, when he opened them again, Sammi and a man were walking out of the café and heading up the shopping centre.

'I promise you, love, as soon as the job is done, I'll be back with you and the kids and I'll be taking it easy.'

He heard a smile in her voice. 'Hopefully soon then. We love you, Logan.'

His smile spread widely across his face. 'I love you too, babe.'

Logan watched through narrowed eyes as Sammi wandered up the centre. He had it all. A stunning wife, two beautiful kids and a twenty-year-old girl at his beck and call. There had never been a time when Logan had lost control of his life. Never. And he wasn't about to allow that to happen now. No woman had ever got the better of him. And if Sammi thought she was a step ahead of him, she was gravely mistaken. First Reece, and now this guy? Logan would rather see Sammi dead than allow her to get away with being unfaithful.

THIRTY-EIGHT

Sammi walked alongside her dad as they headed to the top of the shopping centre. She never ventured out of Dunreath much, so she wanted to make the most of it. As much as Clydebank wasn't that far away from Dunreath, she felt a million miles removed from the place and that made her feel settled.

'I'm just going to head to the bathroom, I'll be back in a minute,' Kev said as they stopped outside the bathrooms in the centre.

Sammi nodded and noticed the bookshop across the way. 'I'll meet you in there.'

'Are you a reader?' Kev asked.

She shook her head. 'Never. But today's about new beginnings; new things. So, might as well take a look around, eh?'

Sammi headed into the bookshop and, just as she began perusing the section labelled *Crime*, she felt a gentle tap on her shoulder. As she turned, her stomach fluttered with fear.

'A bookshop?' Logan asked, flashing his bright white teeth at her, reminding her of the bite he'd given her outside the café. 'You?'

'Yeah,' she replied coolly; all the while inside she was screaming. 'It's not really *your* thing, is it – reading, I mean? What are you doing here, Logan? Did you follow me or something?'

He narrowed his eyes and raised a brow. 'Who's the guy?'

Sammi swallowed. She had nothing to hide, so why was she so nervous about telling Logan who Kev was?

'You lost your tongue?' he pressed, before lowering his voice. 'You will if you don't tell me who he is.'

She believed every word he said.

'Not that it's any of your business, but he's my dad.'

Logan's eyes widened and then he looked out towards the bathrooms. 'Your *dad*? As in the one who's in and out of prison constantly?'

Sammi turned her eyes back to the bookshelf and began aimlessly scanning the spines, trying to distract herself from the feeling of nausea in the centre of her throat. 'Correct,' she replied.

'So, what? You just happened to bump into each other here in the shopping centre?'

'No, we arranged to meet up. He messaged me last night and I agreed to meet him.'

Logan ran a finger across the books lying on the table in the *Crime* section and began walking slowly around it. She watched him, trying to contain her frustration and anxiety. Now more than ever she knew that she was going to leave him. If the bite hadn't spurred her on, the threat of more violence if she didn't conform to his expectations definitely did. She couldn't live her life in fear any more. It was exhausting if nothing else. But then, he could kill her if she tried to leave him. It was an impossible situation to be in.

'Right. Well, aren't you going to introduce him to your fiancé?' Logan asked with a smile, picking up a book and pretending to read the back of it.

Sammi's stomach rolled, this time with such ferocity that she had to suppress the urge to gag. Swallowing down the threatening bile, she licked her lips and said, 'He's only just met me properly for the first time. I think that's enough for one day. Maybe the next time?'

The words left her mouth so sweetly that she hoped his softer side would respond. Not that his softer side often came out, but she could only hope.

He twirled the book around in his hands for a few seconds and she noticed the title. *All Liars Die*. He traced the title with his finger, glanced at her, then placed the book back on the table.

'Okay,' he shrugged. 'I can see why you'd want to wait. I'll catch up with you later.'

Stunned by his response, but not fooled into thinking it was genuine, Sammi forced a smile and replied, 'Thanks. I really appreciate it.'

He leaned in, and she flinched, bracing herself for another bite. Instead, he kissed her on the cheek and then simply walked out of the shop. She watched him go and wondered what the hell had just happened. They'd been so unnatural with each other. Gentle with their words was not how Sammi's relationship with Logan ever went down. She knew exactly what was going to happen. There would be a blowout later and she'd have to prepare herself for it. Unless she didn't go back home.

Steadying herself, Sammi glanced up at the bookshelf and hoped there would be a guide to how to commit murder of your fiancé. Of course, there was no such book. Only fictional titles, all of which didn't speak to her, so she headed out of the shop. Just as she did, Kev was walking towards her with a reserved look on his face.

'You all right? You've gone really pale,' he said.

Nodding, Sammi smiled back at him and said, 'I need to get the bus home.'

'Something I've said?'

'No. Not at all. I just really need to get home. Lots to do. Running a business takes up a lot of time. But we should do this again?'

'You said you wanted to meet your aunty? Why don't I get the bus back with you and we can do it now?'

It was all too much. She couldn't do it right now. And what if Logan was watching? What if he did something to embarrass her? Or worse?

'Another time,' she said, glancing down at her phone. 'My bus won't be long. I'll see you later.'

She began moving towards the bus terminus and all she could think about was the look in Logan's eye when she'd declined his request to meet Kev. He was livid that she'd said no to him.

No one *ever* said no to Logan.

THIRTY-NINE

Sammi sat at the back of the bus and buried her face in her phone. She'd just met her dad and found out she had extended family. She couldn't believe that Jay Graham was her cousin. Her ex's best mate. Both employed by her fiancé. How small the world was, for this to have come about. She'd been living in Dunreath her whole life, had probably passed her blood relatives on many an occasion and was completely oblivious.

She began tapping out a message to Kev.

> Sorry for rushing off like that. I think everything got a bit too much for me. I'd love to meet your sister. Whenever suits. Sammi.

Once she hit send, she opened up her Instagram app and noticed a new message from Reece Lyle. She stared at it a second longer. Hadn't she blocked him from contacting her? Maybe she hadn't done it right. Shaking her head, she left it unread and started scrolling through the stories at the top of the screen. Stacey Solomon, Mrs Hinch, Yungblud had all posted stories. None of them was enough to distract her from Reece's message sitting in her inbox. Why was he *so* insistent? What was he trying to do to them: get them both killed? And Sammi hadn't done anything wrong, she hadn't replied inappropriately. She'd warned him off.

Realising the bus was approaching her stop, Sammi pressed the bell and got to her feet. She got off once the driver had pulled in and stepped onto the pavement. Dunreath Main Street had to be one of the most depressing places in the world. The flats that lined the front street had large parts of rendering missing, some of the windows were boarded up. The secure entry to all three buildings was broken and the doors jammed open. The smell of weed, alcohol and stale urine coming from inside the closes was unbearable to the point where she had to hold her breath as she walked past.

She dreamed of a different life, away from the village. Away from Logan. No longer worried about random messages coming through in case he kicked off. And she would have that one day. Hopefully soon. She was going to leave him. She was. And she wasn't going to allow him to make her stay out of fear, because staying would only cause her more fear, more danger.

'Sammi?'

The voice jolted her from her pleasant daydream and the view of the street surrounding her brought back the feeling of dread. Turning, she saw her dad stood outside the bookies. Frowning, she crossed the road and headed in his direction.

'How the hell did you get here so quick?' she asked with a smile.

'Taxi,' he replied. 'Although, I'm taking driving lessons at the minute, so hopefully I'll be able to chauffeur you around soon enough.'

That would be the dream, Sammi thought. To be able to have enough money to take lessons, pass her test, buy a car and drive it as far away from Dunreath as possible. It was that very thought, about leaving Dunreath in a car, that made her realise she was done. It was time to go; to get away from Logan and this life.

'Sammi? Are you okay?'

'Sorry, was miles away,' she replied. 'I'm just about to head home. But I meant what I said in my message.'

Kev nodded. 'Great. I'll get in touch once I've spoken to Lori. I mean, you've already met your cousin, I'm assuming? Since you knew who he was?'

Sniffing loudly, she nodded. 'Yeah, I've met him. Strange I didn't know he was a relation. I think he went to my school too. Not that I was ever there much; I'm sure he wasn't either. It's probably why he's ended up working for someone like Logan.' That last sentence was said with a sneer and Kev looked shocked. Realising that she'd spoken ill of him and that she'd shown that her life wasn't quite as perfect as she'd made out, Sammi switched her frown to a smile and said, 'Anyway, better get back. Speak soon.'

She headed further into the village, before turning up Glenloch Road towards Logan's flat. As it came into view, she noticed his car wasn't parked outside. She'd made it back before him and the relief was overwhelming. Then it occurred to her, how stupid she was being. She hated Logan. Truly *hated* him. He wasn't the man she'd fallen for a couple of years ago. Now that she had her dad back in her life, could she go right now? Pack a bag and ask to stay with him until she could support herself? Surely after everything, Kev was likely to take her in if he knew she really needed the help? He'd said he wanted to be as much of a dad to her as he could, and she believed him.

She opened the front door and headed inside. Considering Logan's flat was in Dunreath, the place was immaculate. Every wall was crisp white, and the black and grey abstract art piece hanging in the hallway looked expensive. She'd always wondered how much it had cost but had never asked. She wandered through to the living room, taking everything in for the last time. Black leather reclining sofas with USB ports and speakers on the headrests sat on either side of the living room. A white marble coffee table sat in the centre of the room on top of a black shagpile rug. The carpets were brand new and Sammi was never allowed to walk on them without taking her shoes off. Wandering through to the kitchen, the sun shone onto the marble worktops and there was not a thing out of place. The one good thing about Logan was he was tidy, a little too tidy. He liked things a certain way: clean, tidy. Perfect.

It had always struck her as odd that he had purchased a property in Dunreath and not the West End of Glasgow, because he certainly had the money for it. And he'd made the place look like something that had been plucked from Kelvinside, not Dunreath Village.

She needed a bag to pack her things. Not too much, just some essentials and enough clothes for a week. The less she took, the longer it would take for him to notice.

Pulling her phone back out, she selected her dad's number and called him.

'Hi,' Kev said, sounding surprised that he was hearing from her so soon after they'd just parted ways.

'Hi, look, I know this might sound odd, but everything I told you isn't strictly true. My life isn't as perfect as I made it out to be. I'm not as happy as I said, and my fiancé, well, he's dangerous. Could I come and stay with you for a while?'

A moment of silence hung in the air and Sammi had to glance at the screen to check if he'd hung up on her.

'Aww, Sammi. I'm sorry you felt like you had to lie. Has something happened?' Kev asked, concern etched in his tone.

'A million different things that I don't have time to get into right now. But I'm leaving my fiancé. He's not good for me and I just need to get out.'

Another moment of silence. *Shit*, she thought. *He's going to say no.* Of course he was. They were practically strangers.

'Of course you can. But do you feel comfortable staying with me? I mean, we've only just met.'

'You said you had a lot of making up to do and I said I wanted us to build a relationship. I know it's not ideal, but this could be the making of us, couldn't it?'

In any other world, under any other set of circumstances, Sammi wouldn't have to ask Kev for help. But given how dangerous Logan was, *who* Logan was and what he stood for, she had no choice but to take the opportunity in front of her.

'I won't stay long,' she added, in the hope that it would make the request sound more appealing.

'I already said it's fine, Sammi. And you can stay as long as you like. Would you like me to come and help pack your things? Do you need to get out quickly?'

Sammi pulled the holdall out from under the bed in the pristine bedroom, decorated much the same as the rest of the house, and began pulling clothes out from the chest of drawers. 'I'll take five minutes. I'm not bringing much.'

'Okay,' Kev replied. 'I was going to head to Lori's, but if you'd prefer, we can head back to mine now?'

She was nodding, even though she knew he couldn't see the gesture. 'Do you live far?'

'I live in Lambhill. Far enough away for you?' Kev asked as if he'd heard her thoughts.

When she'd gone to Clydebank to meet Kev earlier in the day, she thought it was far enough away that she wouldn't risk Logan seeing her. She'd been wrong. Lambhill was almost ten miles away. It was better than Clydebank.

'More than enough,' she replied, her heart surging in her chest. Now she had to get out quickly before Logan came back.

'I'll just wait here for you then? Outside the bookies?'

Sammi had an involuntary intake of breath as she hung up the phone. Dashing through to the bathroom, the marble matching that of the kitchen, she gathered up her toothbrush, shampoo, conditioner and shower gel, before running back through to the room and throwing them in the bag, not bothering to check if all the lids were secure. Hairdryer, straighteners, brush, jammies and underwear went in quickly after, followed by seven days' worth of clothes. She'd leave everything else behind so Logan wouldn't notice too much was gone, if at all, she hoped.

As she moved towards the front door, she listened for footsteps on the communal stairway. If Logan appeared now, it would be easier to lie. If he found her halfway down Glenloch Road, how would she explain the holdall?

The silence seemed to shatter with a buzzing sound coming from the second bedroom. Turning, Sammi frowned. The buzzing continued, on and on. Whatever it was persisted and Sammi's curiosity got the better of her. Keeping the holdall firm in her grip, she made her way through to the second bedroom: a room she barely ventured into. It was like a half-office, half-gym. A treadmill, a rowing machine and weights sat in one corner, a desk with a computer on it in the other. Again, not a thing was out of place.

As she stepped inside, the buzzing got louder and it was coming from one of the drawers in the desk. Her frown deepened as she pulled the top drawer open and discovered an iPad. The name *Babe* was video-calling him.

Should she answer it?

Just as she was about to hit the green icon, the buzzing stopped. Sammi stood there, foreign iPad in her hand, while a feeling of dread washed over her. Who was Babe?

Buzzbuzzbuzz.

She almost dropped the tablet once it started to vibrate again. The same name flashed up on the eleven-inch screen and Sammi's stomach flipped as her finger swiped the green icon across the glass.

'Hello?' Sammi said awkwardly as she saw the face of a blonde woman fill the screen.

The woman, evidently nicknamed Babe, gave a look of contempt before saying, 'Who the hell are you?'

So taken aback by the question, Sammi's words initially failed her. Then she remembered who she was. Not some stupid little girl, that was for sure. 'I could ask you the same question,' she replied.

The woman frowned and Sammi heard children in the background. 'Why are you answering my husband's iPad?'

Husband? *Husband?*

Sammi blinked in quick succession and shook her head. 'I'm sorry, are you sure you are calling the right person?'

'I think I would know my own husband. So tell me, why are you answering his iPad? Where is Logan?'

Everything seemed to stop then. Time. The flow of air into her lungs.

'I... I don't know. I think he's at work,' Sammi faltered. 'Sorry, did you say *husband*?'

'Yes. And you still haven't told me who the hell you are,' the woman replied, her volume increasing. Her brow creased and her eyes narrowed, although they were glazed with concern. This woman, seemingly Logan's wife, appeared worried. 'Well?'

Sammi stared at the face of the woman on the other side of the call. Was this happening? Was Logan really married? And if so, for how long? No, this couldn't be right. Surely not. Of course, she knew Logan had his fingers in many different pies, legal and illegal. But married?

'I'm...' Sammi composed herself, swallowing down the anger and the fear of what may follow from what she was about to say. 'I'm Sammi; Logan's fiancée.'

The woman's expression froze. Then she let out an incredulous laugh before she replied with, '*Excuse* me? No.' She shook her head. 'No. You're confused. Are you the cleaner or something? Has he asked you to do this for a wind-up? He's got a terrible sense of humour.'

In that moment, Sammi almost felt sorry for this woman. Now, after planning to leave Logan anyway, Sammi would get over this quickly. But this woman was Logan's wife of Christ knows how long. And by the sound of childish laughter in the background, he'd been living a double life long before Sammi came along. A thought entered her mind then. How many more Sammis were there? How many more Babes?

'I'm not confused and, no, I'm not the cleaner. I've been engaged to him for two years; got engaged pretty much as soon as we got together. This is going to sound like absolute bullshit, but I can assure you it's not. I've literally just packed my bags and was on my way out the door, about to leave him, when you called. I genuinely had no idea you existed until I answered.'

The woman's face burned and her eyes became glassy. 'You were on your way out the door? Right now?'

Sammi balanced the iPad on the drawers, leaning it against the wall, stood back and held up her holdall. 'Honestly, I was. And I'm not hanging about, he'll be back any minute. I don't want to be here when he arrives. Sorry, I don't know what else to say.'

The woman's lower lip began to tremble. 'What's your name again?'

'Sammi,' she replied. 'I swear, I didn't even know this iPad existed, never mind that he had a wife.'

Sammi glanced at the name at the top of the screen. Babe wouldn't be her real name. Obviously.

'Look, I'm going to hang up now. Good luck with, well, everything.'

Sammi ended the call, placed the iPad back in the drawer and left the flat. She practically ran down the street, hoping that Logan wouldn't pass her on the way. And even if he did, now that she knew what she did, she would be up for the fight – provided the streets weren't empty of people.

Her entire body began to shake from the adrenaline of what had just happened. She was leaving him for various reasons, but never in a million years did she ever think that he was fucking married.

Kev came into view as she rounded the corner onto the main street and she continued to run towards him. It was obvious he could see that something had happened as his expression changed from a smile to concern almost immediately.

'What's wrong?'

Puffing out her cheeks, she shrugged. 'Oh, you know, just found out I'm engaged to a bastard who's already married.'

Kev's eyes widened. 'Are you *serious*?'

'Deadly. Can we go?' Sammi asked, glancing around. 'I don't want to risk him seeing me.'

'Yeah, of course. There's a bus due in two minutes.'

Kev took the holdall from Sammi's hand and stood to the side as the bus came down the hill. She climbed onto the bus, nodded to the driver and headed straight up the stairs of the double-decker. She'd get a good view of Dunreath, and be able to see if Logan passed as she walked out of his life for good.

Her dad sat beside her, the holdall between them. 'Are you all right?'

This was it. She was free.

'Honestly? I've never felt better.'

FORTY

As he slid his key into the door, he noticed that the door itself wasn't locked. Closed, but not locked. He pulled the key out and pushed the door open to its widest, before peering into the hallway. He stood there, stock-still, waiting for some little thieving bastard to run out from behind a bedroom door, knowing they were caught. But nothing happened. The place was silent. It smelled the same. The only difference was, Sammi wasn't home, even though he'd watched her get on the bus to head back to Dunreath after meeting her dad.

Sighing in annoyance, he went into the bathroom, and that's when he saw it. The edge of the bath was empty. Sammi's toiletries were gone. Turning to the sink, he saw that her toothbrush was gone too.

'Sammi?' he called out, already beginning to feel angry. She'd left him and she must have just gone because it wasn't so long ago he'd been with her in Clydebank shopping centre. Or perhaps she'd packed up her things before going to meet her dad? Thinking back, he couldn't recall seeing her with a backpack. He'd have noticed. 'Sammi?' he called again, this time his voice more like a growl, even though he knew she wasn't in the flat. When she didn't answer, Logan stepped out of the bathroom and searched through each room briefly, checking to see what else she'd taken. Cheeky bitch could have lifted anything she thought might be worth a bit as she knew she'd amount to nothing without him.

Satisfied that none of his belongings were gone, Logan pulled his phone out of his pocket and selected Sammi's number. Just as he was about to hit call, his phone rang. It was his wife.

Now's not the fucking time, he thought before answering. 'Hey, babe, what's up?'

'You!' she screamed. 'You're what's *up*!'

Holding the phone away from his ear to avoid the shrillness of her voice, he replied with, 'Wow, what is going on? What am I supposed to have done?'

She sobbed on the other end of the line and he listened carefully. 'Is it true?' she cried, and Logan's brow furrowed. This wasn't just a coincidence. Sammi was gone and his wife was screaming at him down the phone.

'Is what true?' he replied, trying to seem calm and controlled but concerned at the same time.

She fell silent, as though trying to compose herself. Logan listened as she took a few deep breaths and said, 'I spoke to your *fiancée* today. Seems as though she's had a lucky escape.'

Logan gripped the phone so tightly in his hand that his knuckles strained. Of course this was the reason Sammi had left. She wouldn't have dared otherwise.

'I have absolutely no idea what you're on about, babe.'

'Oh, don't give me that, Logan. *Sammi?* The girl said she was your fiancée, had absolutely no idea that me or the kids existed. I mean, who even are you, Logan? How long have you been lying to me?'

Gritting his teeth, Logan tried to compose himself. This was the last thing he ever thought would happen. He'd managed to separate both his lives so delicately up until now. They lived almost ninety miles apart, and no one in Dunreath knew Logan was married. No one in Dunreath really knew Logan at all.

'I tried to video-call you earlier, the kids wanted to say hello to their daddy face to face. Your fiancée answered your *fucking* iPad.'

Closing his eyes against the reality of what was going on, Logan wanted to crush the phone in his hand. 'Can we discuss this in person?' he asked calmly.

'Are you *kidding*? You think I want to be anywhere near you after this? You've been engaged to this girl for two *years*. And by the way, what age is she? Because from what I could tell, she looked about eighteen years old. Is that what you're into? Cradle snatching?'

Logan opened his mouth to reply, but she continued.

'Don't bother coming back here to try to reason with me, or wriggle your way out of this, Logan. We're done. I'm taking the boys and you will *never* see us again, do you understand me?'

Logan bit down on his tongue so hard he could taste blood. 'Babe, you can't take those boys away from me. I'm their dad.'

'Should have thought about that when you started planning a second life with this Sammi girl. Looks like you've messed up on both ends of your relationships because when I spoke to her, she was already on her way out the door with her bags packed. Jesus, Logan, two break-ups in one day? You're doing *really* well for yourself.'

The line went dead and Logan took the deepest breath he could manage, before launching his phone at the bedroom wall.

As the phone lay in pieces on the floor in front of him, Logan tried to work out what he was going to do next.

He couldn't go to Galashiels to fix his marriage. Firstly, she said she wouldn't be there anyway, and if Margaret and Ronnie knew about this, they'd never tell him where she was. There was no point. If he was honest with himself, he wasn't sure he had the energy to deal with his marriage. His wife had served her purpose, to a degree. Now that he was setting things up in Dunreath, that was what he needed to focus on. He had a job to complete here. A demolition that needed to be done with precision.

A sudden sense of calm washed over him as he bent down to retrieve the shattered mobile phone at his feet. He'd buy a new one and transfer everything over. It wouldn't be a problem and it wasn't like money was an issue. He had plenty of it.

No matter what happened with his wife from now on, Logan promised himself he'd finish what he started. Dunreath was the place to be able to do that. Blackhill Court was the heart of it all. When he was done, he'd take his boys and they'd never see their mother ever again.

FORTY-ONE

Lori stood in front of the mirror like she did every single day since escaping the tower with Steph. She glanced down at the branding on the outside of both her breasts and both inner thighs too. Four saltire symbols forever scarred her skin. A memory that something horrendous had happened to her, even though she couldn't remember when they'd been put there. In some ways, she was thankful for that. In others, she wished she could recall because it might help her get over it better. The mental pain of the aftermath, however, was very much still there. That was something she'd never forget, even though she wanted to. And now with the knowledge that the remains of only one of them was in that basement, she was more unsettled than ever before.

Pulling her clothes on, Lori moved out to the hallway to find Jay stood in his security uniform.

'You just in?' she asked, sick at the thought that he was still working for Logan Greer. After discovering those remains, Jay should have run for the hills. Now they were having to walk on eggshells in case Logan Greer did anything to hurt either Jay or Reece.

'Aye,' he replied quietly. 'Did some overtime.'

Lori shook her head. 'Why?'

'Well, if you hadn't noticed, Mum, we're not exactly rolling in it, and I've already betrayed my boss once. I'm trying to keep on his good side. I want that money he promised me, although I doubt that will happen now; I need to prove myself now more than ever and I need to know what he's thinking when it comes to Reece.'

Raising a brow, Lori tried not to allow her everyday anxiety to get the better of her. 'Has he said anything to you about Reece?'

Jay shook his head. 'He tried to get Reece to come back to the site so they could discuss it. But Reece stayed clear. I mean, Logan didn't say he was going to do anything, but that wasn't the impression I got.'

Lori's stomach lurched. 'I can't even imagine; I don't want to. The guy has a reputation; we know that. Maybe you need to get out of there, Jay.'

'I can't, Mum. I need to keep him on side. If I leave now, I think it will make things so much worse. I'll stick with it for now, hopefully I can keep Reece out of trouble. But he doesn't do himself any favours.'

Lori frowned. 'What do you mean?'

'The Sammi thing? She's Reece's ex and, yeah, I get that he couldn't have predicted the future. But still, texting her is like saying you want to commit suicide.'

Lori's jaw dropped open. 'What the hell is he playing at?'

'He's an idiot. Said he's not into her like that any more. I don't believe a word of it and, if Logan finds out, he won't either. Sammi told Reece herself to stay away from her for his own good.'

Sighing loudly, Lori wondered how much worse things could get.

'And he hasn't said anything to you about her or Reece in the last few days?'

'Nah. She hasn't been at the café for the last two days. She's disappeared, by what I can gather. I'm hoping there's nothing in it, but Logan seems a bit preoccupied. Hopefully he's not done something to her.'

'Maybe she left him?' Lori said.

'Hmm,' Jay replied sceptically.

Lori could only hope that was the case. Not just for Reece's sake, but for Sammi's too.

'Look, a change of subject here. Mind I told you my brother came over the other night? Well, I wondered if you fancied meeting him? He's got his own place and he's doing really well since his last stint in prison.'

Jay shrugged. 'Aye, fine by me. When?'

'Well, I'm going to meet him and his daughter today, actually. Just for a few hours, but it gets us out of this shithole for a while.'

Jay yawned. 'Give me a couple hours to get a kip and then I'm all yours.'

She smiled and watched as he headed into his bedroom and closed the door. A little escape from the chaos of what their lives were like right now would be blissful. It was unfortunate they'd have to come back to Dunreath and face it all again.

FORTY-TWO

Sammi sat by the window and stared out onto the main road. Not that there was much to look at. Lambhill, or at least the part where Kev stayed, seemed to be mostly residential. The odd shop here and there from what she'd seen. And a pub. Compared to Dunreath it was relatively quiet. Sammi liked that. She'd never known peace like it.

'Cuppa?' Kev asked, walking into the living room.

'I'm okay, thanks,' Sammi replied with a smile. 'You know what?'

Kev looked on expectantly.

'I've been more relaxed here in the last two days than my entire life living in Dunreath. Especially the last two years with *him*.'

Kev didn't say anything. He simply sat down on the sofa and leaned back, like he was ready to listen to her.

'Do you find it peaceful here?' she asked.

'I've been peaceful since I got sober. I mean, every day is a battle not to use, or to drink. But when I think about the road I was on, the life I *wasn't* living and the death sentence handed to me by that consultant, I'd take an internal battle over that any day of the week. Having your own space, your own peace of mind, beats being stuck in a spiral of anxiety because something or someone brings it to your life.'

Sammi nodded. She completely understood what he was talking about. She'd never truly understood just how unhappy she was living a life with Logan until she left him two days ago. When she discovered he'd been living a secret life and she was the other woman, it had been the thing to solidify her decision and to know she was doing the right thing in leaving, even though she'd already packed a bag.

'What time is Lori coming at?'

'Should be any minute now,' Kev replied, glancing down at his watch.

Just then, there was a chap at the door and Kev stood up quickly. She could tell he was nervous.

As he made his way out to answer the door, Sammi turned her attention back to the window and looked out onto the street. An elderly man walked past with a newspaper tucked under his arm. He was holding a dog lead, with a tiny dog on the end of it.

'Hey.' She heard a voice as Kev opened the door.

'Hi, come in,' Kev said.

'This is Jay, your nephew.'

Sammi got to her feet and suddenly felt nervous herself. She had only just met her dad two days ago. Now she was staying with him in his flat and about to meet blood relatives for the first time. Even though she knew who Jay was, it felt different being introduced as his cousin.

'Sammi is through in the living room,' Kev said.

Sammi glanced down at herself, wondering if she looked smart enough. Not that anyone would care what she was wearing in this kind of situation.

Silence, followed by footsteps as everyone entered the living room where Sammi was stood, feeling like a prize cow.

Kev entered first, followed by Lori and then Jay.

'This is my daughter, Sammi.'

'You?' Jay blurted out.

Sammi narrowed her eyes and reminded herself that she'd had two days to process the news that she was related to him. This was a shock, brand new in the moment for Jay.

'Yes, me,' Sammi replied, before opening up her arms and saying, 'Surprise,' then immediately regretting it. She wasn't a prize at the circus, for fuck sake.

She turned her attention to Lori, whose eyes were wide and mouth slightly agape.

'You're that girl from the café,' she said. 'You're engaged to that Logan Greer character.'

Sammi glanced down at the floor and cleared her throat. 'Not any more. I left him two days ago when I found out he's married with kids.'

Kev glanced between the two and Sammi shrugged.

'I served Lori and her friend the other day in the café. They saw Logan being a prick to me and pretty much stopped it.'

Lori shook her head. 'I'm sorry if we made things worse.'

'You didn't,' Sammi replied with a smile. 'I'm sorry if I was rude to you. I was just nervous because he was doing it in public. I didn't want things to escalate, you know. He's very calculated, though; he never gets too angry in front of people. Saves that for me behind closed doors.' *Or outside the café itself*, she thought, recalling how he'd bit her hard on the lip.

'Sammi is staying with me for a while, until she can get herself sorted after leaving him. Which I'm so glad you did,' Kev said, before he manoeuvred around Lori and gestured for her and Jay to have a seat on the sofa. He'd laid out glasses and a jug of water on the coffee table in the centre of the room and began filling them without asking if anyone wanted any.

'You weren't rude. We got what you were doing,' Lori said. 'From what I saw the other day, you're well shot of him.'

Sammi nodded. 'Yeah, definitely agree with you on that one.'

Lori gave a warm smile and said, 'And now that I know you're my niece, I'm happier knowing you're away from him.'

Jay reached over for a glass of water as Kev sat down next to him. 'So, you're the long-lost uncle?'

Kev nodded. 'I am that. And there's a long-lost aunty out there somewhere too.'

'Yeah, I heard she got taken into foster care years ago.'

'Best thing that could have happened to her,' Kev said. 'But maybe one day we'll all get to reunite.'

The four of them chatted; very briefly, about life. What they'd done over the years, which wasn't much. Where they'd been, which was nowhere, and what their future plans were, which wasn't a lot except for Sammi's dad. He wanted to, one day, own his own restaurant or go into private catering, working for himself. It was the first time she'd ever heard anyone from Dunreath express any form of aspirations. If her dad, a recovering drug and alcohol abuser, could do it, then maybe she could too?

'I didn't know he had a wife,' Jay said. 'Never talks about her. I suppose he wouldn't, given he was engaged to you. So, how'd you find out he's married?'

'Jay!' Lori said, giving him a backhanded slap on the arm.

'No, it's okay,' Sammi replied. 'I've nothing to hide. I'm not the one who lied the entire way through our relationship.'

Lori pulled her lips into a thin line, giving that sympathetic half-smile that people did when they didn't know what to say.

'So, what did happen?' Kev asked.

'Long story short, I was packing my bags to leave and his wife video-called him on an iPad. I didn't even know he had an iPad, let alone a fucking wife. Anyway, when I saw her name come up on the screen, I just decided to answer it.'

The three of them looked on as though they were listening to some shit podcast and it made Sammi laugh.

'And that was kind of it. She asked who I was, I told her, she went off her nut, I apologised, hung up and left.'

Kev gave an inward whistle and sat back on the sofa. 'Well, like Lori said, you're well shot.'

Jay was staring at her in silence, like he was trying to work something out.

'What?'

'Why did you and Reece keep your relationship a secret?'

Lori nudged him and gave him an icy stare.

Sammi sighed. 'He told you then?'

Jay raised his hands in mock defeat. 'I'm not judging you, by the way. I just think this could escalate his suspicions with

Reece even more. You know, he said you guys were flirting, then you leave. Logan might blame Reece for that.'

'He's got more to worry about now with his wife knowing his secret than Reece flirting with the fiancée he should never have been with in the first place,' Sammi retorted.

Lori shook her head and took a sip of water. 'It's a wonder he's not on one of those Are We Dating The Same Guy pages on Facebook.'

Sammi hadn't heard of that kind of thing. 'Jesus, I'll bet there are some red flags on there.'

Lori smiled but said nothing and it planted a seed in Sammi's head. What if Logan was on there? What if Sammi wasn't the only one he'd lied to? What if he was on the lookout for someone far easier to control than her?

'You still working for him?' Sammi directed the question at Jay.

'Aye. Site supervisor now.' He said it like he was proud but she could tell it was a front.

'And Reece? He still there?'

'Nah. Wasn't for him,' Jay replied bluntly. 'The job, I mean.'

'He left? When?'

'Few days ago.'

Sammi was quiet. Had he left because of her? Had he left because he had been messaging her? Was Jay right? Had Logan threatened him because she'd left?

'Anyway, can we stop talking about him? He's no longer in my life and was truly never mine to begin with. I think Lori's right: I've had a lucky escape. It's the wife I feel sorry for.'

Kev quickly changed the subject, began talking about cheffing, all things food and the hospitality industry. He spoke passionately about it, and she hoped that, one day, she could get to a place in her life where she had a purpose.

FORTY-THREE

Lori smiled as she watched her brother chat with his long-lost daughter. Not so lost, having been living in Dunreath her entire life. In normal circumstances, Sammi might be angry about the whole thing, but she didn't seem in the least bit annoyed. Maybe she was just grateful that Kev was in her life now, helping her to get her life together and stay away from Logan. If only Jay could do the same.

Lori noticed that most of the water Kev had poured earlier was gone, so she leaned forward and picked up the jug from the coffee table. 'Drink, anyone?'

Sammi nodded. 'I'll take one, thanks.'

Lori got to her feet and moved around the table. Just as she was about to begin filling Sammi's glass, the jug slipped through her fingers, landed on the carpet and water sprayed up and all over her and Sammi.

'Oh shit, I'm *so* sorry.'

Sammi jumped to her feet. 'It's fine. It's only water.'

The fronts of their T-shirts were both soaked and Lori felt like an idiot.

'Honestly, it's okay. Look, come through to my room and I'll get us both a change of T-shirt. We look about the same size, I'd say.'

Lori smiled at her new niece and followed her through to her bedroom.

'I'm so sorry,' Lori repeated. 'I feel like an idiot.'

'Honestly, I've dealt with far worse working in cafés and pubs. I'd rather water than stale beer or hot coffee,' Sammi replied, leading Lori into her bedroom and pulling a drawer open in the far corner of the room. She removed two black T-shirts and chucked one across the room. 'That should fit you until your own dries.'

Smiling sheepishly, Lori picked the T-shirt up off the bed where it landed. Sammi pulled her wet shirt over her head and Lori froze. The marking on Sammi's side, just under her bra line, jumped out at her. The redness of it, the bumpy scarring. It looked new, maybe only months old, possibly a year.

Narrowing her eyes as she stared at it, she noticed it wasn't just similar. It was absolutely identical to the ones on her own body. Same as the ones Steph had too.

Sammi pulled the new T-shirt over her head and turned to see Lori still drenched in spilled water. 'What's up?'

Lori snapped out of the shock and licked her lips. 'What was that on your side?'

Sighing loudly, she shook her head. 'It's nothing.'

'Nothing?' Lori replied cynically.

'Are you getting changed?' Sammi asked, and Lori could tell she was trying to change the subject.

Lori's heart began pounding in her chest so hard she felt her breath catch in her throat. 'Did someone do that to you?'

Sammi rolled her eyes. 'Fine, if you must know, it was Logan. We got into a fight one night and as punishment he did this to me.'

Lori stared at her, eyes wide with fear and a thought inside her head that she didn't want to believe, *couldn't* comprehend. 'You got into a fight and he did *that*?'

'I didn't want to have sex one night. I was on my period. He got angry and…' The words trailed off and Sammi looked more concerned about Lori's reaction than the scar itself. Sammi sighed. 'I'm okay, honestly. But with Logan, if he wants you to do something, you do it. Unless you want a hard life.'

Lori's mouth filled with saliva. 'Jesus fucking Christ.'

Sammi's expression became etched with concern as Lori's knees buckled and she fell onto the bed.

'Oh my God, are you all right?'

Taking deep breaths and attempting to stem the sudden sense of nausea, memories she'd rather forget flooded her mind. 'Erm, no, I'm not.' Lori glanced up at Sammi and took her hand. 'The man who gave you that scar, it was *definitely* Logan?'

'I think I'd know if it wasn't,' Sammi replied with confusion. 'It *couldn't* have been anyone else?'

Sammi sat down next to Lori and pulled her hand away. 'No, I'm not mistaken. I remember him doing it. The ring is fucking massive and it burned like a bastard. Imagine being such an arsehole that you burn your partner with your ring because you don't want to have sex. Fucking knob, I hate him.'

Lori's eyes filled with tears and her hands began to tremble.

'Look, Lori, I don't know you very well but you're kind of scaring me. What is wrong? Why are you so upset about my scar?'

Lori wiped away tears and tried her hardest not to let the sob that gripped her throat escape. 'I have the same one. Well, four of them, actually.'

Sammi's face scrunched as she leaned back. 'What are you talking about?'

Lori nodded and removed the wet T-shirt. Pulling the bra cup down a little, she showed the branded saltire scar to Sammi. Turning, she showed her the one on the other breast. 'I have one on the inside of each thigh too.'

Sammi stared at the scar, her eyes narrow as she processed what she was looking at. 'Are you telling me what I think you're telling me?'

She thought about the scars on her own body and how she had got them. Not that she had a full recollection, but enough to know it was brutal and traumatic. No, she thought, there was no way this was an innocent coincidence. It just wasn't possible.

'Lori? Did Logan give you those scars? Were you two a couple or something?'

Lori opened her mouth to speak but the sound of knocking on the bedroom door stopped her.

'You two all right in there?' Kev called through.

'Yep, just coming,' Lori called back as cheerfully as possible. Turning to Sammi, she said, 'Keep this to yourself. Don't tell a soul about this, I mean it.'

Sammi shrugged. 'I don't even know what I'm supposed to keep quiet. I don't get what's going on.'

Lori nodded, sucked a huge lungful of air in through her nostrils and said, 'Good. Keep it that way.' She pulled on the dry T-shirt, got to her feet and opened the bedroom door. 'All sorted,' she replied to Kev.

Moving through to the living room, she sat down next to Jay and tried as hard as she could to stay calm. But all she could think about was the missing second body in the basement of tower three.

There was no doubt in her mind now. One of them, either Ped or Jambo, had survived and was now living their life under a new alias right under Lori and Steph's noses.

Logan Greer was *not* who he claimed he was. Question was, who was he? And what the hell was he going to do next?

FORTY-FOUR

Logan sat in the Portakabin on his own, with the council letter in his hand. The very piece of paper which, hopefully, granted his planning permission application to be able to build on the land the towers stood on now. His stomach fluttered with excitement as he ripped the envelope open and unfolded the letter.

As he scanned over the words, his excitement hardened in his stomach, turning to anger. The bastards had rejected him. No reason whatsoever. A flat-out no. That was it. No way of building on the land. Now he owned something he could do fuck all with.

'Fuck!' Logan growled as he slammed the letter down on the desk. He picked up the landline and dialled the number at the bottom of the letter. But before he could finish, his mobile rang. It was Davie. Logan put the receiver down and answered the call. 'Davie? I hope you've got good news for me.'

'Not exactly,' Davie replied, and Logan closed his eyes. Today was going from bad to worse and it wasn't going to be long before Logan exploded.

'What's the fucking problem now?' Logan said through gritted teeth.

'The suppliers down in London; they're withholding the next shipment.'

Logan's eyes shot open and he got to his feet. 'Why?'

'Something about quality control. Apparently some of the product was tampered with and punters have died as a result. They don't want to put anything else out until it's taken care of.

They didn't say as much, but it sounds like territory issues to me. Regardless, it means we've nothing to sell once the stock we already have is sold out.'

Logan began pacing the Portakabin. 'This is fucking ridiculous. The council have fucked me over and now this?'

A moment of silence and then, 'What do you mean, the council have fucked you over?'

'They've rejected my application to build on the land once the towers are down. That's a shit ton of income just gone. And now this? I'm going to have to find another supplier up here.'

'Fuck, sorry, mate. That's a lot of shite to be hit with at once. I'll keep my ear to the ground, keep you updated with what's going on down there. Although, I have to say, I don't think the team are going to be best impressed by this. They all rely on the income, Logan. We're going to have to act fast to get another supplier before our current stock runs out. Otherwise—'

'Otherwise what?' Logan said sharply. 'They're a bunch of teenage boys, Davie. What are they going to do?'

Davie sighed down the line. 'I'm just worried that their loyalty will be tested if they stop getting paid.'

Logan shook his head. 'Loyalty? Tell me, Davie, have you found out who else is stealing from me? Because it seems to me that their loyalty is already questionable. Here's the deal, you find the second little arsehole who decided to steal from me and give him the tanking of his life and I'll sort supply issues.'

Before Davie had a chance to answer, Logan ended the call and slammed his phone onto the desk next to the council letter.

What a shite forty-eight hours Logan was having. His wife had told him she was taking the boys and leaving him. Sammi was gone. The council rejection and the supply issues on top of that made him feel like he was going to explode. He didn't give a shit about Sammi, not really. Throughout most of his life, Logan had perfected the art of control. This was the first time in a long time he was losing control of his life, and it didn't sit well with him.

Rubbing at the side of his face, his skin tingled beneath his beard as he stared up at the towers. The date of the demolition had been set. One week from now, he'd finally be able to start pulling those towers down. One at a time, piece by piece. The plan had been to start to make money from the land. Something good had to come from this place and he was utterly determined to make it all work, for it all to come together. The community had rallied round him. The local media and West and Clyde Council were backing him; or so he'd thought. He needed to keep up the persona that he was going to do what he promised and clean up Dunreath. Logan would continue to keep his nose clean and show his professional, caring side. He'd go to the local councillor, bung him a few grand for his back pocket. He'd be able to sort the formality of planning permission, he was sure of it. There were always local councillors and MSPs looking to earn a bit on the side, and there were always dodgy ones lying in wait. Logan would happily line their pockets if it meant getting construction started almost as soon as the Clydeview Towers site was cleared.

'Boss?' Jay's voice penetrated his thoughts. 'You all right over there?'

Logan turned, his hand falling from his face. How long had he been standing there? 'Aye, just thinking about the demolition. It's only a week away. I was thinking about the land and what it will look like, that's all.'

Logan picked up the letter and slipped it into his trouser pocket. He didn't want anyone knowing about the rejection.

Jay smiled at him and Logan tilted his head. 'How's the family doing, Jay?'

His expression fell, just a little. But Logan knew the question would have felt like a threat, especially after Jay had betrayed him.

'Erm, aye. All good, thanks.'

Logan nodded. 'Good. Your mum, she's okay, is she?'

Jay nodded slowly. 'Why do you ask?'

Pursing his lips, Logan shook his head. 'No reason. Just like to check in with my staff, make sure everyone's good. You know, good home life means you perform better at work. And that's what I care about.'

Jay's shoulders relaxed a little and Logan cracked his knuckles together. He couldn't let things fall apart. Not yet. Not now. Not when his plan was so close to being executed. But he did need to let his anger out somewhere, otherwise he might show a side of himself to the people he didn't want to, and he couldn't afford that right now.

'Right then, best let you get back to work,' Logan said, moving away from Jay and back into the Portakabin.

He sat down behind his desk, picked up his phone and placed the iPad on the desk. He should have kept the bloody thing at the site all along – that way, Sammi would never have discovered it. A rookie mistake and one he couldn't fix. Not that it would affect his plans for the future. He'd take his revenge whether Sammi and his wife were in his life or not.

Unlocking the phone, he opened up the Instagram app that was signed in on Sammi's account and clicked on messages. She'd read Reece's last message but hadn't replied.

As he was about to close the app down, three little dots danced around the bottom of the chat box.

He rubbed his hand across the wiry hair of his beard and waited to see what Sammi was going to say.

> What do you want, Reece?

Logan narrowed his eyes and wondered how Reece would respond. What the hell was he playing at? The young lad was on a death wish if he thought he'd get away with sending private messages to a gangster's girlfriend.

Three dots danced around the screen again. Reece was in the middle of composing his response.

> You... It's always been you. I still feel the same way as I did back then.

Logan stared at the words for what felt like an eternity and then a loud and sudden burst of laughter escaped his lips. He still felt the same way? What was that supposed to mean? Back when? Did she have a history with Reece that Logan knew nothing about? He was a wee boy compared to Logan with fuck all to offer.

He banged his fist down on the table and gritted his teeth. 'I'm going to fucking kill him.'

> Well, I'm single now. So, do your best 😊

For some reason, those words seemed to be the thing that tipped him over the edge. On their own, he might have let it go, for a short while at least. But on top of everything else that had gone down over the last two days, and especially in the last few minutes, Logan felt like his blood was boiling. This anger needed to be released or he was going to end up ill. Getting to his feet, Logan moved around the desk and out of the Portakabin in time to see Jay making his way up the yard.

'Oi, Jay, come here, eh?'

Jay stopped, turned and hesitated, before walking back down the yard towards Logan. Once stood in front of him, Logan stared into the face of the young lad who was so keen to impress when they'd first met. Now was the real test.

'I need you to do something for me,' Logan said. 'And as your boss, I won't take no for an answer. Not unless you want things to go catastrophically wrong for you.'

FORTY-FIVE

Jay sat in the driver's seat of the van and did exactly as Logan told him: *do not ask questions, do not speak unless spoken to and, under all circumstances, do exactly what he is instructed to do.* None of those things sounded appealing, but when Logan pointed the gun into the back of his neck, Jay had no choice but to do everything Logan said. He had absolutely no doubt that Logan would shoot him right through the neck, the bullet exiting his throat and blood spattering up the front windscreen.

He emptied his mind of the images and hoped that whatever Logan was planning wasn't going to be as sinister as he imagined, although, with a gun involved, he expected the worst.

'Do you know who we're looking for, Jay boy?' Logan asked quietly, his tone and the nature of the question sending a chill up Jay's spine.

Jay shook his head.

'Your best buddy, Reece Lyle.'

Jay stared out of the window onto the road ahead, which led up the hill towards Blackhill Court.

'You got anything to say about that, Jay? You got any questions as to *why* I'm looking for your buddy?'

Jay tried his best to contain the tremors running through his hands as he gripped the steering wheel. Yes, he thought. A million questions, but he knew the answer to the first one. Either Logan wanted to grill Reece on his knowledge of the body Jay had shown him, or Logan had found out Reece was messaging Sammi. Neither option would end well for Reece, especially not when Logan was holding a gun to the back of his neck.

'Why are you looking for him?' Jay asked quietly, desperately trying not to move a muscle so that Logan didn't see it as an attempt to escape.

'You sound a wee bit terrified, mate. You all right there?' Logan menaced.

'Having a gun pushed into the back of your neck will do that, boss,' Jay replied, trying not to sound cheeky and set Logan off.

'Ha, yeah. Fair dos,' Logan said, yet he didn't remove the gun. 'Well, you see. Your wee pal, Reece, my *ex*-employee, he's been a little bit stupid. A big bit stupid, actually.'

'What's he done?' Jay asked, trying to sound unworried, unfazed. He failed terribly.

'Oh, come on now, Jay boy, you know what he's done. Firstly, he walks off my site without so much as a goodbye, then he decides to try to get into my bird's pants.'

Jay grimaced at Logan's choice of words. He parted his lips to defend Reece but thought better of it. If he tried to stick up for Reece, he could end up dead. What was he supposed to do? Lying would make it worse, but the truth wouldn't help either. Telling Logan about the history between Reece and Sammi would be like pulling the pin from a grenade.

Not only was Reece his best mate, but now Sammi was family. He couldn't work out how he was going to get himself out of this or protect them.

'So, I want to have a little word with him,' Logan continued, bringing Jay back from his thoughts. Getting involved with Logan Greer was about the biggest mistake Jay had ever made in his life. He should never have applied for the job. He'd heard the rumours before he'd sent his application in but it hadn't worried him. If only he'd known then what he knew now.

'And you need me for that?' Jay asked.

'Well, he sees me, he's going to run a fucking mile, isn't he? He sees you, then he's not going to think anything's up.'

Jay's stomach lurched at the thought of what the hell he was being forced to do. The fact that a gun was being held to the back of his head was a clear indication of where Logan's thoughts were at. He couldn't even text Reece to warn him to stay away from the estate.

The evening was still warm, the air hot and sticky, adding to Jay's panic. He wanted to ask what Logan expected him to do but the words simply would not come.

'Ah.' Logan breathed the word out, Jay feeling the breath on the back of his neck. 'There's our boy, heading home to his mummy. Stephanie, isn't it?'

Jay swallowed so hard his throat clicked loudly. This wasn't happening. Every word that came out of Logan's mouth was a threat.

Logan's promise of ten grand was long gone. None of it mattered now. The money, the idea of getting out of Dunreath for good. All that Jay cared about now was stopping Logan from killing Reece.

'Right then, slowly does it, Jay boy. Into Blackhill Court we go.'

As Jay slowly eased the van into the estate, he saw Reece in the distance and, in that moment, he realised how horrific the situation was becoming. The horror sat in his stomach and what made it worse was he could do nothing to stop what was about to happen. He wanted to cry, call out to Reece to run and hide. But in reality, all he could do was what he was told. Drive straight for him.

FORTY-SIX

Lori sipped from the glass half filled with Diet Coke and felt the warmth from the evening sun on her skin. It was hard to forget she was in the middle of a cesspit, yet still she tried to soak in the little moments of calm amidst the chaos that was her life.

'So, Sammi's your niece? That's fucking mad, isn't it?' Steph said, picking up her wine glass.

'It's all mad, Steph. Everything about this life, this place. It's like living smack bang in the middle of a lunatic asylum.'

Steph snorted. 'Careful. You're not allowed to say things like that any more.'

Lori rolled her eyes. 'Me offending someone by my choice of words about this place is the least of our worries, Steph.'

Steph took a long drink from her Pinot Grigio and frowned. 'What do you mean?'

Lori cleared her throat. 'When I met Sammi yesterday, I spilled water over us.'

Steph gave a cautious smile. 'Good start.'

'She took me back to her bedroom at Kev's to give me a spare T-shirt. When she took her own off, she had what I thought was a tattoo.'

'Right?'

'Only, it wasn't a tattoo. It was a scar. *Our* scar, Steph. The saltire.'

Steph's eyes widened, and she placed the glass down on the table. Suddenly, the world seemed smaller, more silent. 'Are you sure?'

'Never been surer of anything.'

'So, how'd she get it? And where was it?'

Lori sighed loudly. 'Under her bra line, on her side. I had to do a double take, but it was definitely the same one we have.'

Steph guzzled back her wine and poured another generous glass. 'Did you ask her about it?'

Lori explained how she showed Sammi her own scars and how the conversation went; how she asked Sammi never to breathe a word of it to anyone.

'Fuck,' Steph whispered. 'And we know there was only one body down in that basement.'

Lori felt her hands begin to tremble. 'Steph…'

Steph sat back in her chair and stared out at the estate. Her breath quickened and she started to panic. 'Lori, it's him. It's Logan. He didn't die.'

Lori nodded quickly. 'Yeah, I know. There's no other explanation.'

'What *the fuck* are we going to do, Lori? He'll soon discover that we know, if he hasn't already. Then what? We just wait for him to come and try to finish us off?'

Lori got off her chair and crouched down in front of Steph. 'I think we need to tell someone.'

Steph's eyes darted between Lori and the estate. 'Who the fuck do we tell? The polis? Because they ain't going to fucking help us, Lori. Are they? You've heard about how he's embedded himself in the local news and with the council. They think the sun shines out his arse because he's trying to clean this place up. They'll never believe us.'

Lori bowed her head. Steph was right. 'We can't just wait for this to blow over, Steph.'

Steph raised her trembling hand, wine glass in her grip, and glugged it back. Lori sat back in her seat.

As they both glanced over Blackhill Court, Lori watched as Reece walked towards their building. Glancing further back, she saw Jay sitting in the driver's seat of a van. His expression spoke a thousand words and Lori's stomach dropped.

FORTY-SEVEN

Jay eased the van into the edge of Blackhill Court and pulled the handbrake on. Logan's chin was practically on Jay's shoulder, watching as Reece approached the centre of the estate. His own flat was just out of sight. A few inches further and he'd be able to see the veranda in which he was certain that his mum and Reece's mum would be sat, chatting and looking out over the shitehole it seemed no one could escape.

'You see that?' Logan said in an almost whisper. 'He's messaging my girl. I think they've got history between them.'

Jay closed his eyes briefly and, when he opened them again, he watched as Reece tapped on his phone. 'How can you be sure?'

'I've been reading the messages he's sending to Sammi's Instagram. He said he still feels the same way as he did back then. You know anything about that?'

Jay fell silent and prayed that Reece would move quicker into the building, giving Jay more time to think about how to get himself and Reece out of this mess.

'An answer would be good, Jay,' Logan said, pressing the gun harder into the back of his neck.

'No, I don't know anything about that.'

'You're lying for him. Move,' Logan said. 'Now.'

Jay put the van into first, let the clutch up and moved slowly along Blackhill Court.

'Get the speed up,' Logan said, pressing the gun harder into the back of Jay's neck.

He did as he was told, and realised what was about to happen. There was no way he could stop it without getting himself killed in the process and, if Jay died, he wouldn't be able to stop Reece from dying too.

'Logan, please think about this. Reece doesn't mean any harm. None of us do.'

'Aye, I bet your mother thought the same back in the day.'

Jay's stomach flipped then, so violently that saliva pooled under his tongue. He swallowed it down and felt his entire body begin to tremble. What the hell was he talking about? The fear he felt began to turn to fury.

'What's that supposed to mean?' Jay said, his teeth clenched together.

'Don't question me, son, or I'll blow your fucking head off right now. *Don't* underestimate me.'

Jay unclenched his teeth and closed his mouth. What the fuck was Logan talking about? He desperately wanted more from him, but how could he ask that now when he was driving towards his best friend with a gun at his neck?

'Right, window down, just a little,' Logan said. 'Shout on him.'

Jay's throat immediately dried up, like he'd had sand poured down his neck.

'*Fucking* shout on him,' Logan growled.

Tears began to pool but Jay knew this was a life-or-death situation for himself. He could throw the van into first and put his foot down, throwing Logan off his seat. But how likely was it that it would go the way Jay saw it in his head? Not very.

'Reece?' Jay called, half-heartedly, but it was enough for Reece to hear him and turn around.

The pressure of the gun against the back of Jay's neck released and three loud pops rang out right next to his ear. The sound was so loud a sharp pain shot through Jay's head. Had he been hit himself?

Reece crumpled to the ground and Logan shouted in his ear to drive. The sound of Logan's voice was muffled as the gunshots still rang loudly inside his head. As if on autopilot, Jay put his foot down and flew out the other end of Blackhill Court and on to the main road.

'Get us out of the village. Go to the site. Now!' Logan shouted, his voice ringing in Jay's ear along with the sound of the gunshots.

Jay did as he was told, not knowing whether he'd survive this. Not knowing whether Reece would either.

'Did you have to shoot him?' Jay asked as he flew along the A82 towards the derelict site of the Clydeview Towers.

He heard Logan shift in his seat, before climbing into the front passenger side of the van and turning to face Jay. He was rubbing at his shoulder with his hand as if the gun going off had hurt him.

'Let me put you straight on something, Jay boy. If you fuck me over, you die. End of story.'

The words were so blunt, Jay had no response. There was nothing he could say to argue the point. Reece had been right all along. Logan Greer was a nutcase. Now Jay was getting to see the full wrath of him, and the terror he felt in the pit of his stomach made him feel sick.

'Your mum fucked me over once.'

Jay's head snapped round to look Logan in the eye, and when he did, he was staring down the barrel of the gun which had just taken out his best mate. 'What are you talking about?'

'About twenty-four years ago, your mum tried to kill me and my best mate with Stephanie to help her. Only thing is, it didn't work. I survived. Don't know how, your mum packs a fucking punch, I'll give her that.'

Jay's hands trembled on the steering wheel as they pulled into the site. He parked the van outside the Portakabin and pulled on the handbrake. He looked around. The place was quieter than usual. Eerily quiet, like people knew what was going to happen.

'Why did she do that?' Jay asked, desperate to keep Logan talking for as long as possible. The longer he talked, the longer Jay had to live. 'What happened?'

'All in good time, Jay boy. All in good time. Now, kill the engine,' Logan said. 'Get out slowly, and walk towards tower three.'

Jay hesitated but, as Logan pushed the gun towards Jay's chest, he got out of the van. There was no point in running. Instead, he did exactly as Logan asked; nothing more, nothing less. He felt himself tremble, not just on the outside, but on the inside too. He took a steadying breath, hoping that Logan couldn't see his fear.

As Jay moved through the entrance lobby of tower three, the basement door was already open.

'Down you go,' Logan said, pressing the gun into his back. 'I'll be back with food and some water. Oh, and your mum.'

Jay stared down the staircase, knowing what was down there, and felt the need to beg Logan for mercy. He kept his mouth shut.

'By the time you know everything about what that bitch did to me and my pal down there, the dem will have already started. This tower will come down on top of you both and you'll become nothing but sand.'

'Logan, mate, please.'

'I'm not your fucking mate. I never was.' Logan then held out his hand. 'Phone. Now.'

Jay knew he had no choice. If he tried to fight this, he'd end up another pile of bones at the bottom of the stairs. If that happened, he'd leave his family in grave danger. Handing Logan the phone, Jay felt utterly helpless.

'Now, are you going to walk down those stairs yourself, or do I have to shoot you down?'

Jay closed his eyes, took a deep breath and stepped down. One, two, three. The door behind him slammed shut and he heard the sound of a click. The door was locked and he was trapped with a two-decade-old skeleton for company.

How the hell was he going to get himself out of this?

FORTY-EIGHT

Her pounding footsteps reverberated up through her legs as she ran across the green towards Steph. Heart pounding so hard she felt it in her throat, Lori winced at the sounds coming from her best friend.

'Please, somebody help me!'

Lori stared down at Steph as she cradled Reece in her arms, the blood from his torso seeping onto her clothes as she screamed with terror.

'Lori! Do something!'

She froze in that moment, unable to process what she was looking at. A loud ringing sound rattled inside her ears as she tried to breathe. Reece had been shot. The gun. The van. Jay's face. She couldn't process it all.

A sudden jolt of reality hit her and Lori pulled her phone out, called for an ambulance. She kept back from Steph so she could hear the call handler on the other end of the line. A man stepped forward and took off his hoody before placing it over Reece's wound and began applying pressure.

'Lori, do something!' Steph screamed again, seemingly unaware that she was already on the phone.

People were starting to gather, approaching slowly with caution to watch as Reece bled out on the ground in his mother's arms. Lori saw phones in hands, filming, taking pictures.

'What the fuck is wrong with you all?' she growled, walking over to one of the spectators and knocking the phone from his hand. 'Get a fucking grip, the lot of you.'

People lowered their phones, mumbled quietly. No one knew what to do. As much as Blackhill Court was the depths of hell at times, nothing like this had ever happened – not in Lori's lifetime at least.

'Which service do you require?' the handler said.

'My friend's son, he's been shot. I need an ambulance,' Lori replied as her eyes fixed down on Reece. Steph's screams had become less intense. The man seemed calm as he pressed down on top of the hoody, although there was still a lot of blood.

As the call ended, Lori could barely recall the questions she'd been asked or the answers she'd given. All she could focus on was the scene in front of her as she tucked her phone away and went to Steph. She was at Reece's head, allowing the man, who Lori didn't know but recognised from around the area, to focus.

'Reece? Reece, can you hear me?' Lori lowered her voice.

His eyes darted up towards her, wide and confused.

'Lori, what the hell happened there? Why did Jay shoot him?' Steph cried.

'It wasn't Jay,' Reece croaked. 'It was Logan Greer. I saw his face. Jay was the driver.'

Lori and Steph exchanged a glance as the sound of sirens in the distance grew louder. The man kept his face neutral. It was obvious he didn't want to be involved in any of it. She couldn't blame him.

'Jesus,' Steph sobbed. 'Reece, you hold on, okay. We'll get you help.'

Lori felt like she was suffocating. Logan was the shooter and Jay was with him. Whoever *him* was. Ped, or Jambo. Either way, Lori had to make sure Jay was safe. Because if Logan had shot Reece, he could be about to do the same thing to Jay. He'd be coming for them all.

The estate was suddenly surrounded by police vans, armed officers and an ambulance edged its way in.

'Mum.' Reece's voice was a mere whisper. His breathing had changed, it was shallower. Lori closed her eyes. She prayed that he'd make it. But with the amount of blood and the look on Reece's face, she wasn't sure he would.

'Don't talk, Reece,' Steph sobbed. 'This man's helping to stop the blood. And look, the ambulance is here. You're going to be okay.'

Lori's eyes pooled with tears behind her closed lids and she couldn't bear to watch. She'd known Reece all his life. He was like a son to her, the way Jay was to Steph. He couldn't die. Neither of them could. Lori wouldn't allow it. She'd do her best to stop that from happening. The same way she'd managed to stop Ped and Jambo from killing her and Steph.

'Lori?' Steph sobbed.

Lori fell to her knees next to Steph and looked down at Reece. He was pale, lips blue.

'Mum,' Reece whispered again, this time the emotion heavy in his voice. 'Please don't let me die.'

FORTY-NINE

Sammi sat back on the sofa and typed the name Logan Greer into the Google search bar at the top of the screen on her phone. It had occurred to her that she'd got into a relationship with Logan very quickly. He'd showered her with all the right things – gifts, compliments, love – and she'd fallen for it.

Clicking on the first search option that came up didn't show her anything she didn't already know. Instead, she went to images and scanned over them slowly. A lot showed the logo for his demolition and security companies. There were a few *Dunreath Gazette* articles that showed his picture; all of which she'd already seen.

Scrolling a little further down the page, she came across a photograph with a Facebook link beneath it. She clicked on it and the page opened. She stared at it. The picture was of Logan with a woman. Sammi recognised her immediately. It was his wife. The image was date-stamped as April 2019, but it was definitely the same woman Sammi had answered the iPad to. She read the caption.

> The Home-Start Network – Foster Families
>
> We would like to thank local businessman, Logan Greer, pictured here with his wife. Mr Greer has worked closely with The Home-start Network for a number of years now, making sure that the charity has enough funds to cover the essentials for children coming to us from various situations. Tonight's event was hosted by us, and Mr Greer came along to support the charity, joined by his wife and family.

She stared at the image through narrowed eyes. Logan worked with a charity for foster kids? Really? There had to be something more to that, surely? She thought about the drug-dealing side of his business and wondered if the charity was somehow involved in that? Maybe he used it as a front to make him look good or something.

Raising a brow, she sighed and glanced out of the window in front of her.

'What you looking so frustrated about?' Kev asked, slipping his jacket on.

Sammi sighed. 'I'm just so annoyed with myself that I didn't see Logan for what he was a lot sooner. Still, at least I'm not married to him, unlike this one.'

'You're on her social media?' Kev asked, sounding shocked.

Sammi shook her head. 'No, I was actually looking for things about Logan. I realised I know nothing about his past and I wanted to see if there was anything online about him from before I met him. He doesn't do social media so I went to Google and I found a picture of him and his wife.'

A look of surprise crossed his face. 'Can I see her?'

Sammi held the phone out to him, and when he took it from her and looked down at the screen, his expression changed. Eyes narrow at first, before slowly widening. Then he parted his lips and said, 'You've got to be *fucking* kidding me.'

Getting to her feet, Sammi moved around so she could see the screen too. 'What's wrong? Do you know her or something?'

Kev nodded. 'That's my sister.'

Sammi let out a laugh. 'You're at it.'

'I'm not. I swear to you right here, right now, that's my and Lori's sister, Charley. The one who was taken into foster care twenty-four years ago.'

Sammi took the phone from him and stared down at Charley's face. She studied her features. Eyes dark like Kev and Lori. Nose a little turned up at the end with a slight ridge in the middle. Same jawline. Same smile.

'Oh my God,' Sammi whispered, then stared at the caption again. 'That's why he works for the charity then? Because she was fostered. It makes sense now.'

'Can I see that a minute?' Kev asked, taking the phone back from her. He stared at the image and Sammi could see the disbelief in his face.

Kev sat down, stared at the screen. He used his fingers to enlarge the photo of Logan and he studied it carefully.

'I think I know him,' he finally said after moments of silence. 'Well, I used to know him. A long time ago.'

'Did you grow up together or something?'

Kev cleared his throat and shifted in his seat. He looked uncomfortable. 'I owed him money; technically still do. He's dangerous, Sammi. The most dangerous drug dealer I'd ever come across in my time as a user. Wouldn't think twice about cutting off a finger or a full hand if you didn't pay up. Then he just disappeared. I was expecting him to come looking for me when I got out of jail. He never appeared. Rumour had it he'd been arrested, some people said he'd moved out of the country. Others thought he was dead. But no one seemed to know for sure where he'd gone. And now, twenty-four years later, he's married to my estranged sister and engaged to my *fucking* daughter.'

Sammi's heart pounded against the wall of her chest. 'This can't be happening. This has to be a coincidence.'

Kev got up, began pacing the floor. 'It's *not* a coincidence. He's done this on purpose.'

Sammi's skin prickled at the thought that Logan could have done something so calculated.

'So, you think he's married your sister and started seeing me, all because you owe him a couple of hundred quid? That doesn't make any sense.'

Kev crunched his teeth together. 'It wasn't a couple of hundred quid, Sammi. I said I'd deal for him to work off some debt. But it didn't quite work out that way and I ended up owing him thousands, Sammi.'

'What do you mean, didn't quite work out that way? Did you keep the drugs for yourself or something?'

Kev raised a brow. 'It's a bit more complicated than that.'

Sammi looked on at him expectantly and he sighed.

'I suppose I'll need to explain myself to Lori anyway. Look, I was a shithead when I was young; we all know that. I'm surprised Lori ever looked in my direction again after what I did to her.'

'What did you do?'

'I hid the drugs under her bed. Then I went on a bender. When I came back, the drugs were gone. I think she got rid of them, thinking she was helping. I suppose she was. But I'd never have thought this would happen two and a half decades later.'

She frowned. 'You think he'd still call in that debt after all this time?'

Kev puffed out his cheeks. 'Yeah, I do. He was ruthless back then, Sammi. And it seems nothing has changed.'

FIFTY

Lori watched as the ambulance doors closed before it drove off with Reece and Steph inside, blue flashing lights, sirens and being escorted and trailed by police. She was aware of the man who'd held his hoody on Reece's wound as he spoke with an officer. He was shaking his head, saying that he hadn't seen anything other than Reece lying on the grass, bleeding out.

'Ma'am, if you could focus,' the officer said as Lori looked on, wondering if she'd ever see Reece alive again; wondering if she'd ever see her own son alive again.

'Yes, sorry,' Lori replied. Should she just tell him everything? Go right back to the start, that night twenty-four years ago. Then she remembered what Steph had said: how the council and local media held Logan in such high regard. A wealthy, well-intentioned businessman who wanted to clean up the village. No one would believe such a man would do such terrible things. They wouldn't believe any of it. Not only that. They'd committed a crime all those years ago. Murdered two men (or so she'd thought) and left their bodies to rot in that basement. 'No, I'm sorry, I didn't see who shot Reece.'

The officer nodded. 'You're *absolutely* sure about that? You saw nothing and no one at all?'

'It's all such a blur. We were just sitting on my veranda, up there.' Lori pointed. 'Next thing, a van approached. Reece was walking across the estate and then he was down. Steph started screaming. I don't really remember much after that. Or before it, to tell you the truth.'

Nodding again, the officer looked at her with a strange scepticism, and it unnerved her. He had no idea what she was going to have to do to protect her family, and that was if it wasn't already too late.

'I'll be in touch,' the officer said, moving across to the central area of the estate, which was now surrounded by crime-scene tape. Lori turned her back on him, glanced up at her flat and wondered what she was supposed to do next.

She walked across the grass and into the building, climbing the stairs towards the front door. Her phone rang and she pulled it out.

'Lori,' Kev said, before she'd even had the chance to say hello. 'Lori, are you sitting down?'

She sighed. 'I think you're the one who needs to sit down, Kev.'

'What do you mean?'

'Reece has been shot. Logan Greer was the shooter and Jay was driving the van.'

The words were so blunt; her entire body completely numb.

'*Jesus.* Are you okay? Is Reece dead?' Kev asked, his voice quieter now. 'Where's Jay now?'

'It came out of nowhere,' Lori said without answering any of Kev's questions. She explained what happened, just as she had to the officer, and tried her best not to fall apart.

'Fucking *hell.* How do you know Logan was the one who shot Reece?'

Lori pushed open the front door to her flat and took a deep breath. 'Because Reece told us as he lay in Steph's arms, bleeding all over her.'

She stepped inside and moved through to the living room. The veranda door was still open; Steph's wine glass still on the table, her own glass of Diet Coke next to it.

'Oh shit, Lori. I can't believe it. Why did he do it?'

She swallowed hard. Could she tell him? Could she say it out loud? If she did, she'd have to tell her brother everything.

About what happened to her and Steph all those years ago and how she'd made the link to Logan being part of her horrific past. She'd have to tell him it was her fault because she got rid of the drugs that Kev was supposed to sell for him.

'There's so much to it, Kev. Can you come over?'

She heard Kev take a breath. 'I mean, yeah, of course I can. Let me just call in to work. I'll be there as soon as I can.'

Lori nodded. 'Okay, get here quicker than soon, Kev, and bring Sammi. You can't let her out of your sight. Logan is a loose cannon.'

FIFTY-ONE

Sammi stared at him, her heart thumping hard in her chest. Reece had been shot. Logan pulled the trigger. Was this because of her relationship with Reece in the past? Had Logan found out and used it as his excuse?

'I'm not stepping a foot inside that fucking village after what he's done. He'll fucking kill us all,' Sammi said in a panic.

Kev shook his head. 'I know you're scared, Sammi. But we *have* to go. Reece has been shot. I can't leave you alone here. He could have followed us here. He could be watching you right now, waiting for you to be alone. I'm not putting you at risk like that. Come on, the taxi's outside. I'll keep you safe, I promise.'

Sammi snorted. 'You can't keep that kind of promise. How can you? He married your sister. You said yourself you don't think that's a coincidence. He's been planning something against you for a long time by the sounds of it, and when he finds out you're my dad, it'll fuel his fire.'

They both stood in silence for a few moments. The terror in Sammi's chest made it hard to breathe. But she knew her dad was right. She couldn't be left alone.

'I swear to God if I had a passport I'd be fleeing the country right now,' Sammi said, before gesturing for Kev to leave the flat.

Kev locked the door and Sammi followed her dad downstairs and out of the building. He held the taxi door open for her and she climbed in.

The journey back to Blackhill Court was silent, and all Sammi could picture was Logan pulling in front of the taxi to block it and pointing the gun at them. He would be furious with her that she'd left, that she'd lied to him about Reece.

Almost half an hour passed by before the taxi pulled up on the edge of Blackhill Court. A police cordon had been set up around the green in the centre of the estate and Sammi felt sick.

'Oh aye,' the driver said. 'Looks like there's been an incident.'

'Aye, seems so,' Kev replied before he paid the astronomical fare. They both climbed out and Sammi stood next to him; almost felt herself reach for his hand. She was utterly terrified, but still, she barely knew him. She couldn't bring herself to call him Dad yet, never mind hold his hand.

They moved around the cordon, officers stationed at either side of it. Sammi glanced over at the grass and, to her horror, saw bloodstains on the grass. Her heart almost skipped a beat as she thought about the pain Reece would have been in; the fear he must have felt at the time. Was he dead? Had Logan done what he'd set out to do? A man like him didn't shoot to injure.

A crowd had gathered at the far side of the estate and Sammi followed Kev into the close and up the stairs, where Lori was waiting for them at the door. Her face was pale, her expression filled with terror. When she saw Kev, she burst into tears.

'Hey,' he said, pulling her in for a hug. 'It's okay. You're going to be okay.'

'I'm not worried about me,' she sobbed, pulling away and moving into the flat. Sammi's stomach flipped. No one was going to be okay if Logan was on the warpath with a gun.

They all moved through to the living room and sat down on the sofa.

'He did it because of me,' Sammi blurted out. 'Reece and I used to go out a few years back. He must have found out. He accused Reece of flirting with me a few days ago. That's the only reason I can think of.'

'Not just that,' Kev replied. 'It could be because I owe him money.'

Lori's eyes darted between them before finally resting on Kev. 'I'm sorry, Kev. If I hadn't got rid of those drugs under my bed, this wouldn't be happening. He told me you owed him money and he'd take it in some form or other if he couldn't get it from you.'

Sammi felt sick and glanced towards her dad.

'When did he say that? Today?' Kev's volume increased; his voice laced with frustration.

Lori shook her head. 'No. He said it to me twenty-four years ago, not long after Mum and Dad died. You were in prison and...' Her voice cracked and she went quiet.

Sammi closed her eyes for a moment. This all had to be a dream. It couldn't be happening.

'What do you mean, twenty-four years ago?' Kev asked.

Lori puffed out her cheeks and Sammi opened her eyes.

'About two months after Mum and Dad died, me and Steph went on a double date...'

As Lori told her story, the blood in Sammi's veins ran cold.

FIFTY-TWO

Logan sat with his feet up on the desk and watched as all the machines were delivered to the site. The high-reach excavator made his heart sing as he imagined it getting to work. He'd get to watch the buildings come down, one at a time. He'd get to see the land be freed from them; he'd finally be free of them. The memories would remain, of course. But he'd make new memories. Vengeance for him and his best mate, who was still down there.

The soft strip of the towers had already been completed. Windows, doors and partitions all removed. All he had to do now was begin.

'Okay,' the man said, appearing in the doorway with his clipboard. 'If you could read over and sign here to confirm all machines have been received.'

Logan got to his feet, moved around the desk and towards the door. He took the clipboard and read over it. High-reach excavator times two. He nodded and read down the short list. Fifty-ton crane. Demolition curtain times two. Masonry crusher. That one made him smile as he stepped out of the Portakabin and took in the machines in front of him.

Looking down, he took the pen from the top of the clipboard and signed and dated the bottom of the page.

'Cheers, mate,' the delivery manager said, before turning on his heel and leaving.

Logan approached the crusher and stood in front of it. He'd been in the demolition game for a few years now. He knew his job well. And he knew how to make it work in ways that it wasn't supposed to.

Lori Graham and Stephanie Lyle were going to pay for what they'd done. And Logan was going to revel in every second of it. He'd had the privilege of seeing Steph watch her son get shot. He got to see Lori clap eyes on her son as the driver. And now, Jay was down in the basement of tower three. Reece would hopefully die if he hadn't already. Soon, Lori and Stephanie would join Jay down there, next to Jambo's bones. His remains would be the last thing they'd all see before the building came down on top of them.

'Almost two and a half decades,' he said quietly. 'And *finally*, my day is coming.'

FIFTY-THREE

Both Kev and Sammi stared at her, open-mouthed and utterly horrified by her revelations.

'Jesus *Christ*,' Kev whispered, his face pale like he was going to throw up.

'I can't believe you went through all that,' Sammi said.

'This is all my fault. If I hadn't hid those drugs under your bed…'

Lori shook her head. 'No, Kev. He has exploited all of us. He's a horrible, narcissistic psychopath. I shouldn't have flushed the drugs. I should have left them for you to sell.'

'We both know I wouldn't have done that. I'd have taken them myself and I'd have been killed a long time ago.'

Lori sobbed and wiped at her tears.

'I'm so sorry,' Kev replied. 'I should have done better by you. I mean, how can you be okay after what happened?'

Lori sighed. 'I've somehow learned how to deal with it. I don't feel as traumatised as I should. I mean obviously I am and, in the beginning, I was. Who wouldn't be? But so much time had passed and I knew they weren't coming back. Until they did. Well, one of them anyway.'

Lori noticed the exchange between her brother and niece and narrowed her eyes.

'Lori,' Kev said. 'I'm not sure how you're going to take this, given how what happened to you was my fault to begin with; I was going to tell you this before I knew Reece got shot.'

'What is it?'

Sammi cleared her throat awkwardly and readjusted herself on the couch. 'Remember I told you that I found out Logan was married and I spoke to his wife?'

Lori nodded and glanced back at Kev.

'He married Charley,' he said.

The words hung in the air and Lori raised a brow. 'Charley who?'

Sammi cleared her throat again. 'Your sister.'

Sticking her chin out and feeling an incredulous laugh escape her lips, Lori's eyes darted between the two before she shook her head. 'Fuck off. There's no way.'

Kev glanced down at the carpet where his feet rested. 'Sammi found a picture of him on Google at a foster-family charity event back in 2019. He was standing next to his wife. It was Charley. I saw her with my own eyes.'

Lori stood up, the sudden feeling of nausea hitting her like a tidal wave. 'A charity event? No. That can't be right. How is that even possible, Kev?'

He stood with her. 'I don't know, Lori. But he did it. And I don't think it's a coincidence either. Not after what you've just told us. I think he planned it all.'

She began pacing the room. Back and forth. Back and forth.

'Okay, let's get this right. After I managed to get me and Steph away from whatever fucked-up plan he and his sick pal had for us, he hid in plain sight for twenty-four years, married Charley, fathered two kids with her, got engaged to your daughter, shot Reece and has taken my son to fuck knows where.'

Kev and Sammi were silent.

'Does that sound right to you? I mean, does it sound plausible?'

Sammi closed her eyes. 'For someone like Logan? Yes, it does.'

Lori stopped pacing, stood still and looked up at the ceiling. 'The bastard. He's been planning his revenge all this time.'

She thought back to that night. How had he managed to survive? She'd watched them both die, hadn't she?

Pulling out her phone, she tried Jay's mobile for the eighth time. She wanted to believe he was still alive, that he was okay. Still no answer and now her thoughts were spiralling. What if he was already dead and Logan was getting rid of the evidence?

'I need to find Jay,' she said, grabbing her keys. 'I need to help him.'

Kev waved his hands. 'Woah, aren't the police trying to do that?'

'I didn't tell them Jay was in the van. In fact, I told them I saw nothing.'

'Why the *fuck* did you do that?' Sammi shouted.

Lori gave her a dead stare. 'Because he's held in high regard with the council and the media around here. No one would believe someone like me from Blackhill Court over a well-respected businessman. And I was fucking terrified. I've gone through my entire life thinking I'd murdered two lowlife drug dealers and left them to rot. He's gone from a lowlife to the high life. I can't let him get away with what he's done.'

'This is Ped we're talking about, Lori. You remember him from back then. He's an utter fucking nutjob. Surely you haven't forgotten that?' Kev said. 'If it hadn't been for prison, he'd have killed me back then. And now, it seems he's worse than ever.'

Lori ran a hand over her face and her stomach sank. It was him. Ped. And now, he had her son.

'I can be a fucking nutjob too if I'm pushed into a corner. Reece is dying because of him. And he has my son. You think I'm going to back away from him?'

Kev shook his head and grunted in frustration. 'I'm not going to let you do this.'

'You don't get to *let* me do anything, Kev. No one does. Jay's my boy. That freak has him and I will do whatever it takes to stop him from harming Jay.'

Sammi puffed out her cheeks. 'Everyone needs to slow down. The only person who might be able to stop Logan is

Charley. If she can talk to him, maybe she can convince him to stop?'

Silence hung heavily over the room for a few moments, before Lori nodded. 'I'll do it.'

FIFTY-FOUR

Steph paced the floor in the family room at the Queen Elizabeth Hospital in Glasgow. An armed police officer was stood outside the door, as well as outside the operating theatre where Reece was having life-saving surgery. It was only life-saving if he didn't die, and the surgeons had told Steph to prepare for the worst. She didn't understand what was happening to her son's body. The surgeon had tried to explain it but the words were lost on her.

She couldn't get Reece's last words to her out of her head. *'Please don't let me die.'*

What was she supposed to do with that? How was she supposed to tell him that she could stop him from dying when she knew she couldn't? She couldn't unsee the look on his face, the terror in his eyes. And she knew how that felt. To know that you were teetering on the edge of death and there was nothing you could do to stop it. The night Lori had saved their lives would forever play in her head like a horror film. Over and over, pleading with whatever God existed to help them get out of their predicament.

'What is taking so long?' Steph shouted, pulling at her hair. The armed officer stood to the side and the surgeon walked into the room.

'Please, Ms Lyle. Have a seat.' He gestured to a nearby chair.

'Did you save him? Is he dead?' she said, the words leaving her mouth rapidly.

The surgeon gave a single nod. 'Reece is still with us, but the next twenty-four hours are going to be critical. We need to keep a *very* close eye on him for any signs of internal bleeding. We were able to remove the bullets. Three in total, but the damage is significant.'

The bastard hit him with every shot, Steph thought. 'And he's awake?'

'No. He's in an induced coma.'

'Can I see him?' Steph said, her voice quivering with fear.

'You can.'

Before she knew it, she was being led by the surgeon and escorted by the armed officer down a long corridor. To her right, she was able to glance down to the ground floor, into the heart of the hospital, which to her looked a little like a food court in a shopping centre. She could smell the soup from the café beneath her. Normally she liked the smell of fresh cooking; in that moment, everything around her smelled like death.

'You can stay the night if you like? We can arrange for somewhere for you to sleep so that you don't have to leave him during the critical hours after surgery,' the surgeon said, before stopping outside a door.

'Yes, please,' Steph said, already planning on phoning Lori. 'And thank you. I really can't leave him right now.'

The surgeon gave her a sympathetic smile before opening the door.

Reece was lying in a bed that was positioned at a forty-five-degree angle. He was hooked up to machines; wires everywhere.

'Oh my God,' Steph said, the emotion catching her voice as she moved to his bedside.

'The nurse will be around soon to do some observations. Can I get you anything? A cup of tea, coffee?'

Steph stared down at her son and closed her eyes. 'No. Thank you.' She pulled the chair next to the bed around so that she could sit facing Reece and lowered herself onto it. 'I'm not leaving your side, Reece. You hear me? When you wake up, I'll be here. Just don't take too long, okay?'

Pulling her phone out, Steph found Lori's number and hit call and Lori answered immediately.

'How is he?' Lori asked.

'He's alive, but critical. They removed three bullets. The fucker hit him with every shot. I'm going to stay at the hospital.'

'You should,' Lori replied.

'Has Jay come home?' Steph asked, knowing it was a ridiculous question. Of course he hadn't come home. Like Logan would ever let that happen.

'No, and I haven't heard from him. He's not answering his phone, Steph.' Lori's voice trailed off. The emotions inside Steph clawed their way up and into her throat.

She closed her eyes. 'What are we going to do, Lori?'

'You are going to stay exactly where you are. I will handle this.'

'But how?' Steph asked, turning to see the armed officer outside the door. 'Are you going to tell the police?'

There was a pause, a bout of silence.

'Lori?'

'No police. You called it, Steph. The bastard is loved by the highest suits in the area. They'll never believe it. And he'll be protected because he's injecting so much money into the local economy. I'll handle it my way. You stay by Reece's side. He needs you.'

Steph swallowed the lump of terror in her throat. 'Are you going alone?'

Silence again. Then, 'I don't even know where he is. But I think he'll want me to find him. I tried to kill him to save us, Steph. He's come back for us. I think, in this instance, I have to go alone to stop anyone else getting hurt.'

Steph closed her eyes again. This was a real, living nightmare which had lasted over two decades. 'Be careful,' she quivered.

'I will. And you too. Don't let Reece out of your sight.'

'I mean, we have our own security,' Steph said, although her attempt at humour was lost on both of them. 'If Logan was to come to the hospital, he wouldn't get very far.'

No laughter came from the other end of the line. Only silence and a true sense of fear.

Lori turned her voice to a whisper. 'I'll make sure he dies this time, Steph. Trust me.'

Lori ended the call, and Steph put the phone down on her knee. She took Reece's limp hand in her own, gave it a gentle squeeze and cried silent tears, hoping and praying that Reece would survive and Logan wouldn't.

FIFTY-FIVE

Charley got off the train at Glasgow Central and took in the smell of the city. It smelled the same as it had when she'd left; when she'd gone to be with her foster family. She'd been lucky to get away from the hellish life her blood parents had made her endure. Now she was back, and her entire life had been turned upside down.

When her sister, Lori, had phoned her asking for her to come back to Blackhill Court today, something in the pit of her stomach told her that she had to go. Lori sounded emotional and, after practically begging her, Charley had agreed. She'd just found out her husband had been living a secret life, so why not try to reconnect with her family? She was an adult now and hadn't seen Lori in a very long time. The only thing was, Lori had mentioned that their older brother, Kev, was back. She hadn't seen him in over two decades. She couldn't begin to imagine what he would look like now.

She glanced up at the information board and noted that the next train for Singer station was leaving in just five minutes. In less than half an hour, she'd be back in Clydebank, a stone's throw from Dunreath and Blackhill Court. The very thought made her feel sick to her stomach, and yet, here she was.

Her mind wandered back to her conversation with Margaret and Ronnie earlier. They'd voiced their concerns about her going back to Dunreath; Margaret had tears in her eyes as they spoke, worrying that it might bring back some trauma from her childhood. Margaret reminded her of how broken she had been when she'd first arrived from the children's home.

'I'll be okay, Margaret. I'm a big girl now. And my sister just wants to reconnect. With everything going on with Logan, I figured this could only be a good thing.' She had left out the fact that Kev was going to be there. She didn't want to worry Margaret any more than she already had.

Ronnie had smiled and placed his hand over Charley's. 'We will look after Callan and Thomas until you get home. Won't we, Margaret?'

Charley pulled her small suitcase behind her, half jogging, half running towards platform seventeen. The train was relatively empty as she got on and took a seat, facing forward. Always facing forward while travelling, otherwise she'd throw up, and she didn't need another reason to feel sick. Not today.

Resting her back against the seat, Charley pulled out her phone and realised she hadn't changed the screen saver yet. She stared down at the image of her and Logan on their wedding day and something twisted inside her. Married at home with just Margaret, Ronnie and a few of her foster siblings when she was twenty years old. Things had been perfect. He'd been the most attentive husband, always supportive, always loving; or so she'd thought. She laughed bitterly at herself. How could she have been so stupid? All those years of working away, building up his business to provide a good life for her and the boys, had been a front for him to be able to shack up with whoever took his fancy. Sammi probably wasn't the first.

Charley had always known he'd be a good dad if his skills as a husband were anything to go by. How had this happened? Why hadn't she seen this coming? Could it be because she'd married him too young? She'd never had a relationship prior to Logan and the only good role models she'd had in her life were Margaret and Ronnie. They'd been the only healthy relationship she'd ever experienced. But she'd started seeing Logan before she'd gone to them. It wasn't until she was sixteen that she told them about him. They'd never approved of Logan, although, being the kindest people on the planet, they'd never stifled her feelings about him. They'd only ever warned her to be careful with him; to understand that everything concerning her life was her choice. But were their concerns spot on? When she was sixteen, he was twenty. She was fourteen when she first met him, he was seventeen, about to turn eighteen. And when she'd discovered his infidelity via that video call, the girl, Sammi, looked very young. At most twenty. Was that his thing? Did he like his women young? Was that why he'd shown an interest in her? The thought made her stomach heave.

'Only marry him if that is what you truly want, and not what you think you should do because someone else wants it,' Margaret had said.

Of course she'd wanted to marry him. He'd been good to her, hadn't he? Up until a few days ago, when she found out he was living a double life.

Staring down at his face, she saw a different person now. Someone she didn't know any more. And in spite of this, Charley couldn't just shut off her feelings for the man she'd been married to for seventeen years, had two beautiful boys with. Something about it all just didn't sit right with her. Why would he jeopardise what he had for some twenty-year-old girl from Dunreath of all bloody places?

The train pulled out of Glasgow Central and Charley's stomach rolled again. This was it. She was going to come face to face with her brother and sister.

She leaned her head against the window as the train stopped at each station. People getting on and off at Partick and Anniesland, unaware of who she was and the mess her life was in. As the train passed through Westerton, Drumchapel and Drumry, Charley's stomach flipped intensely as she knew her stop was coming up. She gripped tightly to the handle of her case as it was announced that the next stop was going to be Singer station, adding that the train's destination was Helensburgh. What if she couldn't get off? What if the fear of what she was about to be faced with was too much to bear and she simply couldn't move?

As the train came to a stop, Charley forced herself to stand and, as the doors opened, she stepped onto the platform and glanced up the stairs to the exit leading onto Kilbowie Road.

'This place hasn't changed one bit,' she said under her breath, heading towards the bottom of the stairs. She was the only one who had got off the train, strangely.

Once at the top, she rounded the corner and there he was. Stood in front of her, having aged relatively well considering what he'd done to himself over the years, was her brother. She just about recognised him.

'Charley?' he said, almost asking rather than stating.

'Hi, Kev,' she replied. 'It's been a long time.'

He smiled a little and there was a hint of sadness in his eyes. She felt it too. This man was her blood. She'd missed an entire lifetime of being part of her family. The family that was ruined by drugs and alcohol.

'How was your journey?' he asked.

'Oh, you know? Laced with anxiety and fear about coming back to this place.'

Kev nodded. 'I felt the same last week before I knocked on Lori's door. Come on, I've got a taxi waiting. I'll take us back to Lori's.'

They got into the taxi, Charley somewhat hesitantly, and as they drove up Kilbowie Road, everything about her childhood was coming to her in waves, waves that were already beginning to suffocate her.

The taxi ride was silent. She took a sharp intake of breath and tried to remind herself that everything back then was still there: back in the past. The thing she struggled with was having to face it all because, in just a few minutes, she'd be there, right in the middle of where she grew up. Or at least, where she survived for the first fourteen years of her life. The last time she'd been in Blackhill Court was when her parents had died.

As the taxi pulled into Dunreath and headed towards Blackhill Court, Charley took deep breaths. In and out. In and out.

'That's fifteen quid exactly,' the driver said, pulling on the handbrake and turning to face Kev.

Kev handed over a twenty and opened the door. Charley got out and Kev took her suitcase.

'Lori's in that building now,' Kev said, noticing that Charley was looking up at the windows of their old home. The images of her parents lying dead on that mattress they called a bed came to mind almost instantly. She hadn't thought of that image in years; hadn't thought of them in a truly long time. Now, being back in the estate was conjuring up bad memories.

Charley looked towards where Kev was pointing and realised that Lori's flat looked directly onto the old place.

'How can she look out to that every day and not be affected by it?' Charley asked, feeling the emotion beginning to build already.

Kev sighed. 'I have no idea. I'm having trouble with it myself.'

Charley looked around. The estate hadn't changed at all. Most of the flats looked like they had the same windows, the same doors. The edges of the pavements still dipped in the same places. She remembered every detail as clearly as though she had last visited the day before.

'Shall we?' Kev said, interrupting her thoughts just as nausea was beginning to set in. Strange how memories of the past can weigh heavy on your stomach.

They headed into the flat and upstairs, where the front door was open and Lori was stood waiting for them.

'Charley,' Lori said, and then tears began streaming down her face. 'I can't *believe* you're here.'

Charley couldn't believe it herself. Dunreath set her uneasy. Staring at her sister, Charley couldn't help but feel out of place. There was a clear difference in appearance between them. Lori looked older than her years. Charley did not. She supposed good living, fresh air and good food – or lack of those things – were the reasons.

What she hadn't expected was to feel the same emotion displayed by her sister. After years of being absent from this so-called family, with just the odd phone call between them and no real connection, Charley thought she bore no emotional attachment to her blood family. It seemed she was wrong.

'Neither can I,' she finally replied.

'Come here, you,' Lori said as she stretched out her arms. As much as she didn't want to, Charley leaned in and gave a small hug. She hadn't hugged her sister since she was fourteen years old.

Pulling away, she sighed and said, 'So, how are things?'

She noticed Lori glance between her siblings and the unease settled in her stomach as she walked through the small flat – the same layout as the one she'd grown up in, minus one bedroom.

Once inside the living room, Charley saw a third person. At first, she didn't recognise the girl. Then the memory came, her face framed by an iPad screen. The woman who claimed to be her husband's fiancée.

'You? What the hell are you doing here?' Charley said, her voice venomous.

'Charley,' Kev said, stepping between them and looking her in the eye. 'This is my daughter, Sammi.'

Charley's brow furrowed. 'Your daughter? Is this some kind of joke?'

'I just want to say sorry for all this. I swear, I knew *nothing* about you,' Sammi said, her tone solemn.

Charley scoffed loudly. 'Is this an ambush or something?'

'Charley,' Lori said. 'We asked you to come because, one, we genuinely do want to see you. But there's something bigger going on, and I'm so sorry to say it, but your husband is at the heart of it all.'

Pacing back and forth, Charley began to control her breathing. 'Lori, you better start explaining what is going on. Why is my husband's bit on the side standing here? I mean, this can't just be a coincidence, can it?'

Everyone was quiet and Charley took in each of their faces.

'You're right. It's not a coincidence. Your husband is Logan Greer,' Lori continued. 'And I'm so sorry to say this to you, Charley, especially when we haven't seen each other for such a long time. But he's been lying to you the entire time you've been married, most likely the entire duration of your relationship.'

Charley rubbed at her throat, trying to ease the spasms in her airways. She took long, steady breaths and tried not to panic.

'Why do you say that?'

She noticed Kev staring at her and the sympathy in his eyes made her feel humiliated.

'Charley, Logan Greer used to be my dealer back when we all lived here. I owed him a lot of money around the time Mum and Dad died. I did a runner and then…' He cleared his throat and glanced at Lori.

'Back then, Logan went by a different name. He called himself Ped, and he had a mate called Jambo. Me and Steph went on a double date with them and…'

Charley zoned out; sat down before she fell down as she listened to Lori tell her story.

Her husband had tried to kill her sister, and she'd left him for dead in self-defence. That was why he'd married Charley. He'd wanted revenge and it seemed he had all the time in the world, because his revenge had been a slow process.

Logan was a liar. Her marriage was a lie. And she'd been the last one to see it.

FIFTY-SIX

'Are you okay?' Lori asked as Charley sipped on some water.

'I'm fine,' she replied. 'I was just hot and overwhelmed by everything.'

Lori gave Kev a concerned glance and Charley shifted in her seat.

'I'm a big girl, Lori. In spite of what you might think.'

Lori took in her sister's features, all the while in a silent panic that the longer she sat on her hands doing nothing, her son could be dead or at least on that road.

'Lori,' Charley said, taking Lori away from the thoughts of what might be. 'I'm so sorry for what you both went through. But can I ask, how do you know for sure that Logan is this guy, Ped, or whatever you called him?'

Lori stood up and pulled up her T-shirt. Kev turned away and Sammi stood too. They showed her their saltire scars and Charley's expression soured.

Lori's eyes filled with tears. 'I only realised when I saw Sammi's scar. Steph has them too.'

Charley stared at her with wide eyes and an open mouth. She shook her head. 'No.'

Lori wiped away her tears. 'No?'

'This can't be happening. It can't.'

Kev shifted on the sofa next to her. 'Charley, I get it. You don't want to believe it. Of course you don't.'

Charley turned sharply towards her brother. 'That saltire. Anyone could have that ring.'

'We didn't say it was a ring,' Sammi said, and Charley closed her eyes before running her hands over her face.

'He has a saltire sovereign as his wedding ring. Apparently it belonged to his dad, who died when he was a child.' Charley let out a sob and then quickly composed herself. 'He used to burn Logan with it as a kid.'

That would explain why he had decided to do that to Lori and Steph, and Sammi too. And how many other women out there had that same scar? 'Hurt people hurt people, or so the saying goes,' Lori said. 'But that doesn't excuse his abuse towards any of us, Charley. It doesn't.' Charley sobbed into her hands and Lori waited for her to compose herself, then she took her hand and said, 'Charley, he's been the master manipulator of all of us. He went after you when you left the estate, he groomed you, sweetheart. He abused me and who knows how many others over the years. I know this sounds crazy, but it's true. Logan's a complete lunatic and he needs to be stopped. He's already shot Reece and—'

'Who?' Charley said, sniffing loudly and wiping away tears.

Lori tilted her head back and stared up at the ceiling. There was still so much that Charley didn't know.

'Stephanie's son. Logan shot him earlier tonight because I left them for dead in those towers all those years ago. He has my son and I need you to help me to find him. You might be the only person who could help stop Logan from killing all of us,' Lori pleaded.

Charley began pacing the floor. She looked harassed. Then she stopped, sucked air into her lungs and stood in the middle of the floor. 'Where is he now?' she asked, eyeing each of them.

'Probably hiding out in one of his businesses,' Sammi replied.

Charley frowned. '*One* of his businesses?'

'Yeah, the café, the pub, the demolition site; he owns the security firm manning it. He could be at any of them,' Sammi continued.

Charley's face flushed and Lori could tell she'd been none the wiser about any of it.

Pulling out her phone, Charley glanced down at the screen. 'I blocked him when I found out about you, Sammi. If I'm going to be able to help, I need to find him right now.'

Lori felt her eyes pool with tears once again. 'He's dangerous, Charley.'

'Yeah, all the more reason for it to be me who goes to him. He'll think I'm here to discuss our marriage. He won't know I've seen you all. It has to be this way.'

In awe of her sister's bravery, Lori pulled her in. 'You can't go alone.'

'I have to.'

FIFTY-SEVEN

Lori sat on the front step outside her flat in Blackhill Court and looked up at her old place. Living there with two drug-addicted parents and two siblings had come with its fair share of stresses. But nothing like how she felt now. If someone had told her back then that she'd be faced with the man who'd abused her and her best friend two decades later, in order to save her son, she'd have laughed in their face and accused them of being high on drugs. Now she knew she had no choice but to go back to the past.

'Are you there, Lori?' the voice said down the phone, his voice making her shudder.

'I'm here,' she replied quietly, trying to stop the panic from spewing out of her. 'Where's Jay? Where's my boy? Is he still alive?'

'And are you alone?' Logan asked, ignoring her questions.

'I'll do whatever it is you want. Just give me some proof that my boy is still alive. Please.'

Silence, followed by footsteps and then a loud knocking sound. 'Tell her you're still alive, eh?'

The distant sound of Jay calling for her made her heart surge and her stomach roll all at once. He was still breathing, but for how long?

'I'll ask you again, Lori. Are you alone?'

'Yes, I'm alone. Now, what the fuck do you want, Ped?'

Just saying his name made her skin crawl. Was she ready to look him in the eye again? No. But there was nothing she wouldn't do for her son, or Reece, for that matter.

'My *name* is Logan. And I think it's obvious what I want, don't you?'

'Not really,' she said, trying to make herself sound as calm and unfazed as possible, which was ridiculous; they both knew she was terrified, although not for herself, and he'd be banking on that.

Lori noticed the stone next to her foot. She picked it up and started scraping it along the step next to her shoe.

'What I do know is that you shot Reece and, as much as you might have a good aim, he's still alive, and the doctors think he'll pull through,' she lied. 'Sorry to disappoint you.'

His throaty laugh felt like it crawled out of the speaker and wrapped its slimy fingers around her neck.

'To be fair, to know that you and Stephanie are suffering because of what's happening to your boys is good enough for me. What's disappointing is that *you're* still alive, Lori.'

Lori forced out a laugh. 'No, what's disappointing, you abusive, evil prick, is that *you're* still alive. I made the rookie mistake of assuming you were dead when, really, I should have checked. I should have rammed those nails from that old plank of wood into your throat.'

'Ooh, seems you've got a huge set of balls, speaking to me like that when I could snuff out your boy's life in a second. I suppose being dragged up in Blackhill by your druggie parents toughened you up. Not sure you'd be so fucking cheeky if you were stood in front of me, would you?'

'Suppose they were good for something.' Lori bit the inside of her cheek so hard, the iron taste of blood on her tongue was immediate. 'Tell me, how's my sister these days? You know, the one you're married to?' The words left her mouth before she could stop herself. Fuck. She'd landed Charley in the shit now, but she couldn't change it.

Silence followed the question.

'You sought her out, didn't you? For revenge? Or do you like them young, Ped? Because she was just fourteen when you went after her, wasn't she?'

The sound of his breath down the line made Lori's skin crawl, making the hairs from every follicle on her body stand to attention.

'Revenge was a bonus,' Logan replied. 'Charley was young, impressionable. Everything I was looking for in a woman.'

'She wasn't a woman. She was a child, Ped. That makes you a paedophile, you know that, right?' Lori said, as she got to her feet and stepped down onto the pavement. If he was stood in front of her now, she'd gouge his eyes out. His words made her feel sick.

'Hardly. We didn't sleep together until she was sixteen. And, I mean, I could have just come looking for you and Stephanie. But where's the fun in that? I'm the type of person who likes to feel like I've earned the outcome of my plans; I don't seek instant gratification. I much prefer the long game, if that makes sense.'

'Nothing you say or do makes sense to me,' she said through gritted teeth. 'Now, where *the fuck* is my son?'

'If you want to see Jay again, then meet me at the third tower. Now. I have eyes on every inch of this site, including inside each of the six towers. I'll know if you've come alone. And if you don't, I'll make sure that Jay's voice begging for mercy is the last thing you hear before I fucking kill you. Am I clear?'

Lori closed her eyes and tried to breathe through the immeasurable sense of terror each word carried. He'd injected his poison into each and every person she'd ever cared about. She had to play this properly.

'I said, am I clear?'

Eyes stinging from the tears behind her closed lids, Lori nodded, cleared her throat and said, 'Yes. I heard you.'

A shiver ran up her spine at the sound of his callous laughter before the line went dead.

She pulled the phone away from her ear, stared down at the screen where Jay stared back at her. Her baby boy. The baby she'd never planned for, yet he'd given her everything she'd ever needed. Stability, a reason to get up in the morning. After what had happened with Ped and Jambo back in 2001, Lori had often wondered if there was ever a good reason to keep going; to keep breathing. Jay was the only male in Lori's life who'd treated her with any kind of respect. Jay's dad had been a one-night stand and he'd disappeared off the face of the earth before she'd even realised she was pregnant. Her own dad hadn't even known the meaning of the word respect, and her brother, he was too off his face most of her life for him to know that the word even existed, let alone what it meant.

Lori turned, looked up at the building where she lived and wondered if she'd ever see it again.

FIFTY-EIGHT

Logan stood with his back to the basement door, tapping the phone on his chin as he listened for sounds of movement beneath him. Jay had been silent since Logan had left him, other than to call out to let Lori know he was still alive.

Pushing himself off the door, Logan turned and used the top corner of the phone to knock on the door.

Tap. Tap. Tap.

'Mummy's on her way, Jay boy,' Logan sang.

'Fuck off,' Jay shouted back.

'Ha, I can see you take your big balls from Mummy. Can't say I'm surprised she's got a mouth on her, given what she did to me. Not that she finished the job properly. Well, not on me, anyway. Poor Jambo, he didn't deserve to die the way he did. And he certainly doesn't deserve his final resting place to be down in that fucking pit with you. But what was I supposed to do? Move him? That would have raised too many questions, created too many issues for me. If I'd done that, we might not be here today, waiting for that final, dramatic climax.'

'You're a fucking lunatic,' Jay called back. 'She only hurt you to get away from you.'

Logan nodded, then a sudden sense of rage came over him. He slammed his fist into the metal door and shouted, 'I'm a lunatic because your mother tried to fucking *kill* me. Smashed me over the head with a fucking piece of wood with nails sticking out. I've still got the fucking scars to prove it.'

He remembered that moment as though it was just yesterday, the scars on his face tingling as the images came into his head one after the other. It wasn't so much the act of violence against him but the hours that followed.

'So many people are dealing with their past traumas these days, Jay boy. You know, going to see a therapist has become a bit of a trend. Everyone seems to have one.'

'You need a fucking straightjacket and a padded cell,' Jay called back, his voice a little more enraged than before.

Logan laughed loudly. 'Aye, maybe. But if that was the case, then I wouldn't be getting everything I've ever wanted. You see, Jay, *this* is my therapy. This is justice. Poor Jambo never got his, so I'm taking it for both of us.'

A sudden bang on the other side of the door made Logan jump and he stood back.

'Let me fucking out of here!'

The shock turned to humour and Logan began to laugh. 'What, before the party has started? No chance. The demolition is scheduled for tomorrow, Jay. But I've brought it forward. You and Mummy are getting a sneak preview of what it's like to see a building fall to the ground. You get front-row seats. Well, not front row *exactly*. Call it an immersive experience.'

Silence followed, and Logan could only imagine the look on Jay's face as he picked apart what he'd just been told. It wouldn't be an easy thing to digest, to know that you were going to die by being crushed by a falling building.

'You'll never get away with this,' Jay shouted.

Logan ran a hand over his well-groomed beard. As much as it was neat and tidy, it was thick enough to cover the scars Lori Graham had left behind.

'Oh aye? Well, your mother got away with what she did for almost two and a half decades. By the time I'm done with you both, you'll be nothing but dust, quite literally. You see, with a demolition like this one, about ninety-five per cent of all materials are usually recycled. And I'm going to include you and your mother in that. Bones can be crushed down into dust. Oh, don't worry. I'll make sure you both fit in the crusher, even if I have to cut you into tiny fucking pieces.'

Another few thumps from the other side of the door before silence followed. Logan imagined what it would feel like to know that Lori Graham had suffered before her ultimate demise. To know that her son died a painful death before she did. It would be glorious after what she did to him.

Then he'd move on to Stephanie. Without Lori to protect her, and her son on the brink of death, she'd be the easiest target of all.

FIFTY-NINE

Charley stood with her back to the Dunreath Arms, which apparently her husband owned and she'd known nothing about. She hadn't even known that he was living in Dunreath while working. He'd made her believe he was through in Edinburgh. And she'd believed him, like she'd believed all his bullshit. Her bag hung by her leg as she stared out at the village and the uncertainty of her future life. Her entire relationship with Logan had been a lie. Her entire life one big theatre production, and yet she'd been the only one not in on the script.

Thomas and Callan came into her mind. Their dad, the man they adored, was not real. Yet they had Logan's blood in their veins. Would they turn out like him? Not a chance. Charley would put every effort into making sure that never happened.

What Logan had done was truly evil, and there was no way that she could walk away and say nothing. She had to confront him, at least about their marriage.

Was Logan a killer? A lunatic like Kev said? Had he really tried to hurt her sister back then? Had he really sought her out for revenge? How sick and twisted did someone have to be in order to do something like that? Something so calculated? Bringing kids into the whole thing was a step too far, surely?

'Here, hen? You waitin' fur that taxi?' A woman around Charley's age interrupted her thoughts. She took in the woman's appearance. She was bedraggled, more than a bit worse for wear. The woman reminded Charley of her mother.

She shook her head. 'No, you go on ahead.'

The woman flashed a toothless smile at Charley. A pang of sadness hit her then. What had happened in this woman's life that left her looking the way she did?

It could have been you, a voice whispered in her head.

And the voice was right. Life could have gone a very different way for Charley had she not got away from Dunreath. Margaret and Ronnie were the only parents she'd needed in life. They were wonderful; still very much a part of her life now and wonderful grandparents to Callan and Thomas. And as much as they'd gently warned her of their thoughts about Logan, they'd accepted her choice to marry him even though he was much older than her. She was twenty at the time, and he was twenty-three. That didn't seem like such a gap, but when she thought about meeting him at fourteen and he'd been seventeen, she knew now that was all kinds of wrong.

The driver rolled down the passenger window and leaned over. 'You've been warned already, Francesca, you're barred from our firm.' He sounded irritated.

'Whit the fuck fur? Av no done anyhin!' the woman suddenly screamed, making Charley jump. The sound of her voice, the slow, slurring words, transported Charley back twenty-four years to Blackhill Court, building six, flat three. Growing up in that place, Charley thought all people spoke like that. It hadn't been until she went out into the real world after being taken in by Ronnie and Margaret that she realised she'd lived in a very different place to the rest of the world. Well, the majority of it anyway.

'Aye, maybe not today. I'm warning you, even attempt to open the door and I'll phone the police. Do you want to end up in the jail again?'

The woman, Francesca, tutted loudly and moved away, sticking a finger up on each hand as she walked backwards.

'Fucking hell,' Charley whispered, remembering why she had been glad to leave Blackhill Court behind, grateful for the life she was living. Or at least had been living, up until a few days ago. Up until she realised the truth of who her husband was.

Pulling out her phone, she glanced down at the family screen saver and, as if on cue, a car drove past with all its windows down and music blaring. That song. The song she and Logan danced to at their wedding. 'City of Blinding Lights' by U2.

The car stopped right in front of her as it joined the queue for the red light at the end of the road, and her chest felt like it was going to explode. Her throat constricted as she stared down at Logan's face. His smile. His eyes. All so attractive, all so comforting, yet now she felt like she didn't know him at all. She was married to a stranger who'd apparently done some horrific things.

She looked up at the pub once more and fought back tears as Bono's voice sang the words to her very favourite song. The lyrics hit different now. She missed Logan, of course she did. But she missed the version she knew of him back then. She missed the feeling of normality; of knowing her life wasn't a lie.

Breathing deeply to contain the unease inside her, Charley glanced down the street towards Clydeview Towers. She could just about see the top of each of the six buildings. She'd already checked in at the pub and the café. Logan wasn't there. That left the demolition site. A place she had never visited when growing up in Dunreath. A place she had no idea her husband owned now. A taxi pulled up beside her, joining the queue of traffic, and she bent down to peer in to the driver.

'Excuse me, can you take me to Clydeview?' she said to the driver who'd just threatened the woman with the police.

'Aye, hen,' he replied with curiosity in his voice.

Charley was already climbing into the taxi. 'Thank you.'

'Nae bother, love,' the driver said, setting the meter. 'You know that place is closed off to the public, don't you?' he said. 'Those flats are due to be demolished tomorrow. If you want to watch the demolition, you need to do it from the very top of the village itself.'

She only nodded as she put on her belt, and the driver pulled away from the pub.

Charley glanced down at her phone again. Her two boys' faces smiling up at her, Logan's full of lies and deceit when, before, it had just been full of happiness.

SIXTY

The machines Reece was hooked up to began beeping loudly and quickly and Stephanie's heart surged in her chest. Immediately reaching for the call button on Reece's bed, she began pressing it over and over, screaming for help.

Getting to her feet and rushing around the bed, Stephanie pulled the door open and rushed down the corridor, shouting for nurses and doctors to help her son.

Everything from that moment was a blur. It was like she'd lost her ability to see and hear properly, as blood rushed in her ears while she was told to wait outside the room.

They worked on Reece for what felt like hours, and nothing seemed to be happening. He was dying and there was nothing anyone could do to stop it.

'Come on, love. Try to breathe,' a woman said to her, and Stephanie turned to see a woman wearing blue scrubs, with a concerned look on her face.

She wanted to tell the woman to go away, to leave her alone. But then, did she want to be on her own when the inevitable happened?

'What's happening?' Stephanie asked the woman.

'They're doing everything they can to save him, sweetheart,' she said.

'They will, won't they? They'll save him,' Stephanie asked, although she knew it was futile.

'Let's pray they can, love,' was all the woman said. Because how could she say that, no, her son wouldn't die?

Staring through the window as someone pumped at Reece's chest, wires sticking out of everywhere as his lifeless body lay on the hospital bed, Stephanie felt like a grenade, clutching at the pin in the hope that she wouldn't explode.

Then something happened. A change in the atmosphere. Everything and everyone seemed to stop. Everything went quiet.

'Time of death is sixteen forty,' one of the doctors said.

Stephanie banged her hands on the glass outside the room where Reece's body lay with strangers surrounding him. Her mouth was wide, attempting to scream, but no sound came out. She was paralysed as a nurse closed the blinds inside the room.

The woman in blue scrubs next to her wrapped her arms around Stephanie's shoulders as she collapsed to the floor, unable to comprehend what was happening. It was a nightmare. She had to be able to wake up from it. But as her screams intensified and the pain of the enormity of her loss expanded in her chest, Stephanie knew that she was never going to wake up. Not from this. This was real. This was happening.

'I'm so sorry for your loss,' the woman said, sitting down beside her, and Stephanie heard the emotion in her voice.

She glanced up at the nurse, who she could barely see through the tears. 'Please, tell them not to stop. He can't die. Not my boy. Not like this.'

The nurse had tears in her eyes, yet she fought back, kept her composure. 'I'm *so* sorry, sweetheart.'

Getting to her feet, Stephanie sat down on the chair outside the room and felt every inch of her body tremble as she pulled her phone out of her pocket. Hardly seeing the screen, she found Lori's number and hit call.

Lori answered, but Stephanie couldn't get her words out. All she could do was cry, loud and long wails echoing off the walls of the hospital corridor.

'Steph? Try to breathe,' Lori said so quietly down the line, Stephanie could barely hear her.

Swallowing down the hard lump in her throat and attempting to compose herself even just for a second, Steph tried to form the words on her tongue. 'He died,' she squeaked. 'My baby boy, he's gone.'

Lori was silent.

'You need to protect Jay,' Stephanie continued. 'You need to get him back. Get him home.'

Again, she was met with silence.

'Lori...' Stephanie almost choked as she tried to speak.

Lori's voice wobbled on the other end of the line and then she let out a sob. It set Stephanie off again and both cried down the phone to one another.

'Be with Reece,' Lori finally said. 'You need to focus on yourself. Do *not* come back here. You're safe at the hospital.'

'What are you going to do?'

'What I should have done twenty-four years ago. I'm going to finish what I fucking started. He won't get away with this, Steph. I *promise* you that. I'm doing this for Reece; I'm doing it for all of us.'

Stephanie tried to protest but it was too late. The line was already dead. And soon, Lori would be too.

'Shit,' she said, tears still cascading down her cheeks. '*Shit.*'

'Something I can help with?' the nurse said.

Stephanie glanced at her and then at the armed officer standing guard outside Reece's room.

'No. Nothing.' She got up and went into the hospital room, sat down by Reece and stared at him. He looked like he was sleeping. Peaceful and blissful. Unaware of what was unfolding in the real world. He wouldn't have to go through any more pain; any more fear.

She leaned over and pressed her lips against his forehead, held them there for as long as she could. His skin was beginning to turn cold, and it broke her heart that she'd never feel his warmth ever again. She'd never get to hug her son. Never get to tell him good night. Never have him bring her a cuppa, or her favourite slice of cake. She'd never hear his voice again.

Pulling herself into the standing position, Steph let out a long, laboured breath and tried her best to compose herself.

'I'm going to get him for you, baby. You didn't die for nothing; I'll make sure of it.'

Reluctantly, Stephanie headed for the door and placed her hand on the handle. Turning back, she took one last look at her son. The last time she'd ever see him was now.

'I love you, baby boy. I hope you knew that.'

SIXTY-ONE

This was it. It was time. Lori would swap her life for her son, and she would have no qualms about doing so. She was going to fight Logan to the very death. She had no other choice.

She stood outside the gates of the site and looked up at the towers. As much as tower three was the setting of her nightmare, the rest of the buildings made her feel just as scared of going any further. She could turn and walk away, but Jay didn't have that option, and she wasn't about to let Logan Greer take another young life in the name of revenge. There was no going back now. It would be just her and Logan. Face to face.

Heading towards the entrance, a Portakabin sat to the right just inside the gate, and Lori cursed the day Jay applied for the job as security guard for the site.

The towers loomed high above her with thick grey clouds hovering over them. Funny that, she thought. The sun never seemed to shine in this part of Dunreath.

The towers were spaced evenly, with enough space for car parks between them. Not that a lot of people who had ever lived at Clydeview owned a car. Might have stolen one, but never owned.

She glared at the third tower, the horrific memories coming thick and fast. Agreeing to go on that double date and getting into that car with Steph was the worst decision Lori had ever made in her life. If she had just said no, she wouldn't be stood here right now. Or maybe she would? Logan might have got to her some other way. It seemed he'd been hell-bent on getting his revenge, and he'd gone to some serious lengths to do so.

Glancing back at the cabin, Lori took a breath. The lights were off, the door closed. Logan would be waiting for her at the third tower. She'd come alone, like he'd requested. She needed to show she could do what was asked of her. If she deviated in any way, he'd kill Jay sooner than planned.

She began to walk slowly towards tower three, taking each and every step as steadily as she could. Glancing from left to right, it was abundantly clear that there was no one else on the site.

The sound of rushing footsteps on gravel from behind made her turn and, as she did, a shovel connected with her cheek, making it feel like her face had just exploded before she fell to the ground.

SIXTY-TWO

Sammi stared down at the handwritten note she'd found in the kitchen and read it aloud.

> *Gone for a walk to clear my head and work out how to help Jay. Back soon. Lori.*

Kev shook his head and took the note from Sammi's hand. 'What the fuck is she doing just disappearing like this? And now of all times. *Jesus.*'

'You think she's going to do something stupid?' Sammi asked, a genuine sense of fear rushing through her. 'Now that I think of it, it wasn't the best idea to let Charley go by herself either.'

Kev began to pace the floor.

Sammi raised a brow. 'Lori could get herself killed.'

Kev nodded. 'She's walking right into the path of a nutjob if she is headed his way. We need to find out where he is; we need to stop this.'

Sammi thought back to when she'd first met him. Logan had made himself look like a stand-up guy. A businessman who cared about her. He'd thrown the hook right to her and she'd caught it with both hands.

'We?' Sammi exclaimed, then shook her head. 'He won't hesitate to do us all in, Kev. I'm a fucking idiot for ever getting involved with him.'

Sammi pulled out her phone and searched for Logan's number. Raising the phone to her ear, she held up her hand when it started to ring. 'Logan?'

Kev's expression turned to shock, mouthing the words, 'What the fuck are you doing?'

'What the fuck do *you* want?' Logan answered, the anger in his voice palpable.

'I wanted to say sorry for leaving. I got a fright when I answered that iPad. I had no idea what I was doing and I regret it. Could we meet? Talk things through? I want us to give things another go.'

A bout of silence fell over the line and, for a moment, Sammi thought he'd hung up.

'Nah, we're done,' he said, his tone blunt and full of truth. 'I was stupid getting into a relationship with a daft wee lassie like you when I had a real wife at home.'

Sammi narrowed her eyes, the sense of anger translating down the line and seeping into her bones. 'Or are you angry that you got caught? Not just cheating on your wife, I mean. For getting caught living a double life? In one life you're Logan and in the other one you're Ped: the drug-dealing, sexually abusive narcissist trying to get revenge on the Graham family.'

Sammi glanced up to see Kev's eyes on her, wide and full of terror.

Silence again on the line, although this time she heard a breath catch in his throat.

'You still there?'

'Yer da tell you about me then? Mad junkie Kev still on the gear? Aye, before you ask, I knew he was your old man. I knew his missus, if you can call her that. Loved the gear, your ma. Was always looking for ways to pay rather than cash. I obliged, of course.' Logan laughed and it was a menacing sound.

'So that was why you got involved with me? You knew I was his daughter?' Sammi said, dumbfounded that she'd been duped too.

'Is he there with you?' he asked, ignoring her question.

Sammi glanced at Kev. 'He's here.'

'Put him on.'

She held the phone out to the man who'd only just come back into her life. They were trying to build a relationship, having missed out on each other for years. Logan could put a stop to that, and very quickly if he wanted to, and now she regretted everything she'd just said to him on the phone.

Kev took the phone and hit the loudspeaker icon. 'Ped?'

'Ah, Kev, my old mucker. How the *fuck* are things?'

Kev closed his eyes for a moment and, when he reopened them, Sammi saw something different in his expression.

'Old mucker? That's something we never were, Ped. You were my dealer, that's it. I was just an idiot who kept coming back for another fix, building up more debt than was ever possible to pay back. And you knew exactly what you were doing, you piece of shit. Preying on people like me, and worse, just to line your pockets.'

'Och, come on, Kev. Don't be like that. You were the biggest junkie in the estate, there was no way you weren't going to come to me for drugs on the daily. And I'm glad you did. You were my biggest source of income; until you stopped fucking paying. Speaking of money, you still owe me.'

Sammi heard the crunch of Kev's teeth. 'I owe you fuck all. You took what you thought was yours when you lured my sister and her best pal to that fucking building.'

Logan's laughter sent a shiver up Sammi's spine. 'Aye, well, I'm not finished with any of you just yet.'

The line went dead and Kev stood stock-still, holding the phone in his hand.

SIXTY-THREE

The pain radiated from her cheek, all the way up and around to the back of her skull. The bastard had hit her hard, but not hard enough. Lori was alive and that meant there was still a tiny glimmer of hope that she would be able to put a stop to what he was planning to do to Jay. No one else mattered, not even Lori. If she had to die to save her son, then so bloody be it.

Her left eye was glued shut and, as much as she tried to peel it open, the lids wouldn't move.

She sucked in a lungful of air and tried to move. Nothing happened, other than pain everywhere.

'Welcome back to the land of the fucking living,' his voice snarled from somewhere close by.

Opening her right eye, Lori wondered if she'd either gone completely blind or if she was in the deepest, darkest part of the tower, because she could not see a thing.

'Aren't you going to say hello to your boy?' he said. His voice teased out a snigger and it made Lori's skin crawl. 'I mean, you're going to be saying bye to each other very soon, so you'd best do your talking now while you can.'

Rising panic flooded Lori's chest as she tried to move again, this time feeling a rush of pins and needles in her legs. She was lying face down in the foetal position with her legs and wrists tied together.

'You might not have finished the job twenty-four years ago, Lori. But I'll make damn fucking sure I finish you and your fucking boy tonight. Good news, the demolition starts tomorrow. And you two get front-row seats to the fucking show.'

She tried to keep herself composed, calm, but all she could think about was where Jay was.

'Where is he?' she said and, as her jaw moved while she spoke, another pain shot through her face to the back of her skull.

'He's lying right next to you,' Logan replied, before a sudden bright beam of light was shone into her face. Squinting against the light, Lori could just about make out the outline of her son. As her one good eye adjusted, her vision became clearer, and there he was. Lying facing her in the same position as she was. Some kind of gag stuffed into his mouth with tape across his face. His eyes were wide with fear, and blood stained his face.

'You can't do this,' Lori said. 'You'll never get away with it. People know I'm here. People know I've come to see you after what you did to Reece.'

She was lying, of course. And now she could have kicked herself for not telling anyone where she was going. Although if she had, they'd have only tried to stop her. And she didn't have a plan. She hadn't thought any of it through. All she'd wanted was to get to Jay, and Logan had gladly led her right to him.

Why the fuck hadn't she just told the police? How stupid was she for thinking she could deal with this on her own? All these years, she'd worried that if she'd ever come clean, she'd be sent to prison for murder even though it was self-defence. Violence against women was rarely taken seriously back then. And she was just a young kid. Barely sixteen and, with a family reputation like hers, she suspected no one would have believed her anyway.

'You're not a very good liar, Lori,' Logan said.

'You are, though. Aren't you? You're the king of lies. I mean, seeking out my baby sister and marrying her just to exact your revenge on me and my brother? What the fuck is that all about?'

Jay's eyes were wider again, shaking his head furiously at her, as though he was worried that she'd make things worse, make him angrier somehow.

'It's all about what you said. Exacting my revenge. I wanted to take everything from Kev and you and that bitch of a pal of yours. So, I did. Or at least, I've started. Charley was a surprise. I didn't expect to like her, never mind fall in love with her. And my kids? She'll never take them away from me. Those boys will carry on my legacy long after I'm gone.'

How he spoke about his kids made her feel sick. Logan was evil, through and through.

'You're only capable of loving yourself. You're a sick fuck, Ped,' Lori growled. 'She'll never let you anywhere near those kids.'

'You made me that way. You and that bitch Stephanie. If it wasn't for you, I'd be living a normal life.'

Logan paced slowly back and forth in the small room he was keeping them in. It was familiar. The smell, the sense of dread it gave her. And then she remembered. This was where he'd kept them back then. Fear turned to terror, but she refused to show it.

'And what about before us? Your dad?'

'Whatever you think you know about me, you're wrong.'

'Your dad used to burn you with that ring, didn't he? That's why you're so fucked up in the head. It's nothing to do with me and Steph. You were a mess before you met us.'

Logan stopped, bent down to retrieve something. It was large as he strode over to her and shoved it in her face. 'This is what made me who I am today, Lori,' he spat. 'My best friend has lain down here for fucking years because of you. He was like a brother to me. The only person to accept me for what I was. He was there when my life was shit, and you took him from me.'

Lori tried to back away from the human skull staring her in the face. Its greyish colour and dark caverns where the eyes used to be made her feel instantly nauseous.

'When I came around that night, when I saw him lying there, I vowed I'd get you. I vowed I'd take you the fuck out. He didn't deserve to die like that. You stole his life from him, and me. This way, Jambo gets to watch as I take justice for him.'

A rush of saliva filled Lori's mouth and vomit spewed onto the floor, missing Jay by centimetres.

'You want to know what happened that night after you and that bitch bolted?'

'Not really,' Lori said, spitting bile onto the floor and mouthing an apology at Jay, who'd already closed his eyes and was trying to turn away from the pool of vomit near his face.

'Well, you're going to fucking hear it,' Logan spat. 'Because you need to know what you did that night. You need to know why your life is going to end here tonight.'

SIXTY-FOUR

2001

Ped opened his eyes and looked around. He couldn't see a thing, the basement was too black to even see the outline of his hand as he held it up to his face. The iron stench of blood, however, was overwhelming. A sudden awareness of the pain in his face took over and, moving his hand towards the sticky surface of his cheek, he winced at the touch.

Getting to the sitting position, Ped felt every bone in his body scream in pain. The back of his head, the side of his face, his abdomen. And his leg. He was sure it was broken.

'Jesus fucking Christ,' he hissed as he tried to stand up, the pain in his leg unbearable. He needed to find Jambo and get them out of here. He needed to find those little bitches and put an end to them and fast, otherwise they'd go to the police and they'd both end up in jail. Ped was owed too much money from his punters, there was too much money left to be made. He couldn't go to jail. He had endless opportunities to make money on the outside, and he wasn't about to let two little bitches like Lori and Stephanie stop him in his tracks. 'Jambo, where the fuck are you? Are you all right?'

But just as the words were out of his mouth, the realisation of what had happened began to creep in. The fight. The girls trying to escape. The plank of wood with the nails sticking out of it slamming into the side of his face.

Shit. How long had he been out for? Minutes? Hours? And where the hell was Jambo?

Forcing himself to his feet, Ped looked around, trying to see in the dark. He took an agonising step forward and tripped over something. He growled from the pain as he went down, his leg unable to do what his brain was telling it to.

As much as it was pitch-black, he sensed something near to him. Something large. The smell of blood was stronger down on the floor.

No. Not something. *Someone.*

'Jambo?' Ped whispered, his eyes trying to adjust to the darkness. 'Jesus, Jambo,' he said again, this time realising that he was the only one down in the basement who was alive.

Ped was shaking him now. Desperately trying to wake him, knowing that it was futile. Jambo was well and truly dead. The gouge in his throat, the blood seeping from it and onto Ped's hands told him as much.

Ped sat back and stared down at the silhouette of his friend. They'd been best mates since childhood. Jambo had been the one to make Ped feel better after one of his dad's tirades of abuse, followed by a slap, a kick or a burn. The saltire scars after all these years were still there, although some were beginning to fade.

Ped felt for his dad's ring on his hand. It was still there. That thing was the man's pride and fucking joy. He'd hate to think Ped had it after he'd died. That was enough for Ped to keep it.

He glanced down at Jambo once more. Not only had they been friends since they were kids, they'd been dealing together since they could, as far back as fifteen years old. Stashing ecstasy tablets under Jambo's mattress and selling up to a thousand a week around Dunreath. Things had gone from strength to strength, and they'd moved on to heavier substances, making more money than ever before. The good thing about Ped and Jambo, they knew how to be discreet. Never flashing their cash or showing that they even had money. It kept the police off their backs and, to be fair, no one in the area was ever sober enough to suspect they were ever up to anything. Two pals with similar backgrounds, abusive parents, had come together and made something of themselves. They only had each other. No other family members existed; none that cared enough anyway. It was either become the addict, or supply the addict. Ped never liked being out of control of his body. Neither had Jambo. So they'd decided that dealing was the way forward for quick income.

Now he was on his own. Jambo was dead and Ped was severely injured. How was he going to get out of this? He couldn't go to the hospital, they'd ask questions about what had happened to him. He could lie and say he was attacked, but being believed wasn't something he was banking on. No one would come looking for Jambo. His extended family were dead thanks to the fucking Fyfe brothers.

He'd have to leave Jambo down here. The place where he was murdered would be the place where he'd rest for eternity. The idea ripped him from the inside out.

'Pair of bitches,' he hissed, before a sudden and unexpected wave of emotion took over. His eyes pooled with tears and he wiped angrily at them with the back of his bloodied hand. Composing himself, he said, 'I'll fucking kill them for this, mate. I'm not going to let them away with this.'

Ped dragged himself to the bottom of the stairs and reached for the light. He switched it on and light flooded the basement, beaming down onto Jambo's dead body, his head a mash of blood and concrete.

Ped quickly turned away, tried to suppress the urge to throw up. Closing his eyes, he took a deep breath through his mouth so he didn't have to breathe in the stench of blood. A mix of his own and Jambo's.

'I'm sorry, mate,' Ped whispered, emotion scratching at his throat as he turned out the light.

Dragging himself up the stairs, he reached the top and slipped through the door, hoping that the towers would live up to their expectations and keep him concealed from anyone who might be lurking. Albeit, those people would likely be junkies, off their faces and completely unaware of what was going on around them. He should know, he was their dealer after all.

Thankful that it was dark outside, Ped slowly limped across the grounds in which the towers sat, no longer inhabited by the people who once lived there, and headed towards the car they'd stolen earlier in the night.

It was gone.

'Fuck,' he said under his breath, looking around in the hope that he'd see it. Maybe some kids had taken it, played around with it or moved it. He knew it was ridiculous to think such a thing. The car was gone. Stolen for a second time that night. Then it occurred to him. Maybe Lori and Stephanie had taken it? They were from Blackhill Court, at least one of them would know how to start a car without a key.

Blood burning in his veins, Ped looked up at tower three and gritted his teeth. He was going to have to sort himself out, get cleaned up. He hoped his leg wasn't broken, maybe just a sprain? If he could get himself together, he could go on as though nothing had happened. He'd need to lay low in the home he was living in, but he could get away with that for a few weeks. The staff didn't much bother with him so long as he didn't cause any issues. He'd been there long enough now that they knew to just leave him be, in his room. He needed to get his shit together, make sure he had a roof over his head while he healed physically. If any of the punters questioned him about Jambo, what would he say? How would he explain his absence? That he'd moved away? Would anyone even care?

One thing was for sure. He wanted Lori and Stephanie to think he was dead. If they did, they wouldn't live their lives looking over their shoulders for him. That meant he could go on with life, planning out what he was going to do to them.

As soon as he was eighteen and free of the system, he'd move away. Start again. Then he'd come back in a few years and put an end to them. They wouldn't get away with this. There was no way he was going to let them. No matter how long it would take. They, *especially* Lori, would pay for what they'd done.

SIXTY-FIVE

2025

Lori had managed to manoeuvre herself into the sitting position and now sat with her back to the wall, staring up at Ped; or Logan, as he referred to himself these days. She wondered just how insane he was to think he was the one wronged the most out of everyone involved in this fucked-up scenario.

'So, you see, Lori. What you did was brutal. You let Jambo die. You left me for dead. You took my car and—'

'We took the car you *stole* to lure us to this fucking hellhole,' she shot back at him, still reeling from the fact that he genuinely thought that his actions were justified. 'We used it to escape.'

Logan's eyes were like little balls of fire inside his head as he stared at her. She shifted her gaze to Jay, who still looked as terrified as ever.

'Don't look at him, look at me,' Logan said, jabbing a finger into her face. 'I'm the one running this. You need to know what's coming next.'

Lori wanted to throw herself at him, but with her arms tied behind her she couldn't move much. 'And what's that, Logan? You're going to bring the tower down on top of us? Is that what your plan is?' She almost grimaced at the idea of being crushed inside the very building she'd fled from back in 2001. How was she back here? With him of all people. 'Why didn't you just bring us all here together and be done with it? Why not kill us all right here?' she said, her voice high and full of rage.

Logan shrugged. 'It's more fun this way. Dragging Jay into it, letting him watch as his best pal was shot right over his shoulder. Wonder how he's doing now? You think he's dead yet?'

Lori couldn't speak. She was too angry and she didn't trust herself not to lash out and end up getting another shovel in the face. If she could avoid Jay seeing that at all costs, then she would.

'He's probably not far off it, if I'm honest. You think Stephanie is there with him? She'll get to watch him die. Isn't that nice? There for his birth, obviously,' he smirked, 'and there for his death. It's a privilege, really.'

Jay closed his eyes and Lori noticed tears dripping across the bridge of his nose. Her heart ached for him and for Reece.

'Anyway,' Logan clapped his hands and then rubbed them together, making both Lori and Jay jump, 'here's what's going to happen. Did you see the masonry crushing machine outside?'

Lori felt a surge of adrenaline in her veins.

'Well, there's already a big pile of masonry outside that needs to go through the crusher. We need to recycle ninety-five per cent of the materials from the demolition. So, here's my plan, and it's a good one, so listen carefully.'

Logan was pacing the floor like an excited child who'd just been told he was going to Florida for his summer holiday. The way he spoke about the process of the demolition, it was as though he'd memorised a script for this very moment.

'I'm going to kill you both. But don't worry, I've done my research. So, it takes about six to twelve hours for your blood to completely dry up. That's when I'll put you both through the machine; although I'll probably have to cut you into pieces first, not sure an entire body would fit through it, to be honest. It'll be like ashes but without the cremation. You'll both turn to sand. All you both have to do is decide where you'd like to be scattered.'

Jay sobbed silently in front of Lori, clearly terrified of dying in the most horrific way. Lori's terror hadn't peaked yet, for some strange reason. There wasn't much chance that either of them was going to get out of this situation. Unless she lied.

'When I arrived here, I was going to tell you something,' Lori started. She was lying, making it up as she went along, but she had no choice. She had to scare him into slowing down. 'I was about to tell you that there were armed officers at the hospital with Stephanie and Reece. She's told them everything, about what happened back then, about what we did to you and Jambo. She said that the police were on their way.'

Her throat ran dry as Logan stopped pacing. He turned his head sharply towards her and glared at her through narrowed eyes.

'Funny that, because I don't hear any sirens, do you?'

'They're not going to alert you that they're coming, are they? Not when they think you've got a gun. They'll want to play it smart.'

Logan's brow furrowed and his evil smile crept across his face. 'Nah. You're lying.'

'I'm not,' she said as steadily as possible. 'You go up there and check. You'll see the place surrounded. Steph's a smart woman, she'll know this is where you've taken us.'

Lori prayed to any God that would listen that she was right. Maybe Steph would tell the police everything. Something Lori should have done as soon as Reece was shot. Why the fuck hadn't she just swallowed her fear and done it?

Logan turned his head towards the top of the stairs and kept his eye on the door, as though contemplating that what Lori was saying might be the truth. If he did on some level believe her, then maybe she stood a chance of getting out of here. All the while that she was talking to him, she was gently wriggling her wrists around behind her, trying to free them.

Raising his arm and pointing out his index finger, without looking, Logan said, 'Don't fucking move from there.'

He slowly climbed the stairs and opened the door at the top, before leaving the basement and closing the door behind him.

Lori and Jay were alone in the basement, with just enough light to allow her to see how terrified Jay was.

'Jay, try to stay calm. I'm going to try to get us out of this,' she said. All the while, his eyes remained closed.

She wriggled more vigorously now, twisting and pulling, stretching the tie that bound her hands at her back.

And then she heard his voice from above. Logan. He was talking to someone.

'Someone's here,' Lori whispered.

She could scream, cry out for help. But would that put the person up there in danger too? What if it was Kev, or Sammi? Logan had a gun. He'd shoot them if Lori made a fuss.

She continued to wriggle, hoping that she would be able to loosen the binds enough to slip her wrists out.

SIXTY-SIX

'What the hell are *you* doing here?' Logan said as he stared at his wife.

'Charming, coming from your husband,' Charley replied, folding her arms across her body. 'I came to see you because, one, you're my husband; two, you're the father of our boys; and three, I wanted to see if we could try to work things out. We've been a couple for such a long time. I think that's something worth fighting for, don't you?'

Logan narrowed his eyes, looked his wife up and down. 'You said you wanted a divorce. That I would never see the kids again. And how did you know where to find me? Oh wait, you're in cahoots with your brother and sister, aren't you? That's how you found me.'

Charley blinked, her demeanour calm as always, unlike her brother and sister. Kev, the manic junkie always looking for the next poor prick to rob for drug money; or Lori, the little slapper who spat out a sprog without knowing who the dad was.

'Not in cahoots. Just been in touch, that's all. And I changed my mind about us,' she said smoothly. 'I didn't want to leave things the way we did. Me finding out about your other life via a video call and never actually seeing you again just didn't sit right with me. And believe it or not, you've been the only family I've had since I was fourteen; except for Margaret and Ronnie. You're the father of my kids. Surely that counts for something?'

Logan loosened his shoulders a little. He didn't need this right now, but in truth, he could use this to his advantage.

She peered over his shoulder at the basement door and frowned. 'What's down there?'

'My office,' he answered.

Charley's brow furrowed. 'I assumed your office was out at that Portakabin at the front entrance?'

It was Logan's turn to frown. 'How did you find this place? I never gave you the address.'

Charley smiled. 'You did.'

Logan's jaw tensed. '*No*, I didn't. I told you I was in Edinburgh. The reason I did that was because, if you haven't forgotten, I was having an affair with someone else and I didn't want you to find out.'

A look of shock crossed Charley's face momentarily, before she fixed it with a smile again. 'So, it's true then? Sammi, your fiancée? What age is she again? Twenty? That's a bit old for you, is it not? You normally go for girls in their teens?'

Logan stepped closer, his nose almost touching Charley's. 'What the fuck is that meant to mean?'

'Well,' Charley shrugged, stepping back and unfolding her arms, 'you went for me when I was fourteen. Remember when we first met at that children's home before I was placed with Ronnie and Margaret? You were so complimentary of me. Telling me I was too good to have come from a family like I did? You kind of love-bombed me, didn't you? Tricked me into thinking that you actually liked me, tricked me into thinking you loved me. Fuck, you married me to get me to believe it all. We had kids together, Logan.'

Logan eyed her suspiciously, looking her up and down, wondering where it was all going.

'You went for my sister, Lori, too. Was that before or after me? She was only sixteen; of age, yes. But it's still a sick fuck move to make, isn't it?'

'You shut your mouth,' he growled through bared teeth.

'Ah, there you are. The *real* you. *Peter* Logan Greer. Or Ped, as you used to go by. I know all about you, Logan. I know you kidnapped my sister and her friend. I know what you did to them. The fact you felt that it was justified because my brother owed you thousands of pounds in drug money is just ludicrous. And branding them with that fucking ring? How could you do that after what your own dad did to you? Or was that a fucking lie too?'

'You know that wasn't a lie. You've seen the scars yourself,' he said, his voice still low, growling.

'So, what? The rest of it's a lie? Lori, Kev, even Sammi? They're all telling lies about you?'

Logan felt his insides shift. His stomach whirred as the words left Charley's mouth. Flexing his fingers, he took a breath and said, 'I don't know *what* they told you, Charley, but whatever it was is utter bullshit. I did *not* rape anyone. Yes, I had an affair with Sammi. What can I say? She did something different for me in the bedroom department than you ever did and I just kept coming back for more.'

Charley raised a brow. 'Wow, you're scum, you know that?'

Logan slid his tongue across his top teeth and shook his head. 'You think you've got it all worked out, don't you?'

She laughed loudly and so suddenly it made Logan flinch. 'I think I'm close. We all know who you are, Logan. You're a rapist, a drug dealer. You think you're some kind of gangster when, really, you're just a prick who thinks he can exert his power over little people. I mean, you *are* just a prick, aren't you? It's not like you're working for anyone higher up: a Billy Bigger Bollocks? No one would take you on, you're too unpredictable, too erratic.'

Logan raised his hand so quickly he didn't give Charley enough time to react before he struck her across the face. She cried out and stumbled backwards, hitting her head on the wall behind her.

'Aye, you're right. I am erratic. And I,' he jabbed his finger into his own chest, 'am the boss. I am the gangster you should cross the street to get away from. I am the boss who will hunt you down if you owe me money, whether it's a quid or twenty thousand. And you? You're just as mouthy as your fucking sister.' He placed a hand under her arm and yanked her up. What he didn't anticipate was the blow that was coming his way. She swung her designer handbag, the one he'd bought her for their tenth wedding anniversary, and smashed it right into the centre of his face.

Letting go of Charley, he brought his hands to his face. Blood seeped all over his fingers. She'd burst his nose. There was most definitely a brick in that bag but, just as the thought came to his mind, a second blow came to the back of the head and, this time, his knees gave out, sending him crashing to the floor. He rolled onto his back just as she was about to bring the bag down on top of him and slid out from underneath before it hit. He grabbed at Charley's ankles and pulled her down. A bone crunching echoed around them and Charley let out a scream, but Logan was already on his feet, pulling her towards the basement on her back.

Opening the door behind him, he dragged Charley down the stairs, not bothering that her head hit each step on their descent.

'You'll fucking kill her,' Lori shouted.

'Aye, well I did say I was going to kill you all, didn't I?' Logan sneered back, before practically throwing Charley into the corner. He pointed a finger at them all and said, 'Don't even think about fucking moving because I won't hesitate to come in here and shoot you all in the fucking head.'

Everyone sat stock-still and Logan felt satisfied that he'd terrified them enough to comply.

He climbed the stairs, moved out to the corridor and slammed the door shut before leaning against it. Breathing deeply and trying to stay calm, Logan tried to gather his thoughts. But how the fuck could he stay calm? He'd been ambushed by his fucking wife.

He raised his knee and slammed his foot back onto the metal door, a loud clanging sound reverberating around him.
'Fuck!'

SIXTY-SEVEN

Charley crawled towards Lori, whose eyes were wide with terror.

'He's going to kill us, Charley,' Lori said.

'I know,' she replied, moving around behind her and untying her hands, all the while wincing from the pain in the elbow she'd landed on when Logan had pulled her down to the ground. 'That's why I came. I'm trying to stop him.'

Lori wriggled her hands free and pulled Charley in for a hug. 'I'm so sorry for dragging you into this.'

'Ouch.' Charley winced again and closed her eyes momentarily. 'You didn't drag us into anything. He did.'

'Are you all right? Did he hurt you?' Lori asked in panic.

'No more than I hurt him, the bastard.'

Charley pulled away and stared down at the boy whom she'd never met. Her nephew, Jay. He was tied up, gagged and looked utterly terrified.

'Are you all right?' she asked as she moved towards him.

He didn't respond, only kept his eyes on the door at the top of the stairs while Charley removed the gag.

'He's got a gun,' he whispered once the gag was off his face. 'He'll come back with it.'

Lori was pulling Jay to his feet. 'Yeah, well, he can fucking try it.'

'Mum,' Jay replied fiercely, 'we *are* going to die in here. He's not fucking about. He's going to use the gun he used to shoot Reece. Then he's going to bring this building down on top of us. There is nothing we can do to stop it.'

Charley was staring at him now, knowing that he was right. But how had she managed to miss this side of her husband for so many years?

'What do we do, Mum?' Jay asked, his voice now like that of a young child, utterly terrified that the bogeyman was going to crawl out from under his bed and grab his ankles.

'We don't let him win,' Charley said, turning to see her designer bag at the bottom of the stairs. Logan had somehow managed to forget to take it from her.

'How the fuck do we do that? He's got a gun. He could just stand at the top of those stairs,' Jay pointed, 'and shoot us all in the head. It'll only take three bullets and we're all gone.'

Charley nodded and moved towards the bottom of the stairs. She picked up the bag and slipped her hand inside. 'Yeah, you're right. But he's panicking, Jay. His head is all over the place and he's going to come charging down here, erratic and without a proper plan. All we have to do is take him by surprise.'

Jay raised a brow. 'You're fucking nuts. He's not going to panic. He's calculated. Logan will kill us quicker than you can blink. We're never getting out of here.'

Lori was quiet and Charley was watching her as she stared at the pile of bones on the floor. She studied the skull in particular.

'I have an idea,' she whispered, bending down and picking the skull up carefully.

Charley grimaced. 'Who the fuck is that?'

'This is Jambo. This is the head of the other man who tried to kill me and Steph.'

Jay was silent, frozen as he stood next to his mum. Charley couldn't begin to imagine how it would feel to see her children so terrified, and she had no intention of ever finding out. Logan had to be stopped.

'What happened to him?' Charley asked, her tone hesitant. Did she really want to know?

Lori turned her head, her eyes fixed on Charley's. 'We defended ourselves, that's what happened. All these years, I thought they were both dead.'

'Fuck,' Charley whispered. 'Lori, you must have been so terrified. I can't even imagine.'

Lori shook her head sadly. 'He never did anything to hurt you in all the years you were married?'

Charley kept her eyes on the skull. 'I mean, he always had a bit of a temper. But never with the boys. Only me, at times. If I asked him to come home early from a job, or...' She let the words trail off. This was not the time.

'He has a temper, all right.'

Lori handed the skull to Jay, and he hesitated for a moment, before taking it from her. Then Charley watched as she carefully and silently climbed the stairs to the top. She reached up and unscrewed the light bulb before descending the stairs again.

Now they were all at the bottom, together again. Lori took the skull from Jay and handed him the bulb.

'What the fuck am I meant to do with this?' he whispered, sounding as confused as Charley felt.

'Keep hold of it. The glass will come in handy.'

They all turned back and stared at the skull in Lori's hand.

SIXTY-EIGHT

Peeling himself off the wall, Logan knew that it was now or never. There was no other way. Everyone in that basement had to die. They all knew far too much because of Lori *fucking* Graham, including his wife.

His thoughts ran wildly. What about Stephanie? She was at the hospital with Reece. Was he dead? What if he survived? What if he woke up and told the police? What if Stephanie told them everything?

FuckFuckFuck! Think.

He made his way out of tower three and raced across the site towards the Portakabin. He should have had the gun in the back of his trousers the entire time. He could have had this done by now. Stupid fucking idiot.

Entering the Portakabin, he opened the drawer in his desk and pulled the gun out, before deactivating the CCTV cameras all over the site. He couldn't allow any of this to be recorded, because whether things went to plan or not, he needed as little evidence as possible.

He opened up the computer and went back over the CCTV from when he first arrived on-site with Jay. He highlighted footage from every camera from that moment on and shut down the computer before heading out of the Portakabin and racing back to the tower.

Once inside, he composed himself, slowed his breathing and checked to make sure that the gun was loaded.

By tomorrow, they would all be dead, and the towers would start to come down. Logan would stand back, watch as the demolition team hired to do the job got to work. He imagined his elation as the third tower came down on top of them. The only problem was the remaining people with information. Sammi. Stephanie. Kev and Reece. Hopefully Reece was dead by now. But that didn't help him with the others.

Taking a deep breath, Logan looked at the basement door for a few moments, before unlocking it with his free hand. Pushing it open slowly, Logan pointed the gun into the darkness. Something didn't feel right. It was too quiet. He was expecting crying, pleas to let them go. But there was nothing. Not so much as a breath on the air to be heard.

He reached for the light switch and pulled it, expecting light to illuminate their terrified faces at the bottom. But nothing happened.

'Right,' he said. 'Stop fucking about and get to your feet. All of you.'

Nothing. Not a sound. He frowned. Had they got out? But how the hell could they have done that?

'Lori, bring your Jay up first. You made me watch my best mate die, only seems fair I make you watch your son lose his life.'

His words floated into the abyss and his frown deepened.

'Oi, I said stop fucking around.'

He slipped his hand into his pocket for his phone to use the torch when something came flying at him from the darkness of the basement. It hit him in the face and he staggered back, losing his footing a little before righting himself. He glanced down at what was thrown at him and a sudden rush of anger made him roar. Jambo's skull, cracked and broken, lay at his feet.

'You fucking bitch!'

He raised his gun, ready to fire into the darkness, when the sound of something from behind distracted him. He spun around, arm outstretched, when he saw Stephanie racing towards him. Her arm raised, she brought the hammer down hard, hitting him on the shoulder, but not before he managed to fire the gun. She let out a scream and struck him again, this time across the face. The blow knocked him over and he lost his grip on the gun.

The pain in his face was wild and he was dazed.

'Fuck!' Steph cried. He couldn't see her, but she was close by. Probably bleeding. Had he hit her?

The pain in his face intensified and seemed to sync with every cry coming from Stephanie.

He tried to open his mouth to speak, but nothing happened. Attempting to raise his arms, Logan discovered that he couldn't move. Had she paralysed him, or was it the shock from the pain?

'Are you all right?' a voice called. It was Lori Graham.

'The bastard shot me,' Steph called back.

All Logan seemed to be able to do was blink. What the hell was going on?

'How did you know we were here?' Lori asked.

'I didn't. Call it a good guess, bastards like him always return to the scene of the crime.'

Movement came from his left, and the sound of footsteps approaching made him want to turn in response but, again, he simply couldn't move.

Staring up at the ceiling of the room that housed the doorway to the basement, he watched as three faces appeared above him. Lori. Charley. Jay.

'He's bleeding pretty heavily,' Jay said, staring down at his face.

Where the fuck was his gun? His eyes darted from left to right, but his head remained still. He needed to get to the gun before…

'Looking for this?' Lori asked, waving the gun above him. 'Yeah, I'll keep this for now.'

Lori's face disappeared from his line of sight and he could hear her talking to Steph.

'Stings like a bastard,' Steph said.

'It looks like the bullet grazed you,' Lori said. 'You'll need to get that looked at.'

Steph grunted. 'I don't give a shit if I die now.'

'Fuck sake, Steph. Don't say things like that. He hasn't won,' Lori replied.

There was a scuffling of feet. More grunting.

'What you doing with that?' Lori said. 'You're not doing this. It's up to me.'

Logan stared up at Charley's face. Her eyes pooled with tears, her face strained from holding them in. He wanted to plead with her to help him. Get him an ambulance. Why the fuck was she just standing there?

'You,' Steph said, coming into view. Her expression was pained, her eyes too pooling with tears, which dripped down onto Logan's shirt. 'You killed my boy.'

Jay's head snapped up. 'He's dead?'

Steph's face contorted. 'Yes. This bastard killed him. It was the last bullet that did the most damage.'

Logan lay there, felt himself grow weaker. He couldn't move, couldn't speak, the blow to his head rendering him unable to do anything. But he could smile. And he did, drawing his mouth into the widest grin he could muster, and staring Steph right in the face.

Good, he thought. It was some form of justice for Jambo. Not necessarily his first choice, but it was the one which had the most impact.

Steph raised her arm. The barrel of the gun was in line with his face. He raised a brow – as much as he could – and smiled wider. If he died now, knowing that she would suffer her son's loss for the rest of her days, then he'd take that as a win.

'Wait,' Charley said, placing her hand on Steph's arm.

Charley. Was she having a change of heart? Did she want to try to save him? Or did she just not have the heart or stomach to watch someone die?

Steph didn't move. She simply did what Charley wanted. She waited.

Charley bent down, getting as close to Logan as she could. He wanted to reach out with his hand and strangle her, but movement was impossible.

'I hate you,' she whispered. 'I can't believe that someone like you even exists. You manipulated me. You were calculated. You forced your way into my life, made me believe that you loved me. You were sick enough to have two children with me and all in the name of revenge. Somehow, you managed to disguise who you really are for so long. I can't believe I was so gullible. I believed every word that came out of your mouth.'

Tears streamed from her eyes, but her expression was straight, neutral almost. He wanted to laugh at her, to make her feel disgusted with herself for being so stupid. But he couldn't even smile now. His body was numb.

'How could you do this to me? To the boys?'

He wished that he had the strength to speak. He wanted to tell her that his blood ran in their veins and, because of that, she'd never be free of him.

'I hope your death is long, painful and fills you with so much fear that you fucking shit yourself a million times over. You deserve nothing less.' Charley swallowed hard and got to her feet. She moved away from his line of sight and now Lori and Steph were stood above him.

Steph still had the gun, but by the looks of it, she was struggling with the pain. Lori reached across and tried to remove the gun from Steph's hand, but she wouldn't let go.

'No, Lori. He killed my boy,' she said, her voice breaking. Then through gritted teeth, she said, 'The Bible says an eye for an eye. And I want to shoot his *fucking* eyes right out of his head.'

It was at that point Logan began to drift out of consciousness. He felt a slap across the face, words directed at him, something about not getting away with what he'd done.

He opened his eyes when he felt the gun pressed into his head. Steph's face was so close to him that he could feel her breath and he could barely make out her features.

'After everything you did to us, to my son, you deserve to burn. I wish I could get to watch you die. I really do, *Ped*.'

Steph got up and moved away from him, and the last face he saw was Lori Graham.

Bending down, Lori grabbed at his ankles and dragged him towards the basement door. Suddenly, he tumbled down the stairs, thumping his head off each step. As he landed, Lori rustled around in his pockets and removed his phone, then kicked him swiftly in the ribs, knocking the breath from him.

'You should have died down here back in 2001, Ped. I'm righting that wrong,' she said quietly. 'I should never have assumed you were dead. Your death back then would have been much less painful and a lot less scary. Now you're going to have to endure an entire building coming down on top of you. You'll never survive that and certainly not with that nasty head knock. Enjoy hell, Ped. You'll fit right in.'

She left him down there, with the headless skeleton of Jambo's remains. The door at the top slammed shut, plunging him into darkness. Logan hoped that he'd die before the building came down on top of him.

SIXTY-NINE

The blood seeped onto her top, making her skin wet and sticky.

'We need to get you to a hospital,' Lori said as she helped Steph to walk.

'Absolutely not,' Steph said. 'We can deal with it back at home.'

Steph felt all eyes on her as she clocked the chair and moved towards it. She needed to sit down, take a breath after what had just happened.

'Breathe,' Lori said, helping to lower her onto the chair. Charley's hand was under her other arm. Steph looked up at her.

'Are you okay?' Charley said in a whisper.

Then the darkness descended like a brick-heavy cloud. Reece was dead. Her son. The son who'd been born after all the trauma from Ped and Jambo. The light at the end of her dark tunnel. And now he was gone. Murdered by the same man who'd almost taken her life twenty-four years ago.

'No,' she said, her voice squeaking as she burst into tears, sobs escaping her so quickly she could hardly get a breath. The pain in her side was nothing in comparison.

Lori lowered herself so she was facing Steph. Her eyes wet with tears as she cried with her friend.

'Steph?' Jay asked. 'Is it true? Is Reece really dead?'

She let out a guttural scream and Jay immediately sank to the floor.

'We need to get out of here,' Charley said. 'We need to make sure that any CCTV footage of us is destroyed. If we're to get away with this, then we need to do everything we can.'

Jay stood up quickly, as if rising from the dead. 'The Portakabin. The system for the cameras is in there. I still have a key.'

He pulled open the door and held it there for everyone to go through, each of them still crying.

Charley and Lori helped Steph to her feet and they all walked across the site towards the Portakabin, Steph wincing with each step.

'Where the fuck is all the security?' Lori said. 'Jay, where is everyone?'

Jay looked back. 'He must've sent everyone home. If he was going to do this, then it makes sense.'

Steph watched as Jay went into the cabin first. Once they were all inside, Lori handed Logan's phone to Jay and he slipped it into his pocket. He tapped on the keyboard on the desk and frowned.

'What?' Steph asked.

'The cameras; they're all off.'

'Are you sure?' She winced again.

'He switched them all off. And he's deleted footage as far back as a few hours ago.'

Steph held on to her side and glanced down at the floor. 'I need to get out of here before I bleed all over the place and leave evidence I was here.'

Lori nodded. 'So, we're good to go?'

Charley moved towards Jay and glanced down at the screen. Steph watched her, all the while trying to breathe through the pain.

'You're sure it's all gone? He couldn't have set us up?'

'He didn't know this was going to happen to him. He turned it off to protect himself. There is no footage of us ever being here, including him bringing me here right after he shot Reece.'

The sound of her son's name caught her by surprise through the pain and Steph swallowed hard. 'Right then, let's go.'

Charley and Jay moved back around from the desk and stood with Lori and Steph.

'It's over,' Lori said to Steph. 'He's gone.'

Steph shook her head. 'We said that the last time.'

Jay looked up at the clock on the wall and said, 'This time tomorrow, the first two towers will be down and they'll be starting work on the third.'

Steph nodded. 'I won't rest until that building is on the ground.'

Lori nodded and pulled Steph closer to her. 'And we'll make sure we take it all in. This time, we leave nothing to assumption.'

Steph sighed. 'I should have shot him.'

'Then it looks like murder if he's found,' Jay said. 'This way looks like a pretty awful accident. He owns the site. He's got a head trauma. It could be explained away by him doing some final checks before the demolition starts tomorrow. He tripped, banged his head and died. It's an open-and-shut case.'

Steph gave a weak smile. 'I wish I shared your enthusiasm. You got paramedic skills as well as police investigation skills? I could do with some attention.'

Lori put Steph's arm up and over her shoulder, indicating for Charley to do the same.

'You need to live for Reece's sake,' Jay said. 'That's his justice, Aunty Steph. He shot you, but you survived him. Again. Reece would have been so grateful you did.'

The nausea was setting in now and she knew she didn't have long before she passed out.

Stepping out of the cabin, Jay locked up, and they all turned back to take one last look at tower three.

It would be the last night it would rear its ugly head over Dunreath. It would be the last night it would harbour the secrets of twenty-four years ago.

SEVENTY

FORTY-EIGHT HOURS LATER

Jay let himself into the site, showing his site supervisor badge to the demolition supervisor, who gave him a nod.

Dressed in all his health and safety gear didn't fill him with any sense of safety. His stomach churned as he stood back and watched as the the demolition for tower three began.

It fascinated him that the first two towers were already a pile of rubble. He took comfort in knowing that the third building would be a pile just like it, with Logan Greer firmly buried underneath.

'So, where is Mr Greer again?' the demolition supervisor asked.

Jay shrugged. 'You know, he didn't actually say where he was going. All he said was I was to manage things from here and that you'd do most of the work. Happy for me to sign off on everything.'

The man nodded. 'It's all right for some, eh?'

Jay smirked. 'Aye. Leave us minions to do all the hard work while you swan off on holiday.'

'Ha, all bosses are the same, mate. Doesn't matter what sector you're in.'

The long-reach excavator got to work, with some of the workers spraying water onto the building as it began to fall from its height, stopping the dust from hovering in the air and choking everyone to death.

Once the building was down, this would all be over.

Steph had been right about wishing she'd shot him. Jay felt the same way. But it hadn't been in their best interests to murder the bastard beforehand.

His body would be found, of course it would.

And that would be the end of it.

—

Steph sat on the blanket at the top of the hill, which looked down onto Clydeview Towers, about three miles away. From here, she had a decent view of her traumatic past coming to an end. The sound and sight of the building crumbling from the force of the machines bringing it down soothed her soul just a little bit.

'I wish Reece was here to see this,' she said.

'He'll know,' Lori said, wrapping her arm around Steph's shoulder and leaning her head against it. Steph winced. 'Oh, sorry.'

'It's okay. It doesn't hurt as much any more. Kev's first aid really did the trick,' she replied, glancing over at Kev and winking at him.

He gave a smile. 'I think I went into autopilot when you came in. I thought you were dying.'

Steph replied with a wry smile of her own. 'Unfortunately, no. But maybe one day.'

Lori shot her a look.

Charley stood up and stepped forward, her back to everyone else. She'd been very quiet over the last two days. Not that Steph could blame her. Her entire life had been a lie, and now she had to be okay with her husband and the father of her two kids being buried – hopefully alive – underneath a building.

'You good, Charley?' Lori called out.

She didn't respond; instead, she stood still, her hair floating on the breeze at the top of the hill at the edge of the village of Dunreath. The rest of the spectators were closer than them, a mile or so closer. That suited Steph and the rest of them.

'You think Jay's okay being at the site?' Kev asked. 'You know, he's only young. This is a lot for anyone, but a young, impressionable lad like him, it's bound to have an impact.'

Lori smiled. 'You've really come such a long way from that older brother I remember.'

Steph looked on at the pair. The comment seemed to catch Kev off guard.

'What do you mean?' he asked.

'Well, don't take this as a dig, but I've never known you to care about anyone other than yourself,' Lori replied. 'And since you've been back in my life, you've shown otherwise.'

Steph remembered Kev back then. He had been useless and did only care about himself. She and Lori, along with Charley, were extremely young and didn't understand the full force of what it must have been like to live as an addict. They only saw it from one side and not what it would have felt like to be all consumed by it.

It was nice to see them back together, but she couldn't bring herself to say it, given all she'd lost herself.

'Thank you,' Kev said. 'I've got a lot of catching up to do as a dad.'

Sammi didn't say anything; instead, she sat down beside Steph, slipped her hand through the crook of her elbow and gave it a squeeze. Without looking at Steph and keeping her eyes on the third tower, Sammi said quietly, 'I'm so sorry about Reece. He didn't deserve this. I had a lot of love for him, you know. Logan ruined that for us, and I didn't even realise it at the time.'

A large razor-like lump formed in Steph's throat. That was when it hit her. Reece was never coming back.

She took Sammi's hand and squeezed it so tight she worried she would hurt her. But Sammi squeezed back. 'Maybe in another life you two will get another shot.'

'I feel like it was my fault.'

'You didn't shoot him, sweetheart. None of this is your fault,' Steph replied, tears streaming down her cheeks as she watched the excavator tear down another piece of the tower. Even though it was three miles from where they stood, the sound was still deafening. Not loud enough to drown out Steph's thoughts, her grief. Not loud enough to drown out Reece's last words to her as he lay in her arms. *Please don't let me die.*

Everyone seemed to huddle around them then. Lori, Charley, Kev. They all sat tightly together and watched as tower three was razed to the ground.

SEVENTY-ONE

It was typical that he was still alive. The paralysis was gone and he realised it was most likely the shock of the blow that had rendered him unable to move. Yet, there he was, still waiting to die in the same basement as before.

It was as though no time had passed, as though this was already his hell and he'd been reliving it for twenty-four years.

The sound of crumbling and crashing concrete filled him with terror. He was going to be crushed to death. But then, maybe not? Being in the basement might be what would save him. Once the rubble was clear, he'd be able to get out? If he didn't suffocate first, or die from dehydration.

His body screamed with pain. Why hadn't he died yet? Was this his punishment? To die a brutal death because of what he'd done? Because of who he was?

Tears filled his eyes as he lay on his back, battered and bruised, paralysed yet fully aware of what he was about to go through. Even if he did survive the building coming down on top of him, he wouldn't last long beneath the rubble.

As thoughts swirled around in his head, it occurred to him that his boys hadn't crossed his mind. He didn't care much for them. They were just a product of his plan. Charley would be left to deal with them now. That was how it had always been.

Getting into a relationship with Charley had been tough because he'd had to force himself into it. Logan had always struggled with relationships unless they benefited him in some way. The only person he'd truly felt something for had been his best mate, Jambo. Again, Jambo was a person who brought good to Logan's life. Not just a best friend and like a brother, Jambo was money, muscle for when punters wouldn't pay up. Losing him had been like losing a limb as well as fifty per cent of his business. And Logan had to start over after the incident with Lori and Steph. Lying low had been the only way. Which was why getting with Charley had been instrumental to his plan. But it had backfired.

The sound of crumbling bricks and heavy machinery grew louder and Logan cleared his mind. He didn't want to have anyone's face in his mind when he died. If he could imagine death, then it wouldn't be so difficult when it came.

Closing his eyes, he pictured the colour black. Imagined it swallowing him as the building came down.

—

'Jesus fucking Christ, mate. What the fuck were you even doing down there?' an unfamiliar voice said. Logan tried to look up from where the voice was coming from but his eyes struggled to adjust in the light. 'Your site supervisor said you were on holiday.'

Logan rubbed at his eyes. He was dazed. Confused.

'Am I out?' he asked, his voice weak.

'Aye, one of the lads operating one of the hoses heard screaming coming from inside. We stopped the machines and found you in a basement. What were you doing down there?'

He had to think fast. He was sat in the back of one of the vans just outside the site, someone had thrust a bottle of water into his hand. His head thumped as he tried to remember being found.

'I, erm. Yeah, I was meant to be going on holiday to see my wife. I wanted to do one more check of the site before the demolition commenced. I don't know how I managed to lock myself in. Jesus.' He let out an incredulous laugh. 'I thought I was a goner.'

'If you hadn't started shouting, you would have been. Jesus, man. My heart's in my throat. We should get you checked over,' the man said. 'That's a nasty knock you've got on your face there.'

Logan raised a hand to his cheek and winced. 'Ah, yeah. That's what happened. I tripped. Fell down the stairs. Door must've slammed shut behind me. I left my phone in the Portakabin.'

The man was nodding, as if he was trying to understand. 'Aye, well. Let me get you to the hospital, eh?'

Logan shook his head. 'Nah, mate. I'm fine. Honestly, just feeling a bit rough. I'd rather not waste their time. I'll head home, get a shower and a sleep.'

The man hesitated. 'I really think you should get checked. I'll need to report this.'

Logan shot him a look, took a sip from the water bottle and handed it to him. 'I said I'm fine. All I need to do is let my wife know I'm all right. She'll be worried.'

The man raised his chin, almost as though he was suspicious of Logan. Instead of arguing his point, he simply shrugged and replied, 'You want a lift home?'

Logan shook his head. 'No, I'm fine. Got my van.'

Narrowing his eyes, the man followed Logan's line of sight. 'You think you're good to drive?'

'Look, mate, I know you mean well. But I got locked in a basement, I'm not pissed. It's embarrassing, really. I'd rather you didn't spread this around. No need to report it. I'm telling you I'm fine. And if I die, it's not like I can sue you anyway.'

He smiled at the man, tried to show he was genuine, when he didn't give a shit. All he wanted was to get away from the site, get back to the flat and work out what the hell he was supposed to do next.

The man raised his hands. 'Fine,' he said. 'But please, let me know how you are.'

Logan gave a thin-lipped smile and got to his feet. Considering he had felt paralysed just a few hours earlier, and barely remembered being pulled from the basement, he was surprisingly steady on his feet.

'Safe home, mate,' the man called after him.

Logan didn't look back. Instead, he pulled his key from his pocket, got into his van and drove out of the site.

SEVENTY-TWO

ONE WEEK AFTER DEMOLITION

Lori stood by the front door of her flat and sucked in a lungful of air. She couldn't believe that she was finally getting out of Blackhill Court. After all these years of living deep inside the place she'd suffered all of her trauma, she was finally free.

'I can't believe I'm leaving without him,' Steph said as she stood next to Lori.

'He'd want you away from here,' Lori replied. 'He wouldn't want you to feel guilty about it, Steph.'

Steph nodded, and the look of sadness on her face gripped Lori by the throat. On one hand, she was devastated for her best friend's loss. On the other, she was entirely grateful she hadn't lost her own son.

'How many suitcases have you got between you?' Kev asked, struggling out of Lori's bedroom as he dragged one behind him.

'We've got three each.' Jay smiled.

Sammi laughed and Kev shook his head at her. 'You should be helping me, I'm not exactly young and fit.'

Sammi laughed again and moved through to the bedroom to get one of the suitcases.

'I can't believe we're all leaving this shithole,' Jay said as he stood in the centre of the square hallway. 'I just wish Reece was here to see it.'

Lori took Steph's hand and gave it a gentle squeeze.

'We're all free,' she said. 'This place is going to be a distant memory soon.'

'More like a distant nightmare,' Steph replied.

Kev and Sammi appeared in the hallway again.

'Right,' Sammi said. 'That's it. All suitcases accounted for.'

Lori smiled. She was excited that they were all about to move to the Borders to be reunited with her youngest sister.

'I can't believe Charley's foster family are allowing us all to stay with them while we find our feet,' Sammi said. 'I mean, I'm not even family. Not really.'

Kev shot her a look and placed a hand on her shoulder. 'Hey. You're my daughter. That makes you Charley's niece.'

'If anyone should be feeling out of place, Sammi, it's me,' Steph replied. 'But you don't hear me complaining.'

Lori laughed and took a breath. 'Right,' she said. 'Let's get the fuck out of here.'

Turning, she opened the door and was met with a fist. Falling back, a pair of arms caught her, but she still hit the floor with a thump.

'Everyone get inside, now,' the voice growled. It was Logan.

'Urgh,' Steph groaned loudly. 'Why won't you just fucking *die?*'

The pain in Lori's face caused her eyes to stream, making his face blur behind the tears. But he was there all right. Alive and kicking. Steph was right, why wouldn't he just die?

She was pulled backwards along the floor, and she tried to find her footing. Blinking away the tears, she glanced up to see Logan pointing a gun at her, waving it between each of them.

'Thought I was gone, didn't you?' Logan said. His voice was hoarse and he sounded out of breath. 'That's twice now you two bitches thought you'd done away with me. Seems like I'm unbreakable.'

Lori cupped her nose, the pain increasing, blood pouring through her fingers.

'You know what, Ped?' Steph spat the name out. 'You're not unbreakable, you're just *fucking* lucky.'

He spun his arms, pointed the gun at her and gritted his teeth. 'Did I say you could talk?'

Steph stood up, outstretched her arms and laughed. 'You think you can hurt me? You already killed my son. I'd be relieved if you put one of those bullets in my head right now.'

He inched forward, forced the gun into her head. 'Gladly.'

Lori wanted to scream. Everyone remained still, like they were frozen in fear. Logan was focused, his eyes set deeply on Steph.

'Logan,' Sammi said. 'You don't have to do this.'

He blinked, but didn't turn. Lori knew that he was in a position where he wouldn't be able to kill them all. He was one and there were five of them. One, maybe two of them would get shot, yes. But they'd be able to tackle him, surely?

'Shut it, Sammi. You're next.'

'Look,' Kev said as he stood next to his daughter. 'It's me you want. You're pissed about the money I owe you.'

Logan gave a manic laugh. 'Ha, aye. That among other things. Your sister and her fucking pal tried to kill me. *Twice*. I'm not walking away from that.'

Kev nodded. 'Aye, but have you asked yourself why they did that? You're a fucking animal, Logan. You raped them, branded their fucking skin as if you were labelling them as your own. You killed Steph's boy. You shouldn't be standing here trying to take the moral high ground.'

Lori felt sick. She could see Sammi tugging on the bottom of Kev's jacket as if she was trying to warn him to be quiet. But Lori knew her brother well enough to know that he was trying to distract Logan from shooting Steph. From shooting any of them.

Lori placed a protective arm across Jay, not that it would do any good if Logan did turn the gun on them.

'Go on,' Steph said. 'You shot me last week and failed. Why not try again?'

'Steph,' Lori said, hoping that she'd stop trying to antagonise him.

'What?' She shrugged. 'He's already taken the one person in life who was keeping me here. He's gone now. What else do I have to live for?'

Logan was smiling widely, his eyes glinting under the light. 'You want to die? Like your son did?'

Steph pushed her forehead into the gun and bared her teeth. 'You want me to be scared of you, but I'm not. You're nothing but a piece of shit, Logan. I wouldn't give you the satisfaction.'

Lori felt Jay's hand move her arm away and he got to his feet. 'Right,' he started, but Logan spun quickly and pointed the gun at him. Lori let out a scream and, suddenly, Kev threw a punch, his fist landing on the back of Logan's head. He went down, the gun still in his hand. Jay was on top of him, trying to wrestle the gun from his hand.

'Jay,' Lori screamed again. 'Stop. He'll kill you.'

The men rolled on the floor, Sammi cowered in the corner, Steph was frozen on the spot.

The gun went off twice.

Once the initial silence after the shots wore off, a loud ringing began in Lori's ears. Sammi was still in the corner, crouched on her knees, hands over her ears. Steph was moving now, towards the heap of bodies on the floor of Lori's living room.

She stared at Jay. He was moving, rolling onto his back. He stared up at the ceiling, seemingly in shock.

'Jay,' she said, barely hearing her own voice. 'Jay, are you okay? Are you hit?'

He shook his head as her eyes quickly scanned his body. There were blood spatters all over him. His T-shirt, his face, his arms. Glancing down at his hand, she saw the gun, his fingers wrapped firmly around it.

'Lori,' Steph said, hovering over Kev and Logan.

Lori turned. Logan was face down, Kev on his side, eyes staring at Logan.

'Shit,' she said. 'Kev, you're hit.'

The blood was pouring from him in copious amounts.

'Jay, give me the gun,' Lori said. But Jay didn't move.

'Lori, they're both gone,' Steph said as she stared down at them. Lori's ears were ringing so loudly she could barely hear her.

Kev's eyes were wide open, but there was no life there.

'Shit,' she whispered, before turning her attention to Logan. Reaching down, she took the gun from Jay, who was now getting to his feet. She pointed it towards Logan but she knew she wouldn't have to pull the trigger. With the blood pouring from his head, she knew he was gone. Finally. Gone.

'He shot Kev and dropped the gun. I picked it up and shot him in the face,' Jay said.

Lori felt her heart drop to her stomach. No, no, no.

The words echoed in the room as Sammi began to scream. She rushed from the corner of the room and dropped to her knees next to Kev's lifeless body and sobbed loudly.

Lori turned to Jay, who was staring into space. Steph went to him, took him in her arms and held him close.

Lori nudged Logan with her foot but she could barely move his dead weight. She glared at him, a hatred building from the pit of her stomach. The man had tormented them for most of their lives. He'd killed Reece, now Kev.

'We only just got him back,' Lori whispered, before raising her foot and stamping it down on top of Logan's dead body. 'His life was just beginning.' Another stamp. 'I fucking hate you.'

Falling to her knees, she pressed the gun into the back of his head. She wanted to kill him herself, but she couldn't.

Something caught the corner of her eye. His ring. The one he'd used to brand all of them. Reaching down, she yanked it from his finger and slipped it into her pocket.

Turning, she pulled Sammi into her arms and cried with her.

SEVENTY-THREE

BREWERY DRIVER FOUND DEAD IN BACK OF VAN

Police Scotland has launched an investigation into the suspicious death of a man found in the back of a brewery delivery van in Dunreath. Officers were called out to Old Clydeview Crematorium in the early hours of Sunday following a call from a concerned citizen. Police are keen to speak to a group of youths who were seen fleeing the area around the time the call came in.

It is reported that a small number of drug packages were found alongside the deceased. If anyone has any information regarding the incident, please contact Police Scotland on 101.

SEVENTY-FOUR

ONE MONTH LATER

Lori sat at the large dining table with Charley on one side of her and Steph on the other and Sammi standing by the large bay window overlooking the garden. It was the end of a long day; a double funeral. Lori felt numb, she couldn't even begin to imagine how Steph was feeling.

'It was so kind of Margaret and Ronnie to allow us to have the reception here,' Steph said as Lori nursed a cup of tea.

'Yeah,' Charley replied. 'They're the kindest people I've ever met. I don't know how I'd have got through life without them.'

Lori sighed and took a sip. She knew during moments of stress and grief, people often turned to a glass of something stronger to help settle them. After everything she'd been through, after what she'd seen alcohol and drugs do to the people closest to her, she still didn't want to touch the stuff.

'And the police have shut the case?' Charley said. 'On your end, I mean?'

Lori nodded. 'Yeah. They accepted that Logan was Kev's old drug dealer and that he still owed Logan money. I told them about me flushing the drugs in our house when I was sixteen and said that was the only reason I could think of that would explain why he was there. Jay's still waiting on word, but it looks like he won't face jail time. He was protecting all of us.'

Charley puffed out her cheeks. 'I can't believe he did this to us. I can't believe he used me for all these years to get to you all. I feel so violated.'

Lori closed her eyes. 'They matched the bullet that killed Reece to Logan's gun after what happened to Kev. So, they know it was Logan who shot Reece.'

Steph bowed her head and cleared her throat. 'Some sort of justice, I suppose.'

Lori got up and moved across the kitchen towards the window where Sammi stood.

'Are you okay?' she asked, and Sammi shook her head.

'I only just got him back,' she replied. 'I grew up with nothing, Lori. I finally found my dad. We started to build a relationship, and Logan took him from me.'

She squeezed Sammi's shoulder. 'I know, love. It's all so fucking unfair. Sorry, I don't mean to swear.'

'You're right to. It is *fucking* unfair. It's unfair that he got away with so much for so long.'

'All we can do now, is live our lives,' Lori said. 'As hard as it is to accept that Reece and Kev are gone, we can live now without looking over our shoulders any more. They'd want that for us.'

Lori reached into her pocket and pulled out Logan's saltire sovereign ring. She held it out to Charley.

'I took this from him after he killed Kev. What do you want to do with it?'

Charley glanced down at it in Lori's hand and took the ring from her. She walked across to the bin sitting by the door, opened it and threw the ring inside.

—

Steph stood outside on the patio, overlooking the vast gardens. She thought about Charley growing up here and couldn't imagine what it must have been like to go from somewhere like Blackhill Court to a palace.

Lighting the cigarette between her lips, she glanced up at the sky and the images of her son on the grass that day, bleeding all over her, haunted her mind. They would forever. The sound of the gun going off, the initial shock and confusion. Reece's words, begging her not to let him die. Seeing the doctors and nurses working on him before pronouncing him dead. Those last hours of his life would play on a constant loop forever, and Steph didn't know if she would be able to handle that for the rest of her life.

'Steph?'

Turning, she saw Sammi stood next to her. She too was staring out over the vast garden.

'You okay?' Sammi asked.

Shaking her head, Steph inhaled more smoke into her lungs. 'Nah, not at all. And I never will be again.'

Sammi was silent. She'd be hurting too. How could she not be?

'Reece was a good guy, you know? I'm just sorry I treated him the way I did; you know, leaving him so quickly for that arsehole.'

'He was a good egg, I know that. He didn't deserve to die the way he did. And neither did your dad.' Steph slipped an arm around Sammi's shoulder, gave her a gentle squeeze before she said, 'You mind? I just need a few moments by myself.'

Nodding, Sammi went back into the house and Steph stepped off the patio and walked down to the bottom of the garden, where a small fountain trickled. The sound was peaceful; tranquil.

She perched on the edge of the fountain wall and took a deep breath as she felt in her pocket for the packet of antidepressants the doctor had prescribed for her. Not enough, of course.

Finishing her cigarette, she pulled the half-bottle of gin from her pocket, unscrewed the cap and drank back some.

'Hey.' Lori's voice came from behind her. Steph didn't bother to stop drinking from the bottle.

She swallowed the gin and winced as it burned the back of her throat.

'You all right?'

Steph wiped the back of her hand across her mouth and shook her head. 'Not in the slightest.'

Lori sat down beside Steph and the two of them stared out at the garden.

'I'm going to help you get through this, you know. I promise, you're going to be okay.'

Steph sucked in a lungful of air and let out a sob. 'How will I ever be okay after this, Lori?'

Lori opened her mouth to speak but said nothing. Steph looked up at the sky and closed her eyes. All she wanted was to be with Reece, gone from this world.

'Don't you dare,' Lori said.

Steph glanced at her. 'What?'

'You're not leaving me now. No way. I won't let you. Steph, Reece being dead is the worst thing that will ever happen to you. But I will help you get through it. We're free now, Steph. Logan can't hurt us any more. Do you think Reece would want you to give up on your life now of all times?'

Steph kept her eye on the clouds above her and, for a long while, she said nothing. Was Lori right? Was now the time she could start living?

'But it's so fucking sore, Lori. I'd much rather live in fear of that bastard than live without my boy.'

Tears fell from both their eyes and Lori pulled Steph close to her.

'I know, Steph. I know. But please, don't give up. We have so much life to live now. We're free from him, free from the estate. Live the life Reece would have wanted for you and for himself. Please. Try.'

Steph sighed. 'I can't imagine feeling anything other than painfully sad and angry for the rest of my life. But I'll try. Because you're right, Reece would want me to.'

Looking back up at the sky, Steph blinked away tears and said, 'Not yet, baby boy. Not yet.'

A letter from Alex

This is the first book I've written since my dad passed away in November 2024. I usually write to a soundtrack, but the usual playlist for me was too difficult to listen to. Any music with even the slightest hint of sadness just wasn't the one. So, I wrote the majority of this book while listening to The Prodigy. And actually, I've come to really enjoy their music. If you've finished reading this book, then you might understand why Logan Greer came across so brutally awful – it was the soundtrack ☺

The Fightback was fun to write. Getting to research the demolition trade was more interesting than I anticipated, and I enjoyed that part so much more than I thought I would.

I want to thank you, the reader. If you're returning to my work, welcome back. I hope you enjoyed (or will enjoy) *The Fightback*. If you're new here, then welcome, and I thoroughly hope you come back for more.

If you would like to keep up to date on what I'm currently working on, then you can find me on Facebook, Instagram and TikTok. You can also contact me at alexkaneauthor@gmail.com.

Cheers,
Alex

Acknowledgements

I want to thank my agent, Jo and all at Bell Lomax Moreton. No words needed; you're all wonderful.

Thank you to Keshini Naidoo at Hera Books, as well as the rest of the team.

A special thank you goes to Andrew at Caskie Limited. The initial email from a crime writer must have been a strange one, but you were so incredibly helpful, and I couldn't have written the demolition scenes without your expertise.

Thank you to my husband, who is forever telling me to stop procrastinating and get to work.

Thank you to my mum and mother-in-law for all your help with everything.

Special thank you to Elaine at Daydreams Bookshop in Milngavie. Your support since you opened your shop in 2024 has been incredible.

Last but by no means least, thank you to my readers. Without you, I wouldn't be where I am today.